PRAISE FOR JENN LEES ARLAN'S PLEDGE SERIES

"An enchantingly woven tapestry of found magic and found love. *Of Warriors and Sages* swept me through the portal from our world into one that was as cruel as it was beautiful. At moments quiet and reflective and others bold and fiery, Lees' writing drew me into a story I couldn't put down."
SL Dooley, *author of bestselling Portal Slayer series and the award winning duology The Summertime Circus (Bookfest 2023 Christian Fantasy) and The Cold Moon Carnival (Bookfest 2024) (Anatolian Press).*

'Arlan's Pledge, Jenn Lees weaves two worlds and many characters into this uniquely Celtic portal fantasy.'— *Lorehaven Magazine.*

'This story is believable and magical at the same time—a great combination. Lees is a master storyteller. This is an epic story, and is very well crafted from characters to plot to the story's setting.' — *Melody Quinn Ink & Insights Competition Judge 2021*

The Quest manuscript (now published as *Of Warriors and Sages: Arlan's Pledge Book Two)* achieved semi-finalist in the OZMA Fantasy Book Award 2023 (Chanticleer International Book Awards)

Arlan's Pledge Book Two manuscript reached the Top Ten in Ink & Insights Competition 2021

'Readers will find themselves in a different world as they read the book and see the characters actively mold their own destinies.'— *Monisha Krishnan Ink & Insights Competition Judge 2021*

"The detail... for this story, not just this one (*The Kingmaking Book 3*), but the ones that precede it, is amazing. This is clearly well-thought out... I hope to see this story sitting amongst others of its genre, like LOTR."—*Shreya Gopaulsingh Ink & Insights Competition Judge 2022*

Of WARRIORS And SAGES

Arlan's Pledge

BOOK TWO

JENN LEES

OF WARRIORS AND SAGES

ARLAN'S PLEDGE BOOK TWO

Cover by Fiona Jayde Media

www.fionajaydemedia.com

Map by J I Rogers, Mythspinner Studios

www.mythspinnerstudios.com

RECOMMENDATION: *READ MURTAIREAN: AN ASSASSIN'S TALE* PRIOR TO THIS NOVEL

To our son.

Our adventurer and non-conformist.

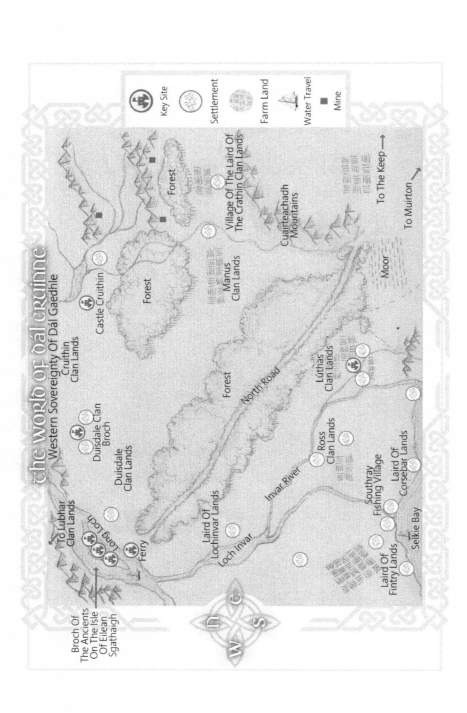

the world of dál cruinne

Western Sovereignty Of Dál Gaedhle

Key Site

Settlement

Farm Land

Water Travel

Mine

To Lubhar Clan Lands

Broch Of The Ancients On The Isle Of Eilean Sgathaigh

Long Loch

Ferry

Duisdale Clan Broch

Duisdale Clan Lands

Castle Cruithin

Cruithin Clan Lands

Forest

Forest

Forest

Forest

Manus Clan Lands

Village Of The Laird Of The Crathin Clan Lands

Cuairteachadh Mountains

Moor

To The Keep

To Muirton

North Road

Laird Of Lochinvar Lands

Loch Invar

Invar River

Ross Clan Lands

Lúthas Clan Lands

Southray Fishing Village

Laird Of Fintry Lands

Laird Of Corsebar Lands

Selkie Bay

N E S W

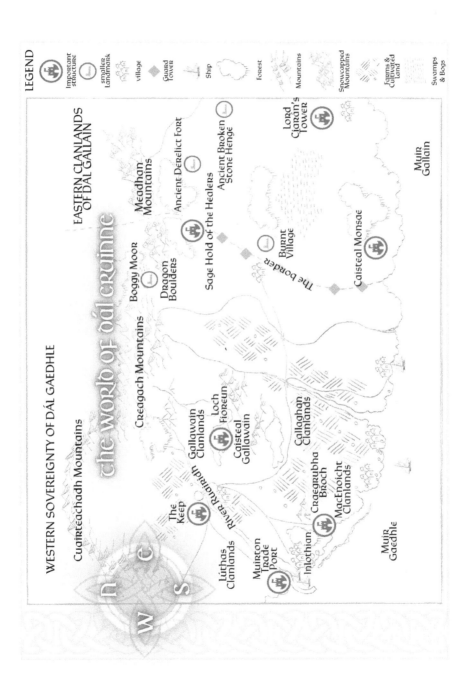

the world of dál eraínne

WESTERN SOVEREIGNTY OF DÁL GAEDHLE

EASTERN CLANLANDS OF DÁL GALLAIN

Cuairteachadh Mountains

Creagach Mountains

Boggy Moor

Meadhan Mountains

Dragon Boulders

Ancient Derelict Fort

Sage Hold of the Healers

Ancient Broken Stone Henge

Gallawain Clanlands

Loch Fioreun

Caisteal Gallawain

Burnt Village

The border

Lord Ciaran's Tower

Callaghan Clanlands

Caisteal Monsae

Muir Gallain

River Ruadhún

The Keep

Cragrubha Broch

MacEnoicht Clanlands

Lúthas Clanlands

Muirton Trade Port

Inlothian

Muir Gaedhle

LEGEND

Important structure

smaller Landmark

village

Guard Tower

Ship

Forest

Mountains

Snowcapped Mountains

Farms & Cultivated Land

Swamps & Bogs

Contents

Dragons from mankind are kept
In dark deep caves where none have slept.
Locked in peace, protected, left
Until the time of their resurrection.
When myths shall pass,
And fables be exposed.
Once more shall beast and man align.
Not for destruction, nor human direction,
But for the revelation
Of truth's intention.

ORAL TRADITION OF DÀL CRUINNE

PROLOGUE

For what price a soul?
All the wealth and fame a world and time may bring
Can be forfeited in but a moment.
An act written in the indelible ink of one's own lifeblood.

SAGE GLIOCAS
(2870-2962 POST DRAGON WARS)

The World of Dál Cruinne
Eastern Clanlands of Dál Gallain,
Post Dragon Wars Year 6053
Thirty Years Ago

Ciarán waited, just as the lady mage had instructed.

Brilliant silver summer sun lit the long glen and a flowing burn slashed argent through the wide expanse of velvet green. Eagles soared high above, and red deer trotted in and out of the woodland skirting the edge of the valley. Ciarán sat astride his stallion upon the ridge, adjusting his soft buckskin breeches and the tartan plaid that lay across his shoulder. He had travelled another day's journey eastward, almost as far as one could go before the saw-toothed mountains cut off the world.

He tightened his grip on the reins and touched the handle of his sword, *Dearg*, that rose above his right shoulder. Warmth seeped into him, and he closed his eyes. A male capercaillie drummed out his territorial warning, and a stag honked in the distance. Behind him—close—the jingle of a horse's tack grew louder.

Ciarán opened his eyes. Clouds billowed in the east, a darkening blotch on an otherwise pristine sky. The approaching horse nickered, its rider drawing the beast to a halt, then light footsteps landed next to Ciarán.

"Shall we?" The speaker, a young man wearing tight velvet breeches with lace frilling the cuffs of his jacket, dangled a basket from one hand and held a bottle of wine in the other. "I do so love a picnic. Grab the blanket, would you?"

Ciarán dismounted, pulled the rolled blanket from behind the saddle and followed, leaving both horses nibbling the sweet grass surrounding the rock-lined outcrop that became a natural viewing platform.

Ciarán's brow tightened. The man dressed strangely and spoke in an odd manner. He had reached the edge of the ridge where he took the blanket from Ciarán, spread it on the ground, and placed the basket and bottle upon it. The man moved with youthfulness and grace, and his slight figure belied a strength and ease for physical things. He lowered himself, sitting on the blanket with the elegance of a dancer. His gingery-blond hair, a mass of curls, framed his perfect face; his features arranged in faultless beauty.

"You are the one I am to meet, yes?" Ciarán asked.

"I am he. The mage directed you to this very place, did she not? Come! This wine is from France." He gave a flick of his head. "You don't know France. It's a world away from here. Ha!" He hugged the bottle and closed his eyes, and his lips turned into a dreamy curve. "Ah, *Paris.*" He opened his eyes with a start. "Believe me, you'll love the sweet berry flavours mixed with spicy hints of oak. Even if you don't, I will." He patted the rug beside him. "Sit."

Ciarán lowered himself onto the rug and the man poured wine into two glazed cups he had withdrawn from the basket. He handed one to Ciarán, then drank from the other, his cheeks sucking in, and an expression of rapture filling his face.

"Try it." He held the cup in salute.

Ciarán sipped the deep ruby-red liquid. Sharp-but-sweet filled his mouth, and the taste of spicy berries lingered on his tongue.

"Try this." The young man's inflection rose as he brought a wheel of cheese from the hamper.

He unwrapped the cheese from the cloth, cut a triangle, and passed it to Ciarán. The piece stuck to the knife; soft, white with specs of blue. He nodded encouragement, so Ciarán tasted. Soft-creamy cheese melted in his mouth, cutting away the berries and oak. Crisp flecks of flavour burst on his palate. They were sharp, strong, and drew want from his taste buds. Ciarán took another mouthful.

"Ah, yes. It's good, isn't it?" He cut another piece and held it out to Ciarán.

The delicate aroma tugged at Ciarán's mouth, which now filled with palate juices. He licked his lips and kept his narrowing gaze on the man next to him.

"Yes, you're right." His companion returned the cheese to the plate and brushed his hands together. "Down to business."

Ciarán sucked the last of the creaminess from his lower teeth.

This one had more than culinary delights to discuss. *By Cernunnos, get on with it!*

"This"—the youth lifted his cup in a casual manner to the valley below— "is all mine. I understand you wish to purchase it."

Ciarán blinked. *The youth owns it all?*

Out loud, he said, "Yes, I do. For how much are you asking?"

Its worth sat on the fringes of Ciarán's mind. He would give all he had for it—although it would be but little since his banishment from Dál Gaedhle and the loss of his clan chief title and lands.

"So, you'd give all you have for it?" his host said, pouring more wine.

Ciarán stifled a flinch. *Does this one hear my thoughts?* "Tell me your price, lord."

"You may pay me what you can for this, but I wish you to work for me." He smoothed down his velvet breeches with a delicate hand.

Ciarán narrowed his eyes. "What would the employment entail?"

"Acquisitions." His rose-bud mouth opened, and he placed a triangle of soft cheese on his pink tongue, eyeing Ciarán from the corner of his eye.

"Acquisitions?" Ciarán grasped wildly at the possibilities of what this young lord wished to possess.

"I collect things." The glazed cup rested on his lips once more, and now his direct gaze did not leave Ciarán.

"What manner of items, my young lord?"

"Everything." Holding the cup, he made a circular journey with his hand, as though to encompass all things and ensure Ciarán had understood. "I want it all, and I can share it with you if you work for me."

Ciarán squinted. "Is there a condition?"

"A catch, do you mean?" He topped up Ciarán's cup with more wine.

"Aye, for it sounds fantastical."

"I'm a powerful man, Lord Ciarán." He reached for Ciarán, the jewels of his rings glinting in the sunlight. "Don't let my age fool you. I can return to you the power you crave, and more. Get you the realm you so rightly deserve. The kingdom denied you by that cheater in the Quest and his crafty wife."

Ciarán's pulse joined the thudding in his head from the wine. *Could this man know my past?* The lady mage had said he would meet the one who truly reigned in this land. Perhaps he also had knowledge of everything.

"It can cost you all to get it all, but then you have it all, don't you?" The man's smile was angelic.

Ciarán pressed his lips together.

"You're thinking *it's too good to be true,*" his host continued and leaned forward. "No. It's true *you* have been prepared for this since birth. Your wet-nurse saw to that when she sacrificed your infant blood to the fire in your sire's Great Hall." His youthful voice hardened. "You're mine, anyway. I'm just claiming you now and offering an impressive deal." The beatific face drew closer. "Take it. You know you want it. Let's start small, like this valley, then we'll work up to bigger things."

Ciarán leaned back from the intense stare.

Ah, but this may be his opportunity to have what he so rightly deserved. Hot resentments re-surged inside him as his hands locked into fists. This could mean wealth and power. More importantly, it would be his opportunity to regain everything that *breugaire* who had wed his love had snatched from his grasp at every turn of his life.

I will take this chance, for none other may come.

"Deal?" The young lord offered a bejewelled hand.

"The mage assured me I could trust you." Ciarán put forth his own hand. "Deal. May I have your name, young sir?"

"Lucien." He drew the knife from the cheese, his hand moving in a haze of lace, and pain flew across Ciarán's palm, leaving his blood dripping with enthusiasm. "You're mine." Holding fast to Ciarán's bleeding hand, his face came close to Ciarán's once more, so near, Ciarán's vision blurred. "I also go by my other name. You may have heard it. *Cumhachd adhar.*"

The day dimmed, pressing onto Ciarán so that he could not move, and the distant cloud, having drawn close, now surrounded their picnic.

Cumhachd adhar. The words echoed in his head. *The Power of the Air.*

Darkness enveloped Ciarán. Pain wracked his body. He turned ice cold with fear. His heart broke as though betrayed, heated with anger, then hatred consumed him. The oppressive feelings weighed like lead upon him.

The lord rose, youthfulness and gingery-blond curls replaced by a man of impressive stature with blood-red eyes and raven-black hair. His beauty was retained in height, strength, and power. Authority emanated from this being now towering over Ciarán, and it was as though his garments dripped anguish aching in horror and dread. Wailing surrounded this fearsomely beautiful creature, reaching a crescendo.

The being vanished, filling the ridge platform with an abrupt silence.

Ciarán gasped in the fresh mountain air and lifted his shoulders, now free of the invisible weight.

On the rug beside him sat a scroll. The deeds of ownership of the land... and his soul.

ONE

— • —

The heart will decide,
Tho' pain and loneliness be the path.
Ever true to conviction.
Ever true to destiny.
This is the way of the victor.

VISIONS AND SAYINGS OF THE BLIND LADY SAGE

Our World, 2018
Kinnoull Hill
Perth, Scotland

Hooves pounded the track through Deuchny Wood.

I cantered my horse. Sitting in the saddle was second nature to me now. The rhythmic thudding of the gelding's tread and the motion of its gait were so soothing to me. Calming to my soul.

I held my face up to the rush of wind and inhaled the earthy forest scents. Warmth surged within and my cheeks stretched tight in a smile. It had paid off—twice weekly lessons at the riding school, and weekends riding the moors and glens of Scotland, had increased my confidence in horses. And in myself.

I hadn't waited for the other riders but streaked ahead. Surrounded by trees bathed in golden sunlight, a lightness filled me, sending my soul soaring. The gelding snorted, and his tread thudded along the track, just like another horse. A war horse—Mengus. Not so big and scary to me now. Although not as large as Arlan's stallion, this strong, sturdy beast on which I'd learned to ride had a pleasant nature.

I cantered past a forest of tall pines. That's how Arlan would return—through a forest.

My heart pinched. Tugging on the reins, I pulled my horse up and wiped the tears away.

1

"Good lad." I patted the gelding's neck, my voice coming out huskily.

But as much as I'd wished it to happen, Arlan hadn't returned. A tinge of heat travelled along my arms once more. Two years of waiting! I took a deep breath in through my nose then blew it out. I needed a good session in the dojo. That always helped to relieve my pent-up frustrations.

I rose in the saddle, easing my seat and stretching my legs, my muscles firm and strong.

Yes. I'm fitter than ever.

"Come back!" I shouted at the forest. "I'm ready!"

My horse nickered, side-stepping beneath me, so I stroked his warm neck. His coat, smooth beneath my fingertips, overlaid solid muscle, and his coarse mane tickled the back of my hand. I turned him and headed down the hill while a tightness in my chest danced with the chill in my middle. I gritted my teeth against them both.

"I will get there. Dál Gaedhle is the land of my birth."

Arlan had said so, and the firm sense of that truth now resided in my gut. That defining moment, the one that would tell me who I was, where I came from... who my biological parents were... was just around the corner. I felt that in my innermost being.

Who was I in this world, anyway? My job at the bookshop maintained its usual regular repetitiveness. And those times I allowed myself to feel awkward—peculiar and downright weird—were fewer and further between. Arlan believed me to be normal for Dál Gaedhle and exceptional for this world.

"And I am," I said out loud to no one but myself. At last I'd allowed myself to feel good about *me*.

I sat taller in the saddle. I no longer let the people of *this* world make me feel odd.

If all I could do was go to Dál Gaedhle and fight for the world I'd grown to love, I'd be happy. Fighting beside Arlan with his sword-brothers—and sisters, too. My heart leaped within me, and I tightened my grip on the reins. *This* was who I was now—horse woman and martial artist, and I *would* get to Dál Gaedhle!

I'd be a warrior. *In a real fight.*

I slowed the gelding to a trot, a dagger of doubt sliding into me then twisting. I may never be with Arlan.

Be with Arlan. He must marry a woman of a noble clan. He said he'd investigate to discover my clan and see if I was of noble birth. But what if he'd found I belonged to an insignificant clan? Or nothing, and I was a nobody? Perhaps that was why he'd not returned.

He'd probably married his princess by now and was happily producing wee Arlans while he did his clan-war-chief thing.

I pulled the horse to a stop and leaned forward, hands resting on the pommel.

I've missed my chance again—two years have proven it.

I shook my head, clearing away those negative thoughts.

"No! Shut up. Believe in him."

Arlan said he loved me. And he'd promised to come back for me.

For me.

Any time I left the cottage could be *the* instance Arlan chose to cross worlds. He'd find the note on the kitchen table, the one I always left for him, and a mobile phone with my number. Surely, he'd remember how to use one. Who knew how long it had been in Dál Gaedhle since he'd left here.

Damn. The portal crossing worlds and time certainly made life complicated.

I pressed my lips together. He'd better have learned how to master a portal! Because I couldn't.

I squeezed my eyes tight. I'd run through that spot on the track to the Iron Age Fort at dawn and at dusk for what seemed like a million times! And *nothing* had happened.

Except for the last time I'd tried...

I leaned back in the saddle as a shiver passed through me.

That attempt had been weird. I thought I'd hit a wall. Not a hard wall... a leathery one that gently pushed against me. Like it had said *no*.

I sighed so heavily it shook my chest. So *I* couldn't go through on my own?

Possibly.

What if something had happened to Arlan? Maybe that's why it wouldn't let me through. Did portals *know* stuff? Perhaps it knew if it allowed me to travel to its other side, Arlan wouldn't be there.

What if Arlan was dead? And he'd died in that skirmish he was sure he'd go back to. Cold walked down my back, leaving the hairs on my neck standing on end.

My eyes flew open. "No. Don't even think it." A gruff laugh escaped my lips. "Who could beat *him*!"

It had been so long since he left. What if many years had passed in Dál Gaedhle? Things could have changed. Perhaps the *badness* that concerned Arlan so much had overcome his land. And his efforts to rally an army of warriors and fight it had failed. That beautiful world he'd spoken of may be no more. That would be bad enough, but it would mean I could never discover who my actual parents were, or how I came to be here.

I needed to find a way there. I needed to know for certain what happened to Arlan.

Arlan's soft whisper as he leaned from Mengus, saying he would come and get me, did a replay in my mind.

When he comes back for *me*, I'll go with him and join the fight for the freedom of his world.

My world.

I inhaled the pine forest's sharp tang, counting my heartbeat, stilling my mind. The forest faded around me, and my eyesight blurred. I recognised what was happening—another vision—and I welcomed it.

Waves roar and crash against a rocky outcrop. Up on the platform of land jutting into the wild seas stands a broch—a wide, squat, round tower. Green fields stretch behind it, dotted by white sheep and ginger-brown cattle. A broad beach lies in front of it, where breakers roll and crash onto the shore, one after the other—endlessly. Salt spray fills my nostrils. My mind grasps at what I see. Extending far behind the broch are the rise of

3

mountains with the air so clear it glints like crystal. A silver sun shines on the land, and on me, its surprising heat warms me.

Humble workers fulfil their obligations to their clan chief in the fields behind this broch. They come to me as sensations. His warriors are their protection and support and the warriors' strength and loyalty belong to their clan chief, who will guide them through the times in which they live. For troubled times are upon them.

The breeze blows off the surf and noble traits flow past me—loyalty, allegiance, and trust—bonds so traditional and pragmatic, yet held with fealty, and a fierceness. Also, love for family, land, and clan chief, and for the highest ruler of the land, the àrd righ—their high king—whom they revere with a violent dedication.

I recoiled, the intensity of those emotions overwhelming me. I'd never seen such devotion to a leader. No such ardour stood out to me in my modern world. The forest came back into sharp definition. Then Deuchny Wood surrounded me once more.

I let the vision go, but the sensations lingered. They were intense, with a rightness to them. I longed even more for that world and craved to be amongst those faithful to their high king. I sensed their leader held as much dedication to his people as they had for him. He would be a good person. An honest person. One who would put his people before himself. Who protected them with all he was worth. With his very life.

I blinked away tears and dug my heels into my horse's flanks. Lurching to a gallop, I rode down the hill, leaning over the gelding's neck till I approached the carpark where the riding school instructor had parked the horse floats.

The instructor waited in her vehicle. She was an amiable enough person, but I didn't regard her as a friend, just an acquaintance. I didn't have many people who I considered friends, really. My mind slid to George, my best friend in this world, and perhaps the only other person who understood me. And the only other person who knew Arlan and his true identity—and believed it.

I cringed.

George still refused to acknowledge how I felt about Arlan, despite how often I'd spoken of my love for him since he rode through the portal two years ago. And of my determination to go to Dál Gaedhle and be with him.

George would have to walk beside me with his eyes and ears closed to not know that I love Arlan!

I gritted my teeth, my insides coiling. Once again, I'd have to make it clear to George. He'd spent so much time coaching me on my Gaelic, and I really appreciated him for that, but sometimes I still got the feeling he thought there was more to our relationship. I'd told him we were only friends, he and I, more than once. But it hadn't seemed to change his attitude toward me—like he was in denial.

I pulled the gelding up at the carpark by the horse floats. He snorted, foam spraying from his bit.

My instructor got out of the riding school's vehicle to meet me. "Where're the others?" She looked past me, her brow crinkling.

"Oh, they're coming."

"You love a fast ride, don't you, Rhiannon?" she asked as I dismounted. "How's that young man of yours?"

My brow tightened. I hoped she didn't mean George. "Young man?"

"George, isn't it? The one you went to Ireland with last weekend. Did you have a good time?"

Oh man, she meant him. *Make it sound platonic, Rhiannon.*

"Yes, we took the ferry to Dublin. George thought it'd be good for me to hear the Gaelic spoken in a different dialect. We hired a car and drove to Newgrange and spent the entire day at the ancient earthworks."

The instructor didn't need to know how that trip had made things even more weird between George and myself. She wasn't the person I'd spill my feelings to on *that* subject. Why can't a man and a woman just be friends? That's what George was to me. A good friend. No, a decent guy who was a *great* friend. And I needed one, like him, who understood what was going on in my life.

I grimaced, and my mount shook his head, tugging at the reins in my hand. The instructor stood with a hand on her hip, an eyebrow raised, and a slight smirk on her lips.

"He's not *my man.*" *Why am I so defensive?* "He's teaching me the Gaelic."

"Oh, well he seems such a nice person, from what you say." She loosened the girth strap, the smirk now a knowing smile. "And he teaches at Oxford. Isn't that what you said?" She peered over the gelding's back. "He must be very intelligent."

I removed the saddle, rolling my eyes.

She'll be thinking of me in terms of shelf *and* past-sell-by-date, *for sure.*

I parked my car in front of my cottage and stared at the field behind it. I could almost see Mengus trotting around the overgrown meadow. He was a magnificent animal compared to the horses I rode—a muscled black war horse with feathering. A nineteen-hand high heavy-horse, but as lithe as an Arab, and as agile as a quarter-horse.

Yes, I knew horses now—Arlan would be proud of me.

Mengus was larger and more beautiful than any of his kind in this world.

Just like the warrior who rode him...

The sky clouded over, so I stepped from my car and strode down the pathway to my door. Beside the cottage, my axe for chopping firewood sat on the block, its blade sunk into the wood. It made me think of Arlan every time I passed it. During his months with me, he'd kept the woodpile stacked for the open fire, his muscles dancing with each powerful blow of the axe. A pulse of heat quivered through me at the memory.

It was my task now to keep the pile stocked, and I made it a good upper body workout.

I reached the backdoor, and a smile tweaked the corners of my mouth. On Arlan's first entry to my home, I'd gestured for him to leave his weapons in the umbrella stand.

He couldn't speak English yet. Sign language had been enough. He'd put down his massive sword, but the blades just kept coming—from belts and tucked down boots. He'd probably had more hidden somewhere.

Chuckling at that memory, I walked through my tiny cottage to my bedroom and dumped my bag, then lifted the lid of the old trunk that sat at the foot of my bed, once my only valued possession. Pulling out my baby rug, I pressed it to my face, inhaling Mum's scent and that special baby smell. I held it up, examining the emblem hand-embroidered into the tartan. Arlan had identified it. The crest of Clan Gallawain—his mother's clan—an eagle flying over a castle on an island in the middle of a loch. It'd filled my dreams ever since Arlan had gone through the portal in the woods on the hill behind my home.

Everything I'd planned to take with me when I went, I kept easy to grab and go. I lifted my sword from the trunk and unsheathed it, then examined its edge. I'd purchased it at the Celtic Festival the very day I first met Arlan. With a whetstone, and recalling Arlan's technique, I'd honed until its edges were a shiny silver against the grey metal.

That'd taken ages.

Then I'd swiped the sharp edges with a soft cloth perpendicular to the blade, just like Arlan had done to his own sword, *Camhanaich*.

Doing sword exercises had helped build up my strength. I'd copied Arlan's dance with his sword, each movement imprinted on my memory from *that* day. I'd googled and found websites showing various sword skills and schools of sword tradition. According to those, Arlan's technique was perfect.

I placed the broadside to my mouth and kissed it, the smooth surface cool on my lips. Doubt zig-zagged through my insides like a rapier.

Am I truly ready? Could I fight to kill? Will Arlan be pleased with me?

My phone buzzed with a call. It was George.

I stared at the ceiling, my shoulders slumped, and I dropped the sword on my bed. I slid to answer. "Hi."

"You okay?" George's voice blared from my phone. I held it away from my ear.

"Yes. What do you want?" Curtness slipped into my tone. I should've regretted my sharp words, but George's cheery voice just reminded me I had to broach the subject again. Tell him we were *only* friends. And it would hurt him... once more.

"I'm at the railway station." George's voice held an uncertain note. "Shall I catch a taxi out?"

"What? Why?" I rubbed my forehead.

"We'd organised for me to stay this weekend. After you'd had your ride, of course."

I stifled a groan. *I could have sworn I'd not agreed to seeing him again so soon.*

"How about I meet you at the supermarket? I promised dinner, remember?" George asked.

"Okay, I'll be there in twenty." I hung up.

Damn. The man was getting eager. Too eager. Especially after our trip to Ireland.

I flopped onto my bed. He seemed to look at *us* differently now. Or had he been for a while, and I'd only just noticed it since our trip? As much as I hated to have to do it, I'd need to put firmer boundaries in our relationship—fences with neon signs lit up saying *friend only* so he couldn't miss them. He clearly wasn't getting the message. He was my one true friend. And you don't get many of those in this life. Well, he was here now, and I couldn't exactly turn him around and send him back to Oxford. The patter of gentle rain rumbled softly on the roof. I grabbed my coat and trudged to my car.

"Shall I put the sparkling white in the fridge?" George stood by the kitchen table, the bag of groceries spilling on the small table-top, and his overnight bag dumped on the floor by his feet. "Dinner just needs reheating. I know you like Indian." His mouth widened in a grin, and his eyes lowered a fraction to my lips. His grin wavered.

I forced a smile and stifled the *niggles* for the umpteenth time.

"That'll be nice," I said noncommittally as I turned the oven on to heat.

"I'll clear this so we can set the table for two." George moved the ready-made curry and naan bread from the table to the narrow bench.

"No, it's okay." I nudged him aside and took the cutlery from the drawer. "I'd rather eat in the living room. It's warmer."

The last thing I needed was a romantic dinner for two over my tiny kitchen table.

George opened the oven and slid the meals in. I walked the few short paces through to the living room and put the cutlery on the coffee table, his stare heavy on me while I scrambled for a way to approach the subject.

The subject that would hurt my best friend.

"He's not coming back. You know that, Rhiannon?" The pot-mitt dangled from George's hand.

I pressed my lips tight.

Just come out with it, George. Don't hold back. Say what you really think!

"Face it. He'd be back by now if he were." George tossed the pot-mitt onto the kitchen table from where he stood.

"Arlan will keep his promise." I faced George full on. "I *will* wait for him."

"Everything you've done is commendable. You can ride a horse now. You're a brown belt and your sensei is pleased with how you're doing with weapons... And your Gaelic is incredible." He pushed his spectacles up his nose. "You even speak it without an accent." A tight laugh escaped. "I never thought you'd do it."

"It's because I heard a real Gaelic speaker—"

"Rhiannon!" George's shoulders stiffened. "I'm sorry, but I can't take this anymore." He stepped closer and, reaching for my hand, took it in his own. He looked right at me; his intense brown eyes were pools of solemnity. "I love you."

The base of my neck chilled.

How do I answer that?

"Be with *me*. I'm here, in *this* world. A man who loves you. You wait for a fantasy. Arlan's not coming!"

Rain pattered on the window while my insides tore. I couldn't deny my fondness for George. He was my friend. *My friend*—that was all.

"George." My voice was quiet, unlike the tumult growing within me. "Do you think I'm crazy?"

"No. But you wait for something that'll never happen." His eyes widened. "All the odds are against Arlan coming to *here, now*."

The rain drummed harder on the window, and George's fingers pressed into my hand.

"I don't believe that." I forced calm into my voice, when I really wanted to *yell* at him.

"Okay, then. This is where we part company." George's voice cracked. "I can no longer do this."

"Do what, George? We are only *good friends*. You know how I feel about Arlan."

"I can't stand this." George's voice fractured around the edges. "I'm going." He let go of my hand.

It slowly cooled.

"Where are you going?" I followed him as he headed for the kitchen. *What? He's leaving?* "George, I'll miss—"

"I can't—*won't* be just your friend." George grabbed his bag from where he'd dropped it on the kitchen floor and spun. "We'd be together if it wasn't for *him*."

I skidded to a halt. "No, George. I've only ever..."

George stomped to the backdoor then turned to me, his face pulled tight, threatening to crack like his voice.

"I'm sorry, George. I... I've told you I love Arlan."

He stepped into the rain, shoulders hunching.

"I'll drive you," I said.

"No. I'm calling an Uber."

"Well, wait inside till it comes." I spoke to his back. "You're getting wet."

"I have a coat." He said, his voice flat. He took out his phone. "Goodbye." He didn't turn around.

I bit my lip. *Damn it.* I'd hurt him. *Really* hurt him.

"I'll wait with—"

George spun, his sharp glare hitting me like a throwing knife. "No. Rhiannon."

I retreated a step, then moved into the kitchen and stood by the sink to watch him through the window. George shrugged into his coat, the rain beating down on him, darkening him with wet.

I'd been here before. Back in high school. I would bury my nose in a book each break-time and stare at the words on the page. Not reading, while other teenagers chatted in their own small groups around me.

Me... sitting alone on a school bench.

I was now on my own once more.

It had been the same as I stood beside Mum's freshly dug grave, my hand trickling dirt over a shiny black coffin six feet below me while her grave filled. Not only covering

8

her coffin, but covering any deep connection my young-adult self had ever had with another.

Blurry raindrops streaked my double-glazed windowpane, like the warm saltiness now trickling down my cheeks. I scraped my tears away, my chest tightening.

With a deeper certainty, I couldn't wait to leave this world where I'd only ever lost and never seemed to have gained. From now on I'd have to just go it alone.

Come for me, Arlan.

Two

— • —

A son of the land
Breath of our ancestors
Substance of legend
Subject of bard song
Arbiter, peacemaker, strong protector
Exemplar in leadership
Courageous in the face of fear
A friend to all
True born of Dál Gaedhle
Our beloved Àrd Rìgh
Donnach Finnbar MacEnoicht

STANDING STONE MEMORIAL INSCRIPTION

World of Dál Cruinne
Post Dragon Wars Year 6083
Western Sovereignty of Dál Gaedhle
The Meadow below The Keep

Words were inadequate.

In truth, none ever expressed a person completely, and those carved upon the standing stone sentinel in the centre of bare earth scorched by a dragon's breath fell far short of encompassing the man's greatness—as far as the unfathomable distance between Dál Cruinne and the Other World.

The numb hollow was still there, right in the centre of Arlan's being. Tears had come, but now they would not. He had none left. The granite sentinel bore the accolades of the late àrd rìgh as a memorial, but chiselled on Arlan's heart was the name of Donnach Finnbar MacEnoicht.

Dadaidh.

A deep heaviness engulfed him again. No chance now to ask Father's forgiveness for being such a selfish, self-centred idiot. Father would never know his son had grown up and now faced his responsibilities.

That I had chosen to fight as you wished, Father, and be the weapon you forged me to be.

Arlan lifted his face to a pale blue sky. White clouds scudded past the silver sun and grazed the tips of grey mountains encircling the valley. The Keep, the seat of the Àrd Rìgh, the High King of Dál Gaedhle, sat in silence guarding the River Ruairidh's one and only crossing to the northwest. The granite caisteal, his home from childhood, would now belong to another.

Muffled chatter, horses' whinnies and the percussive clang of a smithy echoed over from the bailey yard. Arlan stood in front of Father's memorial stone in the meadow just past the bridge at the edge of the village that sat at the base of The Keep. The songs of workers sowing the surrounding fields reached his ears, then the clatter of a horse-drawn cart approaching the bridge drowned out their voices.

Arlan faced the road. A green-robed sage drove a covered cart pulled by a sturdy horse. Three horses, one a war horse, trailed behind the cart. The man beside the driver sat tall, his long greying beard plaited at his chin, and his arm bandaged.

"Muir!" Arlan ran from the meadow to the road, his mouth stretching in a grin as he passed his war horse, Mengus, tethered to the drystone wall.

The sage pulled the horses to a halt and Muir leaped off. Arlan closed the space between them and hugged the veteran warrior, careful to avoid Muir's healing arm, wounded in the skirmish that surrounded Arlan's transport to the Other World.

"How are you, old man?"

"I'm almost back to health, lord. Please, less of the *old man*. My sword and spear will be ready for your service soon."

Arlan gripped Muir's uninjured arm, giving him a gentle shake, then approached the man robed in green who held the reins. "How's my brother, good sage?"

"Prince Kyle lies asleep still. A coma, Sage Phelan names it. He was content that your brother was ready for the journey to you." The man from the sage hold where healers had attended Kyle's head wound, lifted his chin, indicating to the back of the wagon.

Arlan stepped to the opening of the canvas covering and peered inside. Kyle lay with his head bandaged and his face drawn, skinny limbed and like a small child. Beside his inert form sat another sage. Arlan's heart twinged. Kyle had never looked so pitiful. Arlan shuffled his feet.

His brother's rest had given him one of his own. A respite from a lifetime of bullying. No berating. No chiding. No critical comments in front of his warriors. No reminding him that, in Kyle's opinion, he wasn't fit for any charge.

Arlan's face heated, and he stared at his boots.

How can I think such things? Kyle was his own blood. Deriding big brother or no', no one deserved this.

Kyle lived, yet he did not.

11

Arlan gave his shoulders a slight shake then smoothed his beard, attempting to brush away his heated cheeks.

"Sage Healer Phelan advises that a quiet yet familiar environment will be best for Lord Kyle until he wakes," the sage caring for Kyle said.

Kyle's man sat at his feet, head bowed and eyes downcast. "My condolences, Lord Arlan, on the loss of our great àrd rìgh and your dear father. He shall be missed. I promise I'll tend to my charge, your brother."

"Thank you. Assist the sages to Kyle's rooms once you arrive at The Keep." Arlan strode to the front of the cart where Muir collected his belongings.

"You will stay for the *Sàsaichean*?" Arlan asked the sage up front.

"Aye, the sage council summoned us," the man said. "We are thankful it coincided with the improvement in Lord Kyle's condition."

Arlan nodded and turned back to Muir.

"Where's Lord Bàn?" Muir peered at Arlan.

"My sword-brother journeyed to clan lands in the north. To return the body of Erin to her parents." And grieve his lost love.

"Aye, lord. Your warband mourns for our warrior lost in that skirmish." Muir tilted his head. "Ye'll miss your sword-brother."

"Och, well, he promises he won't be long. Did you see any bandits on your way?"

"Nae, we came by the mountains. The refugees are only a trickle at present."

"That's a welcome reprieve, but it doesn't mean Ciarán Gallawain is resting."

"Our caisteals rest not. Those where we stayed overnight were full of activity. Bailey walls reinforced. I heard the ring of weapons forged and warriors trained." He retrieved his horse from behind the cart.

"Aye, all prepare." Arlan untethered Mengus and walked with Muir to The Keep.

"What will ye do, lord?" Muir's rusty voice was always so calm, no matter the situation.

"I'll take my brother to Craegrubha Broch. It's quieter there. And now my father..." His mouth dried and he couldn't finish the sentence. "The Keep is no longer my home."

He passed the high bailey walls where behind, pinks and reds dappled the flowering hanging baskets on the grey stone balconies of the caisteal. Mother's legacy. She was now reunited with Father.

He released a sigh, tinged with a bittersweet happiness for his parents. It had barely been a turn of the moon since his return from the Other World and every day, and every night, his thoughts went to the woman with heather-mauve eyes. The woman *he* would reunite with in *this* life.

Brave, intelligent, with eyes that bore into him as though she could examine the depths of his very soul. Rhiannon was a woman of *this* world. He was convinced of it. Tall and graceful—beautiful, though she knew it not. But of greater importance, a woman with a natural goodness and generosity. His lips lifted in a smile with the remembrance of her attempts at his tongue. George would school her in his language, as he'd promised. Fluency in the tongue of Dál Gaedhle would add to her confidence. She had been shy and self-conscious, stating she felt left out in her world. An oddity. Och, if only she comprehended how she stood out there! Like one of their Greek statues he'd seen on Google—a marble goddess among school children's handmade pottery!

His breath caught. He must find the nearest portal and return with Rhiannon. But so much occupied him here. Deciding what to do now Father had passed and their family lands required a laird was not the least of the issues he must deal with at this moment. Kyle was the eldest and the heir to the role of MacEnoicht Clan Chief, but how could he do so while he lay asleep?

And his own role, the one Father groomed him for since birth, that of War Chief of the MacEnoicht Clan? There was no question as to his assuming it now that Gallawain threatened the very sovereignty of Dál Gaedhle by assassinating Father. Arlan swallowed away the ache, then straightened his shoulders.

I will do my duty. The task for which I was born.

Muir remained quiet and followed Arlan through the open sturdy wooden gates of The Keep and into the bailey yard where the clang of the smithy's mallet grew louder and the *thunk* of hardened-wood weapons came from the practice yard.

Arlan grunted and headed in that direction, passing the smithy's forge to where the farrier stationed himself and performed his duty of attending all the horses of The Keep, including the war horses. Arlan drew a silver coin from his belt pouch and stepped up to the farrier, who bent over the large back hoof of a sturdy horse. The wiry man stood tall, letting the horse drop its hoof, and nodded to Arlan.

"Good day to ye, lord. I trust ye are pleased with yer newly shod horse. Fine animal is yer Mengus, lord."

"Aye, man, and thank you for your skill and faithful service." Arlan tossed the silver coin.

The farrier caught it mid-air, his mouth dropping open. "'Tis mighty generous of you, Lord Arlan."

"Nae. Ye deserve it. You do your work with such ability and... joy." Arlan chuckled and the farrier's face broke into a grin. Then he laughed too.

"'Tis my gifting. Serving these sensitive but sometimes crotchety creatures is ma purpose and also ma pleasure." His smile remained.

Arlan led Mengus to the stables and into the stall reserved for him. A stable hand approached.

"Nae, thank you, lad. I'll care for my horse." Arlan removed the tack, then grabbed a curry comb. Mengus' coat was soon soft and shining black and running smooth beneath Arlan's palms. Warmth radiated from the muscles of his solid war horse—his dear friend.

"Mo dheagh charaid." Arlan patted his stallion's rump.

Mengus turned his long face and a deep brown eye to him and nickered softly. Arlan left the stall, and on his way out from the stables passed Muir busy cleaning tack.

"You're not resting from your journey, Muir?"

"I'll come with you to Creagrubha. So I prepare." It was a statement from Muir, not a question.

"Aye, thank you." Arlan swallowed past a thickness in his throat at the dedication of the man. "I have some errands to attend before we leave. And I must find Leigh. I require his dour countenance, for it will brighten our journey to Craegrubha Broch." Arlan gave a fond laugh. The man was grumpy but knew dogs and fought well. Plus, he had relied on Leigh's loyalty and good sense in the past and would need it now. "He will accompany us and bring the hounds."

"I will find Leigh. He'll be in the kennels with those hairy mutts he loves so much." Muir dipped his cloth in a tub of beeswax and picked up the bridle he'd just removed from his horse. "He can drive the wagon while Lord Kyle's man tends to the invalid's needs. We will pile the fleeces high for Lord Kyle's comfort."

Arlan nodded, then walked on to the practice yard and surveyed the sand. Men and women strove against each other in blunted spear and shield practice. Warrior sages looked on, shouting coarse comments that would hit a warrior's heart as much as their body. Leuchars, the Dál Gaedhle War Chief, stood off the sand on one side with an older warrior sage, their heads bent in deep conversation. Massive, solid, with coppery hair, scarred arms and trunk—no beauty. Leuchars' keen and strategic mind made up for what he lacked in looks. He could reprimand with a stare, grind out orders all day, and punish at the merest hint of an insubordinate thought. He was a trinity, loved and hated and respected, all in equal measure.

Arlan approached and Leuchars lifted his head, dismissing the warrior sage. Arlan stood side by side with Leuchars and faced the warriors in the practice yard, the best way to *not* engage the man's combative instincts.

Leuchars grunted, leaving an empty pause between them—usually the man's version of an invitation to speak. Arlan shrugged and took it as such.

"I'll gather my loyal clansmen warriors and assemble a MacEnoicht warband fit to join the army of the new àrd rìgh when that is decided."

Leuchars grunted again. "Aye, leading your clan warband is your duty and your right, Lord Arlan. I have ordered a troop from The Keep's guard to head to the border and seek assistance from nearby villagers," he said. "They will help repair the border forts and designate villagers to man them. Observe the movement of refugees."

Arlan gave a curt nod. "And Ciarán Gallawain's activities."

Leuchars glanced aside to Arlan under bright ginger eyebrows. "There are many forts. It will take time." Leuchars' voice was deep and unusually soft. "Our land has not faced such a threat in the lifetime of these warriors." He lifted a chin to those thrusting spear against shield on the sand. "Not even in mine." His voice returned to its familiar gruffness. "That small-linked tunic ye have commissioned?"

"Chain maille?" Arlan offered.

"Aye. Such a finnicky task, lord. It will take an age."

"It will protect a warrior from a sharp blade."

"And cost a kingdom. Not *every* warrior, then."

My chain maille tunic may never be ready...

The clashing of blunted spears on willow-wood made a companionable clatter while Arlan stood beside the war chief. His mind wandered to his list of tasks he'd left with Sage Eifion. Arlan could exact no official role from the sage. As Father's advisory sage throughout his reign as àrd rìgh, Eifion had become Arlan's close mentor and confidant.

A bond I will never break.

Eifion was to find the nearest portal, seek a missing baby girl from a noble house in years past, and assign the task of making gunpowder to sages Eifion could trust had the skills required. Arlan's mouth tugged in a wry grin.

"I will investigate the gun powder myself," Eifion had said.

"Nae, Eifion, please. It could be a dangerous thing. I need you. Assign the task to another. Maybe a younger sage with a steadier hand." Arlan's face had stretched in a sheepish smile, as it did now.

A young lad ran up to him, pushing past warriors twice his size.

"My Lord Arlan," the lad panted, "the sages who gather for the sage council request your presence."

"Aye, after I've finished speaking to the war chief."

"Ah... They request your prompt attendance, lord." The lad's voice shook.

"Right now?" Arlan rolled his eyes.

"Aye, lord," he continued with a tremble.

Arlan gave a nod to Leuchars, who dismissed him with a slight bow, then stomped along to the caisteal.

The sages always had something they wished to discuss.

Nae, not *discuss... order.*

What would it be now? How he wished to be on his way to Craegrubha Broch, where Kyle could recover and he himself could regroup. But attending to Father's funeral rites, and the ordering and placement of the memorial stone, which had required his approval, had thus far prevented his departure. Now Kyle had arrived, there could be no more delay. Unless these sages invented one.

Leigh had made a hasty journey to the broch and back, at his request, and had reported that Glen Stewart managed well the lands, stock and clan families. Glen was a gifted administrator of all involved in the keeping of the MacEnoicht clan lands. And he had always done so with Father busy in his role as high king. Glen could continue until Kyle was well enough once more.

As second son, all may think Arlan should assume the role of clan chief, for it was the custom with an heir's death or incapacitation. He fisted his hands by his sides. With Ciarán Gallawain's battle machinations, he had not the time nor the inclination to be clan chief. He would be the War Chief of Clan MacEnoicht.

And there is so much more I can do as such.

Arlan marched up to the double doors of the Great Hall. Ahead, sages robed in various colours denoting their stream of expertise sat in a row near the plinth of the àrd rìgh's throne.

"Arlan." Stepping beside him, Eifion held his commanding voice at a whisper, his robe swishing and his long white hair held at his nape by a leather thong, keeping it away from his wrinkled face.

The tension in Arlan's neck lessened at the presence of his old friend. And, by all that is good, he needed him now.

"What's this about?" Arlan whispered out of the corner of his mouth as they approached the sage council together.

"It is about that for which ye returned from the Other World." Eifion kept his usually imposing voice soft. "Taking up your responsibilities."

"Aye, as War Chief of Clan MacEnoicht."

Eifion opened his mouth as though to say more but was interrupted.

"Lord Arlan." A grey-haired sage in the very centre of the line stood, directing his stare at Arlan. Even from some paces away, Sage Cénell's green eyes bore into him.

"Oh," Eifion breathed beside him.

"*Oh*, what?" Arlan stole a glance at Eifion, who silently shook his head.

"Lord Arlan, I speak on behalf of the sage council," Sage Cénell said.

Arlan stood before them and bowed from the neck.

"We have discussed your situation, young lord. Your lands are under the care of your clansman warrior bonded to your family...?"

"Glen Stewart," Arlan replied.

"Well," Cénell brushed over his reply. "It is decided that you will now assume the role of Chieftain of Clan MacEnoicht." His stern-voiced announcement echoed in the lofty hall.

"My brother has just returned to me. He is away to his rooms to recover from his journey."

"He is well? Awake from his injury induced sleep?" Cénell's brows drew together.

"No, but—"

"Then he is unable to tend to his duties as clan chieftain, and you must fill his place," Cénell clipped his command.

"I am... not trained to be a clan chief. That is my brother's destiny. The warrior sages trained me to defend my clan lands and lead battles, not administer a land." Arlan rolled his shoulders and stretched his neck, Kyle's chiding voice ringing in his head. *You are barely fit to be a leader of warriors. How then could you manage our clan's resources and administer justice?* The role required decisions on stray sheep and cattle thieves. Building and planting. He wasn't a farmer. According to Kyle, if Arlan were clan chief, his people would starve!

"Nae. My brother will recover. He will be clan chieftain. Not I."

"You will do what the council advises." Cénell leaned forward, his voice deepening. Advises? *Ye mean orders.* "I am my clan's war chief. That I *can* do."

Murmurs ran along the line of seated sages, and Cénell tapped his foot.

"Ciarán Gallawain rests not." Arlan scowled down at the sage. "I must gather the MacEnoicht warband and prepare. I would lead my warriors and join with the rest of Dál Gaedhle and the new àrd rìgh—whoever may win that title—and push this threat back and keep our land free."

They would *not* make him do it. Glen Stewart was most capable of administering the clanlands. *I will not perform only to fail. I... am... not—*

Eifion coughed. "Sage Cénell." Eifion's voice rose above the mutterings of the sages, and he lifted his hands for silence.

16

Cénell shushed his fellow sages and raised his eyebrows at Eifion. "Sage Eifion, you wish to advocate for this recalcitrant lord?"

"I wish the council to take into account"—he sighed and turned to Arlan— "this young lord is grieving the loss of his dear father. And his brother lies gravely ill."

"This we know, and that is why he must be clan chieftain. Our concern is for the clan. Now our dear high king and MacEnoicht Clan Chieftain has passed from this life, the clan requires a leader." Cénell thumped his fist into his palm. "We do not know if Lord Kyle will *ever* awaken. Who has survived such a head wound?"

Arlan's insides tightened. What if Kyle didn't survive? His relief at his own peace from Kyle's snide taunts would haunt him for the rest of the life he lived without his brother.

"I will not do it." *I cannot.* "My brother will awaken and be clan chieftain." He spoke with confidence, but bile rose and threatened to fill his mouth with acid. "I'll not be stuck in a caisteal when all my skill lies in a fight. I will *not* leave warriors to die while I scratch a quill over a page recording bushels of wheat bagged and fleeces shorn!"

His resounding voice collided with more muttering from the sages.

"My lord sages." Eifion raised one hand to the council, the other pressed warm and firm on Arlan's shoulder.

The sages finally settled and gave Eifion heed.

"Perhaps we can make some arrangement."

Cénell stood in the centre of the line of sages, shuffling his shoulders and eyes narrowing beneath a crumpled brow. "Go on."

"Lord Arlan has rightly spoken. He is a war chief. Unfortunately, we need them now more than ever. I suggest a castellan, a trustworthy soul from Arlan's clan, performs the administrative duties. Perhaps Glen Stewart can continue to do so until one is appointed, thereby freeing this young warrior for the task in which he will excel."

Cénell's face soured. "It is most unusual."

Arlan's neck heated. "Och, man!" His hands curled into fists.

Eifion pressed more firmly onto Arlan's shoulder and Arlan swallowed his comment.

"We live in extraordinary times, lord sage," Eifion said. "Would you at least consider it?"

"We shall place it on the agenda of our forthcoming council session."

Arlan spun on his heal. "I'll not wait for your decision. I go to my lands to gather my warband. Send me word once the session has decided," he yelled gruffly and marched out of the hall.

He kept his back to Eifion, leaving the outrage and disorder well behind him.

THREE

— · —

The sea waves crash,
The breakers roar.
Pounding my soul.
Relentless. Unabating. Endless.
Time presses on with purpose and design.
Carrying me along like flotsam,
To the shores of the inevitable.

POETRY OF A KING
ÀRD RÌGH RHONAN IUBHAR
(4030-4090 POST DRAGON WARS)

The World of Dál Cruinne
Post Dragon Wars Year 6083
Western Sovereignty of Dál Gaedhle
Craegrubha Broch, MacEnoicht Clan Lands

The salt breeze twirled through Arlan's loose hair.

A wave rolled in as he strode along the narrow beach below Craegrubha Broch. He rushed up to the drier shingle but not before the wave crashed around his feet, then churned the wet sand and rolled out. Seagulls cried above him, soaring on the wind, laughing at his soaking wet boots.

The beach seemed just like himself inside... churned.

He'd returned from the Other World determined to take up his role as War Chief of Clan MacEnoicht and fight against Ciarán Gallawain's threat. He ran his fingers along the rich embossing of the clan chieftain's belt he now wore. The legalistic Sage Cénell had thrust it into his hands as he'd mounted Mengus to leave The Keep. Arlan was to mix the role of chieftain with war chief. Glen Stewart would support him by supervising the day-to-day administration of the clanlands.

Och, there would be little joy in such a task.

He resumed his walk. The breakers continued their roar, their consistent pounding in and receding out blended with the rhythm of his stroll along the sand. Brine spray speckled his cheeks, tightening his skin and leaving salt tingling on his tongue.

He faced the stout, sturdy broch built on the widest section on the cliff with its imposing battlement strategic for defence. He glanced behind, to the far mountains, then in front, way out to sea. The enemy had nae chance of sneaking up on this circular fortification.

Here he'd spent childhood autumns with Kyle before winter's bitter winds arrived. Time with Father—as *father* and not Dál Gaedhle's àrd rìgh.

Arlan stood and inhaled the sea-tinged air, and let the memories linger.

Soft sand melted into the wave-drenched shore where the incoming wave obliterated footprints of gulls tired of flight. No sooner had his boots left their impression in the sinking brine-soaked sands than his footprints joined the seagulls'.

That's how his time in the Other World would seem if he didn't bring Rhiannon here soon.

"A sheachd ghràidh cridhle," he whispered into the sea breeze. *My lovely beloved one.*

Oh, how things had changed since he'd left her. His now higher rank and status would affect their relationship, making it imperative she be from a noble clan.

He would still bring her to Dál Gaedhle, despite all of this. For he could *not* be without her. Clan chieftain would mean naught without Rhiannon by his side.

Nae, life would be naught.

How he missed her. Many a night he'd awoken, his head filled with her. Her floral perfume in his nostrils, his fingertips warm from her skin, and his own flesh trembling at the memory of her touch.

But she was not there. His bed empty. His chest aching.

I need you, Rhiannon. I will come for you soon.

"Och, I need a portal!" He clenched his fists.

The day-to-day running of the broch and its steading lands seemed a burden. Adjudicating disputes was the most time consuming, and as clan chief, it was his ultimate responsibility. Steading holders varied from the grateful to those who felt entitled, and that the laird owed them. Arlan grunted. The arguing and placating took him away from allocating arms and training local clansmen in warrior skills so he could build up a warband.

Glen was capable and had stated he was more than willing to manage the general running of the clan while Arlan attended to his war chief duties, only disturbing him for the resolution of complex disputes.

He nodded to himself. Aye, the steward was a good man who understood where Arlan's own heart—and skills—truly lay.

A dark shape caught the corner of his vision, a shadow rippling along the wave indented sand, came from the direction of the dunes. A cry torn by the wind, increasing in volume, vibrated in his ears. Shocked out of his grumble, he turned, raising his arms to block an incoming blow. Forearm thudded against forearm.

Arlan gritted his teeth against the strength pressing upon him. His breath came quicker and heart beat faster, all contemplations dissolved in the wind and his focus now wholly on the fight. He pivoted, allowing the force of his tall opponent's approach to send them forward and past him.

Arlan set his feet apart, bracing himself for the next move, for spinning to face Arlan, the warrior's yell continued.

A fist travelled to his jaw. He dodged then flicked it away. A foot came toward his midriff. He blocked with his forearm, then threw a punch. The man grabbed his fist, turning it out and locking Arlan's wrist. Arlan spun against the hold, bringing the warrior around where he could ram his opponent's chest with his shoulder. He dug his forward foot into the sand and threw all his weight into the man. Their combined momentum propelled them to the ground. The man spun as they fell, landing on top of Arlan, his hold released.

Panting, Arlan grabbed the warrior's fists and held them outward and away from himself. Blue eyes, a long nose, and a scarred dimple sat inches from his face.

"Ye are getting slow, Arlan." Bàn cocked his head. "Ye, more than anyone, should be ever ready." Bàn smiled fully, stretching his mouth wide and deepening the pits in his cheeks.

Arlan released Bàn's fists and wrapped his arms around his friend, squeezing tight. "Oof!"

"'Tis grand to have ye here, sword-brother." Arlan laughed, kicking Bàn off him and jumping to a stand.

Arlan's smile broadened. A fortnight is a long time to be parted from your best friend.

Bàn nodded, still grinning. "Sage Eifion awaits ye in your hall."

Arlan let out a slow breath and turned to the beach for a last look. Waves crashed into the black rocks at the base of the cliff where Craegrubha Broch stood, and white foam sprayed high. The white crested sea-blue breakers continued their roaring roll onto the shore.

They just kept coming, and like history and destiny, they were unrelenting.

Bàn nudged his shoulder and walked toward the broch. "Come on." His voice was almost lost in the wind.

Arlan reached the outer buildings edging the back of the broch, all drystone in construction. Mengus poked his head out of his stall at his approach. Arlan diverted some paces to stroke his stallion's soft, warm nose and Mengus gave a breathy nicker in welcome. Arlan walked with Bàn past the round squat bake ovens and on by the other drystone constructions, within which venison and fish smoked gently on racks. His mouth watered. Aye, the smoked salmon would be ready soon.

He entered the broch and stepped up the gentle slope of the stone staircase that wound its way along the space between the twin circular walls of the broch and eventually led up to the battlement. He passed the storage rooms, then on to the private chambers, and stopping at Kyle's, he peered in.

Kyle lay in his bed where his man attended him, turning him from his back to his side. He did this often to prevent sores that developed from resting in bed all the time. The healer sages had instructed him to do so, for Kyle had grown thin and the bony parts of Kyle's body, now more prominent, were prone to break through the skin as they pressed against his bedding. Kyle moaned softly while his man servant chocked a pillow behind his back, keeping him in place. Kyle just lay there, helpless.

Bàn's warm strong hand clasped Arlan's shoulder. Arlan pulled away from the entrance to Kyle's room and walked with Bàn to the Great Hall. He ambled to the hearth of the large circular room, which was both wide and tall. The fire pit sat centrally with peat burning lazily on the thick stone hearth-slab. Blue-tinged smoke rose past the upper floor that comprised half balconies, then seeped through the thatched roof. Eifion sat by the fire in a deep, high-backed chair, safe from any draughts.

"Welcome, Sage Eifion. I trust your journey went well and the accommodations for you here are suitable." He leaned forward and grasped gnarled hands in his own and spoke into Eifion's ear. "How goes the search?"

"It will please you to know I have sensed close by something like the energy expressed when you travelled through to the Other World. I believe there is a portal not far from here."

Arlan raised his eyebrows, then quickly relaxed his expression. "Ye sensed?" Arlan recalled how Eifion had been aware of his return from the Other World, despite being leagues away. Perhaps there was more to this man he'd known all his life.

Had Eifion involved magic in his knowing? Surely, not. Magic belonged to mages, such as those reported to be in the employ of Ciarán Gallawain. And those who'd ruined the world so long ago with their involvement in the Dragon Wars.

Eifion remained sitting quietly.

"A portal near here." Arlan dare not address Eifion's method of arriving at this knowledge. "Och, that's grand." His shoulders eased as he stood back. His heart thunked against his ribs. Such close access to the Other World—and Rhiannon.

"Though"—Eifion held up a cautionary finger— "we know not where it enters the Other World. It may be nowhere near where you arrived from the other portal. And you report the young woman stated she met you in a time prior to the one from which you have just returned."

"Aye, this is what Rhiannon claims."

"Then any access must be dealt with caution. You must be able to return to Dál Cruinne. You are required here."

An ache for Rhiannon twinged his chest. If only he could step through and be with her.

Now.

Eifion's brows were lowering. Och, could Eifion read his thoughts in his face? He would divert the attention from himself.

"And the lost wee girl?" Arlan tempered his tone, for he would keep his desperation for Rhiannon to himself.

"Ah." Eifion squinted an eye. "I have heard naught. How far back should I go in my search? Of what age is the woman?"

"In her twenties, but as to when she was born, I am uncertain how that should work, for I speak of Rhiannon. And it seems our timelines, Dál Cruinne's and the Other World's, connect randomly. Therefore, I know not in what time of our history her birth would have occurred."

Eifion's hoary eyebrows reached his hairline. "It is your woman from the Other World of which you enquire. How so?"

"Rhiannon possesses a plaid from Clan Gallawain."

Eifion's mouth dropped open. "From your mother's clan?" He stared at nothing; his eyes unfocused, as they did when his mind went to work. "In my lifetime, I have not known of any girl babes lost to people linked to that clan, except by death. Your dear infant sister one of them. This gives me more with which to work. I shall investigate further."

Arlan joined Bàn, who stood by the fire. He turned his back to its heat, keeping eyes on his boots. *Too* much time had passed since his return. How much longer must he wait until he brought Rhiannon back? All Eifion's searching for a missing bairn would be of no importance if the babe, now grown to a woman, was not here herself. He let out a quiet huff.

"That is a miserable look on your face, Arlan." Eifion's tone held a gentle chiding.

Bàn nudged his elbow, grunting in his ear.

Surely they understood how he missed her so?

Steam rose from Arlan's saltwater stained boots and joined the *lived-in* odours of his clan family home now tickling his nose. The peat fire softly popped, illuminating Eifion's face with an amber hue and highlighting his mouth, which slowly widened into a smile.

"Well? Do you wish me to report the outcome of the sage council?" Eifion snuck his hands into the sleeves of his robe.

Arlan cocked his head, raising an eyebrow. "Ye ken very well that I do. Ciarán readies himself and Dál Gaedhle cannot respond successfully without an àrd rìgh to lead the clan warbands as an army against him."

"The sage council has set the Quest. The victor will be the one who finds and presents a dragon's egg to the council."

Beside Arlan, Bàn's eyes widened, and his own eyes strained as he gaped.

"A dragon's egg?" *What?* "That's impossible."

"Arlan, the Quest has never been a straightforward mission. Of those who compete—those chosen from our clan leaders and their heirs—the winner of the task will rule over all the clans here in Dál Gaedhle. We will not have disordered clanlands such as they do in Dál Gallain, with every clan in the east doing as they wish. I wonder not that Gallawain, the opportunist that he is, has used the natural chaos of those clans to his advantage." Eifion barely held the contempt from his tone. "The land and people require the strongest, bravest, and cleverest to be their leader. The best of our best. *Tòireadh* is a pursuit, a chase, a diligent quest. The awakening of dragons is a pressing issue and surely linked to Ciarán Gallawain's endeavours. The new àrd rìgh must have the skills of leadership and be adept at handling the threat caused by that man's ambitions."

"I envy not those clan leaders who'll compete." Arlan lifted his eyes to the thatched ceiling.

Eifion gave a wry chuckle. "It will be a Quest like none other since the Dragon Wars," he said. "I can assure you of that. I am proud to inform you of another decision of the *Sàsaichean.*" Now Eifion's voice held authority, as though about to make an announcement. "The sage council has decreed, considering your brother's continued incapacitation, that you, Arlan Finnbar MacEnoicht, are the contender from your clan."

"What?" A wave of cold splashed from Arlan's neck to his middle and he shot his gaze back to Eifion, who wore a grin.

Arlan shook his head. Such a task. What if he won? Found a dragon's egg and became àrd rìgh? Leading the Dál Gaedhle clans was a great responsibility. He had seen how Father had handled that very same responsibility and bent under its weight.

The clans were in such a need now that refugees spilled over the borders, pushed by the troubles amongst the eastern clans with Ciarán Gallawain's warbands and mercenaries on their heels. Dál Gaedhle needed a high king who could lead the offensive against Ciarán Gallawain, the banished clan lord who would subjugate all under his tyranny. Arlan wished Gallawain's rule on no one, especially his own people here in the west. Aye, a powerful leader heading an army of clan warbands against this man was imperative. He shook his shoulders, now heavy with an invisible weight.

Arlan dropped his face into his hands and closed his eyes.

He *must* do this. Must compete.

But Rhiannon...

The sage council had ordered him.

He ran his hands through his hair. With Kyle lying on his sick bed, there was none other of his rank in Clan MacEnoicht eligible for the task. His clan needed him to try and win.

Father, you would wish me to quest, I know it.

But Rhiannon...

He was a trained warrior and war chief.

That is what Dál Gaedhle so desperately requires at a time such as this.

Now.

So, I have little choice.

My love will have to wait.

"The task of this Quest must be completed before the next blood moon." Eifion's rich voice broke through his spinning thoughts.

Arlan sighed and lifted his head to Eifion. "When is that, my sage?"

"They occur every two to three years. The most recent one occurred almost three years ago, and our sages who study the sky inform us the next is one turn of the moon away."

"I have one month? I know not where to begin."

"Aye, you do, Arlan." Bàn's tone held a hint of challenge. "We must return to the cave on the moor. Where you met face to face with the fire breather."

"Och, no. Surely there are more placid dragons about."

"It matters not the nature of the dragon," Eifion said. "You require an egg. Any female will be protective."

"Thank you, Eifion, for the reminder of the dangerous nature of the task."

"Aye, it won't be simple." Bàn scratched his short, neat beard. "We may lose some contestants."

"Bàn, you'll compete?" Arlan asked.

Bàn gave a half-smile. "The Sàsaichean has not ordered me, as they have you. A cousin of mine, of the same rank in my clan"—Bàn gave a dismissive shrug— "she may quest."

Arlan's brow tightened, then he looked to Eifion.

"Father won the Quest before I was born." Arlan blinked at the stress in his voice. "How does it proceed? What are the rules?"

"It will commence at The Keep," Eifion said, "and the winner is the first to return having completed the challenge in the allotted time."

Arlan frowned. "But this Quest will be difficult..."

"Collaboration is allowed."

"You mean... a contestant can have assistance? A team of sorts?"

"Aye, àrd rìgh is a role taken by a single person but, as you would have observed from your father—*Tobraichean na Beatha* bless his repose—it is one where a leader deals closely with a group of sage advisers and the clan chieftains all throughout their reign. Thus, the nature of the Quest requires it be a grand task that one cannot undertake unaided." Eifion leaned back in his chair.

Beside Arlan, Bàn shared a knowing look with the sage.

"Bàn, ye *will* enter. Ye can, along with your cousin." Arlan nudged him.

Bàn's mouth was a tight line.

"Och, no! Ye are a better man than I. You never shirked your responsibilities or resented your predestined role, as I did. It took a journey to another world to shake me out of my selfishness. Ye will compete for yourself. You've as much right as I."

"Nae, Arlan. I'll serve you." Bàn spoke low and deep, his eyes never leaving Arlan's. "Ye are the leader for the time in which we live and for what lies ahead." Bàn turned toward the fire and stood opposite Arlan, lifting his chin. His hand went to his sword, its handle raised over his shoulder. "You are the warrior-king."

"Ye believe her?"

Bàn's eyebrows lifted briefly, and for the faintest of moments, his cheek dimpled.

"Believe who?" Eifion asked.

"A mad lady we encountered at the sage hold where the healers tended to Kyle." Arlan kept his focus on Bàn, who now knelt in front of him on one knee, arm muscles tightening with his grasp on his sword.

"I have read her words, Arlan." Conviction wove its way through Bàn's voice. "There's much wisdom, and many of her visions have come true. A warrior king is that which Dál

Gaedhle—nae, all Dál Cruinne—requires. And you are he." Bàn drew forth his sword from its sheath, the soft hiss filling the quiet circular hall. He held it, tip touching the wooden floor. "By my blade, you have my sword-arm and my loyalty. I am your man, warrior king."

"Bàn. Stand, sword-brother." Arlan's face burned that such a one as Bàn would bend the knee and swear an oath of loyalty to *him*.

"Nae, my lord. Not until ye receive my pledge." Bàn remained kneeling, grasping his sword hilt, his cheeks hard and rosy.

Arlan speared a look at Eifion, who sat comfortably in the large chair.

"And ye are unperturbed by the actions and proclamation of Lord Bàn, of House Lùthas, who has every right to enter the Quest for his own name's sake!"

Eifion stood. "He speaks the truth, Lord Arlan. You are our king, and we will name you such. Our hearts are set to do all we can to ensure your success in the Quest, for it is not only we who believe in you, but your warriors also." Eifion stepped closer and grasped Arlan's inked left arm, turning his forearm upwards, the triskele prominent. "For what does this emblem stand?"

"It's one of the many symbols of our world," Arlan grunted.

"This symbol depicts a trinity of the physical, emotional, and spiritual journey that is *life*. Ye are upon your most exacting task. Every sharp word of your father's, every admonition and gem of guidance, even each derisive comment from your brother, has taught you wisdom. A precious gift. More valuable than the wealth of your father's realm. More precious than the love of your people—or of a woman. All have prepared you for *this* task." Eifion smiled knowingly, then continued, "A journey to another world. Decisions made there—to return and embrace your destiny. Everything—battles, hardships, love, loss. All used to bring you to this place in your life. This time in your story, in the history of your land. To mould you into a wise ruler. It is not beyond *Tobraichean na Beatha* to fashion strength and wisdom out of hardship."

"The winner should be the one who can not only defeat Ciarán Gallawain"—Arlan lifted his gaze from his ink to Eifion's solemn eyes— "but lead the clan chiefs in unity. And have the ability to administer judgements that will ensure our people have lives free from fear."

"If only you saw yourself as we do," Eifion said with tenderness. "You have the adoration of your warriors, the trust of your people, and the respect of the clan chieftains."

Arlan's face heated. Such lavish praise coming from the sage—no, the man—he respected the most in this life. He stiffened, for Eifion's words held all the hope and belief the people close to him had in his abilities. He glanced at Bàn, who remained kneeling, weapon grasped tight, and living up to his clan name of *strength*, offering both this and his skill to Arlan.

To a cause. To Dál Gaedhle.

He could reject neither of them. Nor could he fail them.

A weight still dragged on Arlan's shoulders, the mantle of responsibility draping itself on him like the heavy plaid cloak of the àrd rìgh worn by Father in the past. He closed his eyes and raised his face to the high ceiling, and his mind to the heavens beyond.

Am I fit for such a task?
"Ye must be, Arlan." Eifion spoke quiet and low. "For our hope is in none other."

FOUR

— • —

The Pledge to Magic, once vowed, is binding.
Masters may change, powers will tilt, but Magic is all.

MAGE MASTER FÀISTINNAECH
(3310-3380 POST DRAGON WARS)

The World of Dál Cruinne
Post Dragon Wars Year 6083
Eastern Clanlands of Dál Gallain
The Road from the Isle of Eilean

Dull grey sunlight reflected in the puddles scattered along the road.

Vygeas sat astride his war horse, Dräger, the grassy lowlands beside the road gently rising to rolling hills. He raised his hand to his sheathed sword strapped to his back, touching the handle, its leather binding worn smooth from his grip. *Hmph.* He needed familiarity and a sense of normality.

Leynarve insisted she and Aiden, his young knave, walk while he rested upon Dräger. He smiled to himself, the scar on his lip tugging. The Lady Leynarve of Monsae was the daughter of a clan chief of Dál Gallain. Her life had changed since her parents were killed. And *oh*, how he knew it. She had run away from her family's caisteal in Monsae, seeking to leave the trauma of loss and the threat of a forced marriage behind her.

Now she thieved.

On their first meeting, she'd advised him she wished to be known as Leyna.

But he would always name her fully.

He chuckled to himself. Leynarve had rescued him from that mob of assassins on the Isle of Eilean. Found the way out, as she boasted she always could. Her *special gift*, she'd named it. And so, it was. Leynarve also had talents when it came to injuries. She'd advised that the stab wounds to his shoulder and thigh required more healing before he would be fit to walk many leagues at a time.

27

He had led them far, and now a pair of weeks spent wandering the countryside lay between them and their escape from that danger.

Aye, licking my wounds, but free of our pursuers.

Leynarve walked alongside his stallion in her leather armour and breeches at a brisk pace with Aiden. Mild uncertainty, alternating with resolve, flowed from her as a streak of colour, like yellow gorse in flower.

Vygeas sucked his teeth. Perhaps he would never completely understand how his own heightened senses worked. How he connected sensations with a specific emotion—a sharpness, a heat, a particular scent or colour. He searched his mind, his feelings, and his inner self to discover how this magic acted within him. Pondering led him nowhere. Again. He shook his head.

Such workings of the enchantment are beyond me.

If only Leynarve possessed his skill for sensing people's emotions and intentions, she would surely know of his relief at her statement of clemency. The one she gave to him in the back of Fhialain's workshop, while those they had freed from their harsh employer made plans for self-directed trade. Kneeling at her feet, she unable to meet his eyes, he had requested pardon.

Nae, *begged* for it for the second time.

Stating her belief that he had changed; she had offered a tentative forgiveness.

It is such a task, for Leynarve has much to pardon.

Vygeas gripped the reins tighter. His role in her parents' death five years ago, as an assassin in Lord Ciarán's service, was a shame to him and a past to remember no more. If only she appreciated how much her forgiveness had meant to him, to his determination to be the new man he had vowed to be.

Leynarve glanced at him, as though hearing his thoughts. She smiled. Her crooked two front teeth! How his heart leaped at the sight of them.

In the air between them, a wave of affection, streaked with the barest hint of hesitation, wafted a perfume his way. Vygeas' mouth tweaked with a smile of his own, for this was often how he *saw* emotions.

Aiden strode staring ahead. Vygeas chuckled to himself. There was an awkwardness in his knave at the newfound affection between Vygeas and the lady, and warm, rosy glow hovered around the youth. Leynarve had indicated that her resolve to forgive the unforgivable had arisen from a comment of Aiden's.

Aye, this tall lad with dark curls hanging over his eyes, though from a poor hamlet, was a wise old soul in a young body.

Vygeas resumed his surveillance of their surroundings, casting his senses and perception over the environment. A brine-tinged breeze from the Island of Eilean, now far behind them, blew over the hills. He touched the pouch at his belt containing the proof of death of his mark. This last completed hit was the key to his liberation. Success in the task, Lord Ciarán had said, would ensure his reprieve from the gallows.

Vygeas denied it not that he *did* deserve hanging for deserting from the lord's army. He was a warrior, and the killing of innocents in the last battle he'd fought for Lord Ciarán had pushed him too far. With Gille Fhialain and his family safely set to sea to start a new life on another shore, Lord Ciarán need not know of Vygeas' ruse. He let out a satisfied grunt. Seeing Gille Fhialain and his family aboard that ship to sail away, instead of dead in a ditch of Vygeas' own digging, had been Vygeas' first step away from living as an assassin and turning to the direction of right.

Now he would present the finger and signet ring of Gille Fhialain to Lord Ciarán as *proof* of his mark's death, then be free. This was his plan. But that deceitful Lord Ciarán loved the *game*.

"I have searched for an alternative to an audience with this lord but have found none," Vygeas said and looked down from the saddle at his lady companion. "We require a strategy, Leynarve."

"I agree, for I trust not that lord." She turned her face up to him, her melodious voice taking on a serious edge. "He would presume he could dupe you once more."

"He would try to take you, Lady Leynarve." Vygeas softened his usual guttural tones and braced himself for Leynarve's reaction, for she would dislike his next statement. "Ye will not attend but hide nearby."

Leynarve's mouth pressed into a line, then her lips parted.

"Aiden will come with me." Vygeas halted her protest.

She snapped around and faced ahead, treading the road with a heavier foot.

"I dinnae have to stay and mind your horse!" Aiden asked, a flash of surprise splashing out from him.

"We will observe the goings on of Lord Ciarán's Tower then choose a time when the steward of the caisteal is busy," Vygeas said. "That cocky one would be quick to restrain us."

Vygeas' mind flew back to the Isle of Eilean and the storm that had almost wrecked him on his journey to the trading island. How abrupt its ceasing and how sudden the sense that Drostan, Lord Ciarán's mage, had left him with the storm's abating. What had happened to Drostan? Vygeas had strained his heightened perception, only noting Drostan's absence, not discerning how it had come to be so.

Hmm. "I sensed something amiss with Drostan after that storm on Eilean," Vygeas said. "So, it is possible we may be free of mage interference at the tower. We shall try to avoid the steward, but Lord Ciarán will be as cunning as ever."

"I still have your dagger, lord." Aiden's face beamed at Vygeas. Pleasure's aroma trickled over from the lad. Aiden felt so at Vygeas' trust in him, no doubt, and Vygeas' inclusion of him in the plan.

"Aye, ye will require it." Vygeas gave a nod of approval. "For we must fight if they attempt to detain us."

Fumes of anger tinged with annoyance blew from Leynarve, bellowing clouds of deep crimson in his face.

"My lady, ye must stay safe." Vygeas put all the affection he could into his tone. "Remember, Lord Ciarán wants you for your birthright, Lady Leynarve of Monsae. The army of warrior clansmen belonging to the House of Monsae would be his if he were to wed you. The man is ambitious, if nothing else."

"He is also deceitful, ruthless, greedy, despicable and impatient." She twisted to face Vygeas. "What if he takes you both?"

"Och, he will nae, my lady," Aiden interjected. "My Lord Vygeas is a fierce fighter. Ye ken his gifts make him see, in some strange way, the moves others intend to strike at him. We shall be oot o' there before they can even give thought to the pursuit of us." Aiden returned his gaze to the track. "If ye dinnae mind me saying, my lady."

Leynarve turned back to the road, a fist curling by her side, the other grasping the handle of her short sword at her belt while annoyance danced crimson around her.

The road brought them to a forest, the very one where he and Leynarve had first become acquainted, and a warmth filled him at the memory. Their meeting had been a dance of swords as he'd tried out Leynarve for skills and assessed her scent for intentions. Her expressions had flashed with surprise as he pre-empted her every sword thrust and strike. His mouth stretched into a grin.

Blades and bows! She was still magnificent. How he could have gained the trust and affection of such a woman, he would never fathom.

Vygeas continued to ride Dräger through the wood for most of the day on the way to Lord Ciarán's Tower, and a slow grinding rumbled in his guts at the approach.

"Ye will stay at the forest's edge, Leynarve, while Aiden and I spy the goings on in the tower." Vygeas dropped from the saddle. A twinge of pain stabbed his thigh and joined the constant ache in his shoulder.

"You are still healing." The tone of an order dominated Leynarve's voice. "You need an extra blade—"

"Leynarve." He put a mental fist on the harsh words that would come out. "You are not coming. I want you safe. Stay here, I beg you."

Leynarve raised her eyebrows, stunned at his tone. Acid vapours flowed from her, her mouth closing on a retort.

How I long to kiss that mouth once more.

Such a while—an argument, completing a mark, fighting for his life, and escaping a mob of cheated assassins—since he last tasted her sweet lips.

Vygeas leaned forward and rested his mouth on hers, opening it to play with her tongue. Leynarve stiffened at first, then relaxed into his caress and her arms curled around him.

"Please?" he said, once his lips left hers.

She gave a slight nod.

"Ye have kept that blade sharp?" he asked Aiden, who had turned away from their embrace.

"Aye, lord. And I remember all ye have told me of where to stab for a most effective kill."

"You would make a warrior of your knave, V?" Leynarve slid her hands from his neck, her mouth curving up after her use of the nickname she had given him.

"All will need the skills of fighting," Vygeas said. "For if Lord Ciarán has his way, our entire world will be at war."

"But my lord"— Aiden's eyes lit up as he oozed confidence and enthusiasm— "ye plan to fight on the side of the Àrd Rìgh of Dál Gaedhle, Donnach MacEnoicht, did ye not say? And we will win, for his is the side of right, is it no'?"

Vygeas smiled at Aiden's remark.

"Right does not always win, Aiden." Leynarve's tone held up her disillusionment like a placard.

Vygeas' smile turned into a grimace. Aye, life had dealt hard blows to the woman he loved—himself an instrument in the cause of the most severe.

"Whether we win or lose, we must be on the side of right." He raised his head, pouring conviction into his voice. "For as long as I have left in this world, I will be found nowhere else."

Lord Ciarán's Tower

Bram sat leaning on the edge of his cot, breathless. Heat stirred in his throat at the incapacitation controlling the dragon had wrought in his body. A wild, fearsome beast, resisting Bram's willing and magic. He had wrested control from the creature, and it had taken all his strength and skill to guide the animal to his destination.

The Keep in the west.

And the man who was high king.

A disgraceful deed to perform—all at the master's will.

What powerful magic to tame the beast and do Lord Ciarán's bidding!

A month consumed to recover enough to sit up and walk only a short distance and attend a fraction of his daily tasks. He groaned through his teeth.

Even so, while I am weak, Lord Ciarán cannot force me to do what I will not.

The man still insisted on the search for portals and more dragons' lairs. The discovery of each would mean another task followed, all in line with the ambitious lord's plans.

Would Bram ever become affectionate toward his new master?

He doubted it.

The man was a fox. An impatient one, but clever. A strategist who was always many steps ahead of his opponent. He kept his plans close to his chest. At times, Bram had found the lord's intentions difficult to see in his divination bowl. Lord Ciarán was a thinker with a broader vision than was first apparent. What may seem a minor setback, or even a mistake, could ultimately be part of his plan. Bram shuddered at the recollection of the glimpses he'd had of Lord Ciarán's future.

Bram sighed. At least now he had a reprieve. In his impatience, Lord Ciarán had left his tower and headed off with a laird whom he had reprimanded for dallying over the requisitioning of warriors and stores from another laird with clan lands some leagues away. He had announced he would do it himself and left in a simmering rage.

31

The tower was now in a silent watchfulness and a quiet peace, except for when the lord's man bawled out a lesser servant.

Lord Ciarán had also taken with him the man from the Other World, Findlay, determined to discover more of him. Findlay claimed to have come through a portal in Dál Gaedhle in the west after following the passage of three young people. On questioning Findlay, Lord Ciarán had discovered these to be Dál Gaedhle warriors, though Findlay could not vouch for it, being ignorant of such things.

The man was intriguing, bright, and observant. On this journey, Lord Ciarán would assess his true value. Bram sucked in his cheeks. Findlay was like most, who on seeing the influence Lord Ciarán possessed, wished to be under the lord's protection, being a stranger to this world and so on. Findlay, blatant in his hope to win favour with Lord Ciarán, had produced a small black object he could hold in his hands and declared it a weapon he called a *gun*. A useless weapon in this world due to a lack of *bullets* and a substance he named *gun power*.

Or was it gun powder?

Bram shrugged and stood, his legs shaking. But he was stronger than yesterday and even the day before. Aye, forcing activity, as the healer woman had advised, helped to improve his stamina. The divination bowl in the workshop opposite his small sleeping room called to him. He stepped across the landing and entered the dimly lit chamber, welcoming the familiar scents of herbs, all mingled in the air together, leaving none dominant. He limped to the shelves of pottery containers filled with ground herbs and touched the sheaves of vervain hanging from the drying racks above, the leaves crisp between his fingertips.

Much had changed since his arrival at Lord Ciarán's Tower. A heaviness settled on his chest, and he sighed to push it away. Drostan, his beloved master, was dead. And now he held the sole mantle of mage. Lord Ciarán had petitioned the mage masters of Innesfarne to send another junior mage to fill Bram's previous role. So far, Innesfarne was silent. Bram snorted. Lord Ciarán would fume at their reply, which for certain would be a rejection of his request.

It would be so. He wished such a post upon no one.

Bram stepped to the stone divination bowl, now empty of water—evaporated over the course of time since its last use.

Water—vital for all life and the truest element.

He took the water jug from the bench beneath the shelves of herb containers, removed the cork, and poured the clear liquid into the divination bowl carved from stone. Peace filled his soul and the air hummed with its calling. Bram leaned toward the bowl, his soul yearning for the power the water contained, held for him as his conduit. A vision of his master Drostan flitted through his mind—what the addiction to such can mean. He stood back, summoning self-restraint, and bracing himself for his first foray into *seeing* for a month.

He placed his hands on the bowl's edge. A cool wetness met his fingertips and without hesitation his soul dived in then rose above the narrow round tower of the caisteal. From here, the surrounding land lay before him. A stone henge stood to the north some leagues away, but a stirring in the forest that skirted the road to the tower caught his spirit's attention. He flew toward it.

Silent walkers slid between the trees. One tall man in a grey hooded coat with a sword at his back, long hair tied warrior-style, and face scarred. Another, a lad with the long lanky limbs of youth, followed, his movements noiseless, like the warrior's. They worked as a team. Bram sensed more than friendship between them, but they were not brothers. Their focus was on the tower, their intentions not apparent.

Bram moved closer. The man's features gained clarity and Bram gasped.

It was the assassin on whom his master had sought revenge!

This Vygeas was once a prisoner given a chance at freedom. Drostan, resenting him for some past misdeed, had pursued the man after Lord Ciarán had tasked Vygeas with an assassination. The completion of which would give Vygeas his freedom from the hangman's noose for his crime of desertion from Lord Ciarán's army. Or so Lord Ciarán had said. And now the warrior returned. Come to obtain what was promised, no doubt.

Bram hovered beside the warrior and the lad. He should seek revenge on this man. The one who had caused the death of his beloved master! Inflict such pain as he himself had suffered on holding the dying form of Drostan.

Bram paused, his spirit hovering in the foliage and his mind filling with recollections of Drostan enthralled in his magical energies while he gripped tight to the stone divination bowl, body arched in rapture, and face filled with expressions of delight.

Nae. The cause belonged not to this assassin, but to his own master's addiction to magic, his desire for vengeance, and the consequences of both.

Dealing out revenge leads to murder upon murder. On visionary forays into divination, Bram had *seen* the images of these deaths trailing behind Lord Ciarán's form.

I will not yield to such desires. Too much death haunts me. I will avoid all I can.

The warrior's eyes flicked in Bram's direction. He looked at Bram, his eyes widening. "Who are you?" The warrior drew his sword.

"What is it, lord?" the youth asked.

Bram retreated, flying back to the bowl, and returned to his body now drenched with sweat and heart pounding his ribs.

The warrior had sensed him! *What special gifting does the man have?* For a magic resided within the man's form.

Bram hobbled to his cot, dragging heavy limbs, and lay down, fatigue engulfing him.

The loud voice of the lord's steward echoed up the circular stairs of the tower and hit Bram's ears.

"Well, the lord n' master ain't 'ere, is he? Who else is gonna see 'im?" His voice rose like gravel grating rock. "It was t'other mage that 'ad to do with 'im so this one can, 'an all." The heavy steps of the lord's man clomped up the stairs, gaining in volume. "Oi," he shouted into Bram's open door and glared at Bram lying on his cot. "You can come deal with this one." He stabbed a meaty finger at him.

Bram sat up and scooted to the edge of the bed.

"'Tis that scarred assassin returned." The lord's man scratched his stubbled cheek. "The lord did nae say what tae do if this one came back." He looked thoughtful—as thoughtful as possible for this man. "I could throw him in the dungeon—"

Bram sent a *numbing* to the servant's mind, dulling any initiative he may have considered.

"No, man," Bram said. "I will attend him. I know what is required."

FIVE

— • —

Our legends record that once placed under lock and key, the dragons slept. As well the key, in the place where all the knowledge of this world's realms resides.

DRAGON SCROLLS OF INNESFARNE
DATE OF TEXT UNKNOWN

The World of Dál Cruinne
Post Dragon Wars Year 6083
Eastern Clanlands of Dál Gallain
The Library, Lord Ciarán's Tower

Leyna climbed hand-over-hand.

Hooking her toes into cracked stonework and missing mortar, she scaled the wall of Lord Ciarán's Tower to where the large hall next to the round tower abutted the tower itself. No one had spotted her flight across the stone-paved courtyard, nor it seemed, her spider-crawl up the wall, for no one had cried out the alarm. The burly manservant had previously strutted across the courtyard like he owned the caisteal. Only moments before she had begun her ascent, he had walked by her as though in a stupor while she flattened herself to the tower wall.

Vygeas would know she had left her position in the forest, for he constantly cast his senses across his environment, and she had learned that he always sought to detect her location. He was protective of her.

It was sweet, but also annoying. She could look after herself!

She was assured of Vygeas' silence. Reprimanding her now—if he dared—would only draw attention to her presence. She couldn't suppress a smug grin.

Leyna crept along a windowsill and peered through a narrow window into a hall where a fire raged in an enormous fireplace. It was the great hall of this tower. The place where the laird held audience. A young man trod with care across the stone floor, his posture stooped as though in pain. He stopped in front of the fire, then turned and faced the entrance to the hall. He wore the black robe of a mage and had hair just as

35

black except for a broad streak of grey from his left temple. The mage was handsome, with a chiselled chin, but dark ringed beneath his eyes and he staggered to a nearby chair, leaning heavily upon it.

Leyna frowned. No laird to receive petitioners? No Lord Ciarán, then.

She breathed a relieved sigh. The entrance doors to this hall opened, pouring daylight onto the darkened-wood floor.

Vygeas and Aiden entered and walked toward the man, who nodded his acknowledgement. It appeared Lord Ciarán *was* absent, and the tower caisteal's quiet plus a mage receiving V, confirmed it. Vygeas held his shoulders wide but not tensed—relaxed and sure of this meeting, perhaps sensing this man was no threat. Vygeas would not have entered if this young mage had dulled his gift of heightened perception.

Leyna continued her ascent until the third floor, where she crept across to the round tower's only open window. She placed her toes on the narrow ledge of stone lip that ringed this storey, and gripping the stonework above with her fingertips, sidled along to the window, then paused. No sound came from within.

Leyna slipped through the window, then dropped to the floor. The chamber's fireplace was bare and chill, matching the cool touch of air on her face. She examined the room, squeezing her nose against the odours hitting her nostrils. Shelves filled with books and scrolls lined the walls. The musty stench of old and the inky scent of new permeated the air, which was heavy with knowledge oozing from animal skins and parchment texts. More scrolls and sheets of vellum lay scattered across the desk in the middle of the room. A bronze statuette of a dragon held down an edge of a scroll. Whoever spent their time here, most likely Lord Ciarán, had left in a hurry.

The door to the library stood ajar and no noise ascended the stairwell. Leyna peeked through the crack of doorway to the narrow circular stone stairs.

Empty.

No shouts to restrain the unexpected visitors came echoing up the stairs.

All well with V and Aiden, then?

She slid to the desk. If this was Lord Ciarán's library, what was he reading? She perused the scroll beneath the dragon. The parchment was cold to her fingertips, hard and cracked in sections, and the writing in an ancient tongue. Some characters caught her eye and her lips skewed in a grin. A sage-tutor of years past had insisted she learn extinct languages. Rapped knuckles now bore fruit. One figure represented the word *dragon*.

Footsteps echoed up the stairwell.

The scroll spread beneath a dragon effigy would be important to Gallawain. And if it was valuable to him, it must be worth silver. Five years with a band of thieves taught her skills a lady should never know.

Or use.

Leyna grabbed the scroll, leaving the dragon effigy wobbling in the wake. She shoved the document in her chest armour then slid out of the window. She perched on the edge of the windowsill, her banging heart inside her chest was like a war drum, and her hands slippery on the cold stone caisteal wall. The door creaked open behind her, and Leyna crept away from the glazing.

"'Oo left that open!" The gruff voice belonged to the servant who'd stridden around the caisteal as though it belonged to him. Meaty hands pulled the glazing shut and clicked a latch tight.

Leyna released her breath, waited until the man's footsteps receded, and turned to make her descent. Halfway down she spied Vygeas and Aiden exiting the tower. They strode from the courtyard toward the forest. Leyna continued to creep down the side of the tower in silence then, covered by the poor light of late afternoon, tread carefully through the tower's courtyard.

"You what!" Vygeas' firm grip tightened around her upper arms. His face, dappled by late sunshine passing through the forest foliage, pierced her with a glare of annoyance.

"I'm here, V. Unharmed. And I have something interesting to show you."

"Ye snuck into Lord Ciarán's library, my lady?" Aiden's voice rose, his inflection strangling his last word.

"Oh, be not surprised, Aiden"—Vygeas faced Aiden briefly— "for she is a cat on a roof."

"Ye tell me naught, my lord, for I crawled every roof of Eilean with her." Aiden leaned against the nearest tree trunk, his mouth curling into an appreciative grin.

Leyna stood taller and handed Vygeas the scroll.

"What if we were in danger?" He took the scroll without glancing at it. "What would ye have done then? And dinnae say ye would have come to our rescue!" Vygeas' commoner accent came through his angry words.

"V, I knew all was well. I observed you with the mage before I explored."

Vygeas' shoulders relaxed, and he let go of her arm.

"I take it all went well?" she asked. "For it was not Drostan."

Vygeas straightened, his eyes unfocused on the scroll in his hands, and his face tossed by emotions. "Drostan is dead. His apprentice, now Lord Ciarán's only mage, reports it was due to over-imbibing in magic."

"He told you this? Why?"

"The mage... held no hatred toward me. His aura was benevolent. And the steward who runs the place and tormented me when I languished in Lord Ciarán's dungeon, at first displayed his usual antagonistic demeanour. But on returning from announcing us to the mage, he looked right through us. Hmm." Vygeas tapped his thigh. "Also, whilst Aiden and I were approaching through the forest, I sensed a presence. It must have been the mage aware of us drawing near. Perhaps he"—Vygeas wriggled his fingers in the air— "dulled the caisteal steward with magic. We would not have fared so well with Lord Ciarán in attendance. The mage, Bram, paid me then sent me on my way with a parchment declaring a reprieve of my death sentence. It was as though this mage wished for my freedom from the man." Vygeas paused for a thoughtful moment. "It may be the young mage wishes for some freedom of his own."

Vygeas unrolled the scroll Leyna had handed to him and regarded it, then his forehead creased, pulling at the scar on his right eyebrow and accentuating his confused expression. "What language is this? These pictures mean nothing. Why do you claim it such a prize?"

"It is ancient Ionan."

Vygeas' puckered scar deepened.

"My father's sage taught me to read it." She rubbed the knuckles of her right hand. "I believe it speaks of dragons."

"Dragons do not exist." Derision laced Vygeas' tone.

"Don't they?" Leyna placed her hand on her hip. "Then why is Lord Ciarán so interested in them?"

"What? This is all mythology." Vygeas' words grated out. "You risked yourself for a fantasy, Leynarve."

"If dragons piqued the curiosity of Ciarán Gallawain, the contents of this scroll may be worth the knowing." Leyna grabbed the rolled parchment from Vygeas. "It will be silver in our pockets at the least."

Vygeas released a heavy sigh. "Come, we shall seek accommodation at the nearest inn this night. Aiden—"

"I ken, my lord." Resignation filled the lad's tone. "I ready the horse."

Leyna scrunched her toes inside her boots, her tired feet longing for some respite. "It does not appear to be much, but the food was edible." She gestured to the tavern in the middle of the village. Paint peeled from the swinging sign, a picture of the fabled red beast from which the *Flying Dragon* derived its name. "I dined here the day before I met you. Assassins huddled in a booth on that occasion."

Vygeas grunted. "We shall keep our heads down and dine in our room. And purchase decent fare. For along with my freedom from Lord Ciarán's service, the mage granted me payment for completing that last mark." He turned to Aiden, who led his war horse. "Aiden."

"Aye, lord, I ken." Aiden sighed and hung his head. "Take Dräger to the stables."

"No lad, ye shall find us a room"—Vygeas took the reins from Aiden whose mouth hung open— "while I stable Dräger."

"Aye, my lord." Aiden's eyes brightened, and he grasped the small bag of coin his master passed to him, then strutted into the tavern.

Leyna grinned at Vygeas. "He adores you. You know that?"

"What?" Vygeas led Dräger, frowning.

38

Vygeas settled Dräger in a stall, paid the ostler, and pulled his grey hood over his head. Leyna got out her cap, put it on—tucking her hair inside it—and walked with Vygeas to the inn, entering by the back way.

Inside the inn, a blare of chatter and clanking tankards hit her. In the corner by the stairs that led to the upper floor and rooms, Aiden bartered with the landlady, a harsh-voiced woman with a kind heart, from what Leyna recalled. The aroma of roasting venison hit Leyna's nostrils and, beside her, Vygeas' stomach grumbled. His face drew tight at the clatter filling the room. She had seen it before. The excessive sound would be battering his hearing, for Vygeas had avoided noisy crowds whenever possible.

He glanced sideways at Leyna, then strode to the landlady and began a conversation. Leyna couldn't catch his words, so she stayed put, examining the room. She had learned one can discover much from being a quiet observer.

Candles burned in sconces placed along the walls above the booth seating at the edges of the common room. Smoke from the open fireplace hung low in the air, mingling with the scent of ale, tobacco-sticks, and unwashed bodies. Conversation hummed through the place, interspersed with exclamations that echoed off the stone walls. Patrons called to the serving women for more food and drink. The locals, wearing leather vests over loose linen shirts and warm breeches of sturdy material, relaxed in their usual gathering place, but their faces held grim expressions.

Leyna ambled to the stairs. She would discover the cause of the furrowed brows.

"Aye, it was." The loud comment came from the booth nearest Leyna. "Ma cousin telt me. His brother-in-law sent back word. Donnach MacEnoicht is *dead*. He an' his personal guard was burned to ashes by a fire-breathing dragon, so they were."

She slid her gaze to the booth, slowing her amble further. Beside the speaker, one listener's eyes went wide, while his other companions showed no surprise.

"Where have ye been that ye did nae ken that?" the informer of the àrd rìgh's demise asked his neighbour. "News is all over the place. There's a dragon awake in Dál Gaedhle."

"Nae," another man interrupted. "Tha beast is all over Dál Cruinne, for ma uncle's uncle saw it fly from near the Central Meadhan Mountains here in Dál Gallain, aye."

Leyna spun back to Vygeas, who had turned from the landlady, his forehead like rock. He beckoned her with a lift of his chin, then went up the stairs with Aiden. Leyna strode through the crowded room and straight up the stairs behind Vygeas. She entered their accommodation, which had two beds with linen of questionable cleanliness, a table and one candlestick.

Leyna shut the door tight behind her and pressed her back to it. "Dragons."

"Aye. The air was thick with questioning and anxiety." Vygeas grimaced. "Enough to give me a stabbing ache to the head."

"*Dragons*," she repeated, piercing Vygeas with the most pointed stare she could muster. She pulled the scroll from her leather armour. "I didn't risk my life for a myth. Lord Ciarán is behind this." She waved the scroll in Vygeas' face.

"The àrd rìgh is dead." Vygeas' voice was flat.

"They need another," Aiden piped in. "The landlady said they've set a quest."

"*The* Quest," Leyna corrected. "*Tòireadh*. Where all the clan chiefs of Dál Gaedhle, or their heirs, compete to be the high king of the western regions of the land. It is usually a task requiring physical and mental prowess."

Aiden snorted. "Well, this one certainly is, my lady. The landlady said they are to find a dragon's egg. Who can do such a thing?"

"Who indeed?" Vygeas held out his hand to Leyna. "Show me that scroll, Leynarve, if you please."

"Oh, you are interested now?" She set her hand on her hip.

"It may assist in winning the Quest."

"Assist who in winning? For, as an heir of a house of Dál Gallain and of the east, I cannot enter. And you, V..."

Vygeas' cheek muscle flickered.

"Surely there is a worthy contestant in Dál Gaedhle?" Aiden asked. "Does not Donnach MacEnoicht have heirs? Wouldn't they be able? Made of the same noble substance as their father?"

"He has two sons." Leyna opened the scroll and spread it on the rickety table.

Someone knocked on their door with a heavy hand. "Vittles," a gruff female voice called.

Aiden opened the door to a serving woman holding a platter containing a cut of venison, roasted vegetables, and bread rolls. The woman barged in and headed for the table. Leyna whisked the open scroll off in time for her to clunk the wooden board down.

"Tha's a feast for a king. Ye are all hungry, aye?" She stood with her hand outstretched, and her pointed stare directed at Vygeas. A maid entered with tankards of ale and placed them on the table with a clatter, ale slopping over their sides, then bustled out. The serving woman's right eye squinted at Vygeas. He dipped his hand in his pouch at his belt and pulled out a coin.

"The patrons are tense this night, madam." He held the coin over her upturned palm.

"Aye, the Àrd Rìgh of Dál Gaedhle—"

"I ken this." He kept the coin poised.

"Lord Ciarán amasses an army."

Vygeas tilted his head.

"I could tell ye more, but..." She poked her tongue out the corner of her mouth.

Vygeas inhaled through his nostrils, dug into his purse, and held two small silver coins over the woman's hand.

"'Tis said he owns a powerful mage who can control dragons." The woman snatched the silver from Vygeas' hand and strode out, slamming the door behind her.

Vygeas remained staring at the door, frowning.

"V?"

"It is not Drostan. So, unless Lord Ciarán has another mage, it must be..."

"That feeble man?" Aiden scoffed then stepped to the platter covered in roasted fare dripping in gravy.

"Perhaps such a task weakened him." Vygeas tilted his head. "What does the scroll tell us, Leynarve?" Vygeas removed the dagger from the top of his boot and, joining Aiden at the table, sliced the haunch.

Leyna held the scroll up to the light of the lone candle and ran her vision over the faded characters painted in a dark ink with a fine brush. Vygeas stood beside her, chewing a slice of the succulent meat and peering over her shoulder.

"What kind of script is this?" Vygeas asked. "They are not runes, ogham, nor letters..."

"Each character represents a word. This here"—Leyna pointed to one— "means home." Then she pointed to the character that had caught her attention in Lord Ciarán's library. "And this one stands for dragon."

Vygeas *hmm-ed* around a mouthful of meat. "What does it tell us?"

"Aye, my lady," Aiden asked. "What does it say about dragons and finding their eggs?"

Her forehead tightened, and she peered closer, the Ionan script's meaning sketchy. She spoke the words in her head, feeling the rhythm of the language once more, then with clarity, she read the portion of text again. Straightening her shoulders, she looked Vygeas in the eye.

"It is not what is says. It's what it doesn't say."

"What do ye mean"—Aiden's face scrunched behind the chunk of meat he held to bite— "my lady?"

Leyna concentrated on the faint characters finely brushed on the scroll. The venison's gamey aroma blew from behind on Vygeas' breath as he leaned over her shoulder. Rowdy singing rising through the floor from the tavern's main room downstairs, combining with the muffled clanking of pots below from the scullery staff tidying up from the evening meal, all became vague background noise while the scroll spoke to her the history it recounted.

"Leynarve?" Vygeas' deep voice pierced through the thrall evoked by the script.

Leyna swallowed and removed her focus from the characters.

"I shall read it to you," she announced.

Vygeas' hazel eyes gazed down at her through thick lashes. A puckered scarred eyebrow rose in expectation.

"Please do, my lady," Aiden said. "For I can bear the suspense nae longer."

"*Thus, the Dragon Wars ended,*" Leyna began. "*Many clan chiefs returned to their lands in shame. In the west, the clan chieftains of Dál Gaedhle came under the rule of one àrd rìgh, Àeon Breathnach. Dragons used by men, those surviving the cruel mastery of the mages, were set free or slain. The females in captivity were forced from their nests, and their clutches of eggs confiscated.*"

"What happened to their eggs?" Aiden's excited comment came around a mouthful of roasted vegetables.

"Did your mother nae teach ye to no' speak with food in yer mouth?" Vygeas spoke his sharp reprimand to his knave over the top of Leyna's head.

"It is a good question," Leyna said.

"Aye, and...?" Vygeas tapped his thigh.

"This is the written record of this history. Legend says they stored the scripts of the day and other artefacts of the time in the treasure of knowledge at the Broch of the Ancients. Sages speak of this place in awed tones. So far, this scroll mentions neither."

"We are speaking of six thousand years of history and legend. So... does the history cancel out the legend?" Vygeas asked.

"It is possible some people have rewritten history to serve their purposes." Leyna allowed her cynicism to slip into her tone.

"Would there be an egg there?" he asked. "At this Broch of the Ancients? An artefact of the time? Or perhaps, the sages there were charged with its safekeeping."

"An egg would be rotten by now." Aiden turned up his nose.

"Or preserved," Vygeas suggested.

"Does it have to be a live one?" Aiden asked.

"I'm sure we could discover other helpful information concerning such an egg in this Broch of the Ancients." Leyna faced Vygeas. His brow dipped, and his fingers danced at his thigh. "V?"

"Where is it?"

"The Broch of the Ancients is on the island that sits in the Long Loch, Eilean Sgathaig," Leyna answered. "It is way in the west. We would pass The Keep of Dál Gaedhle and the clan lands of House MacEnoicht to get there."

"Then we shall seek Donnach MacEnoicht's sons," Vygeas announced.

Aiden's mouth gaped open, poised over a bread roll.

"Why?" Prickling rose up the skin on Leyna's neck.

"We shall offer our services to the son of Donnach MacEnoicht who challenges for the Quest."

"We are from the east, my Lord Vygeas." Aiden dropped the roll on the platter. "We have no right of it."

"No, but I desire to help." Vygeas turned concerned eyes to Leyna. "If I wish to fight with the man against Lord Ciarán, I must prove myself. For the son of the àrd rìgh will be wary of one who was once in the employ of Lord Ciarán Gallawain. How better a way than to assist him to win?"

"And demonstrate your loyalty and undying devotion." Leyna finished the line of argument for him, her chest tightening at the implications of such.

"What if he is nae a good man, lord?" Aiden blinked beneath his dark, curly fringe.

Leyna joined Vygeas in a stare directed at the young knave, the muffled noises from the tavern below filling the space left by their silence.

Vygeas lifted a heavy shoulder. "I must meet the man. If he agrees and we journey to the Broch of the Ancients, this will be enough for me to know him."

"Know him?" She echoed with Aiden.

"Aye, *know* him. If I am to align with his cause and fight against my old lord, Gallawain, I must be certain he is honourable and worthy of my efforts. For I will not proceed then find I must retreat and risk the gallows once more. My allegiance, apart from my very life's blood, is the most precious thing I can pledge."

Six

—·—

Portals are a sentient magic. They perceive. Intentions and desires are the key to unlocking the traverse between worlds. In possessing such discernment, the magic has been known to work as a gatekeeper.

SECRET SACRED WRITINGS OF THE SAGES
LOCKED SCROLL 34
GRAND MASTER LLEW'S PRIVATE LIBRARY
ISLE OF INNESFARNE

The World of Dál Cruinne
Post Dragon Wars Year 6083
Western Sovereignty of Dál Gaedhle
Craegrubha Broch, MacEnoicht Clan Lands

Night-time quiet filled the broch.

No early morning shuffles or murmurs of servants attending their morning tasks. Only the continual rhythmic rumble of the breakers against the rocky outcrop on which Craegrubha Broch sat. A dog barked in the yard and a lone bird chirped. Arlan paced his candle-lit quarters, brow tight and shoulders sore with holding them just as taut.

Would that I could stop thinking on the conversation of yester eve!

He huffed, placing his hands at his waist. Eifion's mention of a possible portal nearby had tossed its waves through his mind all night. He rubbed his gritty eyes, and an inner urgency filled his belly.

So close—a portal to Rhiannon's world. Or so Eifion thought.

Eifion had not spoken of its workings. What if all portals were the same? He could go to her world and find her then, having noted the place, wait until a sunrise or sunset, and return home. With Rhiannon.

It would work. *I have done it before. I could do it again.*

But what of his responsibilities here?

"I would not be long away, surely? For I came back but a day later last time."

43

The Quest.

He sighed. He must do it. It was his responsibility. But in truth, he desired to lead a warband and be part of the army that would defeat Ciarán Gallawain. But to be àrd rìgh and lead the clan warbands?

He must compete.

Must win.

But what if I return not from Quest...? To retrieve a dragon's egg was no easy task.

"And I, more than many, ken what face to face with a dragon entails."

A flash of vertical-slitted pupils in a leathery, pointed face rose to his remembrance, just as the dragon had risen from its rocky cave below where Arlan had stood that day. The day the dragon who killed Father had awoken from its lair. A shudder passed through him.

He grabbed his sword, Camhanaich, from where she leaned by the wall and grunted at the blade's impotence against such a beast. If only the cannon were ready.

He *must* go through this nearby portal and discover where it entered Rhiannon's world and find her there, wherever *there* may be. He could die in the Quest and never see her again. His vision misted. He shook the would-be tears away, an urgency stirring in him.

He tensed his arms, Camhanaich's handle digging into his palms. *I will go.*

He grabbed his best kilt and wrapped it about him. Rhiannon had mentioned that on their first meeting he wore a kilt, the tartan of which she'd described as muted tones. Aye, those who wore kilts in the Other World sported tartans of brighter colours. Maybe this kilt, in a tartan of soft green, was the one. He strapped his sword and another blade to his back and stepped along to Bàn's door. He knocked the faintest of taps and the door opened. Bàn stood there wearing breeches, plaid, and blade.

"Aye, I kenned ye would wish tae try," Bàn whispered. "At sunrise, is it?"

Arlan gripped Bàn's shoulders, and without a sound, hastened him along the winding stairs and outside to the stables where night held onto dark, its chill dampening Arlan's bare arms. He grabbed a torch and lit it, illuminating the stable yard, the horses stirring at their approach. Mengus poked his head from his stall and nickered a soft greeting.

"Ye are sure of the place, Bàn?" Arlan spoke low.

"Aye, for Eifion behaved a wee bit odd at the spot. Stopped his mount and walked around the wood muttering thanks it was not *beul an latha* nor *beul na h-oidhche.*" *The dawn of day nor the dusk of evening.*

Arlan chuckled softly. "Och, that will be the place."

Arlan saddled and mounted Mengus, then rode from the broch's outbuildings without a word. Bàn rode beside him on the stretch of road leading from the broch, the pre-dawn hush joining their subterfuge.

Bàn turned off the main track. "We came by a shortcut." Bàn led him through to another track entering a small copse, then he slipped off his stallion.

"This is it?" Arlan jumped off Mengus onto the damp ground of a sparse wood of silver birch, though the trees were thick and heavy with their late spring foliage. "It is barely a wood."

Bàn lifted a shoulder and let it fall. "The old man got exceedingly excited over your *barely a wood*."

Arlan squinted. "I'm not sure how long I will be in Rhiannon's world"—he pointed to the ground— "but I will determine to come back to here. It worked for my return to you, Bàn."

"Aye, ye will brother, or I'll win the Quest for you." Bàn face twisted in a lopsided grin. "Dinnae joke."

"Och, it's almost daylight. On ye go. And give that beautiful woman of yours a big sloppy kiss, aye?"

Arlan's mind returned to the time Rhiannon had dressed for him as a Celt. Wearing, she said, the same clothing she had worn on the day she'd first met him at that Celtic Festival. His thoughts filled with a vision of her in a chain maille top, long boots, a swathe of tartan around her waist, and holding that heavy sword which was very much too large for her... This *costume*, as she named it, would suit his world the best. Arlan straightened his shoulders, then strode between the trees.

Arlan stepped back into the small copse where Bàn awaited his return. Bàn stood with arms folded, staring at his boots. The daylight about him was dim, and the shadows of early morning barely formed. Bàn lifted his head, eyes wide and jaw slack.

"What? Did it no' work? I'm sorry, Arlan, for I was certain the old sage knew of what he spoke—"

"Och, it worked." Arlan placed his hands on his belt and bent his head forward, savouring the moment a slightly younger Rhiannon, dressed as a Celtic warrior, was so surprised at his caress. Her slim body had trembled in his hands while she allowed him to hold her to himself and place a passionate kiss on her lips.

"And?"

"Aye." Thoughtful pleasure welled from within and echoed in Arlan's tone.

"Ye were nae there for long. The sun has not yet fully risen and ye have been gone but moments."

"Nae. I spent the whole day." He dropped his hands from his belt and stared at Bàn. "The portal opened at the grounds of an old caisteal. I saw Rhiannon arrive at the festival where those attending dressed as Celts and princesses and warriors. She'd told me of such. There were some decent blades for sale, also. George was with her, so I waited until the man was out of view and..."

"She knew you?"

He shook his head. "It was before my journey there. The first journey for me. It was her past, when she would first meet me."

"And you have left her there? Was that no' the whole reason for this foray into a portal? To retrieve your love?"

45

Arlan clenched his fists. "I couldn't bring her through. It would've meant bringing her by force, for she did not know who I was, nor of the love we would share."

"Ye kissed her?"

He grinned and nodded, a tingle still lingering deep within him.

"And she let ye, even though she knew you not?" Bàn's blond eyebrows lifted.

"Och, she is a good woman. I surprised her, but she had noticed me and stared with interest at my approach." Arlan stood taller, then shook his head and released a sigh. "Och, Bàn... to hold her again." His voice frayed at the edges. "I must return for her in a time she will ken me."

"Arlan, ye must prepare for the Quest, that is what ye must do. *This*"—Bàn waved his hand toward the thin wooded copse— "was a risk. You cannae take another. I ken you pine for her so. Ye were exceptionally miserable last evening." He slapped Arlan on the shoulder. "But ye mustn't try again till after you have won the Quest."

Arlan glared at his friend, then looked away from Bàn's intense but honest expression. "Och man, ye have become so serious."

"'Tis a serious time, my brother. And ye need to focus on your task. For yourself. For me. For your warriors. For your woman, when ye bring her back, needs to ken the people of Dál Gaedhle have a warrior king to lead them."

"Aye, I cannae deny that. Ye are being my conscience once more. A nearby portal leads to her, so I must send warriors to watch her before the connection is lost. Ensure she's safe until I can go. Oh, how I wish Eifion were more expert in these portals!"

"I shall go." Bàn rested his hand on the dirk at his belt.

"Och, no." He scratched his chin. "I'll send others, but I must inform them of her world and teach them some of her tongue. English, the language she speaks, is one of their hardest tongues, or so Google says, yet many speak it."

"Google?"

"A wise... sage." Arlan waved his hand in a dismissive manner. "Not many ken the Gaelic, though."

"The Gaelic?"

"The equivalent of our tongue. Nae, I think I shall assign this task to your sister and Angus."

Bàn flicked his head in query.

"Angus and Morrigan are young and shorter than you or I and look much like the youth of Rhiannon's world. They would pass as one of them most easily." Arlan lifted his chin. "And Angus, coming from Muirton, has seen some sights in that the seaside town of trade, I'm sure. Perhaps no' easily shocked or flustered at strange things."

"Aye, he lived on the streets for a wee while until his lord benefactor took him in. Will be canny with finding his way around the Other World."

Arlan gave an abrupt nod. "When they arrive today, I shall ask."

Arlan stood at his hearth in the round hall, the heat from the peat fire taking the chill from his back, but the warmth that filled his chest and infused his being came from another source all together.

His warriors knelt before him, their naked swords set in front of faces wearing serious expressions. He surveyed them one by one, a lump forming in his throat. The veteran Muir, the man he trusted in all things battle. Leigh, who knew animals and could employ them like weapons. Douglas, a warrior he couldn't do without. Angus and Morrigan, young but good fighters both. Adele, a mean-looking woman who fought just as meanly but with a tender heart that poked through at surprising moments. Eifion stood to one side with Bàn behind his warriors, who gave their oaths in the same manner as Bàn.

Heartfelt. Earnest. To the death.

All to be faithful to *him*.

Arlan swallowed.

"My friends, rise. I thank you for your pledges of service to me. In return, I promise my protection and support. I will endeavour to not disappoint you, in service or in friendship."

Smiles sprang on faces lifted to him as his warriors rose to their feet.

Eifion stepped forward. "Arlan, may I speak freely on an important matter?"

"Aye, Eifion," Arlan said.

The sage approached and Bàn's face contorted a touch, as it did when he sought to hide a grin.

"What did you think you were doing!" Eifion's resonant voice filled the broch's round hall.

Arlan's breath stilled in his mouth.

"Did you think I would not discover your use of the portal?" Eifion had stepped to be a pace away from Arlan. Although much shorter and slighter in build than he, Eifion was formidable. Arlan's feet acted of their own volition and took a step back from Eifion, just missing the edge of burning peat.

"I needed to see Rhiannon—"

"And you did?"

"Aye." Arlan's cheeks heated.

"And yet she is not here." Eifion gazed around the hall in a dramatic manner.

"Nae, well, she didn't know me. It was before I'd met her and we..." Arlan's words dried up at the stern expression on Eifion's face.

How does he do it? I feel like a child rebuked!

Morrigan stared at the floor and both Muir and Douglas averted their gaze. Arlan gritted his teeth against the heat rising to fill his face.

"By all that is good." Eifion's voice was low and deep. "I know not how you achieved the journey to her and back again without my assistance."

"I managed on my own in the first place..." Arlan allowed a minuscule shrug of his shoulders.

Eifion's eyebrows drew together. "You risked the portal uncertain of the outcome?"

47

"I held a vision in my mind of Rhiannon dressed for our world. I wished not she should enter strangely attired." He shrugged stiffly. "But it was the wrong time, for she knew me not."

"And to come back?"

"Of home and Bàn awaiting me."

"Hmm." Eifion's hoary brows remained joined above his nose while his gaze wandered the room.

It had worked. Why the dressing down?

"I have determined to send warriors to protect Rhiannon until I can go for her," Arlan said, straightening his posture. "And when I do, I will go in a time when she knows me—"

Eifion spun and faced him, brows in his hairline.

"After I have completed the Quest, Eifion. Panic not!"

"So, who?"

"Who?"

Dragon's breath! I would've sworn the sage would say nae to any further foray through a portal.

Who indeed? Arlan's mind scrambled, assessing in moments the benefits and risks of sending each member of his sworn warrior band. His conclusions remained the same.

"I propose Angus and Morrigan to be the ideal travellers. They will fit well into the Other World."

"Will ye go?" Arlan directed his question to Morrigan, who had inspected the floorboards at her feet throughout Eifion's interrogation, and Angus, whose eyes showed their white all round and locked on his.

Morrigan lifted her head, blinking. "It is another world, my lord."

"Och, it shall be grand, Morrigan." Angus' body vibrated and he bounced lightly from foot to foot. "We shall observe your lady from a distance, Lord Arlan. We shall protect her also, shall we not?" He glanced at Morrigan beside him. "It is a dangerous world from your accounts of fires and *riots*." He turned to her then. "Lady Rhiannon might need you, Lady Morrigan, for she may not like to approach a warrior who is a man if she chances upon our spying." He turned glinting eyes back to Arlan. "We shall be discreet, my Lord Arlan. Keep our distance."

Arlan grinned at Angus' enthusiasm. "Lady Morrigan, I chose ye both, for ye work well together. I trust you, but if you don't wish this..." He waved his hand.

"Forgive me, Lord Arlan, I will go as you ask," Morrigan said. "We've faced dragons in Dál Cruinne. There can be naught fiercer in the Other World."

His other warriors left the hall to attend to horses and chores after their journey to Craegrubha. Eifion sat in the high-backed chair against a wall, eyes closed and hands resting on his lap, clasping a freshly plucked twig from the ash forest nearby. For the rest of that day Arlan instructed Morrigan and Angus in the tongue of Rhiannon's world, concentrating on phrases most useful. They caught the language with speed.

"To purchase food, ye must attend their markets they name *super*," Arlan explained.

Angus shrugged. "We shall hunt, lord."

"Nae, do not! You shall risk arrest for poaching. Buy the food with the coin ye can get from selling the jewels I shall give you. And for travelling from where the portal opens in the Other World in the grounds of the caisteal, to Rhiannon's wee village"—he screwed his mouth to the side— "ye will have to travel in a very large cart on long lines of metal. They call it *rail*." He rubbed his fingers through his beard, then scratched harder. "Maybe I'd best explain to you the moving cart they name a *car*."

Arlan's steward, Glen, threw peat on the fire in the centre of the broch's hall. Arlan followed the sparks as they flew upward, cooling and disappearing just before passing as fine ash through the circular thatch roof. He turned to his warriors gathered around his fire, nudging aside the deerhound that had followed Leigh in and, on deciding its place was the warm hearth, had spread its lengthy frame along the entire hearthstone.

"I am pleased and ye have impressed me." Arlan looked at Angus and Morrigan. "I believe you should go tomorrow."

Bàn's brows knit. "Are ye no' a wee bit too eager, my lord?"

"I can tell them all else they need to know tonight, and they can go through at tomorrow's dawn."

Angus sat taller, and Morrigan smiled. Her command of English would be enough to get by.

Douglas covered his mouth, mumbling a curse. "Pardon, ladies."

The others shuffled where they stood.

"Is it not too soon, Lord Arlan?" Adele asked. "I understand your wish to see your woman safe and here as soon as able, but are they prepared enough?"

"They are ready." Eifion spoke behind them.

Arlan looked across to Eifion, and his warriors turned to face the sage.

"What they know will suffice." Eifion's voice was deep with command. "Lord Arlan, it is well. They may go and seek your lady. I shall supervise their journey through the portal to the Other World. We must trust in their desire to come home for their return journey. From what I have read in the scarce ancient scrolls of which I have access"—Eifion scowled at Arlan— "plus your recent endeavours, this appears to be all that is required for a successful traverse."

Arlan stood with his troop in the copse, the edge of the sky pinking, indicating it would be a rainy day, but he cared naught about the weather. He returned his attention to his two warriors dressed in leather breeches and linen shirts and shouldering cloaks to conceal their weapons—short swords. These he ordered they only slip from their hiding place if dire circumstances prevailed.

"Find the quickest route from the country caisteal to Rhiannon's village. Engage not. Observe her from a distance at first. Choose your time to approach, if ye need to approach at all." He placed three jewels in Morrigan's trembling hands, ignoring the tremor in his own. "These are the gems ye can sell for coin at a shop named *Pawn*. Sell one at a time and go not to the same shop to do so. Ye may raise suspicion. If needed, purchase a car. It is much like driving a wagon, I believe. Rhiannon drove always." He shrugged. "I have told all I can of such things. Although a small card is required if a guard asks for a licence. I know not how ye would get one." Arlan frowned.

"Worry not, Lord Arlan." The corner of Angus' mouth tweaked, and an uncommon look of assurance filled the young man's features. "Their world is like ours, from what ye say, and there are always those who can obtain these things... Perhaps not by means ye would like nor wish to know." He gave a small cough. "Another jewel may be required... lord."

Arlan dipped into the purse tied to his belt and handed Angus a ruby.

Bàn hugged Morrigan and slapped Angus' back. Eifion stood off to one side and leaned against a tree, and the others stood back. Arlan's temples rang with the beat of his heart.

Silver light escaped beneath the cloud along the horizon and the young warriors stepped into the small wood, then disappeared.

"That was it?" Douglas asked.

"Wait"—Bàn held up a hand— "for yestermorn, Lord Arlan returned in an instant."

Arlan held his breath, and a silence filled the small copse. If they did return immediately as he had, there would be more news of Rhiannon. Moments passed, his shoulders tensed, and the sun continued its rise, the silver glowing orb now sitting above the horizon.

"Och well, that was a disappointment, if ever I've had one," Douglas said.

Aye, it is, but not in the way you think, Douglas.

Rain pattered on Arlan's head, coinciding with its drumming on the leaves of the scraggly trees of the copse. A strong hand gripped his shoulder.

"Come, Lord Arlan," Bàn said in his ear. "Let us await news of your woman in a drier place."

Arlan returned to the broch with his warriors and Eifion, then sat with them around the fire in the hall, discussing his plans for the Quest. If only his need to partake and win were not so pressing, he would have gone himself and returned with his Rhiannon. Aye, Eifion and Bàn were right. It was too much of a risk to venture another journey himself.

By evening, the rain had ceased. He rode to the small wood, Bàn by his side and the others close behind. Wet-green leaves, sodden from a day's rain, sat stark against trunks washed a brighter white. Eifion put his arm around one of the spindly trunks.

Och, the man loves trees!

Arlan stood in the cold awaiting Morrigan and Angus' return until the darkness of night surrounded him, his breath loud in his ears while the birdsong settled. Bàn coughed, breaking the quiet.

"My lord, Douglas and I shall stay in case they return," Leigh offered.

"Ye need not be here all night." Arlan clenched and unclenched his hands. "The portal will open again at sunrise."

"Even so, my lord"—Douglas stood beside Leigh— "we will stand guard."

"Aye, this is wise." Eifion let go of the tree and stepped closer to Arlan. "Our knowledge of these portals is limited. Perhaps an active one may make it possible for others to transport to our world. Someone should watch here."

Arlan's shoulders drooped. "Send word the moment they return."

"Aye, lord."

Arlan rode back to Craegrubha with his diminished troop, a weariness between his shoulder blades and in no mood for chatter. His head ached from lack of sleep from his night disturbed by thoughts of portals. He went over, once more, all the possibilities of what he could do to obtain a dragon's egg, although he'd exhausted all ideas already.

More research is what I must do. He gave a tired nod. If only he had Google.

Glen roasted a haunch of mutton for their evening meal. Arlan ate among the quietness of low-voiced conversations, only broken by his orders for Glen to send portions out to Leigh and Douglas at the portal.

Arlan bade his friends goodnight and trudged to his sleeping quarters. He stepped into his small chamber and, closing the door behind him, leaned against the wood. His room was dim and empty. He'd become so accustomed to Rhiannon in her room nearby. Arlan threw himself on his cot and sighed.

If only she were in my bed now—in every sense of the word. Ciest mo chridhe. My darling.

He would never find another such as her, and he'd wed her the moment she arrived.

Sleep eventually came, along with dreams of dragons, and flourishing blades, and a woman warrior with long russet hair.

Pounding rattled his door in the early hours accompanied by Bàn's shouts through the timbers. Arlan opened his eyes, his night candle now a flickering stub in a puddle of melted wax. He ran to the door and flung it open.

"Arlan, they returned once barely light." Bàn grabbed Arlan's upper arms, his wide eyes reflecting the glimmer of the candle flame. "Och, brother"—his shoulders heaved— "they've been in the Other World for six turns of the moon!"

Seven

— • —

Life twists and turns on a meandering path,
And is never straight for long.
An obstacle in your track
Can bar your way,
Or send you on the path to the shortest route home.

VISIONS AND SAYINGS OF THE BLIND LADY SAGE

Our World, 2018
Abernethy, Scotland

I raked through my bag.

Hairbrush, lip gloss, old train ticket... *Eww!* Something else *old* but unrecognisable and squishy. I threw it into the bin. My phone was right at the bottom of my bag, as usual. Drawing it out, I checked for any missed calls.

None.

I looked up George's number and checked again for missed texts or calls... for the sixth time this month.

Six being the number. It'd been that long—six months since I'd last spoken to him. Knowing George, he'd interpret any form of communication from me as a change of mind. And possibly—no, most likely—think he could come and start the intimate relationship he wanted.

That point between my shoulder blades grew cold.

I'd never felt like that about George. And even if I had felt something, I could never be unfaithful to Arlan, the man I loved.

I shut the cottage door and strode down the path to my car, shucking my bag on my shoulder. Halting at my gate, I gave a soft snort.

"I love Arlan, but they'll probably never allow me to love *him*." I stomped to my car, gripping tight to the strap of my bag. How on Earth could I prove my parentage?

"And why does it matter so much?" I mumbled while I unlocked my car.

When I finally *did* get to Dál Gaedhle... If I did...

Man, I needed a distraction.

"I'm going to Glasgow!" I shouted out loud.

They'd once named it the Cultural Capital of Europe, after all.

Just as well I'd decided to go out for the day. Even if it was on my own. Sitting around at home moping wasn't getting me anywhere.

I drove to Perth railway station and caught the train to Glasgow Queen Street Rail Station. I arrived and I stepped onto the platform beneath the Victorian arching ironwork supporting a roof with clear sections. Squinting at the sun's glare, I put on my sunglasses. Did they have structures like this in Dál Gaedhle? From what Arlan had said, it had seemed to be all stone castles and brochs.

I strolled out of the station past shops, stepping out of the shadow of the buildings, the sun's warmth touching my head and shoulders. *Hmm.* My heart twinged a little. Last time I was in Glasgow... was with George...

I walked all the way through the central shopping area, then further on to the Kelvingrove Art Gallery and Museum. The dusky yellow sandstone building, in the Spanish Baroque style of the late 1800s, looked out across a park.

Joining the crowd gathered at the museum, I stepped carefully to avoid colliding with others milling about the entrance. Scots and tourists alike must've been *getting their art on* today. The art gallery *did* have many fine pieces.

I entered the museum, my footsteps joining others ringing on the hard stone floor. Children's voices lifted to the high ceiling of the main hall as they ran past couples both young and old. I wandered through the hall and the smaller galleries, pausing at the second exhibit to let the crowd clear before I could lean in to read the information beside it. Then at the third. Same at the fifth.

I sighed. My shoulders had lifted to my ears, hunching against the grating noises surrounding me. The people in the crowd were so physically close to me.

Something in the edges of my vision caught my attention, but when I turned... no one in particular was looking at me.

Huh. You're becoming paranoid, Rhiannon.

I needed some air. And some space.

Outside was Kelvingrove Park, a green parkland dotted with small woods intersected by the River Kelvin. I ambled along a meandering bitumen path for about fifteen minutes, past statues, fountains, and bandstands with the whoosh of traffic distant and the chirping of birds close by, and the tension in my shoulders eased.

Sitting on a park bench, I closed my eyes and let Arlan's descriptions of Dál Gaedhle float through my thoughts, giving birth to a vision. Red deer trotted out through the edge of wild forests. Birdsong filled my ears... the drumming call of the capercaillie and a wood dove's soft coo. The mild scent of heather—the perfume of the mountainside—melded with the tang of pine and rain on the wind. Voices murmured and armaments clattered in castles' bailey yards, where warriors prepared for battle.

I bit my lip against the welling tears. It now seemed more like home to me than here. That world spoke to my soul, whereas this world... I let out a sigh and wiped the tears away.

Arlan was in *that* world. The land of Dál Gaedhle, and he would be fighting for it.

"And I will too!" I sniffed.

My hand rested on the bench seat, the flaky paint rough beneath my fingertips. Surrounded by the relative calm of the park, I drew in the fresh wood-scented air, then took my homemade sandwiches from my bag.

A young couple strolled past hand in hand, gazing into each other's eyes. I pressed my lips together, dropping my vision to the empty seat beside me. For a flash, the indelible impression of Arlan's back while he rode Mengus into the portal rose in my mind. Repressing a sigh, I shook my head and returned my gaze to the couple.

They both looked like they'd just come from a photo shoot. The woman was drop-dead gorgeous, with long wavy blonde hair and fine features but fit-looking, and her tight sleeves moulded to her slim, muscular arms. The man was tall and well built, like he worked out in a gym regularly. He wore his dark blond hair in a bun.

I cringed and pretended to be obsessed with the ham filling in my sandwich while they passed.

Never understood man-buns.

I ate my lunch, then walked out of the park at Clifton Street, passing a few blocks lined with terraced houses. I turned a corner into Sauchiehall Street, and a feeling that had sat in my subconscious all day came to the fore again, like I'd just missed *something*. Now a prickle rose on the back of my neck.

I spun. Leaning against a wall just behind me, the couple who I'd noticed in the park stood kissing—passionately.

Snorting a quiet, embarrassed laugh, I turned and walked on.

At least *someone* was having a romantic day.

I ambled down Sauchiehall Street, scrunching my mouth. Something about that couple brought Arlan to mind. Lately *anything* could, but they truly did—young, healthy, beautiful, and, just like Arlan, exceptional-looking human beings.

Perfect.

Terraced housing changed to shops and cafes. I'd reached the mall end of Sauchiehall. Tables and chairs under bright umbrellas shaded patrons enjoying their meals and coffees. The atmosphere had a European feel. A double row of trees lined the centre of the mall, and I walked right down the middle of them. A breeze blew, the leaves chattering in its wake above me, and the warmth of the sunny day filled me.

At the end of the tree plaza, a waist-high billboard caught the corner of my vision. I turned to face an A-frame sign for a teahouse. Some Earl Grey wouldn't go astray, so I followed the sign's direction down the lane, passing the pub on the corner, an Indian restaurant closed till evening, and an old draper's shop. The lane was quieter away from the main drag of the busy mall and ahead, the tea shop's sign hung above its door.

Walking toward it, I crossed the entrance of a small alley. A clatter echoed out of it. I glanced in. Two large industrial waste bins sat opposite each other at the far end.

"No!" a man's cry funnelled out of the alley. "No—" His voice choked off.

I halted, the man's stress-filled tone gripping me. A thud—like a heavy object coming down on a chunk of meat—and a *crunch* echoed from behind one of the industrial waste bins. I cringed, stomach roiling at yet another dull *thunk*.

Then nothing.

Quiet filled the alleyway, drowning out the faint distant street traffic.

Maybe I should help?

The man who'd yelled might be hurt and need medical attention. It'd sounded like a mugging. But his attacker could still be around and stepping into danger wasn't the wisest of approaches—lesson number one at self-defence class.

A man rose from behind the left metal bin—greying, brow set, deep-creased cheeks. Blood spatters sprayed lines across his face and neck in bright red.

His sharp gaze hit me, his brown eyes connecting with mine, and his teeth bared.

A fraction of time—but long enough to embed *that* man's features in *my* memory.

I turned and ran.

On reaching the end of the lane where it entered Sauchiehall Street mall, I stopped. Raking through my bag for my phone—nearly dropping it with fumbling fingers—I dialled 999, spinning on my heel to face behind me into the lane.

The man came out the small alleyway, fast-pacing it toward me.

I snatched my phone from my ear and continued running into the centre of the mall where, a couple of shop fronts back, dawdling shoppers perused the shop windows, but were too far away to be of any help. The man's expression filled my mind—an acknowledgement that he'd seen enough of me to recognise me again.

Surely, he wouldn't follow me into the mall, all blood splattered like he was?

I wouldn't wait around to find out.

"Arlan, why haven't you come back for me yet!" I ground out under my breath.

I sprinted out of Sauchiehall Street—as best I could in my dress-shoes—and turned to my right past more shops. Following the footpath as it crossed the road over the M8, my thigh muscles burned, but my eyesight was sharp and clear—like when I'd fought in competitions. I paused, panting, and snuck a peek behind.

The man was no longer following me.

The only people I could see were shoppers emerging from the mall and a woman with two kids walking across the pedestrian crossing.

My panting had returned to heavy breathing, but a churning roiled my stomach.

I have to get out of here.

Charing Cross was the closest station, and the most public place. Now the entrance loomed right in front of me. Feet burning in my court shoes, I swiped hair from my eyes and went straight down the escalator, flinging a glance behind me every few seconds. There were only other commuters standing dull-gazed on the escalator steps—*but not that man.*

The train to Glasgow Queen Street Station was arriving at the platform.

How did I get here? Man, making my way to the platform had been just a blur.

I hopped on, and with my knees knocking, fell into a seat. I scanned the carriage—an old man reading a newspaper and a woman with so many shopping bags it was a wonder she could hold them all. The young couple from the park, who'd been kissing at the top of Sauchiehall Street, had just jumped on.

But not *that* man.

I settled my breathing and willed my heart rate into submission. Swallowing, I forced saliva past my dry mouth while the train lurched forward, and I sunk into the seat. An electric whine filled the small carriage travelling beneath the great city of Glasgow.

A Good Samaritan—that was usually me. *But not now.* Not when I needed to keep a low profile. Stay unnoticed. It would be so much harder to slip out of this world if I was a witness in a court case. I was guilty, but only of wanting so badly to be with Arlan.

My phone began to buzz in my hand—or maybe it had been for a while. I answered, my fingers shaking so much it was difficult to *slide* to connect.

'Emergency services. You made a call.'

"Oh, yes." *When had I hung up on that one?* "There's an injured man in a lane off Sauchiehall's mall," I rattled into my phone. "I'm on my way home. I'll report it at the police station once I get there." I hung up before the operator responded.

I glanced around the carriage again. It had slowed, and the next stop was Glasgow Queen Street Station. People rose from their seats and moved to the doors, grabbing handrails, not one person looking at me. The train came to a halt.

I expelled a breath, long and slow, then stood. Good, my legs were only slightly shaking now, and I could walk without collapsing. I stepped off the carriage, took the escalator up to the next level of Glasgow Queen Street, which led to the ScotRail Station platforms, then waited for the train to Perth. The train pulled into the station and the words *Rèile na h-Alba* painted beneath a window passed my view. The wind in the train's wake stirred my hair as the engine's whine came to a stop. I took a sneaky glance to either side of me.

No sign of *that* man, nor any suspicious types. The attractive couple, the same ones I'd spotted throughout the day, hopped on through the door at the far end of the carriage. I stepped aboard, a shaky giggle escaping me and the strap of my shoulder bag digging into my hand.

I chose a seat facing the direction the train headed. The train left the platform, its acceleration gently pushing me back into the slightly softer rail-seating. Out the window, city buildings rolled past, then suburbs, and soon green fields alternated with housing. The train rocked gently, and the wheels over rails *click-clacked* rhythmically. The tension in my arms receded a little, and the prickle at the base of my skull disappeared.

At the top end of the carriage, the attractive couple sat snuggled close, their seats facing my way. I landed my vision on them, and the man's eyes darted away from my direction. Moments later, my vision rested on them again. His gaze flicked off me once more.

Perhaps they'd seen something, too. They'd been close behind me for most of my stroll through the mall.

I stood and walked down the aisle to their seats, bumped by the rocking motion of the train. The seats opposite them were empty, so I sat. The man straightened, and the woman tightened her grip on his arm, but she smiled at me. That was enough.

"Hello." I directed my greeting at the young woman.

The man remained silent, and very still.

"Hallo," the woman answered, her accent strong—perhaps Scandinavian? That fitted in with their exceptional good looks and blond hair.

Well, they all speak English there, don't they?

"I've seen you both quite a bit today." I smiled. *It might break the ice with the foreign visitors.* "We're both doing the same tourist-type things."

The woman smiled thinly. The man's eyebrows dipped, and his mouth tightened. Actually, all of him did. He looked like a coiled spring about to be released. Like Arlan when he was wary of—well—*anything*. This young man was very warrior-like.

I chewed my inner cheek. But I *had* to know.

"Did you see what I saw? In that lane? That man?" I hadn't imagined it or misunderstood what I'd seen, had I?

"English not so good, sorry." The young man shook his head in apology, his accent now clearer.

Not Scandinavian. More like Stornoway.

No—not from the Isles of Scotland. But *very* familiar.

I bore my stare into him and opened my mouth to speak.

He stood abruptly. "This our stop." He dragged the young woman out of her seat, and they marched to the carriage door.

The train slowed, and the signs for Stirling Station slid past the windows. The couple disembarked and melted into the crowd of passengers heading off the platform. I scooted to the window on the platform-side of the carriage as the train lurched to a start. The couple, their heads clearly above the commuters surrounding them, stared at the departing train, the lines of their mouths tight and brows crinkled.

EIGHT

— • —

Beat a man once and he'll take it.
Beat him twice, and he'll hate ye.
Beat him every day
For every day and more
And that will be the day that he breaks it.

ANCIENT PROVERB

Our World, 2018
Perth, Scotland

Detective Sergeant Rabbie Findlay ambled through the doors of Perth's Scotland Police Station. The doors were exactly the same as yesterday. Although it was the afternoon shift, his head still ached from poor sleep, and his limbs were heavy, like he'd run a marathon.

Just like every day for these past few months.

In the reception area, sharp tones, holding irritated words, passed between a group at the back of the queue and a man on the bench seats by the wall.

Findlay huffed, leaned into the glass pane in front of the reception desk, and rapped on the window, the glass cold beneath his knuckles. The constable on desk duty took his gaze away from a lad with his face practically against the window who was speaking loudly at him through the purpose-made slits. He met Findlay's eyes.

"Get a handle on that." Findlay pointed over his shoulder with his thumb to the brewing anger at the rear of the line.

"Aye, sir." The officer skittered back from the desk. "There's a young lady reporting an incident. She's in the interview room with Detective McNab. He wanted you in on it."

Findlay lifted his chin in acknowledgement, and the door buzzed. He pushed the door open and swiftly shut it on the rising clamour.

Maybe it was time to take that early retirement package.

Rubbing shoulders with the scum of the Earth and their victims wore him down.

More and more with every passing day.

It was like he was a pencil drawing—a cartoon sketch of a cop, comical, with a big belly and nose to match his own. A giant eraser wiped out a piece of him every time he stepped through this door.

The back parking bay door slammed open, and two officers entered pushing a cuffed man in front of them, accompanied by grunts and colourful, imaginative language coming from their charge. Findlay almost got out his notebook to record their uniqueness. Further emissions of encyclopaedic expletives came. He shook his head.

No. Not enough pages left in my notebook.

The man spat on the floor and skidded on his heels while the two officers headed him to the holding cells.

"Af'noon, Serg," one constable threw over the head of his charge.

Findlay backed into the doorway from the front desk and let the procession pass, side-stepping to avoid another expectoration.

"Oi!" the other constable reprimanded the man in custody as they passed Findlay. "Sorry, Serg," he said over his shoulder once they'd gone by.

Aye, early retirement is looking good.

The light shone above the door of interview room three. He paused and sighed.

Into the breach once more.

He quietly knocked.

McNab's muffled acknowledgement came from behind the door and Findlay pushed it open. Directly opposite him, Detective Harry McNab sat at the desk in the room with the computer screen sitting off to one side. For once, the man faced his interviewee full on, giving the person his complete attention. He was now straightening his tie. McNab wasn't fastidious regarding his appearance. Usually he wore an open, grime-rimmed, tie-less collard shirt containing a portion of his most recent meal, with the not so delicate aroma of tobacco emanating from the unkempt hair that hung in his eyes.

The subject of the interview, a woman, sat opposite. No need now to query McNab's behaviour.

To say this woman was stunning would be an understatement. Tall and slim, with a figure that curved in all the right places, she sported deep-russet hair that hung down her back in waves. Her eyes—Findlay blinked—were violet. Her features were perfectly classical. She dressed simply in a jumper and skirt, with heels that flattered her legs but were otherwise devoid of ostentation.

"Serg, this is Rhiannon Ferguson." McNab stood and gave Findlay his chair. "Miss Ferguson, this is Detective Sergeant Findlay." McNab sounded odd.

He was being polite.

So, the guy does have manners.

"Miss Ferguson has witnessed a crime," McNab said. "A mugging in Glasgow."

Findlay sat. Purple irises. *Wait a minute.* "Miss Ferguson, do you live out Abernethy way?"

The young woman's lips parted, her fine, amber-tinged brows drawing together.

"I'm sorry, but I remember a call out to a cottage a couple of years ago," he said. "A disgruntled neighbour."

Her eyes widened slightly, then returned to normal with a visible act of her will. Her lips thinned.

"Your boyfriend had a sword. An impressive one, I recall. You were involved in re-enactments?"

"Yes." She eased into her seat a fraction. "But he stored and transported it according to law, and you were okay with it." Her lips tightened in a glacial smile.

"I'm sorry, that isn't any issue here." He pulled the report sheet closer. "Please, tell me what happened in Glasgow this afternoon." He glanced at the written report while she relayed the events. "So, in the short time you paused at the end of the lane you heard no further sounds from the alleged victim?"

"That's right. I wasn't going to hang around to find out. His attacker saw me."

"Why didn't you report this to Glasgow Police?"

She uncrossed her legs and sat forward in her chair. "Look, I'm here doing my civic duty. I was scared. He knows *I* know what he looks like." She enunciated every word. "I wanted to get away from there and leave Glasgow, fast."

He ran his tongue along the back of his teeth. She'd naturally felt scared but had remained sharp.

"McNab will show you some mug shots." He moved aside to give McNab access to the computer keyboard. "Let's see if you recognise anyone."

"Can you tell us some details about the man you saw, please, Miss Ferguson?" McNab clicked the computer keyboard. "What do you recall?"

"He was pale skinned. Greying hair. Tall. I saw his head and shoulders above one of those industrial waste bins, and they stand pretty high. He had brown eyes. Deep-creased cheeks."

"Clean shaven then?" McNab asked.

"Yes."

McNab clicked the keys once more, bringing up the files of known male Caucasian offenders born in the 1960s that fit her description. He spun the computer so Miss Ferguson could see the screen. Findlay rose to leave.

"That's him," she said with conviction. "Number four. There."

Findlay turned back from the door and peered at the image she was referring to. The *number four* Miss Ferguson had pointed out was one Iain McCarthy, a known participant in a crime syndicate in Glasgow. Known but as yet not apprehended. If this were all true, and he didn't doubt the honesty of the young woman sitting in this interview room, it could turn messy.

"Very well, Miss Ferguson. We'll see what reports we receive from Glasgow. Ye called an ambulance, ye say?"

She nodded.

"Here's the information on victim support. We strongly recommend you organise some counselling." He handed her the pamphlet from the pile on the desk. "You go home to that boyfriend of yours and stay low until if and when we need to contact you."

"I..." Her face tightened, and she opened her mouth again to speak but seemed to change her mind.

"Is that okay?" he asked.

"He's not at home. He's not my boyfriend." Her frown changed to a forced smile. "I'll be fine. If I have any trouble, I'm a brown belt." She stood and walked out.

If she had any trouble from Iain McCarthy, a brown belt would be no help.

But that was all moot, with nothing to corroborate her report.

McNab wrote and filed his report and emailed a copy to Glasgow City Centre Police Office.

Findlay grabbed his coat and headed for the door through to reception.

Another shift over. Tick.

"Serg," McNab grunted from his desk. "Just received an email report of a presumed gang mugging in Glasgow. They found the victim in an industrial waste bin in a lane off the mall section of Sauchiehall. He's now in ICU in an induced coma with serious head injuries." McNab gave him a look Findlay knew well.

Findlay took a tube of mints from his pocket and popped one into his mouth.

It never really took away the sourness, but it was always a start.

"Get onto our colleagues at Glasgow, then get Miss Ferguson back in."

NINE

— • —

I reach for you.
You who live light years away,
Though but a slip through a door
That spans our universes.

VISIONS AND SAYINGS OF THE BLIND LADY SAGE

The World of Dál Cruinne
Post Dragon Wars Year 6083
Western Sovereignty of Dál Gaedhle
Craegrubha Broch, MacEnoicht Clan Lands

Chattering voices blared out of the door to the main circular hall.

Arlan hastened up the gently inclining stone stairs of his broch, entering the hall with Bàn on his heels. His troop gathered around the central hearth, warming themselves against the cold of early morning, the rafters of the hall ringing with their laughter. Douglas and Leigh wore the damp of dew, while Muir and Adele looked fresh from their sleep. Morrigan and Angus dressed in jeans, T-shirts, and leather jackets of the Other World.

Douglas chortled and slapped Angus on the back. The young man stood with his hands reaching out to the heat of the peat fire, his face flaming as red as the burning peat. Arlan approached. Angus stiffened then stood tall, brushing the playful punches of Douglas away, then gave Arlan his full attention. He held a white rolled tube.

"Lord Arlan." Angus and Morrigan bowed.

"Ye have returned whole, my friends." Arlan stood by the hearth, his insides jittering.

Douglas whispered some words Arlan couldn't hear, and Leigh and Adele sniggered.

"What amuses you?" he asked.

"We shall let your travellers report, my Lord Arlan," Douglas replied. "It shall be relayed soon enough."

Arlan turned back to Angus, whose face held a scowl. Morrigan stood beside him, dimples deepening and covering her mouth with her hand.

"Though some in their frivolity are ignorant of what we know"—Angus glared at his fellow warriors who stood off to the side, then faced Arlan again— "your Lady Rhiannon is well, lord. Two and a half full cycles of seasons have passed since you left, from what we understand."

"Tell me"—Arlan sought to settle the thudding in his chest— "was a bespectacled man with her?"

"Nae, lord," Morrigan answered. "She is quite alone. She works in the shop in Perth and rides every weekend."

"She attends warrior school," Angus interjected.

"Warrior—? Aye, ye mean self-defence classes." The tightness in Arlan's neck muscles eased. "So, she has done all I suggested."

"Her habit is to place a flat rectangular object on the kitchen table whenever she leaves her home." Morrigan paused, her cheeks brightening. "It is what they call a *mobile phone*."

The others released a collective murmur of inquiry.

"A phone. So I can call her on my I return." Arlan observed. "And ye ken this how?"

"Morrigan broke in—" Angus said.

"The door was an easy nudge." Morrigan's tone held a note of apology, but she glared at Angus.

"She is well and safe." Arlan's voice was breathy, even to his own ears. "That's all the knowledge I require."

Both Morrigan and Angus glanced down at the white roll of paper in Angus' hand. Morrigan's cheeks pinked, and Angus shuffled his shoulders.

"My Lord Arlan, yesterday Rhiannon rode a train to the big city they name Glasgow, a massive place with many caisteals and markets." Angus blinked beneath a frown. "It makes the village surrounding The Keep, and indeed the caisteal itself, appear provincial."

"Why then do ye look so concerned?" Arlan grated out.

"Aye," Bàn addressed them both in a reprimanding tone. "Tell your warrior lord what concerns ye so."

Angus held out the object he clasped tightly. "My Lord Arlan, your command of Lady Rhiannon's language is far better than ours. I feel what is contained in this scroll they call a *newspaper* will complete the tale we shall begin."

Angus recounted that he and Morrigan had followed Rhiannon into Glasgow, where all three witnessed a beating. While Angus spoke, Arlan scanned the newspaper and found the article on the incident in Glasgow.

"They claim this man who was beaten may not survive, and they search for a gang lord." The hairs on the back of Arlan's neck rose. "Ye say you all saw it. And no one else?"

"Aye, Rhiannon fled," Morrigan answered. "After she arrived at Perth, she went straight to the police."

Arlan read the rest of the newspaper item, his arms growing cool, and daggers pricking the base of his skull.

They seek a gang lord... The severely injured man may die... Rhiannon is the only witness.

"I must return and bring Rhiannon home," he announced.

"Nae, Lord Arlan." Eifion's commanding voice came from behind Arlan.

Eifion walked into the hall.

"Eifion, if the man dies then it is murder, and the one who killed him is... Ach! I ken not fully how it works in Rhiannon's world"—Arlan waved his hand around searching for the words— "but they guard those who have seen crimes committed by powerful bad people. Chieftains of crimes with an entire clan to do their evil actions. If the police wish the person who saw the deed to testify to their king's representatives—so they can throw the chieftain of crimes into a dungeon for the rest of his life—they hide them away from the chieftain's clan warriors, so the person remains safe." Arlan shook his head briefly. "No, not just from the chieftain's warriors, but they move the person away from everyone they know. They give them a new life somewhere else."

He took a breath. Maybe some of what he said would make sense. He searched his memory for what they called it when the police hide a person in this situation. He had heard it on the Tee Vee news. "Och!" He snapped his fingers. "They will put Rhiannon into *witness protection*, and I'll never be able to find her!" The hall echoed with the last of his words.

Eifion's face hardened. "Ye most definitely will *not* travel through a portal again, Lord Arlan, Clan Chieftain of MacEnoicht and contender for the Quest to be Àrd Rìgh of Dál Gaedhle. Your personal happiness, or attempts at such, must take second place to your responsibilities here."

"I have said—"

"You will not go back for Rhiannon *ever*."

"I promised I'd go back for her. And I must do it now or—"

"What if you did not return to us? You will *not* risk it. Do you hear me, Lord Arlan? *You* must not go. You have a—"

"*Quest to win*." Arlan pressed his lips together, biting on the next words he would say. That *Tòireadh* meant nothing to him compared to Rhiannon.

But that would be untrue. His love for Rhiannon held importance to him, to his heart and to his future, but the Quest, and winning it, was truly vital to himself, his sworn warriors, his clan—his world.

His own desire to go to her and personally bring her back could not be fulfilled. He must subjugate his longing to the greater need. His muscles burned with the clench of his fists by his sides, the newspaper scrunching in his hand. "Aye, Sage Eifion."

"My lord," Morrigan stepped forward and placed a gentle hand on his forearm. "We will bring back your lady."

"Aye," Angus said. "Lady Rhiannon knows us."

"How?" Arlan asked.

"She realised we followed her through Glasgow." Morrigan bristled. "But we needed to ensure her safety."

"Lady Rhiannon approached us, lord." Angus took a short step back. "Once we spoke, she became suspicious. I think she recognised our accent."

"But we left the train without speaking further." Morrigan spoke low and earnestly, leaning into Arlan. "We did not identify ourselves."

"She will come with us." Angus gave a brief nod.

"Aye, Lord Arlan." Eifion spoke, and Angus and Morrigan deferred to the sage. "Your young warriors have done well. They will find your lady and bring her home."

Arlan ran his fingers across his beard, scratching hard at the tufts beneath his chin. *They must return to Rhiannon before it's too late.*

"Take your broad swords. I'll give you silver and gold trinkets to sell. Ye must use a car. Ye will get to Abernethy faster and be able to—"

Guffaws exploded from the side lines, and Douglas pressed his hand over his mouth.

"What amuses you so!" Arlan asked.

Angus' face blazed and Morrigan studied her boots, her downward tilted face barely hiding her grin.

"This is serious! There is nothing funny—"

"Pardon, Lord Arlan, but there is." Morrigan spoke through a suppressed smile.

"We shall go immediately." Red faced, Angus stared daggers at Douglas and then Morrigan. "Well, at this day's dusk."

Arlan put his fists on his belt and tilted his head, his gaze sweeping over his warriors.

"My lord, we beg your pardon." Morrigan's tone was halfway between contrition and bemused explanation. "It is Angus' driving that is most amusing."

"I will do better next—" Angus began.

Voices in the passage outside the circular hall echoed in, and all surrounding Arlan peered toward the doorway, amused expressions turning serious. Glen spoke a word of command and strode into the hall.

"My Lord Clan Chief." Glen gave a quick bow.

Arlan nodded for him to continue.

"Three travellers have arrived. Two warriors and a lad. They..." Glen's fingers danced over his sword hilt and his eyes flicked to Arlan's warriors.

"What is it, Glen?" Arlan demanded.

"They are from Dál Gallain and state they have journeyed the long distance to seek an audience with you, Lord Arlan. They would tell me naught, but maintain they come in friendship."

"Oh, aye, I bet they do." Muir broke his usual silence, and the hairs on Arlan's arms rose.

"Inform them if they wish to meet with me," Arlan said, "they will leave their weapons outside. Search them. I will receive them in my hall with my warriors. They must understand we remain armed."

"Aye, Lord." Glen bowed and left.

Arlan picked up his broadsword in its baldric and slipped it over his shoulder, then raised his eyebrows, glancing at each of his warriors. They straightened and spread to various places around the hall. Muir stood closest to the door. Bàn and Adele remained by Arlan's side. Eifion took his place on a wooden chair by the wall and pulled an acorn from the folds of his robe. The fire crackled and a hush filled the hall, rising with the smoke lifting to the rafters.

TEN

— • —

Like knows like.
Magic recognises the reflection of itself.
Where its path has been,
Which souls its power has touched,
And in whom it still resides.

MAGE MASTER FÀISTINNAECH
(3310-3380 POST DRAGON WARS)

The World of Dál Cruinne
Post Dragon Wars Year 6083
Western Sovereignty of Dál Gaedhle
Craegrubha Broch, MacEnoicht Clan Lands

Golden hues edged in orange spilled from the doorway, tumbling over a crimson streak—a floating vapour from the main hall, dissolving mist-like at Vygeas' feet.

The MacEnoicht clansman warrior left Vygeas, Leynarve, and Aiden guarded just inside the entrance of the broch.

Vygeas stood still, senses stretching.

"What if he will nae see us, Lord Vygeas?" Aiden asked.

"Hush," Leynarve answered.

She knows I am... what does she name it?

Casting.

Wariness, sharp and clear in odour, poured from the clansman guarding them. And now, with the other clansman's report of their arrival, the agitation mixed with delight coming from the hall ceased abruptly. All warriors inside were alert. Vygeas felt another sensation coming from the hall.

Strange. Familiar, but not.

Fatigue weighted Vygeas' limbs and a headache clamped his skull. Beside him, Leynarve's shoulders drooped slightly, her usual perfect posture revealing her own travel weariness. He had pushed Leynarve and Aiden to make quick their journey to The Keep, only to discover from the gossip of the market crowd that of the two sons of their lost àrd rìgh, the youngest would be his clan's contender for the Quest. The older brother and heir to the clan lands had succumbed to a head injury and roused not. Lord Arlan, the man for Vygeas to approach, was staying at the MacEnoicht clan lands. And so, he had hastened here.

Vygeas' brow cooled with sweat, and he loosened his shoulders, willing his body into submission. Of greatest importance, he must emanate *friend*, for *that* he wished to be. The gossips and commentators at The Keep had all spoken highly of this clan chief, many voicing their desire for him to become the next àrd rìgh.

Lord Arlan would have more chance with himself and Leynarve on his side. Leynarve had studied the scroll further, adamant the answer to those who sought a dragon's egg lay at the Broch of the Ancients, in the form of a key.

The clansman warrior walked through the door and returned to them. The lord had called him Glen. His face and scent spoke of officiousness and severity.

"Your weapons. All of them." Glen held out his hand, snapping his fingers in demand.

Vygeas surrendered all, hidden daggers included. Leynarve and Aiden did the same. He would give no excuse for mistrust. He handed over the tungsten alloy blade he had retrieved from the Inberian assassin on the Isle of Eilean, his most recent kill.

"I wish to present this gift to your Lord Clan Chief."

Glen grasped the sword in its plain scabbard. It had no decoration, unlike the custom here in Dál Gaedhle, and the clansman's lip curled with an unimpressed snarl.

"The blade is forged from an alloy of the strongest metal known to man," Vygeas informed him.

Glen took a step closer and patted along Vygeas' chest, waist, and legs, checking hidden places for unvoluntered weapons. The other clansman warrior did the same to Aiden, then approached Leynarve.

"You will not touch the lady." Vygeas lowered his voice to the man.

"Aye, I will," the man answered in gruff tones.

"Treat her with respect, if you please."

The clansman *harrumphed* and gingerly patted Leynarve's waist and checked her boots, then gave a nodding grunt.

"Follow me." Glen spun, kilt swinging, and strode ahead.

Vygeas obeyed, going ahead of Leynarve and Aiden into the broch's round hall. They walked past a warrior, a scarred veteran emanating a skill to rival Vygeas' own with the sword. The eyes of this older man never left him, coming to the same conclusions about himself, no doubt.

Six other warriors stood strategically in the hall. They dressed in breeches without body armour and had scarred torsos to show for it. Swirls of blue ink enveloped every bare left arm from wrist to shoulder. Except for two. Younger than the others, they dressed uniquely among the warband with a leather garment loosely covering their upper bodies and arms.

By the far wall sat a sage, whose stare cut through Vygeas. The man emanated a power, his eyes widening slightly, and a recognition came from him.

This one is a mage.

An earthy scent of leaf litter, freshly crushed underfoot, wafted toward Vygeas from the elderly man's direction.

Standing by the open hearth, a tall man with jet-black hair towered over his warrior companions. Their aromas held him in love and adoration, infusing the hall with a purple mist. They guarded him fiercely, with the same fervour they held to guard their own bodies. Their muscles were tense, ready to use their skills and spring into action if he, Vygeas, made one mistaken move.

Their clan chief stood as straight as a standing stone, and his sculptured muscles spoke of well-tuned skill. The handle of a broadsword sat above his right shoulder. He radiated an authority, a gifting—and a mistrust of Vygeas.

Vygeas must win this man's favour and acceptance, but the strongest emotions in this hall shot forth from him.

Tension and loneliness spiralled their colours equally through his aura. He longed for something or someone, no—he was *afraid* for them, but not for himself. He held a burden. Kingship weighed on him. He wore it already, although not yet won.

The man needs me, though he knows it not.

Vygeas stopped three paces from the clan chief. The burly warrior to his left, a woman, and a tall blond warrior to his right, stood with hands hovering over weapons. The blond man meant to kill him if required, to protect his lord and... no—*brother* filled the perfume wafting from this warrior.

None spoke.

Blades and bows. I will, then. And it will be the truth.

"My Lord Arlan MacEnoicht, I am Vygeas Innësson, former sell-sword and assassin for Lord Ciarán Gallawain of Dál Gallain." He turned to his companions, his senses attuned. Metal rang with the unsheathing of weapons. He tensed his jaw, for he *would* continue. "This is Lady Leynarve of Monsae."

Swords out of scabbards and many paces closer, MacEnoicht's warriors pressed in.

"If I were here in my former role"—he raised his voice above the cries of alarm— "I would not come thus, in the open, and with companions in tow." He glared at the blond one, now the closest to him, and gave him a look that said, *touch my friends and your life is ended. Weapon or no.*

"Halt, Lord Bàn." At Lord Arlan's command, the warriors ceased their advance toward him. "Vygeas has come in peace. We will hear him out."

Slowly, the warriors stepped back a pace, sheathed their weapons, and everyone breathed again.

The sage stood. The immediate glow around him was white tinged with the green of nature. Curiosity spiralled out of this aged man. Youth came from within him. Vygeas' brow tightened—he was an enigma.

"Lady Leynarve of Monsae, you say? But she and her parents were slain over five years ago." The sage stepped to them, closer than any had dared, and addressed Leynarve. "You have a story to tell, my young lady."

"And who might you be, young man?" Lord Arlan addressed Aiden.

Aiden, speechless, echoed awe and slight terror.

"Aiden is my knave, my Lord Arlan." Vygeas rescued him.

"Welcome." Lord Arlan spoke with a kindness, it came with the blue vapour of sincerity.

He introduced his warriors, each by name. Not all came from noble houses. Lord Arlan released the sharp scent of pride at the mention of each one. It was as though he loved them as much as they loved him.

"Lord Arlan." The clansman named Glen held up the Inberian sword to his chief. "The hooded one— Vygeas—wishes to present you with this gift."

"Our condolences on the loss of the àrd rìgh, and your father, Lord Arlan," Vygeas said.

Surprise mingled with pleasure seeped through the other emotions clouding Lord Arlan, and he took the sword in its scabbard from his clansman. He unsheathed it and examined the blade, holding it in a relaxed grip, feeling its weight and balance.

"It is a blade of tungsten alloy." His gaze lifted to Vygeas, lips parted, and awe rose from him. "Thank you." A strong scent, thick with certainty, and the warmth of genuineness, filled the air around the man. Lord Arlan re-sheathed the blade and tucked it in his belt, then tilted his head. "Why do you seek me?"

Vygeas stepped back and gave Leynarve the floor.

"Lord Arlan, we have heard you are the one who will contend for àrd rìgh in *Tòireadh*. It pained us to discover your older brother is unwell." Leynarve paused, giving Lord Arlan time to acknowledge her comment. "We believe we can help you win it."

The room fell silent. Lord Arlan looked at the one named Lord Bàn, who returned his querying stare. Their looks answered each other. These two were indeed *brothers.*

The sage stirred, and Vygeas turned. Sage Eifion opened his mouth, paused for a second, as though noting Vygeas' anticipation, then continued. "How?" he asked.

"Pardon, sage, but the question is *why*, is it not?" The grey mist of mistrust shot from Lord Bàn, forming sharp-tipped arrows that headed toward him and Leynarve.

Leynarve looked at Vygeas; he took a breath and spoke.

"We wish for you to win. I have fought on Lord Ciarán's side for too long." Fountains of disbelief railed at him from those standing nearest. "The man must be stopped. He is a *deamhan...*" The flood of incredulity from the warriors surrounding Lord Arlan washed away his words.

"We believe that you, Lord Arlan, are the one to defeat him." Leynarve picked up where he had left off. "Believe what you think of us, if you wish, but we desire to join the fight on your side. If you will have us."

Lord Arlan crossed his arms over his chest, accentuating his massive shoulders. "I have no side. I'm not àrd rìgh."

"We have something that will assist in your search for a dragon's egg, my lord." Leynarve reached to her leather armour. Weapons sang from their sheaths once more.

Lord Arlan put up a staying hand. "My friends, we need to hear them out."

Leynarve drew out the scroll while weapons snicked back into their scabbards, and Eifion the sage stepped closer, eyes widening.

"From where did you obtain this?" Curiosity mingled with awe radiated from the sage, permeating his personal scent of yew.

"I stole it from Lord Ciarán." Leynarve's head hung a fraction. "I spent five years with thieves." She answered the sage's unasked question. "Part of the story I shall tell you one day, lord sage."

Eifion took the scroll, holding it as though it were a new born babe, and crept to the nearest table where torchlight fell, and with great care, spread open the scroll. Lord Arlan followed.

"Och, it is ancient Ionan," Lord Arlan exclaimed. "Ye have read it, Lady Leynarve?"

"Aye."

Lord Arlan's gaze rested on her. Vygeas needed no special gifting to tell how this had impressed the clan chief.

"What does it say?" Lord Arlan asked.

"Where to find a dragon's egg." Mild sarcasm edged Lord Bàn's comment.

"Actually, no," Leynarve admitted, and all eyes turned to her. "It tells of a key required to access the place where there *are* dragon eggs."

"So, the key has to be found first?" Lord Bàn's eyes narrowed.

Vygeas turned to Lord Bàn's mistrust and scepticism, pinching his nostrils at their scent. "Ye will not obtain an egg without it."

Lord Bàn's voice rose, along with frustration rising from him in scarlet waves. "Ye send Lord Arlan on a quest for a key when his *Tòireadh* is for an egg. Ye waste his time. We've less than a month! You expect us to believe this ploy that will only delay and cause Arlan to lose!"

"You doubt me, Lord Bàn, but truly, I am on the side of the man you call *brother*. If ye wish him to win and be the king we all desire, ye must trust these strangers to your door." He pointed to himself and Leynarve, then addressed the one named Eifion. "Please, lord sage—though I believe ye are more—read this scroll, for I ken ye have the skill." His commoner accent, strong as he spoke with emotion, rang in his ears. "Then, once ye are convinced, we will accompany you on this important task. That which will grant us all success in our quest to save Dál Gaedhle from the evil that crouches at its borders."

The hall fell silent at his speech. He unclenched his fingers, and Leynarve's eyes showed their white.

Aye, I have revealed so much more than I should have.

Without removing his gaze from Vygeas, Sage Eifion spoke.

"My Lord Arlan, I believe you and I, and these our guests, require a private conversation."

ELEVEN

— • —

Hold back your judgement.
Seek the truth beyond what you see,
For a friend may be found in the oddest of guises.

SAGE GLIOCAS
(2870-2962 POST DRAGON WARS)

The World of Dál Cruinne
Post Dragon Wars Year 6083
Western Sovereignty of Dál Gaedhle
Craegrubha Broch, MacEnoicht Clan Lands

"Lord Bàn, please stay. Morrigan and Angus, you two must prepare for your journey. My other warriors, tend to your chores." With a lift of his chin, Arlan dismissed them.

He placed more dried peat on the fire while Bàn watched his back. He took a breath to ease his constricted chest. Rhiannon's plight was dire. He had to put aside his concern—nae, his fear—of losing track of Rhiannon. He could do naught but ensure Morrigan and Angus went through and pray they ended up at the right time in Rhiannon's world.

This sell-sword-assassin-turned-warrior at his hearth intrigued him. He'd rattled Eifion. And they possessed this scroll, which, judging from Eifion's reaction, appeared genuine. Whether putting his trust in them would be a mistake or no' was yet to be determined.

These strangers stirred more issues on top of those already consuming him. He must focus.

The silence behind him bore into his back. He turned to face them. Bàn stood by his side and Eifion remained next to Lady Leynarve at the table. The lady was of noble stock, well educated, with the airs and graces and the olive complexion of the Monsae clan. She was who she proclaimed herself to be, that much was certain.

The grey-clad *murtair* pierced him with his gaze. Scarred and skilled, his torn mouth and eyebrow told of clashes fought head on. A strange one. He seemed to know things. The bond between himself and Bàn. And what did he mean about Eifion being... *more*?

More than what?

"Lord Vygeas, your House?" he asked.

"I have none, Lord Arlan. You well can perceive I originate from peasant stock."

"Yet you are a warrior. And an assassin."

"I *was* an assassin, my lord."

Eifion stepped from the table where he had pored over the scroll with Lady Monsae, his head held high and stern gaze directed at the ex-assassin.

"You are more, and you will tell us if you wish to be part of what we do." Eifion's tone held command. "For I have gleaned enough information from this scroll to proceed without your assistance."

"I mean no disrespect, lord sage"—Vygeas turned to Eifion— "but *ye* are more, and your lord knows it not. It is you who should stand and confess, as much as I."

"You are bold."

"I am honest." Vygeas' retort collided with Eifion's in the air of the round hall.

What is this? He accuses Eifion?

"Let us proceed amicably." Arlan addressed both men, then set his stare on his visitors.

The young man, Aiden, standing behind his lord, wrung his hands. The lady stepped slowly away from the table, her dark brow drawn and her mouth tight. Bàn, still beside Arlan, with his keen eye would have noted Vygeas' veiled accusations of Eifion.

The sword master straightened, the fingers of his right hand dancing on his thigh. His shoulders rose and fell. Arlan gave a slight nod to the man.

"Lord Arlan, we have expressed our wish to be aligned with you. I know you only by reputation, but I perceive you to be sincere, if not pressed. Lady Leynarve and I seek to show our allegiance to you by assisting you to obtain the key to the place where you will find a dragon's egg. We hope that by this endeavour we may win your trust in us and, indeed, assure us you are all they say of you." Vygeas glanced around, first at Eifion, then at Bàn. "You have gathered close to yourself those with unique gifts and solid devotion."

Vygeas chewed his lip, ragged with a scar now accentuated by this action. The man himself appeared as torn as his lip over whether he should divulge... what?

A secret? Knowledge for a few only? *Why the hesitation?*

"Oh, come out with it, man." Arlan blinked at the edge in his own voice. "If ye wish to be part of what I aim to do and what I stand for, I must know you. *Know* who you are. I am what you see. But you... you are something else. You state that my sage, my closest and wisest adviser, has kept his true self from me. And you raise the hackles of my sword-brother. So, if we are to work together, ye *must* tell."

The ex-assassin examined the floor for only a moment.

"Very well." Vygeas raised his head and locked gazes with him. "My Lord Arlan, in my youth, I trained as a warrior despite my peasant status. I obtained an advantage from a mage—a gifting of heightened senses and the ability to anticipate my opponent. That is all. Apart from that, I am like any man." He let out a sigh. "Ye are now among the very few with this knowledge." He grimaced, his mouth playing with that scarred lip, but his eyes glinted.

Bàn rubbed his thumb against his upper lip and let his breath whistle out through his teeth. Eifion nodded knowingly.

"So, if I were to fight you," Arlan asked, "ye would perceive what I would do before I started my move, aye?"

"Aye. Afore ye even thought of it, my Lord Arlan."

"And ye can sense... what?"

"What people feel. That you, my lord, fear for someone ye love very much."

Arlan started, then eased his shoulders down but kept his mouth tight on the exclamation that sought to pass his lips. No, the man had more to say. *Let him speak.*

"Aye, you read minds," Eifion said.

"Nae, lord sage, only feelings and intentions." Vygeas turned a scarred stare on Bàn. "Your sword-brother here is jealous of me, for he sees me as a rival to your affections before we even begin. Lord Bàn, I wish ye to know I could never replace the bond ye have with your king and the brother of your heart. So, please let us be not opponents. For with what we all will face, we need to be allies and friends who are closer than brothers."

Bàn's thumb stilled on his upper lip, his neck pinked, then the colour rose to engulf his face.

So, this assassin-cum-sell-sword hinted at knowledge Arlan didn't possess, most likely having knowledge of Lord Ciarán's plans and methods of battle. Aye, strategies, resources and so on.

Lady Leynarve of Monsae came to stand beside the once *murtair*. Her noble chin lifted and she gazed at the ex-assassin with a gleam in her eye.

Aye, it never ceases to amaze me the difference a woman makes in the life of a man.

He let out a quiet sigh. "A mage gave you these powers?"

"Gifts." Vygeas quirked his head. "I have no power." He glanced at Eifion, whose hands froze in the process of tucking them into his sleeves.

"Why should we trust one who cavorts with mages?" Bàn asked. "He may mock us with deception."

"There is a magic in him," Eifion said with a firm tone, "but he has no power over it. Aye, for the man is no mage. He has a gifting. That is all."

"And ye are well with that?" Bàn spun to face Arlan.

"My lords," Lady Leynarve addressed them, "believe me, even if you doubt the man who admits to involvement in magic for his gift. He is a good man, one reformed. I witnessed the war in his soul myself. And he emerged the victor."

Arlan stood stock still. His own inner battle was still fresh. Whether to refuse his destiny and live a life filled with self-interest, or draw deep on courage and face the predestined path forged only for him. How hard fought was this war with soul and conscience, and how it changed one so.

Possibly this man possessed integrity, though time would reveal if the effects of magic had or had not tainted him with badness. But the noble woman, a deceased clan chieftain's only daughter and therefore heir, stood by Vygeas. Arlan would take her at her word—the one thing by which a clan leader could live or die.

He ran his fingers through his beard. If the lady and her ex-assassin were proven to be true to their word, an alliance with her Monsae clan lands close to the Dál Gallain and Dál Gaedhle border would be strategic.

"We will give you a chance, Vygeas. You and your companions will accompany us to the Broch of the Ancients to find this key of which you speak."

Bàn grunted, stifling a comment.

"Please rest from your journey, dine with us this evening and we shall discuss plans." He turned to Bàn. "Advise Muir he is to accompany our guests for the day. We must leave tomorrow."

"Aye, time grows short." Bàn ushered out the sell-sword, the noblewoman warrior by his side, and his knave.

Arlan stared into the fire's flames, conscious of Eifion standing silently by the table, rolling the scroll while the hall emptied.

"You have something to tell me, Eifion?" he asked into the quiet, then turned slowly to face his sage.

Eifion fiddled with the acorn he'd slipped from his sleeve. "I have millennia of belief that all magic is bad and all mages evil to overcome in order to tell you the truth of me." He straightened. "For I *am* a mage. I use magic, of a sort. I have used it to *see* you, Arlan, and protect you. And gift you. But believe not it comes from a bad place. This is all I can reveal."

Arlan staggered back. "Ye have used *magic* on me?"

"Arlan, it is not the magic that you have seen, such as in the dragon who killed your father, mastered by a mage with power... from... not a good place."

"Och, is there any difference?" he retorted.

Recollections floated around Arlan, misty and vapour-like. Curious comments from Eifion hinting of things he knew. The trials Arlan would face—stating they were not necessarily of *this* world. Eifion whispering in his grief at Father's death that while sitting under the old, gnarled yew tree in The Keep's courtyard, he had witnessed Arlan's return from the Other World.

"My magic is more a request to the good, and for the good. Arlan, I would rather die than perform an action that would harm you."

Arlan started. "Ye have helped me?"

"Aye, you are a natural linguist, but the ease with which you learned the tongue of the Other World?" A hoary brow rose in question.

Arlan blinked. "Aye, it was remarkable. And it harmed me not. But you kept this from me..."

Eifion grasped his arm, peering up into his eyes with such intensity that Arlan willed his feet to remain planted where he stood.

"If I had revealed my skill as a mage, your father would have exiled me. I believe, with all my soul, that I came to your father's court for a purpose. And that purpose was you, son of my heart. You have experienced magic for yourself through your portal journey, and now a man with a gifting wrought by magic confronts you. I see you are ready to hear me. Know me for what I truly am. Only for your good, Arlan. Only ever for your benefit will I employ my energies."

Eifion—faithful Eifion. His guide and mentor through difficult years, and now by his side, determined for him to win the Quest and become àrd rìgh. The man's heart had proven to be for Father, and now for himself. And, most importantly, for Dál Gaedhle.

Eifion had never let him down, and being one with the power to wield magic should not alter this.

He has always been true to me.

Loyal and devoted. Hiding a truth to ensure he remained close.

Can I deny him now?

Eifion's grip remained, a band of tightness encircling Arlan's forearm.

"My Lord Arlan MacEnoicht?" He slowly lowered to one knee.

"Get up, Eifion." Arlan made to raise him.

"Nae, lord. Not until you banish me or order me to remain."

Arlan's heart squeezed, then he lifted Eifion to his feet.

"My faithful and truest sage, I cannot dismiss you. You are the same man. Ye are so much a part of my life... I couldn't do this endeavour without you." He squinted an eye. "But we shall keep your skills a secret for the present. Aye?"

Twelve

— · —

Step out of time and into eternity.
See what is behind,
And know what will be.
Live even though it is already history.
Stretching behind with no beginning
And ahead with no end to see.

CONTEMPLATIONS OF A TRAVELLER
GRAND MASTER LLEW
(POST DRAGON WARS 6000-CURRENT)

The World of Dál Cruinne
Post Dragon Wars Year 6083
Eastern Clanlands of Dál Gallain
Lord Ciarán's Tower

Bram adjusted his broad brimmed hat.

Spring sunshine kissed the herb patch, warming the earth and glistening the morning dew on foliage excited by the urge to burst forth from stem and root. Pond water at the far end of the patch twinkled with reflected light.

Bram trod carefully with his walking stick along the sawdust path he had laid earlier in the season. Prior to his foray into a dragon. His steps were stronger this day, and the herb pots in his workshop were at low levels. He had a task to do. One which always brought him pleasure.

He smiled to himself—the first time in a while—absorbing the peace due to the absence of the laird of the caisteal. But it was sure to not last much longer. He would use the time to enjoy his own planned tasks without interference. Too soon Lord Ciarán would return.

He brushed past lavender, releasing its heady scent, and trod on the creeping thyme that had ventured along the path. The self-sown poppies were only just shooting, small green sprouts uncurling in the spring sunlight. He had used most of the opium in his workshop stores for a draught on an intermittent basis while recovering. He needed to restock the supply. He would take no more, well aware of the effect of too much papaveretum taken regularly.

Vervain grew on the edges of the path and the herb beds. Last season's remaining old stalks, interspersed with new shoots, lined the path to the pond, which drew him forward. He leaned down, grasping older leaves and rubbing the leathery vegetation between his fingers, and picking a handful as he passed.

The pond lay ahead, inviting. Sunlight sparkled on the surface where frogs hopped from lily pads, and above, dragonflies hovered and mated mid-air. Green short grass edged the water and here he headed.

He sat, placing his walking stick beside him with the spongy bed of grass beneath him. He dropped the vervain into his lap, brought his fingers to his nose then breathed in deeply. Lemon scent filled his nostrils, bringing to mind the aromas of his visions, for vervain was the herb of choice to strengthen inner sight.

The leaves of this plant were also useful to relax stressed muscles. Bram rolled his shoulders, easing only slightly the tightness which had remained for nigh on a month.

Aye, he would take some. Naught else, apart from milk of poppy, had worked for the pain from muscle tension remaining after his venture into a dragon beast.

He placed a leaf into his mouth and chewed. The escaping juices soured his tongue, and he forced a swallow of the masticated ball of herb. In some moments it would work, and muscles long tight would relax. From his experience, a leaf or so was very much too small a dose to enhance a vision.

He gazed at the body of water in front of him. Aye, he had been drawn to his conduit in its natural state. The calm was so alluring. He removed his boots and dipped his feet in the silky-smooth surface, nudging aside a stray water lily pad.

He fell back, his head and torso thudding on the bed of grass, the sky filling his vision.

Darkness surrounded him, cold touching his face and bare forearms, and frosting the water covering his feet.

"Come," a deep voice commanded.

Bram's spirit was drawn from his body, as though a fist had gripped it tight and ripped it from his chest.

He knew the rough touch. Had sensed it previously, while divining. Felt the unseen whisper of air. The soundless, oppressive presence prior to the storm of shadow as deep as the Abyss.

His spirit master.

A shudder coursed through his soul. Also his body, though he could not comprehend how he had sensed such in his current form.

"You will *see*," the icy voice ordered, then threw him forward.

What must I foresee now? Were not the previous visions sufficient? Those images streaming behind Lord Ciarán enough horror to witness?

He would ask, but the consequences of questioning his master...? A trembling overtook his spirit's limbs.

His surroundings flashed past him. The herb garden was a blur. Then people, towers, sun and moon, days and nights, weeks and months were a mere elongated streak of colours. His sight darted to and fro to keep up with all flashing by him.

After some moments, his spirit master halted him, jarring him fiercely.

Bram hovered.

"Look!" the glacial voice ordered.

Bram turned his spirit eyes downward.

It was a battle. A bloody one.

Warriors' bodies lay slain, some as though inside out. Horses' hooves churned in men's guts while birds with an appetite for carrion circled above. Torn standard flags hung shredded across the saddles of fallen war horses. Arrows bristled from prostrate forms, hedgehog-like. Broken bows, spears and swords lay scattered in the mud, and bloodied heads rested on spikes. Dogs lapped at the blood of the dead.

Lord Ciarán was there, seated on his war horse with a grim smile on his lips, facing the defeated army.

Bram peered closer at the Dál Gaedhle tartans on the dead and battered. Warriors, their heads bowed, collapsed in the last moments of life. Bloodied, torn, annihilated.

The overcome huddled at the end of a blind valley. A rockface backed them and a wide but steep-sided valley hemmed them in. Lord Ciarán must have trapped them there.

No escape. Certain death, for their forces and war bands seemed less in number than the horde of warriors at Lord Ciarán's back.

"Is this true?" Bram asked, his spirit's voice child-like in comparison to the one who had spoken thus far. "This is the future, aye?"

"Do you doubt me?" His master's voice echoed through the valley, his anger shuddering the trees that edged the arena of war.

"No, master," Bram answered. "I only wish to comprehend the devastation I see in this vision."

"You must fully understand." The invisible hand grabbed his chest then drew him back and up through clouds, so he could see like an eagle.

Dál Cruinne below was map-like. Real, but as though drawn in the same manner as the map scroll in Lord Ciarán's library.

Bram's breath caught at the awe-inspiring sight.

The whole land was a much larger place than he had known. There was extensively more to his world. To the south east, sat the promontory where the Eighlanndian sea rover had conquered the Citadel of Cathair and now named himself laird. And there, Innesfarne, the caisteal of learning perched on the narrow isle. The snow-capped, saw-toothed mountains cut the land mass in half. More lands to the east. Lands of snow and ice, and to the south...

"Look!" An invisible hand grabbed him by the scruff of the neck then shook him.

The shaking finally stopped, and his vision cleared. Dál Gallain lay before him. The River Bàn-rìghinn flowed south to his left and the saw-toothed mountain range to his right. Spread almost in between these, the valley of death was a long wide swathe of green.

"You will tell your lord of this place. He must know." The grip on his neck turned like a vice. "His reward for his obedience, for executing this battle, shall be one that lasts an eternity."

Bram grimaced at the band of pain clasping his neck.

"Yes, master." His voice came out strangled.

He peered past the pain to the valley below, where a portal glowed not far from its wide entrance. The portal sat within a tree-encircled meadow, shimmering open. His heart skipped a beat. He would investigate this gateway further.

With a shove, the hand pushed him away, dragging him from thoughts of doors to the Other World. His hair and arms streamed behind. Part of him laughed nervously at the thought of himself looking like a rag doll thrown backward. Time flew past once more, the reverse of his journey to that future battle.

He landed with a thud, his spirit returned to his body, and the wind knocked out of him.

He gasped for air, his robe sticking to his clammy skin, and his heart beating so hard it would rip itself out of his chest.

Birds twittered in the trees. A dove's gentle coo reached his ears. The calming scent of lemon balm mixed with the remnants of vervain filled the surrounding air. Mayflies hovered close by, dappled by sunlight filtering through the foliage. All was as prior to his vision.

Peaceful past after furious future.

He scrambled out of the water, splashing his feet from the pond then rubbed them dry with the edge of his robe.

Such death and murder!

He scuffed his feet so hard with his rough garment, his skin tore.

Such senseless, brutal war.

No, he would not tell! This vision was just like the others.

Death followed Ciarán Gallawain like a shadow.

Damn Lord Ciarán!

Bram would damn his own spirit master if it were not already the place of abode belonging to that presence.

All in authority over him ordered him down their vile, barbaric path.

I will not encourage it. Not report it.

His grazed feet now burned with pain, so he ceased his frantic drying. He dropped his robe hem and faced the serene pond waters.

"The man can discover this valley of death for himself."

Thirteen

— • —

This world is not the paradise it first seemed. But I am intrigued and up for the challenge. Reconciling this new life with yesterday is over. I am in with Lord Ciarán now, crazy though the guy is. I feel more alive than I have... ever.

PRIVATE JOURNAL OF RABBIE FINDLAY
FORMER DETECTIVE SERGEANT, SCOTLAND POLICE

The World of Dál Cruinne
Post Dragon Wars Year 6083
Eastern Clanlands of Dál Gallain
Lord Ciarán's Tower

Ciarán stood atop his fortress tower.

The cool vapours of the fresh forest air overcame the immediacy of the tower's stale cooking smells and refuse pits. He surveyed the valley beyond his tower, a patchwork of fields planted with the early crops of spring. He would sequester the produce from these fields to provide for his warbands. The livestock dotting the wide expanse of green—meat on the hoof—he would also earmark for his warbands.

Ciarán breathed in deeply and gave a crisp nod, his loud sniff an intrusion to the silence of his lofty vantage-point.

"Yes, in the thirty years of my exile, I have done well."

He would order his lesser lordlings—those with sense enough to be faithful to him—to gather their men and prepare their warbands. It would soon be time.

"Nae, not merely warbands—my army."

He leaned forward, grasping the stone palisade. He had more persuading and bribing to do on those further east who had not yet seen the virtues of his cause—or the error of their ways.

Taking hostages can be very convincing to those who would ignore him. Holding family members in a dungeon can make a warrior lord do much to which he would otherwise be disinclined. Ciarán must send his faithful men at once to attend to the task of... persuasion.

Or kidnap if required.

When it came to numbers of fighting men and women, if the lordlings and their warriors proved insufficient, he would send his own warriors to drag men from the fields. Even farmers and black smiths can fight if necessary!

He must conquer fully the clan lands of the east, then with a united and larger army, he would begin his push over the western border in strength.

So, he required loyal servants under his lordship. Faithful, unquestioning, and ambitious for *his* agenda only. And not looking to the west and a softer, weaker ruler, as chieftains are often wont to do. What could the west give them? He would have the might of an army. He had the magic of a mage—young but with much potential to become powerful, or so it appeared. Ciarán had the wisdom and ambition to rule. He had the backing of his own master—this very kingship promised to Ciarán by *him*.

His knuckles on the battlement wall cracked through the gathering evening.

"But it has been so long in coming."

Ciarán let go of the wall and sucked in a breath.

Findlay appeared to be one such faithful servant, and after a short time of settling in, the one from the Other World had shown his talents to be promising. Cool-headed and observant. And the man chattered not. He had discovered the man owned this blissful attribute during their recent journey to secure supplies and the loyalty of a clan laird further east. It had proven successful.

Ciarán now required a report of the goings on in his tower during his week's absence on this task, for some occurrence had disturbed the servants during that time. Since Ciarán's return, his steward had stridden about with a puffed chest, seemingly eager to share an incident to put another in the *laird's ledger of misdemeanours*, no doubt. Apart from a brief acknowledgement of Ciarán's return, the mage had not shown his face. He would question both.

Ciarán stretched his gaze further. His man had not spoken of that assassin, Vygeas, and the outcome of the mark assigned to him. Nor of the Lady Leynarve of Monsae who had joined the assassin. Yet word was out that the merchant, Gille Fhialain—the mark in question—and his family had disappeared.

"Something is amiss in my tower, and there is certain to be a connection."

He curled his fists, spun, and ran down the circular stone stairs, two steps at a time, and on reaching the floor of his library, he yelled for his man, then strode in, his shoulders easing slightly in his own place of sanctuary. His desk sat in its usual disarray.

But something is not quite the same.

He ground his teeth, searching every document: open, closed, or tightly rolled shut.

The clomp of wooden shoes on hard stone steps gained in volume. "Aye, Lord Ciarán?"

"Return to me with that mage and Findlay."

The footsteps clumped away, speedier this time. Ciarán tapped his finger on his upper lip and continued to scour the contents of his desk.

"My Ionan scroll!"

He bent down to peer under the desk, then he rummaged through the pile of scrolls on one of the shelves. Footsteps ascended the stair, the clomping echo reaching his ears. He stood in front of his desk while the three summoned servants entered his library.

Findlay stepped to one side, his tunic and plaid dusty from their travels but fitting his bulk more neatly than his garments from the Other World. Ciarán's man remained in front of the door, shuffling his shoulders with a gleam of superiority in his eye. The mage ambled in, leaning on his walking stick. His face looked fresher than when Ciarán had left for his journey, but the lad still walked with a limp. Surely, he had recovered by now. His time in control of a dragon had left him with a streak of grey hair.

It looked odd and yet charming in one so young.

"So," he began, "who shall betray whom first?"

The mage blinked, his man puffed his chest further, and Findlay did not bat an eyelid. "My scroll?"

His man let his mouth drop, allowing for an expression of greater stupidity than usual. Slightly amusing, for this should be impossible in such a one. The mage's shoulders eased a touch.

So, if not the scroll, what was his guilt?

"Mage, report to me all the goings on while I was absent." Ciarán clasped his hands behind his back, for he would keep control and not slap into oblivion the one standing in front of him.

The mage recounted his day to day activities in which he engaged himself during Ciarán's absence. After he described the morning meal of the third day, Ciarán put his hand palm forward in the mage's face.

"I shall be patient." He spoke through his teeth and halted momentarily, for, indeed, he *had* exhibited quite a degree of self-control. "What unusual visitors have graced this fortress during my absence?"

The mage's guileless expression changed in gradual steps to one of resignation.

"The assassin returned, my lord." He hung his head slightly.

"Ahh."

Naught stirred in the chamber for a few moments.

"'E sent 'im awa' free, my—"

"Silence!" Ciarán glared his man to muteness, then returned to the mage. "Why?"

The mage fidgeted with his stick, then raised his head. "The assassin Vygeas had completed his task. He presented the merchant's signet ring, finger attached, as proof of his death, my lord. You had left no instruction, therefore I sent him on his way."

Ciarán growled deep in his throat, but the mage only returned an innocent expression.

Well, Bram was correct. In his haste to leave he *had* omitted that direction.

"He came alone?"

"Nae, lord, a young knave accompanied him."

"No woman?"

"No, Lord Ciarán." The mage's look was of innocence itself.

Ciarán turned to his man. "I have a scroll missing. Have you entered my library?"

"Nae, lord." His expression held the truth then his eyes widened, and his mouth dropped open with a guilty realisation. He raised a finger. "Ah, now, apart frae when tha' assassin were 'ere an' the windi was open, an' I shut it, mi lord."

Ciarán closed his eyes as tightly as his hands clasped at his back.

"Get out of here all of you," he whispered, "except Findlay."

Retreating footsteps travelled down the stairwell, then Findlay gave a gentle cough.

"I have been robbed of an intriguing document." Ciarán opened his eyes. "It had important uses, I am sure—once I completed my translation of it—what with the Quest for dragon eggs to decide the next àrd rìgh of the western sovereignty of this land."

Findlay looked intent, giving Ciarán his full attention. It was a particularly good quality in the man. He listened.

"I know who has it, but I know not why *they* would desire it."

"You want me to investigate and get it back?" Findlay still spoke an odd version of the tongue, but he was too bright to dismiss on such an issue.

"Nae. There are more pressing matters." Ciarán sighed. "I suspect that mage has done his job and found me a portal but, in his usual fashion, is hiding it from me. With a little help from the lad I have employed as Bram's assistant, the fact will be disclosed to me. You have the experience in portals and their function, so you shall attend when we explore it."

FOURTEEN

— • —

A sliver of connection joins our world to the other, and time moves behind it as a shuttle on a loom.

SECRET SACRED WRITINGS OF THE SAGES
LOCKED SCROLL 24
BROCH OF THE ANCIENTS

The World of Dál Cruinne
Post Dragon Wars Year 6083
Eastern Clanlands of Dál Gallain
Beyond the River Bàn-rìghinn

Reins creaked in Ciarán's leather gauntleted grip and his stallion's tack jingled as it chewed the bit. A journey of a day and a half had brought them to their current position in the east of Dál Gallain, having crossed the River Bàn-rìghinn, the queen of rivers, where it widened and shallowed on its journey to the eastern sea, the Muir Gallain.

Ciarán pulled his stallion to a halt on a grassy knoll. Bram, Findlay, and Galan—the young lad whom Ciarán had employed to assist Bram with his magely business—sat mounted beside him. Bram spied the land ahead.

Ciarán ground his teeth. The mage masters of Innesfarne had refused his request for another mage.

May the blast of hell's ovens bake them.

Bram required assistance picking herbs and stewing them in pots, or whatever he did with them, which took time from his search for portals. Plus, the mage had taken too long to fully recover from his stint within a dragon.

Ciarán's stallion stomped a hoof beneath him.

Time, a resource in short supply. Always gone and impossible to retrieve.

Sunshine, uncommonly bright for these eastern parts, reflected off the burn flowing through the broad swathe of green-brown, slashing an argent path like quicksilver through the vast flat valley before him. Sweat trickled down the centre of Ciarán's back.

He would not remove his leather-plated armour, and even this heat could not convince him to travel unprotected. Not with what brewed in the northwest. Dál Gaedhle had now restored and manned some border forts. Responded to his goading at last... and all would go to plan.

His hunch was correct, and the mage had withheld from him the fact he *had* discovered another portal. Still not close by, but a portal, nonetheless.

There had been more the mage was to tell. Bram could hide naught once Galan had exposed the mage's subterfuge.

Ciarán grinned. He had beaten the information out of Bram.

Bram had emitted enigmatic mumblings of eternity—Ciarán would ponder further *that* message from his master—if a certain battle took place. A grand battle in the east.

A Cath Mòr Làraich.

He pressed his lips together.

The east, when all my energies focus on the west.

But eternity...?

He closed his eyes briefly, bringing to mind his exquisite map of Dál Cruinne, hand crafted by a master cartographer.

Very well, I wish for it all. I shall do my master's bidding... to gain it all.

It had taken a day for the mage to recover enough from his whipping to ride. Ciarán trusted the mage's journey in the saddle so soon after his punishment would emphasise the importance of revealing everything.

Always.

"Lord Ciarán, the portal is a short ride to the north." Bram snapped him out of his contemplations.

"Very well, lead on."

Galan's horse picked its way down the hillside, following Bram's mount. Galan sat a horse well and should train for Ciarán's army, not wash pots for the mage. But strength and astuteness—and a willingness to spy—were prerequisites for the task assigned him as Ciarán's elected assistant to Bram.

Ciarán followed, his stallion treading gingerly. It would be easy for a horse to lose its footing on this poor excuse for a track. His gaze returned to the valley beside them. This sizeable glen would be the ideal place for the battle he envisaged taking place in the future.

Yes, it would do wonderfully for his great and final battle.

An overgrown path led them along the edge of this wide valley to a round meadow in the middle of a forested glade. Bram stopped and dismounted. It was painful to watch, for the youngster walked like an old man, leaning on his stick and limping dramatically. Bram wandered back and forth through the green grass of the meadow and, after conferring with Galan, approached him.

"It is here, Lord Ciarán."

"You are certain?" Ciarán threw his leg over his stallion's neck and landed by the mage. "Show me how it works."

"I can tell you, but I cannot show you until the *time-between-times*, for travel between worlds will only occur at—"

"You brought me all this way and now I have to wait for sunset?" Ciarán's voice rose, but he steadied himself before continuing. "So, we sleep under the stars this night?"

Bram remained quiet.

Findlay dismounted behind him. "I'll set a fire. We need some refreshment."

"How and who?" Ciarán bore his stare into Bram.

"My lord?" The young mage's brow crinkled.

"*How* will we do this and *who* will demonstrate for me at sunset?" Ciarán clenched his fists at his side, shutting his mouth on the acerbic comments wishing to spew out and hit his minion this very moment.

This was too important to waste energy. He required this portal to discover what kingdoms and treasures lay on the other side! According to Bram's divination goblet, there could be people who were easy to subdue and enlist in his battle against the enemy. If so, he would not have to move his cowed and subjugated army far to the battlefield. For *it would* take place in the exceptionally wide glen he had just discovered.

"At *beul na h-oidhche*," Bram said, "my assistant, Galan, will go through to the Other World for us."

"Ah, Lord Ciarán"—Findlay dropped the firewood he had gathered and stepped closer to him— "shouldn't I go? It's my world and I've already done this."

"Nae." Ciarán narrowed his gaze. "You are too valuable."

Besides, Findlay may be eager for his own world and not return.

"Come here, young man," he said to Galan. In comparison to Findlay, this one was expendable. He slid his glare to Findlay. *You are not.*

The youngster looked at Ciarán with widened eyes and walked toward him with head held high.

Hmm. There is hope for this one.

"I would have you not only demonstrate to me the portal and its function but perform some reconnaissance."

"Aye, Lord Ciarán." The lad quickened his step toward him.

"Once through, I wish you to observe and, on your return, report to me everything. Are the inhabitants fierce? Do they have an army? If so, how do they fight? If no army, are the inhabitants placid or vicious? You shall spy for me. Can I trust you?"

"Aye, my Lord Ciarán," Galan said without hesitation, his interest clearly piqued.

"Very well."

Ciarán sat on a log Findlay had placed by the fire now blazing substantially, the blackened pot hanging over the flames coming to the boil. The sun lowered in the eastern sky and Findlay produced dried meats and bread from the saddlebags. Bram and Galan paced the meadow, seemingly ascertaining the portal's boundaries. They conversed with heads together and the lad fidgeted.

Well and good. Galan was eager. He would recruit him to his army after all, and Bram could find another chump to stir his soup of rotting herbs.

87

Ciarán drank the mug of nettle tea Findlay had brought him while the sun edged closer to the horizon.

Bram approached. "Lord Ciarán, dusk is almost upon us. Do you wish to come closer, or will you view from your safe vantage point?"

"Safe? What are you expecting, mage?"

"I do not, in all honesty, know what to expect, but my wish for your safety is utmost."

Ciarán stood, his face tightening, and unsheathed *Dearg*. The sword's clean, sharp edges caught the angles of silver sunlight. He grasped the handle in both hands, strands of his long grey hair floating past his face in the breeze stirring with the approaching night air. Tickling.

Bram took a backward pace.

"I will attend close," Ciarán said. "I can defend myself from whatever may come through from the Other World."

Galan stared and gulped.

"Here, lad, take this." Ciarán lifted his dagger from his belt and handed it to him. "In case you require a weapon. You can fight, can you not?"

Galan nodded, his Adam's apple bobbing.

Yes, it will do him good to see some action.

Mottled sunlight angling through the tree foliage surrounding this small, round meadow dappled Bram's and Galan's clothing while they returned to the area they had paced out. He followed.

"Please stand over there, Lord Ciarán." Bram pointed a pace away and behind him.

Ciarán stepped to the place, repressing a frown while daylight dimmed, and night drew closer.

"Go now," Bram ordered Galan.

Galan walked slowly toward the trees, the sun's last light touching his fair young head. He glanced back at his master, seeking approval. Then he was gone.

"That is it?" Ciarán stepped forward a pace. Maybe he had missed the magical moment. "No flashing light? No rumbling sound? How untheatrical!"

"Come no closer." Bram put up a staying hand. "The portal remains active!"

"How can you tell?"

"Can ye not feel it? See the disc?"

Ciarán shook his head mutely. Naught was there. Just a field. Grass. A slight breeze. Must be some *mage-like* thing.

"So now, mage?"

"We wait."

Ciarán paced across where the mage had indicated the entrance to the portal would appear, which was now a path beaten by his boots. Two sunrises and two sunsets had passed without a sign of Galan's return. Findlay had hunted to feed them, returning with small game and a grin splitting his face. It had rained this past night, soddening their gear.

Ciarán's guts were tight, his head aching, and *impatient* not the word for it.

I must see this lad return this morning or—

"Lord Ciarán." Bram's voice, heavy with relief, broke into his embryonic rage. "He returns. Can ye feel it?"

Oh, that again.

Out of nowhere, the young lad stepped through. Rust-coloured dust covered his breeches, and the dagger in his hand was clean and unused. He hesitated, then moved toward Ciarán.

"Well, speak up, boy!" he yelled. "Show me your worth. I've waited days and I'm not in a magnanimous mood."

"My lord, I ken not how to explain it." The lad's voice croaked, seemingly parched.

That is it. I have waited too long. He picked the boy up by the scruff of the neck until his eyes were level with his own.

"Tell me what you saw," he spat into the whelp's face.

"R-r-round houses made of red clay with roofs of straw. Animals like our own but not." Galan screwed up his eyes. "Horses with black-and-white striped coats. Tall brown long necked creatures—"

"Africa?" Findlay suggested.

"Red... d-d-dust everywhere. There is little water." Galan opened his eyes and slid a pleading stare to Findlay standing beside him. "There was a battle, Lord Ciarán. The pale men rode fiercely and fought with swords. The brown men wielded spears. It was their land, I think, my lord. They were not a-horse. There were... there were..."

"Brown men?" Ciarán took a breath to steady himself with the lad still dangling from his grip. Then Ciarán shook him. Shook him so hard, Galan even stopped speaking the gibberish he spouted.

"Lord Ciarán!" Findlay's voice came through the blare of thunder in Ciarán's head.

Ciarán dropped the lad to the ground.

"Speak!" he roared at the youth. "Show me my trust in you was not in vain."

Galan knelt and collected himself. "My Lord, I have witnessed things I have never seen. I must first find words to describe them."

"Go on!" Ciarán yelled his encouragement, his tone harsh but he did not care.

"Long tubes"—Galan blinked repeatedly— "thick as tree trunks and white like birch, sitting on the wheels of a cart. These trunks spat out smoke. They thundered and the ground shook. It hurt my ears. Dust rose and men fell, but a long way from the trunks."

"What nonsense! Why do you lie to me so?"

"No, lord, I lie not," Galan said, his voice strained.

Ciarán breathed hard. *Should I believe this or just slap the idiot into oblivion?*

Findlay took a step closer to the lad. "This sounds like the Zulu wars of the 1800s."

Ciarán flashed a heated look at Findlay and the man shut his mouth.

"Tell me more," he demanded of Galan. "What was their speech like?"

"Unintelligible to me, my lord. I kenned it not."

"And the brown men's foe?"

"Like us, my lord, but differently dressed."

Findlay raised his hand.

Ciarán lifted an eyebrow. "Ye have an opinion?"

"Aye, from the little history I know, I think he's been to Africa in the 1870s and witnessed the British Army fighting the Zulus. The brown men are the Zulus and they won. But"—he raised a finger— "the 'trunks' that Galan describes are British light artillery. Cannon that used gunpowder similar to what I use in the bullets of my gun."

Ciarán speared his stare back to Galan. "You said men fell when these trunks—cannon—thundered, and they died."

"Aye, lord." Galan hung his head. "There was naught left of some."

"Tell me more."

"That is the most of it, Lord Ciarán."

"No, it is not! It cannot be. You were gone for days!"

"Days, my lord?" Galan turned to Bram. "It was one sunrise to one sunset in the Other World."

Surely not? Ciarán glared at Findlay.

"I wouldn't know." Findlay replied to his unspoken question. "I've only been one way."

"In the records of the Fae," Bram said, "those who travelled to the Other World often returned reporting years away compared to but a short time of absence here." He shrugged. "And the other way round as well."

"Find out why it is so! Must I deal with ignorance? Mages are wise, are they not?"

He turned and strode to the horses. He must be on his way. Bram addressed to his back assurances of researching the matter. Ciarán's mind spun ahead of the here and now. He had wasted too much time! Pondered much while awaiting the lad's return and report. He threw his saddlebags on his stallion while the others hastily decamped.

"Findlay, ride with me," he yelled, mounting.

The Other Worlder threw gear behind his saddle then drew his horse close.

"We have much to consider of this portal and its resources," Ciarán said to Findlay. "Bram must find more of such, and you shall tell me of these British cannons. For now, though, I shall gain Caisteal Monsae and its lands by force for it is vital to my control of that southern border with Dál Gaedhle. I am sure Lady Monsae has some connection to the theft of my scroll, having now attached herself to that useless assassin. I was pleasant five years ago, attacking the caisteal in the usual manner to overcome and own it, but those efforts did not suffice. My warbands have grown since, and now I am certain of success. You shall see what Dál Gallain warriors are capable of. Without guns and, what did you name them? *Light artillery.* Just pure strength and prowess and battle-madness. We shall return to my tower and observe my battle chief preparing."

Fifteen

— · —

No one knows himself until,
Pressed beyond resource and will,
He humbly submits to destiny's plan.
For then will be known what maketh the man.

SAGE GLIOCAS
(2870-2962 POST DRAGON WARS)

The World of Dál Cruinne
Post Dragon Wars Year 6083
Western Sovereignty of Dál Gaedhle
To the Long Loch

The westerly rising sun glinted sparkling riffles off the gentle sea waves.

Arlan took one last look at the ocean surrounding the promontory where Craegrubha Broch sat. The water was unusually calm. He nudged Mengus to join his warriors and Eifion. Also, their new acquaintances—Vygeas, his knave Aiden, and Lady Leynarve, who wished him to call her Leyna. They rode with him along the track that would lead far from his home.

He tightened his jaw. If only he could stay behind with Leigh to await young Angus', Morrigan's, and hopefully, Rhiannon's return. Be there to greet Rhiannon the moment she stepped through to his world—her home. Hold her in his arms and never leave her side again.

But the Quest called him. Maybe she'd understand.

Angus and Morrigan had made a hasty return through the portal the previous sunset. No sign of them at this morning's sunrise. So much rested upon their shoulders. He gripped the reins tighter. This was the most important league of their mission—*to bring home my love.*

Eifion and Bàn had urged him on, and so he had ordered the journey to the Broch of the Ancients, intending to skirt around The Keep. Sages and advisors would enquire of Kyle's health and remind him again of Father's death. Well-meant queries were the last things he wished to face. Plus, all alerted to his presence would watch—including other would-be competitors of *Tòireadh.*

Aye, I need to be wary. Of spies. Of sabotage.

He shrugged. It may be unwarranted *paranoia*, as Rhiannon would name it.

A day's ride took them to the River Ruairidh, where he directed a quiet traverse over the bridge near The Keep, the only place to cross this water course. He tossed a plain cloak over his shoulder and pulled a broad-brimmed hat low over his face. Ordering his warband to keep their eyes down, they by-passed the village below the caisteal, engaging with no one.

Eifion rode close and leaned in. "Arlan, I leave you here. I have some ideas of what to inquire regarding a certain young woman's heritage." He squinted an eye. "And I must check on the progress of those sages I left in charge of making your gunpowder."

"Ah, Eifion, please mention not my journey."

"I shall only speak to those who ask. If some do spy you, perhaps you have a favour to repay your sword-brother, Lord Lùthas, and you travel west to his clan lands to assist." Eifion raised his eyebrows. "That should be diverting enough." He headed for The Keep after wishing the party a quiet, safe journey.

Arlan led them north-westward, his back to the grand caisteal and the slowly sinking sun. They camped beside the road not far along to the west of The Keep, where they ate a meal of rabbit cooked over coals, caught by Douglas and Aiden. They settled down to a chill night wrapped in their plaids, with saddles for pillows. Arlan awoke to the morning light and Vygeas and Leyna readying their mounts.

"Ye are unperturbed by a night sleeping rough, Lady Monsae." He nodded his respect to her with his morning greeting.

"Years of living on the road with thieves toughened me." Leyna tightened the laces of her leather chest armour.

What had the lady lived through these past five years? One day he would ask. Now was not the time. But the leather armour she and Vygeas wore, of that he would enquire.

"I am impressed with your leather protection. I will assign a craftsman to the task of kitting out my warriors, for I mean them to be more suitably dressed for battle with the east. Our tradition of bare torsos brings us more injury and death than victory."

"We must get on, lord." Bàn tightened his stallion's girth. "Two days of travel on a narrow forest track are ahead. Muir, take the rear-guard." He lifted his chin to the veteran.

"Vygeas, ride with me." Arlan threw his leg over Mengus. "Lady Leyna, I invite you to stay near."

Walled in by trees on either side, they rode with Vygeas giving his history in pieces, including how he'd met Lady Leynarve on the way to a hit. And that the successful completion of this assassination was the requirement to Vygeas obtaining his freedom from Ciarán Gallawain. But Vygeas had set the man who was the mark and his family free on a ship, keeping them safe from other assassins aware of the gold reward Ciarán Gallawain had offered to all and any within hearing. The Lady of Monsae, with her skills acquired from years of living with a band of thieves, had saved Vygeas after the event. And now that Vygeas had presented the alleged proof of kill, the signet ring of the mark—with finger attached—to Gallawain's representative, Vygeas was, in effect, a free man.

Vygeas relayed the actions of Ciarán, his battles, take-overs, and personality, portraying him to be a master at manipulation, who relished the effects his machinations had on the lives of others. Arlan inwardly shook his head at his second cousin. Gallawain sounded nothing like Mother. How could they be so closely related?

Mengus snorted. His stallion's ill-ease at such closeness to another stallion was settling a wee bit after the day's journey next to Vygeas' war horse, Dräger. In fact, his own unease had settled somewhat too. The history conveyed by Vygeas and Leyna was shaping to be a convincing one. As with all things, time would show the veracity of their claims. Amongst a noblewoman's graces was honesty, and Leyna had contradicted naught of Vygeas' statements, nor appeared in any way uncomfortable with their conversation.

Laughter sprouted from the middle of the line riding two-abreast. Douglas had taken the young Aiden under his wing and was retelling his repertoire of jokes.

They exited the forest by the morning of the third day and the land now opened to a wide, long valley. Green grass, fed by early spring rain and sunshine, coated the mountains that lay either side of the glen where the Long Loch sat, its depth unfathomable. Stretching ahead in Arlan's view, it wove through the base of the mountains that came to dip their feet in the loch's edge. The deep waters rippled in the breeze skimming the loch, glistening like the shiny edge of a newly honed blade. That same wind off the water stirred the loose hair at Arlan's nape and accentuated the tingle in his body at approaching this ageless place, the home of the Broch of the Ancients—a repository of wisdom spoken of by the wise in hushed tones.

In the middle of the long narrow loch sat the island, Eilean Sgathaig, itself long and narrow. The broch on the green isle looked short and stubby from this distance, but Arlan had heard it was a complex and massive structure where all the knowledge of his world resided.

Or so they said.

"Ah, there it is." He glanced aside at Vygeas. "Now I'll discover if the risk I have taken with you shall prove to be the advantage you claim."

"Please, Lord Arlan, regard it not a risk." Leyna trotted her mount closer. "The scroll I obtained gave much useful information. Do you wish to hear some?"

"Aye, please enlighten me," he said, "for there remains a way to go before we reach the ferry to cross."

Vygeas steered his mount aside, and the lady rode closer to Arlan.

"The sages would tell you," Leyna began, "our histories recount that during the Dragon Wars these animals were treated like slaves and died in the battles like men. But there were those who respected these creatures and believed, as with all wild animals, we must save them from extinction due to the abuses of man. These souls prepared places of refuge where the dragons could hatch their young."

"So, our ancestors didn't intend to kill them all?" Arlan asked.

"That is so, according to the scroll." Leyna looked skyward and squinted, as though recalling the text's contents. "Sages who respected the animals took them to the places of refuge prepared. The scroll records that they mate rarely, their eggs have a long incubation period, and an animal can live for many years. They never cease growing, so one can say the larger the animal, the older it is."

"Then it wasn't a youngster that you sought to fight, Lord Arlan." Bàn had ridden in silence for a time, but now spoke up.

Leyna almost jumped out of her saddle. "You fought one?"

"Och no, the story grows in the retelling." He glared at Bàn. "We encountered the one we believe..." Arlan's words halted as something sharp stabbed at his soul.

"The one who killed the àrd rìgh," Bàn finished in solemn tones.

"It arose from its cave near the Central Meadhan Mountains." Arlan's words came out husky.

"Once again, I am sorry for your loss, Lord Arlan." Leyna pursed her lips. "Yes, the Meadhan Mountains are remote enough for a dragon. That is perhaps where we should focus our search."

"Ye fought it, Lord Arlan?" Vygeas gave him a sidelong look. "The dragon?"

"Nae."

"Aye." Bàn's sharp tone held a hint of reprimand. "Angus and I had to pull our lord back."

Arlan shrugged at Vygeas. "Brave or foolish. What can I say?"

"Their actual numbers have always been few." Leyna broke the silence left by Arlan's comment. "Hence the value placed on a dragon in those wars and a mage who could control one."

A look passed between Leyna and Vygeas, but they said naught.

"What, friends?" Arlan set his stare on Vygeas, who turned his gaze to his lady.

Leyna gave a quick nod. "We are almost certain Lord Ciarán's young mage is one who can control dragons."

"Although we are uncertain whether he is responsible for the dragon who killed your honoured father, Lord Arlan," Vygeas added.

The air was difficult to breathe. The reins grew hard in Arlan's hands, and the world slowed. Could Father's murderer be this mage? Ordered by Ciarán. Aye, his cousin was behind it. What kind of man—boy—would willingly set a flaming beast on a king?

A beast himself!

"Arlan?" Bàn spoke softly beside him.

"This mage...?" Arlan turned to Vygeas.

"He seemed one forced, Lord Arlan," Leyna said.

"He suffered for it," Vygeas said. "He is now a weakling. He has paid a price, lord. Of that there is no doubt."

Was that sympathy in Vygeas' tone?

"He will pay a price if I find him," Arlan whispered.

They approached the shore of the loch, where a short ferry dock stood reaching out into the water and a cart loaded with cut wood waited to cross. Directly opposite this pier, sat another pier on the island, which mirrored the one they neared. A chain, used to drag the barge between the two, bounced out of the water and tugged against the pulley secured to the pole at the end of the short dock. The horses flinched and nickered at the brisk clanking of the dripping chain travelling through the pulley while the ferry crossed the loch from the island to this shore. The mule harnessed to the cart barely flinched and the driver sat with his head bowed, seemingly asleep.

"Ho, there." The ferryman nudged the barge into the dock. "Ye'll hae to decide who's coming on this trip. Firewood goes first, ken." He smiled a gapped-toothed welcome. "Room for five. Nae horses."

"Stay here," Arlan whispered to Bàn.

"But—"

"I must show I trust them." He placed a firm hand on Bàn's shoulder. "You stay here with the horses and the others."

Arlan, Vygeas, and Leyna embarked after the wagon had rolled on. Arlan glanced to the shore where the young knave, Aiden, frowned at his master, then gave a hesitant smile to a comment mumbled by Douglas. The ferry moved, Douglas grabbed Aiden by the arm and they both leaped onto the back of the ferry. Arlan looked at Douglas in question, who only lifted a shoulder while Bàn scowled from the pier.

The ferryman pulled the chain to drag the barge through the water to the other side. He asked Aiden to pull for a distance. The ferryman's face crinkled in humour at the lad's efforts, but Aiden soon got into a rhythm. Arlan's fingers tingled at the loch waters whooshing against the prow of the barge with every pull of Aiden's bringing them closer to the isle. The structures on the long, narrow island came clearly into view.

"Oh, it is more than one broch," Leyna said.

"Aye, mi'lady, 'tis three," the ferryman answered. "Three in a row, all joined by covered narrow halls. The rain does come down 'ard 'ere, like. An' in win'er, 'tis buried deep in snow."

"There are no trees," Arlan observed.

"Aye, lord warrior sir, all used in buildin' or burnin'. 'Ave tae get it frae the forest surroundin' the loch now. Keeps some o' us in good earnin's, so it does."

The barge bumped onto the short pier and the cart rolled off. The ferryman held out his hand and Vygeas dropped coin into it. The ferryman bobbed his head in thanks.

"Do they ken yer a comin'?" he asked.

"Nae," Arlan answered. "Will it matter?"

The ferryman's mouth twisted to the side. "Don't 'ave many visitors."

Arlan led his party along the cart track to the first broch. The dark drystone structure loomed ahead, the height of a bailey wall, and wider and stouter at its base than his home broch. Smaller stone buildings surrounded it, probably housing the chickens and ducks who scratched around the shrubs that lined the track to the broch. The pungent scent of sheep wafted his way, and their bleating echoed off the mountainside closest to the western shore of the long and narrow island.

A woman wearing a pale sage robe had hailed the driver of the wood cart, who continued round to the side of the broch where the cart halted at a pile of wood the height of a man. The lady sage stood in place, receiving her approaching visitors with a hard face, her stare dancing over their weapons.

"Greetings, sage," Leyna said.

The woman's mouth thinned for a moment, then she forced a smile of greeting. "Hello, who comes to our isle?"

Leyna introduced herself and Vygeas, then turned to Arlan. "This is Lord Arlan MacEnoicht, the son of our late àrd rìgh."

The sage made a stiff curtsey.

"My lord, welcome." She spoke briskly, a slight tremble accompanied her hands grasping her robe. "I shall inform our head sage, the Àrd Gliocas." She turned and took a few steps to the broch, then stopped and spun back. "Come, if ye please," she said.

Arlan followed the sage, the others close behind, through the front entrance. The stone-cooled air surrounded him. Ahead, and along the curved walls, nestled doors, presumably the sages' personal quarters.

"Wait here a moment, if you please." The sage ran up the gently sloping stone stairs between the two circular walls of the broch.

"We should have sent someone ahead to warn them," Douglas grumbled. "Nae meat and mead for us."

"The ferryman implied guests were few," Vygeas commented. "They are astir above."

"I need no special gift to discern that, my friend," Arlan replied.

"They are intrigued. And"—Vygeas frowned— "a little reluctant, despite the sage announcing the son of an àrd rìgh."

"What else can ye tell?" Arlan asked. *This gift has some advantage.*

"They are friendly. Nae weapons, but concerned for ours."

"We must make them at ease. We'll offer to leave ours here. Let's show friendship. Everyone, place your weapons against this wall." Arlan did so, and the others followed his lead.

A *tap tapping* echoed down the stairs. Many moments later a man entered the atrium where they waited. Long white hair sat on either side of a pale face with thin, almost translucent skin, the main vein of his forehead a blue streak down his brow. He wore a robe of crisp, undyed cloth tied with a simple woven linen belt. A wide ring of many keys hung from the belt. Gnarled fingers grasped the cane he tapped on his approach and leaned on with every step. Dark brows, the only visible hair retaining colour, dipped with his appraisal of them.

"Lord Arlan." He looked directly at Arlan. "I met your father but once. Ye are his son, there is no doubt of this." He rested his stick's point on the floor in front of him, then leaned heavily on the handle with both hands. He set his stern gaze along the rest of the party. "I am the head sage of this library. You may address me by my title, Àrd Gliocas."

Arlan introduced his companions, and the aged one nodded to each.

"I see you have removed your weapons. Very good." He lifted his gaze to Arlan once more. "What do you seek here?"

"I am about to enter *Tòireadh*—"

"Oh, aye. The only occasion on which your father sought me was as *he* entered the Quest." The old man's lips tweaked with a ghost of a smile, then returned to their severity. "My condolences, my young lord clan chief, on the loss of such a great man."

"Thank you, Àrd Gliocas." He pushed down a bubble of grief rising to distract him from his mission. "You are aware of the task set by the *Sàsaichean?*"

"Aye." The aged sage stood immobile, offering nothing more.

"May we search your library for the information we seek?" Arlan asked.

Àrd Gliocas adjusted the grip on his walking stick, causing it to tap lightly on the stone floor. "We have no dragon eggs here, my young clan chief."

"Aye, but I... we believe you have the means to acquire one."

The old man looked warily at him. "Why do you think this?"

"I have an old scroll, my lord Àrd Gliocas," Leyna said, "that speaks of a place of safety for dragons—"

"A scroll, you say?" Àrd Gliocas' posture straightened at this. "Follow me." He turned and walked up the stairs.

Vygeas spoke aside to his knave. "Stay with the—"

"Weapons and mind them. Aye, lord, I ken." The young man *hmphed* and leaned against the wall.

"Guard my new blade well, young knave," Arlan said. "I'm pleased with the gift presented to me by your lord and lady." He exchanged a smile with Aiden, and a nod of acknowledgement with Vygeas.

Arlan led Vygeas and the others and strode after the sage. Once past the very lower levels of the broch, the ancient turned to a door and Arlan followed him through.

Past the thick inner stone wall, the space opened to a round hall twice the size, or more, of Arlan's own hall. A fire on the central hearth burned, contained in a barrel of iron, with a tall pipe attached and reaching to the roof, where it vented the smoke. The walls, lined with wooden bookshelves, had no stone visible bar the voids that drew the air up and through the structure, as at his own home. A wooden staircase attached to the bookshelves ran a gentle curve around the room, gradually ascending to a balcony.

"So many books and parchments," Leyna exclaimed.

"Aye, the double stone walls, each thick as a man is tall, keep out the moisture," the head sage said. "And, as with any broch, the warm air from beneath us joins our fire's heat and draws up through our halls, keeping the temperature right for preserving our fragile scrolls, parchments, and other artefacts and relics. We have lost little over the years."

"An artefact is what we seek, lord sage," Arlan said.

Murmurings caught his ear. A group of elderly sages, similarly dressed in robes of plain cloth, entered this round hall.

"And ye ken why it's called the Broch of the *Ancients*," Douglas said in a loud whisper.

Arlan glared at him, and Àrd Gliocas coughed.

"May I see the scroll?" Àrd Gliocas held out his hand to Leyna.

Leyna took the scroll from her leather armour and passed it to the sage, whose eyebrows rose and hands trembled on opening it.

"It is of value to you?" she asked.

"Aye, very." The sage barely lifted his eyes from examining the document.

"Do you have any other parchments or artefacts from the time it mentions?" The back of Arlan's neck moistened with sweat.

"From the time immediately after the Dragon Wars, do you mean?" Àrd Gliocas' voice grew deeper.

"Aye, my lord Àrd Gliocas. Please, may we see them? It may assist me in my search for an egg."

"Aye, so ye have said." The sage lifted his gaze briefly from his consideration of the scroll he held in shaking hands.

The sages who had entered walked to shelves and replaced scrolls, bound tomes and parchment, then took others, barely lifting their gazes to Arlan and his companions. Some wandered to chairs placed around the room and read, another went to a desk, and yet two others ascended the stairs. Arlan followed their progress. Further up the height of the broch the space narrowed and here shelves lined the half-balconies, which were wide and supported by pillars, where chests rested on their floors.

The head sage remained engrossed in reading.

"May we see them?" Arlan loosened the plaid over his shoulder, the warmth of the large hall oppressing him.

The sage flinched, and looking up from the scroll, regarded him as though for the first time.

"Oh, yes. Aye. You wish to see the artefacts, aye?" He gave a throaty cough and walked to the other side of the hall, where he opened a door.

It led to the walkway connecting the next broch. The sage walked through to the broch's central hall, which was identical to the one they'd just left. Arlan strained his neck to view the ceiling, where yet another pipe of iron vented the fire's smoke. The top balcony of this broch contained stuffed small animals in cages of glazing.

The old sage tapped his cane, walking briskly through the hall to the next one, holding the scroll in a tight grip. Reaching the hall of the third broch, similarly lined with books and parchment, the old sage turned toward the curving staircase without a word.

The winding oak stair banister ran smooth under Arlan's hand and creaked with each step. Beside him, and across the hall, stood curved walls of shelves filled with spines in varying shades of leather, rivalling the library of The Keep, and any library he'd seen. What of *Google*, and all it contains?

How much would be the size of the physical representation of that amount of knowledge!

"Ye are well, Lord Arlan?" Vygeas asked behind him.

"Aye, fine. It's inspiring, is it not?"

The balcony at the top had scant space for them all to stand. It was warmer here and trays covered in thin glazing, lined the curved outer wall, and displayed objects.

"Here you will find artefacts from the era you seek." The sage retreated to the only chair on the narrow balcony and returned to poring over the scroll.

Arlan gave a slight shrug to Vygeas, and Leyna bent over the trays.

Vygeas stepped closer to Leyna and placed his hand on her narrow waist. "What would the key look like, Leynarve?" he whispered into her ear. "Is it an actual key, or does the term stand for some other object?"

Arlan turned aside to the next tray. Vygeas' tone had been intimate. Leyna was of noble stock. Not so Vygeas. Yet they were together. Not married, but *together*. He sighed, shoulders dipping.

Aye, they defied convention. But he was the son of an àrd rìgh, and a contender for the next high kingship.

He should honour tradition... no matter what it could mean for Rhiannon and himself...

The empty space in his heart that should be filled with Rhiannon now ached. He glanced down. His knuckles blanched at the strength of his grip on the tray's glazing, so he let go. Beneath where his curled fingers had gripped sat a chunky, rusted key; its shank long, throating deep, and key wards intricate. It sat beside a piece of eggshell, about the size of a man's fist, and a shrivelled, dried husk of a... Arlan's breathing stilled. A partial dragon's egg, with a baby dragon not yet fully formed! It looked like a curled, unhatched chick without feathers nor beak.

"What have you found, Lord Arlan?" Vygeas asked.

"Och!" Douglas leaned over his shoulder. "It has been deid a long time."

"A dragon embryo?" Leyna came closer. "Oh, that is a key!" She lifted the clear lid of the case and took out the key, the rust staining her palm a reddish brown. Vygeas placed his hand on hers, then stilled, eyes wide in warning.

The ancient sage, so far engrossed in the scroll, shot up from his seat. "Please do not handle it. It is millennia old and will disintegrate!"

"Pardon, lord sage." Leyna returned the key, her face darkening a shade.

Àrd Gliocas frowned heavily at Leyna, then stepped to a far shelf where longer scrolls poked out half their length.

"This scroll"—he waved the scroll Leyna had handed to him— "speaks of places of refuge for dragons. *This* scroll"—he rummaged through the scrolls poking from the shelf and withdrew one of the longest— "has mapped them." He placed it on a narrow table. "I recalled these maps but have only now found the official notation of them." He sent a crinkled grin to Leyna. "My thanks to you, my lady." He unrolled the map. "Be gentle, for it is fragile." He glared at Douglas, who stood back holding palms up and leaned against the balcony railing.

Arlan scoured the map, and Leyna and Vygeas leaned in beside him. Charts covered the stiff and yellowed animal skin, the ink pale at the edges but darker closer to the middle. The cartography inscribed represented the whole of the land of Dál Cruinne, with an inset detail of a section near the Central Meadhan Mountains.

The floor creaked behind Arlan.

"We've been there, my lord." Douglas leaned over Arlan's shoulder and pointed to the section of the map representing a cluster of mountains, three in all, tubular and broch-like.

"Do not touch," warned the sage, seated back in the chair, with one eye on the scroll and another on them.

"Oh aye, it's near where ye camped, and I found you after I re—" Arlan pulled back the words. He wouldn't mention portals or journeys to the Other World to his new acquaintants until truly sure of them. *A need to know only basis*, as they said in the Other World. A grin tweaked the corners of his mouth.

"Ye are familiar with this place, Lord Arlan?" Vygeas asked over his other shoulder. "Ye could get us there again, aye?" He spoke like he knew, maybe from sensing what Arlan felt. Perhaps Vygeas had sensed earlier his longing for Rhiannon.

Och, naught is private around this man.

He turned to the sage and stepped closer. "My lord Àrd Gliocas, the key in this tray, could it be the one to help us find a place where there are whole dragon eggs?"

"Aye..." The word dragged out from the old one.

"Do you know the place where this particular key will unlock the treasure that I seek?"

The sage loosened his hands on the scroll, allowing it to curl inward, squinted at him, and leaned back into the chair, the creaking of the seat the only noise on the quiet balcony.

Arlan knelt, his gut clenching. "My lord Àrd Gliocas, it is my desire to win the Quest, unite my people, and lead an offensive against Ciarán Gallawain. If this is the key to my success, please tell."

"Aye, it is, but I will not tell which lock it calls home. Ye are the same as any young and ambitious man. Professing noble notions when all ye seek is your own glory."

The senior sage flew out of his seat, brushed past Arlan, bustling his companions to one side with the action of his cane, and strode down the stairs, his cane's loud tapping reverberating through the round hall. Arlan jumped up and followed.

"My lord sage." His voice verged on begging. It may shame him, but he didn't care. "If ye would assist me, I promise to serve Dál Gaedhle."

He descended the stairs behind the mute man.

"I have no desire for glory." He put all his conviction into his statement.

The sage continued to pace on the floorboards toward the broch's exit without looking at Arlan. His cane tapped with each step, but he uttered not a word.

"Our world faces danger," Arlan continued earnestly. "I wish to defend it."

The cane's tapping echoed through the connecting hallway.

"If I must beg you, I will." Arlan now tempered his tone, pulling back on his words. *I must not shout at this sage.*

The old man waved the scroll above his head, indicating silence as they entered the second, and middle, of the three brochs.

"All I need to know—" Arlan began.

A loud *shush* came from those reading in the broch around them.

"—is which place of refuge will still have eggs," he whispered behind the sage, "and if this key is the one that will open it."

The ancient spun, his mouth open, ready to speak, but glanced behind Arlan. "Where are your companions?"

"Please, lord—"

"Are ye deaf?" the sage said into his face.

Arlan let out a long, slow sigh. "No, lord Àrd Gliocas. I will gather my friends and leave."

"Very good. You are wiser than you look," the sage retorted, turned on his cane, and marched through the exit. "Ye can find your own way out." And to those reading he ordered, "Ensure they do not dawdle."

Arlan sat on a log by the shore on the west side of the island, the breeze stirring his hair and tickling the leaves in the nearby stumpy bush. He held a piece of cheese in one hand and a chunk of bread in the other, his uneaten portion of the midday meal, which, in pity, an older sage had provided. According to the same woman, the ferry wasn't due to return until later in the day with stores from a nearby village market.

Leyna and Vygeas had remained close to each other since leaving the broch's hall and whispered together throughout their light meal. A *plop plop plop* caught Arlan's ear. Douglas was demonstrating to Aiden his prowess at skimming stones on the loch's surface, the wind-rippled water obliterating the rings formed from the skipping stones.

Arlan sighed.

I will find another way.

At the least, now he knew where to look—that strange, broch-like mountain cluster. He would beat down any door he could find in or near it.

Maybe he would fail and not become the àrd rìgh. Then not have to make all the decisions required to defeat Ciarán Gallawain and the threat he holds against Dál Gaedhle. Nor shoulder the entire responsibility for all. A familiar shiver ran through him.

Aye, the Quest and all that may follow was a serious endeavour.

Leyna blocked his view of the loch. Standing in front of him, she caught his eye, her mouth curled up at the corners and a dark eyebrow rose.

"Cheer up, Lord Arlan." She grasped his hand, uncurled his clenched fist, and placed a cool, grainy object across his palm.

He held up his hand. The rusted key lay across it; its shank spun, rolling in his palm, leaving a gritty sensation. *What?* His heart seemed to sink to his belly.

"Och, no!" He suppressed his cry. "Ye have stolen it!"

At his hoarse whisper, Douglas and Aiden ceased their stone throwing competition and faced him.

"You require it, my lord." Vygeas' firm tone spoke of justification.

"Nae, we all do." Leyna added.

"Ye are distraught at the theft—" Vygeas began.

"*Distraught* comes nae where near what I'm feeling. Your discernment fails you if you think I can be happy with this action. Thieving is wrong. And from a most hallowed of halls. Where is your respect?" Arlan rose, heat throbbing through his veins.

Vygeas stepped forward and went for his sword, leaving his hand hovering over its leather-bound handle while, with his other hand, he ushered Leyna behind him, shielding her with his body. Douglas stepped toward them, drawing his sword part way.

"Nae, still your arm, Douglas." Arlan raised a staying hand. "We'll resolve this like friends." Arlan closed his hand on the offending object. "I'll no' fight you. But aye, I *am* displeased." He nodded briskly at Vygeas, and Leyna who peered from behind him. "If you wish to continue our relationship, you will accompany me to the ancient one and apologise while I return it."

Leyna blinked, then moved to stand beside Vygeas.

"Lady Leynarve of Monsae." Arlan's lungs tightened, the air in them difficult to expel. "I see what ye have learned during your five years living with thieves."

Leyna hung her head.

"I hope you will relearn manners, and do so rapidly, if you wish—if both of you wish—to remain in my company." Arlan punched down the rage that desired to roar within him.

He couldn't let this ruin his relationship with these two. He greatly needed their aid. He foresaw the benefit of allies in the east, and the Monsae clan would be a start. Besides, all the knowledge he needed to find an egg resided in this young noblewoman's head now that the keeper of the Broch of the Ancients was of no help.

"That man refused us." He breathed out hard through his words. "Why, then, did you take it?"

"We want you to *win*," Leyna said.

He stepped right up to her, ignoring Vygeas' rapid approach and iron grip on his arm.

"This is not the way to do it, Leyna." He shook his head. "Come with me," he commanded and, ripping his arm from Vygeas' grasp, turned and marched to the entrance of the broch.

He snatched a glance behind him. They followed.

They *all* followed. Vygeas was taut as a strung bow. And Leyna quiet, the triumph in her eyes at her revelation now replaced with a downward gaze above pink cheeks. Douglas tugged their red-faced knave along, who peered through his long curls.

The sage they'd first encountered stepped out of the entrance on Arlan's approach. She lifted a startled stare at him then bounced her gaze to his companions, her shoulders stiffening.

"I wish to see Àrd Gliocas," he snapped.

The woman flinched, and her eyes widened.

"Och, no. My apologies, sage." He took a breath and slowed himself down. This startled rabbit would run into her warren and leave him to yell through the halls for her master. "Please, may I have an audience with Sage Àrd Gliocas?" Arlan nodded a bow and smiled as kindly as he could with the tumult in his chest.

The sage nodded. "Please wait here, my lord." She turned on her heel and disappeared into the broch.

Vygeas came to Arlan's side in a flash. "They will wish to imprison her." His harsh whisper came through gritted teeth.

"We'll bargain."

"With what? The favour of a clan chief? Will you pull rank and sympathy as the son of a man who was once the àrd rìgh?"

Arlan flared his nostrils, and he forced himself to calm. He would *not* cause this disagreement to divide them.

"I must be true to myself, Vygeas. Please understand this." He bore his stare into the scarred face, willing Vygeas to comprehend, if not by his words, then by his emotions or intent.

Or by whatever means the man deciphers people!

"My lady's life may be forfeited," Vygeas hissed. "She will receive a flogging at the least."

"We will see," Arlan returned.

The sage approached, her eyes round. "Ye must leave your weapons and come with me, if ye please lords... and lady."

Arlan stepped inside, where he removed his sword and baldric. The others followed his lead, clanking their swords against the inner wall. The sage led him through all three brochs and down a stair to another antrum, where she paused by a door then knocked.

"We have little means of escape," Vygeas whispered.

"Wheesht," Arlan threw over his shoulder.

The door opened with a creak and the lady sage departed. The aged sage stood there, leaning on his staff with both hands.

"Aye?" His voice rose in question.

Arlan stepped forward, bent on one knee and bowed. "We beg your mercy, lord Àrd Gliocas."

"For what might that be?" His tone held an edge.

Arlan breathed deep and raised his head. "We stole this, and we wish to return it having realised the error of the action." He opened his hand to reveal the rusted key.

"We?" A dark eyebrow rose in a pale forehead. "Do you not mean the lightest fingers amongst you? Belonging to the delicate hands of the Lady of Monsae?"

"I beg your forgiveness, lord sage," he repeated.

"Why would *you* beg for another?"

"She is one of mine, and therefore I have wronged you."

"And so"—the head sage stood taller— "you would return the key to your success, thus making it more difficult to win a most exacting Quest? One I admit is the hardest in my memory." He sighed. "Lady Monsae."

Leyna stepped forward. "I ask your pardon, lord sage. I only wished for the success of Lord Arlan."

The old sage's lips danced with a life of their own while he chewed over his decision.

"You, I forgive, Lady Monsae. Not for your sake, but for his." He lifted his stick and pointed its tip at Arlan. "But I retain your scroll for our library."

He then looked down at Arlan.

"And you," the booming voice of Àrd Gliocas rang in the small antrum beneath the broch.

A chill ran through Arlan and sweat cooled his brow. The head sage had granted Leyna mercy. It was his role now as her lord, to take her punishment.

He closed his eyes. *My Quest has finished. Failed before it has even begun.*

"Stand," the Lord Àrd Gliocas of the Broch of the Ancients ordered.

Arlan rose from his knee, stood to his full height and opened his eyes.

"*Tòireadh* is set to find the bravest, smartest, strongest, *and* the most noble person to be àrd rìgh." The sage lifted his head and looked Arlan in the eye. "The key you hold is an intricate antique and useless for your task." He lifted the keyring hanging from his belt and pulled each key around the iron circle until he stopped at a large but simpler key, then held it up. "This will open the lock behind which you will discover what you seek—take it, it is yours, Lord Arlan Finnbar MacEnoicht. I wish you much success, young man."

Sixteen

— ⋅ —

The task shall be derived from the era and most fitting to that history's contemporary narrative. The winner of Tòireadh will be the one who is first in strength, skill, courage and thought. They shall excel in leadership, noble character, humility, and self-sacrifice. For the highest ruler of the land must be the best of us, and willing to give their very self for all.

DECLARATION OF THE SÀSAICHEAN
POST DRAGON WARS YEAR 0

The World of Dál Cruinne
Post Dragon Wars Year 6083
Western Sovereignty of Dál Gaedhle
Long Loch

The return journey to where Bàn, Muir, and Adele waited with the horses by the loch, had been a silent one. On reaching the shore, Arlan leaped the short distance from the ferry to the pier. He pushed away his thoughts from the incident on the island—he would leave it far behind.

Douglas walked Aiden off the ferry. The lad kept his head bowed, ashamed of his mistress' behaviour, no doubt. Or maybe pondering Arlan reacting in such displeasure. Leyna and Vygeas followed silently.

"What's happened?" Bàn held out Mengus' reins to Arlan.

"We obtained the key. Now my Quest has truly begun." Arlan dug in his belt pouch and brought out a newly cast key. He released a long, slow breath and allowed just as slow a smile to creep across his lips. He'd passed a test unaware of his participation. "Àrd Gliocas had doubts and much anxiety over whether the ancient key could survive our journey. He insisted his sage who worked their small smelter, cast a new key from an impression, most carefully taken, of the original." He took the reins from Bàn. "And"—he tapped the satchel over his shoulder— "I have a scroll to give to Eifion. The head sage of the Broch of the Ancients commanded me to deliver but not to look." Arlan pulled his mouth to the side.

"Huh. The head sage has relegated you to messenger boy." Bàn nudged his arm. "But by my sword, that's not all." He nodded, squinting at Leyna and Vygeas.

Vygeas had embraced Leyna and held her tight. He kissed her hair, unashamed of the display in front of them all. He let go and turned to Arlan.

"I owe you a debt of gratitude, Lord Arlan. You saved Leynarve. And once again you have impressed me with your mettle. Although we are abashed that we displeased you so, we are convinced ye are the one with whom we wish to align ourselves."

Arlan stood still, leather reins digging into his grip, tempering the forming words that would shoot from his mouth like arrows and possibly do harm to all.

"Please do not let me find myself in a similar situation, caused by yourselves, ever again." He flew up into the saddle. "We must make haste to The Keep. This Quest waits for no one."

He kicked Mengus to a gallop, not waiting for his party to mount. They'd follow.

For now, he needed to ride.

The Keep, sitting high on its granite monolith, came into view, warming Arlan's soul and dampening it all at once. He swallowed. His parents had lived and died here, the place he once named home. If he won the Quest, it would be home once more.

He put a gloved fist to his mouth, stifling a sob, and kicked Mengus to a trot.

"Our lord is eager to register for *Tòireadh*," Bàn said behind him, and soon many hooves clattered on the road headed to The Keep.

Arlan rode up the natural granite ramp to the double-tower gate, his neck straining. Even after a thousand years it remained an awesome sight. Grey walls rose high, with round towers built at points on the curtain wall for strategic lookouts and defensible posts. Tresses of plants in flower, and more spilling from hanging baskets, splashed shades of pinks and reds on the walls of the caisteal within the bailey. He swallowed at the sight, for it was Mother's doing. She added colour to this *dreich* grey, just as she had to his own childhood.

He rode toward the iron reinforced wooden gates at the top of this natural ramp. Mengus' shod hooves clinked with each grip on the cobbled stones which assisted his climb up the steep incline. Arlan's throat tightened. A young woman had once asked him about such an arrangement of cobbles on a day out at Edinburgh castle in the Other World. Rhiannon, who kenned nothing of horses.

Och, must everything remind me of loves and longings this day!

The guard at the tower gate yelled to those below and the two large wooden gates creaked open. Arlan rode through, followed closely by his troop. Calls of greeting came from those crossing the bailey yard, and armed warriors waved as they passed. The armourer, standing near the rows of spears and shields against the inner bailey wall, turned and smiled, and the master sword crafter left his forge to step out into the sunshine and watch Arlan pass. He would find the time to show the man his tungsten alloy blade. A grin tugged at his mouth, for the master swordsmith would be jealous of such a fine weapon.

A young sage, barely out of boyhood, ran toward Arlan and skidded to a halt in front of the horse rail. Mengus flicked his head and snorted.

"Lord Arlan." The lad gave a brief, breathless bow. "Sage Eifion wishes you to attend him as soon as ye are ready after ye have entered Tòireadh." He bobbed again. The other horses arrived at the rail, nickering and snorting at his presence, and he scurried off.

Arlan slid off Mengus. Stable boys waited for the group to gather their gear, then took the horses to their stalls while Muir directed the others to the caisteal steward who would assign them quarters.

Arlan strode into the entrance vestibule of the caisteal proper, Bàn by his side, their boot spurs clicking on the stone floor. Ahead in the Great Hall, the throne of the àrd rìgh sat on its high plinth. Arlan walked tall, running his gaze over the bronze horse throne overlaid in gold and ornamented in fine filigree lacework, reflecting the beauty and strength of the animals—and the power of the àrd rìgh of the land.

Its seat was still vacant.

In front of it sat the table where he would register his entry to contest in *Tòireadh*.

Arlan's skin tingled all over. With this key, success was within reach. But the most dangerous part of the challenge lay ahead... Facing another live beast—

"My Lord Arlan, such a pleasure to see ye again."

He spun to face a clan chief from the mid-north, from what he could tell by a brief glance at the man's tartan and the chieftain's belt he wore. A young woman held his arm.

"Oh, pardon me, for it has been a while," the clan chief continued. "Ye were but a lad the last time we met. This is my second daughter, Senga."

The woman smiled, revealing perfect teeth, surrounded by full lips below eyes the colour of a green, verdant meadow. Her hair haloed a flaming red around her.

"Your pardon, lord, but I cannae recall..."

"Duisdale. Frae up by the lang loch," the clan chieftain said.

"Oh, aye." Arlan bit down on his tongue, the comment that he'd just returned from there sitting on its tip. The eyes and ears of other contestants were everywhere. A clan chieftainess with her son and eligible heir strode past, their stares turning to him.

"Grand to see you, Duisdale, and your lovely daughter." Arlan shook the clan chief's hand. "But I must register if I am to have a chance at this Quest."

"Oh aye, Mhàiri, my eldest daughter and heir to ma' lands, registers herself. Ye compete with her, Lord Arlan." Duisdale's expression became a touch serious. "Ye'll recall us, aye? And ma' daughter, Senga?"

"Ah, aye, but I'd best get on." Arlan gave a curt nod to the young woman, whose smile wavered, then turned to the Great Hall.

He marched to the front of the hall, passing contenders walking away from the table having proved their eligibility and signed up. An older version of Duisdale's daughter strode past him without a glance. Another stunningly beautiful woman from the north.

Bàn nudged him. "Ye ken ye will get more o' that."

"More o' what?"

"Clan chieftains parading their daughters before you," Bàn replied. "A young eligible clan chief like yourself deserves a good noblewoman for his wife."

"I have a pile of letters on the chieftain's desk at the Craegrubha requesting my perusal of various clan chiefs' daughters." Arlan halted mid-stride, the table to register for *Tòireadh* only a few paces away. "I have my woman. I wait for her," he whispered.

He nodded a greeting to Seamus Callaghan, a worthy contender for the Quest, who passed, staring at both himself and Bàn, but never smiled.

"I ken, but have ye discovered her noble house? For ye maintain she has such origins," Bàn answered in an equal whisper.

"Eifion investigates." Arlan tilted his head, giving Bàn a questioning scowl.

"What?"

"Ye bother me with this now?"

"Och, get registered. We must leave and go"—Bàn slid his gaze around the registration table and those walking from it— "to the place we must be."

"Perhaps Eifion has heard of Rhiannon's arrival."

"No, man! Ye have wasted time already. We must leave. It's more than three days' hard ride away. If the horses were nae so tired, I'd say let us prepare and go now!"

"But if Rhiannon has arrived?

"Lord Arlan Finnbar MacEnoicht." The official sage at the table pointed to an open scroll. "Your eligibility is proven by the *Sàsaichean*. Put your mark here, if you please." He pointed to the place with a quill.

"And Lord Bàn Lùthas." The sage unrolled another scroll.

"No sir, I have put my support behind Lord Arlan." Bàn spoke deeply, with no hint of apology.

The sage's hands halted over the half-unrolled scroll. "Oh," he said, then let the scroll curl back upon itself.

Arlan signed, then walked toward the door of the Great Hall with Bàn by his side. Seamus Callaghan stood at the doorway to the bailey yard, his eyes never leaving Arlan. The hair on Arlan's neck rose, and he hustled Bàn along the corridor and up the stone stairs. They strode along the balcony that faced the inner bailey and Arlan peered out through the wide openings in the balcony's stonework. The stables were opposite, where their horses buried their noses in feed troughs while stable boys curried them down. He arrived at Eifion's chambers and rapped on the door.

"Come in," Eifion's muffled voice came from deep within his chambers.

Arlan entered and strode to where the sage sat in the window recess.

"Ah, welcome back." Eifion lowered the book he held. "Did you find it?"

Arlan relayed the story of acquiring the key, including the behaviour of their new friends.

"Aye, on her parents' murders, Lady Leynarve abandoned her lands and title." A thoughtful frown rested on Eifion's brow. "I wonder how the ownership and current stewardship of those lands, plus the title belonging to it, stand now she has emerged." He looked at Arlan and grinned, wrinkles crinkling further around his eyes. "So, you have met my old friend, Brodie?"

"Who?" Bàn turned from his viewing of the river flowing below Eifion's window.

"Lord Àrd Gliocas."

"Your friend?" Bàn uncrossed his arms.

"Aye," Eifion replied.

"Did ye warn him of me?" Arlan asked.

Eifion tilted his head. "Now, that would be regarded as causing bias. I would never do such a thing."

Arlan squinted, handing Eifion the scroll from the head sage of the Broch of the Ancients. "This is for you from... Brodie. He bade me to deliver but not to peek."

Eifion drew a rush of air into his lungs. "Oh, by all that is good..." He held the scroll like it was a precious jewel. "I... must send my thanks to him." He gazed up at Arlan. "'Tis a copy of a locked scroll in which we shall discover more lore on portals."

"Ye have nae heard from Angus and Morrigan," the comment burst from Arlan, "or you would've told me by now."

"Nae, no news." Eifion's mouth twisted. "Ye should delay no further but get on with your task."

"I understand the pressing matter of a time limitation." Arlan widened his eyes at Bàn. "And now that we ken we have to return to near the Central Meadhan Mountains, we mustn't delay our departure."

"Aye, we should go now," Bàn spoke rapidly, "for it's days away and then we must find the three humped mountain where this ancient dragon refuge is supposed to be."

"Three humped mountain?" Eifion's wrinkles deepened. "Dragon refuge?"

"A clan of our ancestors made a fortress from three close mountains. We've seen the map." Arlan blinked at the eagerness in his own tone. "From what we understand from Leyna's scroll and what we learned at the Broch of the Ancients, after the Dragon Wars places of refuge were made for those surviving beasts. This mountain group is supposed to be one of them."

"We camped near them while we awaited Arlan's return from the Other World," Bàn explained further.

"We have a key that fits a door where, purportedly, one can find the eggs."

"And we must leave soon." Reprimand sat behind Bàn's tone, and he flung up a hand. "But Arlan wants to wait."

"Nae, I do not."

"Aye, ye do." Bàn set his fists on his belt.

"Well, I do. But I ken I cannae. The look on Seamus Callaghan's face! On all their faces." He dragged his hands through his hair. "We must leave this night with no one seeing us."

Arlan screwed his mouth to the side.

Bàn paced.

"I could..." Eifion lifted a finger in thought, then pressed it to his lower lip.

"Aye?" Arlan chorused with Bàn.

"Make them all sleep well," he finished.

"By... magic?" Arlan asked, then shot his gaze to Bàn, whose eyes narrowed at his whispering.

"Nae," Eifion said in a hush, then raised his voice to include Bàn in the conversation once more. "By a celebratory dinner, where you invite all the contenders who gather, then—"

"Get them drunk." Bàn snapped his fingers.

"But ye and your troop must not overindulge in the beverages"—Eifion's stern look settled on Arlan— "for I will ensure they are of a strength."

"Agreed! We will go and prepare." Arlan nodded to Bàn, then raced out the door.

"So do I, then," Eifion said behind him.

Seventeen

— • —

The quality of a king is a land's wealth and a people's treasure.
If their lord be honourable, generous, kind,
Famine, war, and pestilence may strike
But safe be the subjects who live beneath his rule.

WISDOM WRITINGS ON KINGSHIP
SAGE GLIOCAS
(2870-2962 POST DRAGON WARS)

The World of Dál Cruinne
Post Dragon Wars Year 6083
Western Sovereignty of Dál Gaedhle
The Keep

Arlan entered a private room of The Keep, his warriors behind him.

Of moderate size, this chamber came off a passage from the Great Hall and was nestled deep within the caisteal. A long table with bench seats sat by a roaring peat fire, and the room glowed a mellow orange. Soft candlelight reflected off bright tapestries that covered the walls in hunting scenes. Servants lay rushes on the floor and set the table with drink and food.

"There's benefit to having the status of the son of a once àrd rìgh." Bàn stepped through the door with him. "We're in the middle of The Keep. For other contestants to follow us on our journey, they must first navigate the maze of hallways and guards," he whispered.

"All is organised, my lord," Douglas said. "Seamus Callaghan and Mhàiri Duisdale are among those who are still here at The Keep and have acknowledged our invitation. Others have left in haste. Some wondered at your delay, my lord."

"Let them wonder and leave. Fewer eyes to watch our departure."

Chatter echoed from the Great Hall and down the passage to their secluded chamber, drawing closer. More servants arrived with platters of roasted meats, blood puddings and haggis. Manservants barrowed in barrels of drink, ale and whisky, Eifion stepping behind them.

"Place them by the table and tap them," Eifion ordered the men, then he stood beside Arlan. "These are of an exceptional strength." He spoke low into Arlan's ear. "There are more awaiting if required."

Voices blared through the door. Arlan turned. Mhàiri Duisdale stepped into the room, her long, loose red hair flaming around her shapely form. Her sharp green eyes surpassed the beauty of her flowing gown made of expensive cloth. Surrounded by her supporters who would aid her on the Quest, the woman dressed for a feast, not the feat required. The son of the Laird of Muirton strode in, eyeing all. A dour faced Seamus and his brothers followed Mhàiri's group, weapons sitting over their shoulders or hanging from belts.

"Please, my friends." Eifion stood in their path. "Leave all weapons at the door. We celebrate in good faith this evening." He smiled and repeated his entreaty to the other groups as they arrived.

"Please sit, one and all," Arlan said.

His guests strolled to the table and servants filled mugs with *uisge beatha*.

"Enjoy this token of goodwill and I wish us all luck on our Quest." He sipped on the dark, rich, amber liquid—smoky, like the peat-scented room.

But aye, it held a strength. Arlan whistled a quiet breath between his lips. He'd ordered his warriors to touch barely a drop, and the servants to keep the guests' cups replenished. Arlan sat at the head of the table and invited his guests to partake of the meal. They ripped legs off roasted chickens, sliced cuts from venison, and scooped portions of haggis onto serving boards.

Vygeas, Leynarve, and the rest of Arlan's warriors sat between the groups of contenders and engaged in friendly conversation. Douglas had ensconced himself in the middle of Mhàiri's warriors and regaled them with his wit, the women on either side of him leaning closer and draping more of their bodies on him as the evening progressed.

The room warmed, and thirsty clan heirs lifted their mugs to servants who hastily refilled them. The servers placed the sweetmeats on the table, then Eifion stood.

"Lords, ladies, and others—and ye can decide which category you fit in." He paused, allowing a raucous cheer to rise from the assemblage. "Lord Arlan trusts you are enjoying our feast."

"Lord Arlan." The heir of the Laird of Muirton held up his cup. "What a whisky! Such an exquisite distilling. 'Twould be a crime to refuse such an elixir." He sculled his drink and held it out for more, a servant obliging the refill.

"Aye, an' we in Dál Gaedhle ken how tae drink, do we no'?" Douglas roared.

Other comments arose, some of them unintelligible, but most sounding appreciative of the evening's fare. Arlan studied the room. A warrior woman sat in Douglas' lap, Vygeas clinked mugs with the heir of clan Manus, Leyna laughed and giggled with Mhàiri whose dress strap had fallen off her shoulder, and Seamus was looking bleary-eyed into his mug.

"The evening would not be complete without a tale," Eifion continued. "And as sage, I would stand in for bard this night."

Muffled applause mixed with clanks from mugs thumping on the table. The chatter ceased, Douglas moved the warrior woman to the seat beside him, and the room hushed, all present paying attention to Eifion.

"My story for you this evening is of a young man named Cathal. Now Cathal was the son of a clan chief. 'Twas a small clan in an insignificant part of the land. Nevertheless, Cathal was to receive a torc from his father, declaring to all he was the rightful heir and would be future clan chief of his father's lands. Nae matter how small they be."

A chuckle arose from the seated guests, and Arlan cast his gaze along the table. Seamus raised his face from his mug and lifted his empty vessel to a passing servant to fill, then fixed his dulled bloodshot eyes on Eifion.

"Two days before his torc day, when all would witness the clan chief placing the torc about Cathal's neck followed by great feasting and plenty o' drink"—Eifion winked at his audience, who cheered again— "a breathless and bedraggled servant ran up to the clan chief's broch."

"'My lord,' he says. 'Thou must be kind, for 'twas nae fault o' mine. But yer coos hav all run awa' an' I hae searched and searched for the past few days and cannae see a horn nor a wee pat tae guide me to 'em.'

"In a rage, young Cathal's father ordered the servant to be put in the chicken coop and our young Cathal to go look for the cattle. For as ye well ken, coos are proof of wealth, and Cathal's father could not be clan chief without them.

"So off Cathal went, over the hills and through the moors and beside shiny lochs, but spied nae coos. His first day's journey took him far from home and he stopped by a small steading house and knocked on its door, asking for shelter for the night. The farmer, a sole old man, shared a humble meal and allowed Cathal to stretch across his hearth. Cathal slept poorly, not only due to the hard hearth stone, but the farmer's wheezing cough. In the morning, Cathal stepped outside to fields, which were in desperate need of sowing. The sick farmer was not well enough to do his work. So, in payment for the food and shelter he'd received, Cathal hitched the plough to the old heavy horse and spent half the day behind the animal making neat straight lines. He spent the other half tossing the seed in the ground and thus, being a fit young lad, he completed the planting for the farmer. He stayed another night, for 'twas late in the day. The next morning, the farmer was on the way to improved health, so Cathal journeyed on.

"Cathal went further afield with not a sighting of the wayward animals. He spent his whole day wandering by the coast, terrified his father's coos had dropped from the cliff into the sea. He came across a lonely cottage whereupon a lovely young widow approached and offered hospitality, for the day had drawn to a close and otherwise young Cathal would spend the night on a blustery beach. Cathal warmed to the woman in the cottage by the sea and the waves crashing on the shore were not the only things a stirrin' this night. Cathal left the next morn a contented man."

Eifion grinned and ran his gaze along the guests at the table, and the warriors, both men and women, filled the room with whistles and cheers.

"Cathal headed toward home without any coos and dreading his father's reaction. He came across a wee hamlet, its inhabitants poor and harassed. They told him a griffin tormented them, for it had taken sheep and chickens, their food and livelihood. Please, they begged, would he save them from this beast? He could be just the one to kill it. Thus, our brave Cathal lies in wait for the griffin with his *bata* in hand and, while it is distracted claiming the bait—a sheep tied to a stake—he cudgels the griffin to death with his fighting stick.

"With the gratitude of the wee hamlet, our young hero moved on, his head bowed and shoulders slack, for still he would return home without coos after four days of searching. He came upon a near naked beggar, and taking pity on the soul, draped him with his own plaid and offered to share a meal of the last of his dried meat and other rations with the poor man. They built a fire, and the beggar produced a pot from his dirty sack, into which Cathal threw the last of his food and a cup of water from the burn. With the stew bubbling and boiling, the men talked.

"'Why are ye so down cast, young man?' asked the beggar.

"'I am to have my torc ceremony as heir, but now ma father has nae wealth for I cannae find our coos. I'll nae be clan chief, and on ma father passing from this life, ma people will be leaderless.'

"The beggar invited him to gaze into the boiling stew. In it Cathal sees the ill farmer, now well, harvesting a bountiful crop; the widow with a healthy son to receive the lands for inheritance and care for her in her old age; a small hamlet growing in number, with chickens and sheep abounding, and the coos at his father's door now wandered home.

"The beggar stood with him over the flame-licked stew, now a tall, healthy man smiling down on him.

"'Go awa hame tae your father's lands. Ye will be the greatest clan chief your people have known, for ye have a noble heart and have placed your people's needs above your ain. Ye are a worthy one.'"

Applause rang around the room, and Eifion bowed. Arlan raised his mug and servants refilled those of his guests. He eyed the room. His troop looked more alert and their speech less slurred than his guests. The night drew on and Seamus Callaghan's head slowly sunk onto the table, joining others. Manus laid on the floor and one of Mhàiri's warriors stretched out on the bench seat. Douglas gently removed the slumbering woman's head from his lap, and Bàn walked past Seamus, shaking his shoulder. The man did not stir. Arlan crept with his troop out of the room and down to the stables.

"I advised the guards you seek an early exit from the caisteal gates." Walking beside him, Muir spoke out the side of his mouth.

Arlan released a breath. Now severely drunk, his guests would awaken tomorrow with an ache of the head and a sensation that the rushes on the floor now grew on their tongues.

Arlan walked Mengus across the bailey yard. Muir had ensured the guards on duty at the gate tower were those of a fierce loyalty to Arlan as the son of Donnach MacEnoicht. The silence of the dead of night echoed from the bailey walls, only punctuated by the soft cloth-covered tread of Mengus' hooves and those of his warriors' horses.

Arlan walked through the town, his warriors behind him like shadows, passing dwellings still in silent slumber. He soothed Mengus' muzzle to stay any nickers. He'd left the hounds behind. Too noisy for this subterfuge. They'd stir up a dragon. This trip must achieve an egg and minimal encounters with a full-grown creature. He shivered.

Please may any encounters be with a flameless beast.

Arlan led Mengus past the last dwelling, which sat in sleepy darkness. Here he and his warriors removed the dampening cloths from the hooves of their war horses. Leading Mengus, he walked over the bridge and approached the meadow with a single sarsen standing in the centre of the burned circle of earth where once ashes lay and now no plant-life grew.

Arlan left Mengus at a drystone wall, the molten monument to the heat of the dragon's blast.

A murmur began from the rear guard of his troop and rippled toward him.

"Ah." Bàn's whisper came to his ear. "Adele has spotted a movement. Perhaps we are followed. I sent her to investigate, but she came back with naught."

Arlan curled his fist and grunted. "I have something I *must* do. Then we ride."

He stepped into the meadow, his warriors following, now all in shades of black and grey under the light of a sliver of moon. He approached the stone sentinel, thrice the height of himself. A quiet hush hedged his back while his warriors stood watch around him. In the shadow cast by poor moonlight, the inscribed ogham script told of Father's name, rank, and greatness.

Arlan stood in silence while the heaviness he'd pushed aside now rolled back into place.

He grasped his sword's handle over his shoulder, *Camhanaich* singing sweetly as he drew her from her sheath. The long steel blade shone in the moonlight, reflecting in a ripple-pattern every beam the sliver shed his way.

Arlan knelt, the ground's cool seeping through his breeches. He brought his blade to rest its point into the bare dirt.

I mustn't fail him.

"Father," he whispered, "ye rest in the peace of the afterlife. For as long as lands, lives, and loves require my service, my sword shall never slumber in my hands. I will fight for our people until I join you in the sleep of death."

Eighteen

— · —

Tho' the foe be near, tramping at your feet,
And beasts of darkness swarm your door.
Hard pressed, thwarted, threatening defeat.
Impossible the outcome, death a surety, and more.
Tho' warriors, allies, and brothers are replete,
These times in clarity profound, a certainty and sure,
'Tis a task for ye yourself only to complete.
Solely chance it, or never win the score.

SAGE GLIOCAS
(2870-2962 POST DRAGON WARS)

The World of Dál Cruinne
Post Dragon Wars Year 6083
Eastern Clanlands of Dál Gallain
At the base of the Central Meadhan Mountains

Arlan headed for the Central Meadhan Mountains, then veered south setting a pace on Mengus that pushed his warband's horses, pressed himself by his time constraints. By his reckoning, from the sliver of moon on the night they'd departed The Keep, he had less than two weeks till the blood moon. After four full days' ride, his troop had scruffy faces and lines sat beneath their eyes. A heavy ache had settled in his own limbs.

The afternoon sky clouded over, and the mountains were now behind them; their granite peaks still wore their snow cover despite spring's presence. Dark-dusted-white peeked in between passing clouds. Arlan's bare skin chilled and he pulled his tartan plaid over his shoulder. A cluster of three tall rock formations came into Arlan's view, rising less than a league away.

116

He led his troop on, riding beside a forest of tall green pine which carpeted the land between the base of the mountain range and this ancient but deserted rock caisteal. Arlan halted his warriors in front of the fortress.

"Ye are certain of a beast here?" Vygeas pulled his horse next to Arlan, with Leyna and his knave on their mounts beside him.

"Nae, but there's one over that way." He jerked his head to the northwest. "The one we encountered..." His words choked off. *Father, I still cannot bear the manner of your death.* "They like this area. As Àrd Gliocas showed us on the maps that record a safe haven for them here," he managed to finish.

Three tall rock formations, quite broch-looking, jutted out from a triangular sand-stone base. Between these enormous tower-like rocks, stone masoned walls rose high and sat thick at the base. The masonry joined each tower, forming a triangular fortress the size of the average caisteal, and with the gates intact, it would have been impenetrable. The aged wooden gate, rotted and hanging ajar on rusted iron hinges, led to an empty bailey yard.

"Huh?" Aiden spoke as they all dismounted. "So why the key?"

Vygeas stared hard at his knave, who shrugged.

A chuckle rose in Arlan's chest. *Aiden's so like Angus.* His mirth stuck in his mouth. How were they faring in the Other World? *Will I see you soon, Rhiannon?* He shook himself. First, he must complete *this* quest.

Arlan's companions stood with shoulders slumped or fidgeting with their lighter weapons tucked in their belts. Brows crinkled in query dominated their expressions.

"Good question, young knave," Arlan said. "It's obviously not for this gate, but another. And one most likely hidden."

"Spread out, all," Bàn ordered. "We will examine the area."

Each of the rock towers contained a large cave, and after examining all three, Arlan's warriors returned from the caves' entrances shaking their heads and declaring all empty within.

"I'll go around its outer perimeter." Arlan clenched and unclenched his hands. "This fortress must be more extensive."

"Aye." Vygeas' fingers danced on his thigh. "There must be other points of entry." He glanced at Leyna, whose mouth lifted at the corners. "Leynarve is an expert at finding a way where others cannot."

They exited the bailey yard, leaving the broken gate behind them. Arlan sent Muir, Adele, and Douglas to the left of the gate, to examine the west side of the fortress, which passed a front tower. Aiden followed them. Arlan went with Bàn, Vygeas and Leyna to his right, and skirted the eastern side and its front tower.

The ground ran clear and flat beside the wall until they passed the first tower where rubble piled against the side of the still intact wall. This mound, scree at first, turned to larger rocks and boulders. They climbed it and came upon a ridge topping the rubble.

Arlan walked along the ridge with the bailey wall to his left, the rubble covering it for half its height. The third tower, which sat the furthest back from the gateway entrance, now loomed ahead of Arlan. Beside him, Leyna strode close to the wall, peering down gaps and cracks between the mound of debris and the masonry. These gaps appeared with regularity every few paces. Just before they reached the back of the largest of the three natural towers, Leyna stopped and withdrew her short sword.

"I think I see something, Lord Arlan." She scratched stones and dirt away from the wall.

Arlan removed his dagger from his belt and dug. Bàn joined him, and they cleared a space revealing the arch of a doorway, a line of masonry with an obvious capstone above the accumulated rubble.

"Would this be it?" Bàn asked.

"There's only one way to find out." Arlan continued digging.

The others joined him and soon cleared the dirt away, freeing a door handle with a bolt beneath—a padlocked bolt.

Arlan leaned through the man-sized channel they'd made, squatted, and lifted the padlock so the key mechanism faced upward.

"It's still intact. The dry dirt enclosing it has preserved it. Barely any rust."

"That is fortuitous, Lord Arlan." Leyna's voice lightened.

"Aye, it was a concern," Vygeas agreed. "A rusted lock is useless despite a pristine, newly cast key."

Arlan placed the key in the massive ancient lock and turned. It was stiff, but with a nudge it went, and the padlock opened. A collective sigh of relief came from his companions standing behind him. Arlan pressed on the door. The top section moved away from the frame, but the rest didn't budge.

"I shall boot it," he said.

"Ye know not what lies behind it." Bàn's voice was in his ear and his breath on his neck.

Arlan shrugged. "A dragon egg, I hope." He stood and kicked the door, and it flew open. Halfway in, it knocked against something and stopped.

"Ye need light, Lord Arlan." Vygeas trod across the uneven ground away from where Arlan stood by the door.

Arlan twisted for a better view of where Vygeas had gone. The edge of the forest abutted against this section of the fortress and fallen branches and leaf litter lay strewn nearby. All stood silent while Vygeas rummaged on the forest floor.

"Oh," Vygeas yelled. "Come here."

Arlan walked with the others the few paces to the forest where a burn flowed from the side of the rubble-berm just as it merged with the tree line. Steam rose from it.

"It is a hot spring," Vygeas noted.

"Very good for relaxing, but for such we have no time," Bàn retorted.

"Aye, but it could travel underground," Vygeas said. "Ye could encounter it through that door, Lord Arlan. It may arise beneath that rock."

Arlan snorted. "It's not all I expect to encounter."

Vygeas grabbed a sturdy stick plus dried bark and leaf litter to wrap around it for a torch.

Arlan grunted to himself. Matches would be helpful. A torch with a long-life battery from the Other World would be even better. But any light would announce his arrival like a firework.

"Och, no. Nae torch," he said. "I cannae alert any female dragon to the thief who seeks to steal her eggs. I'll trust my night vision."

"Your what?" Bàn raised his brows.

"Oh, never mind. First, I'll see if I can see."

He ran back to the door, and feet first, slid into the narrow gap.

Warmth hit him, and a salty tinge of minerals, animal scent, and the sharpness of excrement came on the breeze funnelling along to him. All was silent, and he allowed his eyes to grow accustomed to the dimness. The end of the tunnel glowed.

"It's a tunnel to deeper places, but I can see well enough," he reported over his shoulder. He turned to eager faces. One had narrowed eyes and a crinkled brow.

"What do you know, Vygeas?"

"Lord Arlan, there is a life force down there. Wild. Have a care."

"I expected nae less, Vygeas." Arlan slipped further into the doorway, pushing it fully open.

Bàn made to follow him.

"Nae, Bàn. This part I must do without the help of others."

Bàn peered into his eyes for a moment. "I'll be here when ye return, Arlan."

"Aye, ye had better be."

"And then"—Douglas glanced aside to Aiden while they walked beside the wall— "the young lady proceeded to—"

"You'll stop right there, Douglas." Adele spun to face him. "Dinnae corrupt the young lad."

"Aw, but I wished tae ken." Aiden pouted.

"*Wheesht.* Stay untainted for as lang as ye can, lad." Adele scowled down at Aiden. "It all ceases too soon."

"What does?"

"The innocence of youth."

"She's only angry because she never had a childhood," Douglas whispered into Aiden's ear.

"I heard that," Adele threw sideways at him.

They marched the perimeter past the first rock tower, until the clear path turned to debris and rocks that rose high against the fortress.

"The wall is still intact," Muir said, "yet there is all this rubble made to look like the defences are broken."

"A ploy to confuse?" Adele asked.

"Maybe," the veteran grunted.

They walked further on till almost at the broch-like rock tower that sat at the back of the fortress. They skirted the stone debris and came across a gap in the berm of scree and rocks, where there was a break in the wall. It was large, with rubble and boulders mounded high on either side of the opening, forming a sheltered lead-in to an entrance.

Adele strode forward. "It's dark, and a warm breeze blows from within."

"It could be the entrance our lord seeks." All jocularity had left Douglas' tone. "He'll wish to enter." He turned to Aiden. "Go tell your master, lad. He's certain to be by our lord's side."

Arlan counted fifty paces, all sloping downward, while his hand ran along the wall beside him, its roughness bumping his fingertips. The scent of life and minerals, and the warmth of the breeze, grew as he drew closer to the glowing end of the narrow tunnel. He halted where the tunnel finished. Light streamed in thin beams like fingers from a crack in the cave ceiling. Ripples of light danced on the rock above him, adding white streaks to the yellow sandstone. Below and to the side a ways, the beams hit a clear pond that glowed pale-aqua. Mist rose, heating and humidifying an entire cave about half the size of the Great Hall of The Keep.

If his sense of orientation was correct, this sandstone cave sat under the base of the fortress above. It would have supplied heating and hot water to the once inhabitants. Perhaps now it provided a warm home and an ideal place for a dragon to lay and hatch her eggs.

The rocky floor undulated, rising from the underground thermal spring to where he stood at the end of the narrow access tunnel. There were boulders, with carcasses and old bones scattered in between, also wool, plus the coarse hair of wild goats, from what he could tell. Apart from the brightness of the cave by the spring, the rest stood in shadow. Rock shaped silhouettes lay to his right and, other than trickling water, all was still.

If this was a dragon's lair, where were the eggs? If there *were* any eggs.

Arlan released a breath that shouted into the silence.

Something stirred. A shuffle on dirt. A boulder moved.

Och, no. An enormous head, very spiked—and very much like one he had seen before—rose far to his right.

A shiver passed through him, marching sharp claws down his spine.

So then, definitely a dragon's lair.

The beast settled, the silhouette lowering to rest, accompanied by the gentle hiss of air passing through slitted nostrils. Arlan lowered his hand from *Camhanaich's* handle. A sword would be useless against such a creature. He clenched his fist by his side, his jaw mirroring the action.

But I must do it. He moved closer, searching for a nest.

Vygeas sensed Arlan's anticipation—mingled with the raw odour of fear—as he slithered further into the cave. *Aye, the man is cautious, and must be sly.* For he has to cheat an intelligent creature of one of its own young. He envied him not. Bàn leaned on the doorway, arms pressed above the half-door height of the access. If his lord needed a quick escape, he would be there to pull him out.

Bàn bent low and peered in, then leaned back. "The tunnel goes downward. Not immediately a cave, nor anything similar to a caisteal in nature, like these natural broch-like towers around us."

The familiar scent of Aiden rushed toward Vygeas, sweaty, dark fear and heated excitement bouncing off him in alternating waves of deep colour and pungent scent. Aiden ran around the east corner of the fortress, red-faced and droplets travelling down his temples.

"My lord," Aiden shouted.

Leyna hushed him. Aiden clamped his mouth tight till he stood next to Vygeas. He looked over at Bàn, who now sat on the rubble, his feet still in the doorway.

"Oh, you have found an entrance..." Aiden hesitated.

"Lord Arlan has gone in," Leynarve said.

"We have found one also." Aiden frowned under his curls, now hanging over his eyes with droplets of sweat dangling from each tip. "So, there are two ways in. Ours is much larger than this." He chewed his lip. "Douglas ordered me to tell ye, and I guess he meant for ye to come and Lord Arlan enter there. But..." Now fear's darkness dominated, wafting from his knave.

"Is it big enough for a dragon? Perhaps the dragon's entry to its lair?" Vygeas placed his hand on Aiden's shoulder, who jiggled his head in a nod, spraying Vygeas' hand with droplets of moisture.

The lad's gaze had not left Bàn who had half slid into this narrow entry.

"What if Lord Arlan chases the dragon out?" Aiden's whole body trembled.

Vygeas looked at Leynarve, then at Bàn. "If there is a dragon in there, it will not be happy once our lord is successful."

"We must ensure Lord Arlan's means of escape." Leyna's tone held urgency.

"And the safety of all." Bàn lifted himself from the doorway. "There is enough rubble around—"

"We can block it." Vygeas finished for him, then spun to face Aiden. "Take us there."

The contents of the cave had become clearer as Arlan's sight adjusted to the dimness. A round pile of twigs and other things—feathers and wool—sat some paces away to Arlan's right. Three large eggs, four times the size of an eagle's, nestled in it.

He stepped closer, the ground where he placed his feet still dark to him, and the nest some paces away. He took another silent step. His boot tip caught something, and it knocked against a rock protruding from the cave floor, a slight echo marking the movement.

Shuffling came from the dragon's direction and Arlan stopped dead still, listening through the thunder of his pounding temples. The animal sighed, like a hound on a warm hearth, and settled back to its rest.

Arlan lifted his foot to step closer, and the object he'd previously knocked caught again on his boot and spun. He leaned over and clamped his hand down on it, stopping it from grinding against the loose gravel on the cave floor. Egg-shaped, with a soft and rippled texture, it certainly felt like an egg. He lifted it.

It *was*, but smaller than the ones in the nest.

Perhaps the runt of the litter and discarded as not-quite-right.

Maybe the developing hatchling inside had died or suffered some deformity. Birds could detect this. Fowl at the broch would toss one of their own eggs out of the nest and leave to die. As a child, he'd played with the soggy skin-stretched dead body cracked out of one.

But this leathery egg was whole.

A dragon's egg—all he had to gain to win *Tòireadh.* He lifted a shoulder briefly.

Aye.

Arlan tucked the egg into his plaid. It sat lukewarm against his body. He pulled his plaid tightly across his shoulder, securing it into his belt. He turned, his foot crunching on the cave floor.

A grating of gravel came from behind. Arlan turned his head a fraction, keeping his body immobile. The animal rose, a dark spikey shadow growing taller. Ice flashed across the back of his neck despite the steamy heat surrounding him. Maybe his lack of movement would deceive the beast. Perhaps they responded to fleeing prey.

The dragon stood higher, almost filling the height of the cave. She stepped closer to her nest, her long graceful neck arching over her eggs, then nudged each one with her snout, as though counting them.

"Stop, Aiden." Vygeas turned. "Ye were just before the far back tower, ye say?"

"Aye," Aiden replied, breathless.

"Then it is closer that way." He pointed in the opposite direction to where Aiden had begun to run. "Wait. If we are to block the animal's exit, we need tools." He ran down the scree to the forest near the burn and stopped at a sturdy but not too thick tree. He drew his sword from its sheath. "Forgive me," he said, and chopped the tree.

"Go the way your master said and tell the others to block the entrance," Bàn called to Aiden. "It's surrounded by a mound of debris like this, aye?"

"Aye." Aiden bobbed then ran.

Vygeas and Leyna soon joined Arlan's warriors. Douglas stood with the burly lass, Adele, and Muir at the large break in the bailey wall. On either side, rubble piled high to form a berm, making a sheltered, short passage that led into an opening beneath the fortress.

"It is possibly the entrance to a dragon's lair, Vygeas," Adele said, standing with a rock in her hand.

"Possibly?" Douglas scrunched his nose. "Surely, it *must* be. Sweeter smelling farts come from young Aiden here, than the stench wafting oot o' that opening. For sure, an animal resides in there."

"Stop debating and come assist me," Muir said, then climbed the left-hand mound of rubble where a massive boulder perched.

Vygeas clambered after Muir, and Leynarve and Adele followed. Vygeas shoved the log he'd cut into the space between the boulder's base and the smaller rock Adele had placed there, which would act as a fulcrum.

"Ye all keep away from down there," Vygeas ordered, once the mechanism was in place.

Blades and bows and bloody double-sided battle axes! His head throbbed. *This is why I wish to work alone!*

So many strong emotions caused the usual ring of pain to his head. The band of warriors surrounding him were worried for their lord and anxious for their own lives. Anyone could discern this, but scents and colours beat upon him like a forge master's hammer.

Douglas and Aiden scampered away from the gap in the wall, which a boulder of this size would only partially cover. Perhaps they would have time to complete the blockage before the animal thrust herself against it.

Vygeas held the log, the lever of this rustic device, and Adele and Leynarve leaned against the boulder, while Muir grabbed the lever with Vygeas.

"Say when, V," Leynarve said.

"When," he replied.

They all heaved.

A *snort*, accompanying air moving through widened nostrils, filled the cave. The dragon's tongue flicked from her mouth; its tip forked. She slid it in and out rapidly. Like a lizard, she sought to taste Arlan on the air.

His brow cooled with sweat, magnifying his presence to her sensitive tongue, no doubt. He moved slowly, turning gradually, then taking backward steps to return to the access tunnel, risking the dragon noticing him, but he had no choice.

The dragon snapped her head to face his direction, then stepped closer, a beam of light flashing across her tail flicking behind her. Long and black, with a barbed end, it snapped like a cat annoyed. She had legs and clawed feet but slithered like a snake.

Icicles formed in Arlan's gut, clawing at his innards.

But the awesome beauty of this creature! *If only we weren't enemies.*

He stepped back one more pace closer to his escape. She raised her head, poised and ready to strike. With a loud swoosh, wings jutted from her back, cutting out the light from the crack in the ceiling and filling his vision with black.

Behind her, a grating, like rocks coursing over each other, echoed throughout the cave, ending with a grinding thump reverberating at the far end of the cave. The dragon turned, breaking their impasse, and letting the dim light back into Arlan's eyes. He turned and ran, charging down the long narrow tunnel. Behind him, a roar, like trapped thunder, drowned out a thud and more grating against rocks, which came from deeper within the cave. He glanced over his shoulder. The dragon's snout protruded through the man-sized opening of the tunnel.

He ran on, reaching halfway along the tunnel. Behind him, the dragon breathed in a large intake of air. Its breath sucked wind toward him from his narrow exit now acting as a funnel. He sped up, while the air gushed past him and toward the dragon who filled her lungs. His pounding muscles burned.

He grunted. *A burning of another kind may engulf me if I don't escape this tunnel in time!*

His heart rocked his ribcage like a sword belting a shield.

Father, I may join you soon!

"Bàn!" His desperation screamed back at him off the walls of the narrow tunnel.

The light from the door grew brighter and a shadow hovered over it. A blast of heat pushed him onward. He stumbled but kept his footing. The door remained open and Bàn leaned in.

"Arlan!"

"Give me room!"

Heat hit Arlan's back and caught the wooden door. He scrambled forward on the scree and broken stones, twisting his body sideways away from the flames shooting out from the half-doorway above the mound of rubble. Bàn grabbed him and dragged him to the side, grunting. Fire scorched the ground.

An acrid stench of burned leather and hair hit Arlan's nostrils. He glanced down; flame licked his boots and breeches at the calves. Bàn patted him down. Arlan pressed his legs into the loose dirt, the backs of his boots and breeches now burned away. The flames died but the singe stung his nose.

Bàn ran his grip down Arlan's smouldering plait. "Ouch! That bites."

Arlan's calves stung. He lay on his back, lungs heaving, heart drumming out of his chest and *thunking* an echo into his head. The lump of the egg in his plaid moved up and down in time with his breath, while it slowly returned to normal. He swallowed hard to remove the cloy of burned leather and flesh from his tongue.

"Are ye alright, Arlan?' Bàn's brow beetled as he peered at the remnants of Arlan's breeches. "Any more of you aflame?"

"Nae, I think not. But my hair is a wee bit shorter."

"That is the least of our concerns. The others discovered a larger entrance."

The beast's roar blasted through the gap beside the boulder that now semi-blocked the entrance that Arlan's warriors had discovered. Muir's and Adele's postures froze for a heartbeat.

"That confirms it is a dragon's den." Vygeas grabbed the wooden pole used for a lever.

The bolder now in place only covered half the height of this opening.

"We need to block this entrance completely. There must be no way out for the dragon. It will surely be enraged." Vygeas climbed down the rubble then headed to the other mound of scree. "We shall do the same on this side of this entrance." He grabbed a suitable stone for a fulcrum on his way up the mound.

Muir, Leynarve, Aiden and Adele, followed Vygeas to the top of the other pile of rubble, where another sizable boulder lay close. Adele put her back straight to the boulder and lifted while Vygeas dropped the stone and pole in place. They positioned themselves and heaved again in unison. This boulder grated, then tumbled, wedging between the boulder already in place and the other side of the gap.

"Wedged and stuck, I hope," Douglas commented.

They all scampered down from the mound of scree and rubble to the boulders now blocking the entrance. They kicked, dragged, and shovelled dirt to fill the gaps between the boulders and stones already in place.

"The animal within may scurry closer at any moment." Leynarve brushed dirt from her hands.

"Aye, we should find Lord Arlan and leave," Adele said.

They turned to the direction of the tunnel entrance where Bàn waited for Arlan.

Vygeas sensed urgency, and a massive cloud of concern, plus pain mingled with triumph.

"They come. Get to the horses." Vygeas skidded down the scree and turned to the way that led to the front of the fortress and their mounts. "They will follow. We must ready the horses to ensure we are away before the animal devises a way out of there!"

They ran to their mounts and untied them from their tether line, the animals whinnying and flicking their heads at their haste. Vygeas took the reins of Arlan's black stallion, a massive beast, and one only the likes of Arlan could handle. Douglas readied Bàn's horse.

Arlan and Bàn ran toward them. Arlan limped as he ran, the lower section of his breeches in rags and flapping with each stride. A small bulge protruded from the plaid crossing his chest. Sharp and acrid, the scent of burned flesh filled the air around Arlan, and stung Vygeas' nose and eyes.

"The dragon's flame caught him," Bàn shouted. "He's injured." The deep magenta of worry flew ahead of his words and hit Vygeas with force.

"I am fine." Arlan's tone had an edge to it, of the kind Vygeas had heard many times afore—his injuries spoke for him.

"We shall get him to the sage hold. It's a day's ride," Bàn shouted up to Douglas, who gave a brief nod.

"We know the way," Douglas yelled, jumping from his mount. Then he assisted Bàn to get Arlan into the saddle.

"I can ride," Arlan snapped. His brow creased in the middle—the look pain gave to all people.

"Wherever it is, we need to move," Vygeas said to Arlan. "We are unsure how well our barricade will hold."

Arlan gave a stern nod, and they kicked their mounts to a canter.

Nineteen

— • —

For the dragon proved difficult to tame, hence the employment of a gifted and skilled mage adept in the use of one. Closeness of the mage to the animal from hatching was imperative. But it must never be forgotten that a dragon is a wild creature, a fearsome beast, and ever will be.

DRAGON SCROLLS
INNESFARNE
DATE OF TEXT UNKNOWN

The World of Dál Cruinne
Post Dragon Wars Year 6083
Western Sovereignty of Dál Gaedhle
The Sage Hold of the Healers

Arlan's calves stung with their burn.

He clenched his jaw, as he had done for the past half day that was now dimming to night. It sent shooting pains to his skull, mirroring the hurts in the lower half of his body. He'd cantered Mengus for hours but despite the gentle gait, each thump of his legs against his stallion's flanks sent stabbing agonies from his calves to his thighs. Heaviness attended every part of him, and his skin cooled, tightening with the saltiness of sweat. In front of him, Bàn was just a blur with a blond head paling in the scant moonlight.

Grey rows of low grape vines passed his vision—the vineyards of the sage hold. He let out a long sigh that ended in a groan. He'd soon be off Mengus and able to rest.

Aye, I require the services of their healers.

The shadowy shape of a large wooden fortification built on earth works, loomed nearer. A soft glow of light seeped through the gaps between the vertical planks of the high walls of the sage hold. The gate opened and a lone sage, a muted figure in the darkness holding a lamp, stepped toward them. It was the one they called Jakodi.

"Hail, friend sage," Bàn said, and Jakodi's attention turned to him.

"My Lord Bàn, ye are arrived at a late hour but we greet you nonetheless." Jakodi glanced at the party, then his stare landed on Arlan and travelled to his torn breeches.

"Our Lord Arlan is injured," Bàn told the healer. "Once again we require your expert care, for our lord was burned by a dragon's blaze."

"A dragon's—" Jakodi gulped. "Greetings, Lord Arlan." He stepped closer and ran his vision over Arlan's right leg.

"Sage Jakodi, thank you for your hospitality. It is nothing serious. I just need—" Arlan's mouth dried mid-sentence. "I'm thirsty." His husky voice was far away.

Everything seems far away.

"Please, come in," Jakodi said, then whispered instructions to the junior sage behind him, who scurried off. "Sage Bayrd is on his way." Jakodi directed them to the infirmary, where the warriors dismounted.

Arlan moved his leg and stifled a yelp.

"I'll help you down." Bàn came to his side, his voice thick.

"Here, let me assist." Sage Bayrd held a lantern high. "I shall inform Sage Phelan. He will attend you."

Arlan's legs trembled. He took his feet from the stirrups and lifted one leg over Mengus' neck, avoiding a graze over the rough hair of his mane, and swivelled around to hop down. He landed, his knees buckling. Bàn grabbed him tight, a band of strength at his upper arm, stopping him from crashing to the ground. Muir rushed to his other side and his strong hands gripped tightly.

Bàn and Muir assisted him to walk to the chamber where Bayrd had directed them. Bàn laid Arlan on a cot. The sheets were soft to the touch of Arlan's hand, but a fierce sting erupted in his calves at the contact. Everything stung them—even with the touch of air they burned all over again.

A fire crackled low in the hearth, staving off the chill night air in the comfortably warm chamber, but Arlan's forehead cooled. He turned onto his stomach, bearing his calves upward, and someone, probably Bàn, removed what remained of his boots. Footsteps left the room. The room spun. More feet shuffled closer, and voices murmured over him. A jug clunked, and liquid gurgled into a cup.

"Here, Arlan." Bàn put a cup to Arlan's lips. "The sage says you lose water through your... where ye were burned, and he says ye must drink."

Tilting his head back on an awkward angle, Arlan sipped down the liquid.

"Sage Phelan is coming," Bàn said.

"Aye, I'm thirsty." Arlan laid his head back on the pillow. "But water, Bàn? Nae *uisge-beatha?*"

The door opened and two sets of feet trod in.

"My Lord Arlan." The official but calm tones of Sage Phelan spoke to his back. Arlan moved to turn. "Nae, Lord Arlan, stay still. I shall examine you."

Moments passed with much tutting from the healer. Arlan's heart sank. The man would be straight with him, and his quiet exclamations indicated something dire.

"Och, your legs are a mess, man." The healer's tones were severe. "Have you dragged yourself through the dirt?" Without giving Arlan time to answer, Sage Phelan gave brisk orders to his assistant to cleanse his wounds, then call him back. "Then I shall be able to see the condition of your skin, or what remains of it." He *tsked* then strode out.

Arlan breathed out long and hard. The bed was comfortable, except for a lump near his belly.

"Och, no." Arlan lifted his upper torso from the cot and removed the leathery dragon's egg from his plaid. "Would ye believe I almost forgot about this? Please put it somewhere safe, Bàn. I cannae lose it."

Bàn took the egg from him and placed it on the hearth, then turned and faced Arlan, his mouth askew.

"What?"

"Ahh... I might get that whisky. They mean to clean the grit and such from your wounds. Ye may require it."

Bàn left. It wasn't long before a young woman entered with a bowl and clean rags. She laid them on a bench to the side. Bàn returned soon after.

"I, um, thought Lord Arlan may need this," Bàn said to the junior healer.

The young sage sniffed. "Aye well, it may be a good idea."

A cup clunked on the small bench, Bàn poured, and a liquid glugged. A familiar aroma wafted to Arlan's nose. It was a ripe malt field rippling in a summer breeze. A warm hearth on a winter's day. Clan and friendship. The hands of ancestors past touching him in his present.

Bàn nudged him. "Here, wake a moment, Arlan. Take a sip."

Arlan took the cup and sculled the warm spirit. Bàn repeated the process three more times.

"He may have had enough now," the young woman said, and a cold sting began where she pressed the wet cloth onto his calves.

The sting burned, and the burn went on fire, and the room swam.

"Nae, Bàn, keep the drink coming," Arlan said through a grimace.

And Bàn did until the world tilted, and the room blurred out.

Birdsong came to Arlan's ears, thudding in his head and joining the tightness of his neck. His lower legs hurt less than the previous evening, but they were heavier. He reached down. Soft cloth—bandages smooth to his touch, covered both calves.

He turned his head to the window; the light of the morning sun glowed through his eyelids. He opened his eyes, then shut them against the glare. His eyeballs ached as though they were boiling hen's eggs about to split and spill their contents into the pan. Like the aftermath of a night in a tavern celebrating a fighting-pit win.

He groaned, still lying on his stomach, and the clamp on the back of his neck grew tighter.

Odd, for a hangover—as Rhiannon would call it—never usually gives me such a feeling.

The clamp on the back of his neck wriggled.

"What!" He reached under his hair. Tiny feet scurried around his neck. He sat up and the feet, attached to a smooth body, scampered under his chin.

"Och!" He grabbed something warm and long.

It squeaked. He tossed the small narrow body onto the bed. The creature turned in a circle and faced him. Big eyes, with pupils like a cat's, peered at him from a lizard face. It blinked, its eyes seeming to jump as reptilian second lids closed over vertical pupils then opened again. It scurried onto Arlan's belly, up his chest, round his neck, and under the hair hanging down his back. The clamp to the back of his neck returned.

"Ah...?" Arlan's hand remained poised just behind his head.

Beside the fire, a torn dragon's egg, surrounded by a clear viscous liquid, sat collapsed on the hearth.

"Och, no!"

His belly shook, and mirth bubbled up from within, while his head pounded, but he couldn't stop. The creature squeaked and wriggled.

Arlan placed his hand at the nape of his neck and tiny feet scampered across and onto it. He curled his fingers around it gently and pulled the creature out.

He widened his eyes and peered closer.

A baby dragon sat in his hand.

Tiny and red, about the size of a rat—but so much prettier—it fit in the palm of his hand, its tail curling around his wrist in a possessive manner. It looked directly at him, right at his eyes, tilted its head, and did the bouncing-blink again.

His mouth stretched in a grin.

The runt of the litter and, with a red hide, not black like the mother dragon, it also qualified as a reject. Its pinched snout had two small slits for nostrils, and dark holes for ears sat on either side of its head. Its scaled skin was smooth on his palm and its heart beat against his fingers, while tiny claws gripped tight to him.

Arlan held still. His eyebrows drew together, a knot of discomfort in the centre of his forehead. Then something stirred inside of him, and his face softened.

This wee thing won't last. Oh, let it sleep in my hair, if it will.

"Ye will be a curiosity to show the others." His gaze drifted to the remains of the dragon's egg. "Oh..." He squinted one eye.

Someone tapped at the door, then Bàn entered. The creature scampered up Arlan's arm and back into the hair at his nape. Bàn's eyes rounded, but he said nothing. Sage Phelan followed him in.

"How are ye the day?" The grey, hoary-haired sage retained his wolf-like appearance, the same as on Arlan's previous visit. The occasion the man had attended to Kyle's head wound.

"Thank you, much better. I appreciate your ministrations, if not the discomfort inflicted by your junior sage's attempts to clean my burns."

"It was out of no desire to give my assistant pleasure that I ordered your injuries cleaned. Your wounds must remain so. They are not deep, your boots having shielded your calves somewhat, so your burns should heal but will scar. If they fester, however, this will be dangerous for you. Hence, keeping them clean is imperative. I am aware ye are one always in haste to return to wherever ye have come from, so I have spoken with your troop. One of your warriors"— he frowned— "who was not with you on the last occasion, has experience with wounds and has agreed to tend to your dressings with salt water regularly until ye heal." He paused for breath. "So ye can go as ye always must, or so it seems. And ye must drink plenty of water." With a nod he left the room, not waiting for a response from Arlan.

Bàn shut the door behind the healer sage, then spun to face Arlan.

"What've ye got in your hair?"

Arlan pointed to the broken dragon egg by the hearth.

Bàn blinked, mouth agape. "It... hatched?"

Arlan nodded, then held his head with both hands.

"Och, I need that water, for someone is inside my skull trying to get out and banging with a war hammer something furious."

Bàn poured water from the pitcher on the stand and brought the cup over to him. Arlan took a long draught then held the cup out for more. Bàn tipped the pitcher, and while he did, the hatchling scurried out from behind Arlan's hair and along his arm. Bàn stepped back, let an expletive fly, splashing water on the floor, Arlan's hand, and the tiny dragon. The hatchling, unperturbed by the shower, placed a claw on the rim of the cup, leaned in, and drank. After a few laps, it poked its forked tongue out rapidly into the air in Bàn's direction, then shook like a dog.

The side of Arlan's mouth tightened. "It knows not what to make of you, Bàn."

Bàn scowled. "What will ye do with it?"

Arlan sighed. "I must keep it."

"Whatever for?"

"To prove that the contents of that broken egg"—he lifted his chin in the direction of the hearth and the collapsed leathery egg— "was a dragon, proving it is indeed a *dragon egg.*"

"Ye could kill it and still prove the same."

"Bàn! Nae! The poor wee mite will die soon enough. Let it have some life."

"Have ye gone soft?"

"Och, no. But he's... *cute.*"

"*Cute?*" Bàn's eyebrows got lost in his hairline.

Arlan held the hatchling close to his face and grinned at his use of Rhiannon's word. The baby dragon blinked at him, then scurried along his arm and under his hair.

"Och, let's go." Arlan let his shoulders ease. "I must get to The Keep and present my evidence to the *Sàsaichean.* And Rhiannon—"

"May be there, aye," Bàn said. "But first ye have someone to see."

Arlan lifted his chin in query.

"The Blind Lady Sage has agreed to meet with you," Bàn said.

"Isn't she insane? How can she agree to meet with me?" Arlan rose then ambled along behind Bàn, a stiff walk was all he could muster with thickly bandaged, painful legs, and the war hammer continuing to pound inside his skull. The baby dragon remained gripping his neck, hiding beneath his hair.

"And what made ye think I wanted to see her?" Arlan asked.

Bàn slowed to walk abreast with Arlan and raised an eyebrow.

Arlan waggled his head slightly—until it hurt. "Aye, I do wish to see her. I would like some clarity on her comment to all in the hall of this sage hold on our previous visit. Why did she announce me, there and then, as their warrior king? I was not even a clan chief at the time. Did she, through her madness, believe it herself? And know some would scoff." Arlan huffed. "Sage Bayrd choked on his food. I couldn't tell if he was angry or embarrassed at her actions. And you, my sword-brother, took her at her word."

Beside him, Bàn was silent for a few paces.

"Her minders say they'll let us see her," Bàn finally said. "Ye can ask her yourself."

Arlan rounded a corner past the infirmary where a sage waited beside smaller buildings. He was the same one who, on their last visit, minded those with troubles other than of the body.

"Follow me." The sage opened the door beside him.

The room, about the size of a meeting room off the Great Hall of The Keep, had few furnishings, and an iron grid shielded the front of the hearth. Crying drifted out from a corridor to their left. The sage marched them through the room and along another short corridor. The sharp scent of old urine lingered in the air, also the pungent odour of unwashed bodies. He stopped at a door to the left, and with his hand on the door latch, he paused.

"Giorsal is not as clear minded today as one might wish." The sage looked at Arlan. "But she is calm and amicable. I believe she will do you no harm."

Arlan swallowed, Bàn raised an eyebrow, and the sage unhinged the latch and opened the door.

The room held a simple cot, a table and chair, and one opening looking out onto a small courtyard filled with flowering plants. A woman stood by the window, sunlight streaming onto her long grey hair peppered with amber. She wore a simple gown of homespun cloth dyed a beige. She turned at the creak of the door, her clouded eyes searching the room and settling in Arlan's and Bàn's direction.

"Giorsal, you have visitors," the sage said in gentle tones. "Do ye wish to come closer?"

The woman stepped a pace across the rushes on the floor, the scent of lavender rising from her tread. Her minder nodded encouragement to Arlan.

"Good day, Lady Giorsal, I am Arlan. It is so nice to see you again." He surprised himself with how much he meant it.

She stepped right up to him and placed cool fingers on his face. She was a tall woman and she reached him without stretching. Her fingertips traced the line of his brow, nose, and jaw, then retraced his eyes, lips, and beard. She smiled, beard growth flicking against her hand.

"Ye are a handsome man." Her voice was a soft whisper.

Arlan couldn't draw his gaze away from her. Her eyes were that of a blind person's, no light shone in them, yet flecks of pale mauve dotted the white, and they held intelligence. She spoke more, half words of nae sense, then she turned away and wrung her hands, her incoherent language continuing for some moments.

Her sage minder shrugged. "Her times of clarity are unpredictable, my lords."

Bàn shook his head. "I hoped she would say more to Lord Arlan of her comment about him. Her announcement at our previous visit."

The sage leaned closer. "Her proclamation of Lord Arlan as warrior king?" he whispered.

Bàn screwed his mouth to the side and nodded while the old woman's babblings continued. Then Giorsal turned back to Arlan, and Bàn stood straighter. Giorsal focused on Arlan, her blind eyes seeming to peer into his soul. She stepped closer and a warm and caring smile crept across her face.

"Ye need not be told more, for ye know what ye must do. Haste ye home, mighty king, for your destiny, with all the love, loss, and victory it holds, beckons ye."

Arlan breathed deep, filling his lungs with lavender's perfume. All at once an urgency to return to The Keep hit him. He turned to go, grabbing Bàn's arm and nodding his thanks to the sage in the same movement.

Bàn opened the door, and Arlan limped out behind him.

The Blind Lady Sage's voice echoed through the open door. "Harm not the wee one."

TWENTY

— • —

As the salmon to the spawning riverbed, so love courses up the burn, the current ever hurling it further awa' frae its destination.

POETRY OF A KING
ÀRD RÌGH RHONAN IUBHAR
(4030-4090 POST DRAGON WARS)

Our World, 2018
Perth, Scotland

People stood waiting in the reception area of Perth's police station.

I strode past them all, their expressions ranging from tight to bored, and went straight to reception, ignoring the grumbling behind me.

"I'm Rhiannon Ferguson. Detective Findlay wanted to see me."

"Aye, miss, I'll let ye in," the officer on reception duty said then buzzed the door beside the desk. "Just come through." He waved me forward.

I pushed the door open, stepped through and the officer came to my side.

"One moment, Miss Ferguson, just need to inform Sergeant Findlay that you're here. He's in with some big wigs frae Glasgow." He winked and strode down the corridor to an interview room. After a brief exchange through a half open door, the officer turned back to me. "Come along. Sergeant Findlay is ready for you."

I approached the door, which the duty officer held open for me. Findlay stood by a table, lips pressed together, and directed me to sit. A man and a woman sat on the opposite side, both dressed in blue suits and wearing official but determined expressions. The man glanced at my legs below my skirt.

I should've worn my jeans.

"Thank you for coming today, Miss Ferguson." Findlay smiled a welcome.

He seemed genuine.

"This is Inspector Michelle McDougal and Sergeant Frank Boyle." He indicated to his colleagues seated across the table. "They're detectives from Glasgow."

"Yes, thank you for coming in, Miss Ferguson." The woman smiled. "May I call you Rhiannon?"

I nodded.

"Rhiannon, we have here your formal report stating you had witnessed what you thought to be a mugging in Glasgow yesterday. We are profoundly sorry you saw such violence. I'm sure Sergeant Findlay has given you contacts for the Victims Support Programme." She glanced at Findlay, who nodded.

Findlay had kept his eyes on me the whole time, like I was a specimen under a microscope, and he was waiting for my reaction to what he knew was coming. My neck prickled.

"The man you identified as the perpetrator," Inspector McDougal continued, "is a gang boss. A man we believe is responsible for many other crimes."

Now this is making sense. I held my bag on my lap and gripped it tighter.

"Please, don't be alarmed"—Boyle raised his hand in a staying gesture— "but we feel your safety is in question."

The prickle on my neck now stabbed daggers.

"Now that you've seen what you have your life won't be the same," McDougal said sending a glare in Boyle's direction then returning her gaze to me. "We truly regret this, but unfortunately, it's the nature of the crime we are dealing with. Our plan is for Detective Findlay here to organise a member of the police force to watch your home for the next few days. If the victim does succumb to his injuries, then unfortunately you will be our only witness to a murder." She gave a sympathetic frown. "We can't exclude the possibility of the need to take you to a safe location until after the trial."

What? Wait, did they mean what I thought they meant?

"Are you talking about witness protection?" I'd gripped my bag so hard my knuckles cracked. The thumping in my temples registered the slow but steady rise in my pulse rate. I willed myself to settle.

The detective gave a slight shrug. "We aren't speaking of that, only having a constable stationed outside your residence for a time."

"No." I spoke firmly.

Findlay, who'd stood back to give the Glasgow detectives the floor, now sat on the desk beside me. It creaked a little, and I caught a glimpse of his shirt. It gaped between the buttons over his large belly.

"You're a witness to a mugging, Miss Ferguson, involving a Glasgow gang." He leaned forward, his shirt gape widening. "Your testimony may convince a jury of a criminal's guilt. But we need you to be safe. We'll keep an eye on you."

I looked him in the eye and shook my head.

Findlay tilted his head a fraction. "I understand it's an inconvenience for you, and it's not our lives being turned upside-down, but your safety is our ultimate goal. We'd rather not have to remove you from your current situation."

"What if it did become a murder?" I looked at McDougal. "Would I have to go into witness protection then?"

"Let's not get ahead of ourselves," Findlay said.

I pressed my top teeth on my lower lip and tried with all my might to not glare at Findlay.

What if Arlan comes back and I'm not there 'cos you've whisked me off to some safe location?

I glanced at the other detectives. They must have thought I was a straightforward case. No family, no man, a second-rate job in a dusty old bookshop in a dying shopping centre. That was how they would see it, relieved at how easily they could move me from my cottage without notice, and no one question it.

And if by some freak chance Arlan found me, wherever the safe house was, I'd still be under their surveillance. I ground my back teeth. The police would never let a tall, muscled man with lots of hair, and armed with a very long—and very sharp—sword anywhere near me.

"I'm not leaving my cottage." I squared my shoulders.

"We're not asking you to leave your cottage." Frustration snuck out of Findlay's otherwise professional tone.

Not yet, you're not.

"We just want you safe, Miss Ferguson," he continued. "We understand this can be a little unsettling. Now, an officer will escort you home and watch your cottage until the situation becomes clearer."

"You mean, if the guy dies?" I asked.

Boyle's eyebrows lifted, and McDougal looked down at the papers on the desk with her mouth scrunched to the side.

"Let's just take it one day at a time," Findlay said. "Your life shouldn't be too disrupted. You can attend your place of work, like normal. A police officer will keep an eye on you."

So, not a safe house... for the moment. The spot between my shoulder blades that had grown tight during the whole conversation now eased a little. But they would still be observing me, virtually guarding me. I shot up from my chair and hastened down the corridor. I had to think of a reasonable way to avoid the watchful eye of my minder. Devise a plan for if—no—when Arlan turned up at my house, so he wouldn't attract any attention.

Yeah, right.

"Ah, Miss Ferguson," Findlay called from the doorway, "please wait for the constable to accompany you home."

I stood at the kitchen sink and looked out the window. On the hill where the Iron Age Fortification stood, the late afternoon sun bathed the surrounding green foliage in gold. An unmarked police car sat parked directly in front of my cottage, and the lone officer sitting at the steering wheel looked like he was just out of high school. I'd met him at the police station. Constable Brown had introduced himself, then followed me home to my cottage. Once home, he'd informed me of Sergeant Findlay's orders, insisted he check out my cottage—to ensure it was safe for me to enter—then assumed his duties as watchman.

I chewed on my lip, staring out my window and trying not to imagine the young constable's reaction to a Dál Gaedhle warrior.

Another car, a tiny two-door, veered around the corner of the street. It came up to the kerb outside the cottage, barely slowing, bounced then rode over the kerb and onto the footpath, where it skidded to a halt. The driver then put the car into reverse, and drove back and forward repeatedly, a little way each time, gradually getting the car into some semblance of *parked*.

The policeman stood from his car, put on his hat, and marched over to the vehicle. Both doors opened, and a tall man and woman got out. A chuckle rocked my chest. It was like clowns emerging from a circus car.

A gasp stifled my laughter.

It was the attractive couple from my day out in Glasgow! They spoke to the officer, and from the strained expression on his face, he had difficulty understanding their strong accents. The two foreigners looked toward my cottage, and seeing me at the window, waved and smiled. They couldn't hide their Dál Gaedhle accent from me on the train yesterday. Or their strong physiques, their beauty, and their warrior-like alertness. There was no other explanation to their presence outside my cottage today—they *must* be from Arlan's world.

"Yes!" I punched the air, then thrust my backdoor open and flew down the path, a plan forming in my mind as I went. "Yanni! Svein!"

Well, they do look more Scandinavian than anything.

I ran up to the woman and gave her a hug. She was tall like me, and our embrace fit.

"These are my cousins from Norway," I told the officer. "I haven't seen them for ages."

My mouth stretched in genuine relief at seeing these two people and I grabbed the woman's hand, ignoring the stuttering comments from the policeman, then dragged her inside with the young man following behind. I strode through the cottage and straight into the living room.

Checking we were out of the line of sight of the kitchen window I asked, "Arlan sent you, didn't he? So, what's the plan?" A tingle travelled right through me at having said it all in fluent Gaelic.

But why hadn't Arlan come?

The warrior smiled through a wispy beard, the tightness around his eyes relaxing. "I'm Angus, and this is Morrigan, and I'm so glad ye speak our tongue." The relief in his voice was almost palpable.

"Lord Arlan wishes us to bring you home immediately," Morrigan said. "He apologises for not coming himself, but he contests in *Tòireadh.*" Her face broke into a warm grin. "Ye are brave and quick witted and ye belong with us." She leaned over and hugged me again. Angus coughed and looked at the floor.

Warmth enveloped me. On the outside, from the warrior's body heat, and on the inside, at how easily they had accepted me. Tears prickling, I let go of Morrigan and wiped my eyes.

"Wait." I squinted, trying to translate. "He contests in the *pursuit?*"

"The Quest, ye would name it," Angus said.

"Oh, yes, that's right. Arlan spoke about that. So, that means his father, the àrd rìgh has..."

"Aye, my lady," Morrigan answered, her tone now solemn. "Killed by a dragon."

"A what! A dragon? But they're only in fairy tales."

"Ah, nae. Though I know not what a *faerietail* is," Angus answered. "But we believed them to be myth until we encountered one on our way home to The Keep once Lord Arlan had returned from this world. Lord Arlan sought to fight it, but Lord Bàn and myself stopped him."

"*Wheesht.*" Morrigan scowled at Angus.

"Arlan was going to fight a *dragon?*" I blinked, stilled by this admission. I shook myself. "How did his father die... *by a dragon?*"

"Fire breather," Angus said.

I flopped onto the couch with a thud. They stood near me in silence for a few moments, the light inside the house dimming from the setting sun.

Angus cleared his throat.

"Our Lord Arlan requests we bring ye home, for he fears for your safety. We informed him of the incident in Glasgow yesterday and he believes those who oversee your laws here will put you into protective witnessing."

"Witness protection, you mean?" I pointed to the front of the cottage. "Well, a policeman watches my home. Lord Arlan is probably right." I let the corner of my mouth lift. *Lord Arlan* sounded so important from the way these two spoke of him. "Why is Arlan competing in the Quest? Isn't that up to his brother?"

"My Lady Rhiannon, Lord Kyle was injured in a skirmish." Morrigan looked at her boots. "He does not awaken."

"Oh, I'm sorry to hear that." I slunk deeper into the couch. Serious injuries with no modern medicine—that was Arlan's world. "Wait. Does that mean Arlan is now... clan chief?"

"Aye," they both spoke at the same time.

My heart seemed to tumble into my belly. If Arlan was a clan chief, that meant he was even more important in his world to those around him. I chewed my lip. What if he won the Quest and became àrd rìgh? Then they'd never let him marry... me.

If he even wanted to, anyway.

I snapped out of *that* line of thought. It would lead me nowhere.

"We shall leave immediately," Angus ordered. "We have our weapons—"

"You'll not harm that policeman." I jumped up from the couch. "He's just doing his job."

Angus' mouth gaped for a moment, then he blinked and closed it.

I strode to my bedroom. "I'll go pack. We'll wait till much later, after he nods off," I said over my shoulder. "Then we'll leave."

I stuffed a change of clothes into a backpack that already held my baby-rug—a plaid in the tartan of House Gallawain with the clan crest embroidered on it—my only proof of my origins in Dál Gaedhle. I pulled my sheathed sword with its belt and my shield from the trunk and leaned them against the couch, all ready to go. I strode to the kitchen, then peered outside. In the dim light, the policeman ate what looked like sandwiches.

I threw pies and sausage rolls in the microwave. The microwave pinged and I dished up, then sat with the Dál Gaedhle warriors at the table to eat.

"All together, we have been here for six turns of your moon," Morrigan said.

"We have watched ye all this time." Angus grinned. "And discovered your world."

He faced Morrigan, the warmth in his eyes unmistakable as their gazes locked. A buzz went between them, the air filling with the electric tension that surrounds two people in love. No doubt this world had not been all they'd explored.

Morrigan cleared her throat. "It's such a relief, that we have arrived and the Scotland Police have not yet hidden you."

"Arrived?"

"Aye, after Glasgow we went home, reported all to Lord Arlan, and now return on our lord's orders."

"Oh. I hope we get back to the same time you left." An itch inside niggled. I had to know, and these two could tell me. "Now that Arlan is clan chief, has he... married?"

"No, my lady, he waits for you." Angus smiled with confidence.

"But I'm not noble. Won't a clan chief need a noblewoman?"

Angus' face dropped. Then he flinched and glared at Morrigan. "Why do ye kick me?" he whispered in a hurt tone.

Morrigan stared at her half-eaten sausage roll.

"Morrigan?" I asked. "What do you know?"

Morrigan looked up from her plate, her expression almost pitying. "In our world it is always done that those of position have to wed for alliances, and aye, that means nobles only marry nobles." She glanced over at Angus.

Angus swallowed.

"Lord Arlan has charged Sage Eifion to discover your family heritage," Morrigan added.

Angus frowned. "Ye know this how, Morrigan? Do not give Lady Rhiannon false hope."

"I heard Lord Arlan speaking to Bàn." Morrigan faced me. "Bàn is my brother. He and Lord Arlan are close. Sage Eifion will find out." She finished with a nod.

"And if I'm not?" I asked.

Angus rose from the table, his chair screeching beneath him, then his empty plate clattered in the sink. "We must watch for this man of police to sleep," he ground out, leaning on the sink and facing the window.

Morrigan chased the last pieces of her sausage roll around her plate with her fork.

I stared down at my partially eaten pie, my stomach growing cold.

"If ye are not from a noble clan, Lord Arlan will marry a woman who is." Angus spoke over his shoulder while he remained at the sink. His tone held an edge. "For that is the way of it."

TWENTY-ONE

— • —

With the breath of dawn
I sing my song,
And find my work begun.
The last shout of day—
My hymn,
When journeys' courses run.

SECRET SACRED WRITINGS OF THE SAGES
LOCKED SCROLL 12
BROCH OF THE ANCIENTS

Our World, 2018
Abernethy, Scotland

"It's 3 a.m. and this guy's still awake. Boy, he's dedicated!" I turned from the window. "Just as well the portal is only up the hill. It takes about fifteen minutes to walk there."

"Nae, my Lady Rhiannon." Morrigan stood next to me at my sink, her brow crinkling. "We go through on the grounds of the Highland Caisteal. Where the Celtic Day took place."

"Near Inverness!" I couldn't stop my pitch from rising. "But that's two hours away." I paced my small kitchen, almost bumping into both Dál Gaedhle warriors. "We'll need to leave here soon to get there by sunrise."

My mind flicked through a list of possibilities. It *was* desperate. If this guy didn't go to sleep on the job soon, Angus' option—which surely would involve their weapons—could even be a plausible one. Maybe.

But I had some sedative tablets in the bathroom cupboard.

"I'll make him a 'coffee' to help him keep 'awake'." I made air quotes in the appropriate places.

141

"Huh?" Angus' brow scrunched.

"Lady Rhiannon will prepare him a sleeping draft in a hot beverage," Morrigan explained. "Once he has succumbed, we can leave."

"You're doing a sterling job." I held the mug out to the young policeman, wearing my pyjamas, dressing gown, and fluffy slippers for effect. "But I thought I saw a yawn," I teased.

"Why are you still up?" He hesitated only slightly, then took the offered drink.

"I haven't seen my cousins in *forever*! It's just so great to be with them." I glowed inside.

Well, I meant it.

I padded back to my cottage through the dark night. Angus opened the door for me.

"If he drinks it all, it won't take long." I strode past him to my room where I dressed in jeans and jumper and wrapped my sword in my coat. Twenty minutes went by.

"His head has dropped to the side." Angus was peering out the window. "I think our guard is asleep."

"We're taking my car." I picked up my stuff.

Morrigan's shoulders eased, and she let out a quiet giggle. Angus glared at her.

"If he wakes, he'll see your wee car and, hopefully, think we're still inside the cottage," I said.

"I will get our weapons." Angus, still frowning at Morrigan, crept out of my door.

He returned moments later with their swords, then both warriors followed me to the back of the cottage where I parked my vehicle. They loaded their blades into the boot, then clambered into the seats.

I drove the two hours to the highland estate near Inverness, my vision flicking between my side and rear vision mirrors almost constantly. No car followed us—no bright police lights caught my eye. The A9 was deserted this early morning but my hands still sweated on the steering wheel. Nothing—absolutely nothing—would prevent me from going with these two Dál Gaedhle warriors.

Angus and Morrigan directed me in the dark to a rickety gate down a country lane just outside the castle grounds. Here, I parked the car. Morrigan hugged me and thanked me for my driving, then we got out our gear and strapped on our swords.

Angus and Morrigan entered through the gate into a forested area, walking like they were familiar with these woods, so I followed. We reached a section of thick growth deep in the ancient forest while the sky lightened with dawn approaching.

"We must hasten." Morrigan lengthened her stride. "We have still a short way to go and *beul an latha* is upon us."

A path of sorts emerged from the long grass that had grown in a narrow clearing of trees. Morrigan and Angus passed by brambles and tall weeds. I followed close, avoiding the thorny growth of a large clump of blackberry sticking across the track and threatening to cling to my jeans. A high wrought iron gate, with two brick gate posts, stood in the only gap in the forest on the opposite end of this clearing, with a wire fence extending either side of it. It looked purpose built to cut off this section of the property from walkers on a country hike expecting a right of way path. We hastened across the clearing to it.

"Oh, they have locked it." Morrigan pointed to a chain that passed through the gate and round one brick pillar.

"Aye, the laird has noticed our use of it." Angus drew his sword.

My insides hummed, stirring with the ringing of metal. Angus swiped his blade downward and broke the chain, sending it clattering to the ground.

"Right, that's as far as you go," a deep voice called behind me from the other side of the clearing.

My shoulders stiffened, and Angus spun. Morrigan's sword sung from its sheath.

"Your sleeping pills did nae work for long, Miss Ferguson."

I turned. It was Sergeant Findlay, his face like hard rock, and he stood at the edge of the bramble patch.

"Young Brown radioed in," Findlay continued. "Miss Ferguson, please understand you'll be safe with us. Most likely safer than with your *cousins* here."

The sun's glow now hinted at the horizon. Angus tensed beside me—that coiled spring once more—and Morrigan drew in a breath.

Angus kicked the gate open. "We cannot delay," he whispered to me.

I nodded. "But don't wave your swords around. He might think you mean someone harm."

Angus lowered his sword, then strode past the gate. I followed him through with Morrigan, who slid her sword into its sheath.

"Who are these people, Miss Ferguson?" Findlay called to my back, then let out a grunt.

I didn't answer but followed Angus striding to the deeper parts of this ancient forest.

"Miss Ferguson, can you hear me?" Findlay yelled across the clearing, his tone tightening. "What're you doing?"

"Keep going," I said to Angus. "We can't miss it." I hurried further along, facing straight ahead, focused on Angus' muscled back and stepping double-time to keep up with him.

"Miss Ferguson. Rhiannon! Are you safe with these people?"

I kept going, ignoring Findlay.

"Are they forcing you, Rhiannon?"

A *click* came from the policeman's direction. I spun. Findlay hadn't come any closer, he seemed entangled in the blackberries. He'd unbuckled his handgun from its holster and pointed it at Angus, who'd turned with me and now held his blade in a challenging stance.

"Detective, please!" I took a step toward Angus and, pressing my hand on the broad side of his blade, moved it aside so I stood in front of him. He grunted.

143

"These are my friends, and they're taking me home," I said. "We must get to the p—I'll *not* miss it! I'm safe, but I'm sorry I won't be able to testify. I really am. But I can't see how I could and still—" I bit off the words. Either I'd help put a criminal away for a long time, or I'd go to Arlan. I gave a shaky sigh. *No, being with Arlan wins. Every time.* "Please don't hinder us." I nudged Angus's blade, indicating for him to lower it.

He did, then I turned with him, and we continued through the gate, increasing our pace. Morrigan marched behind me.

"Do not follow," Morrigan shouted to Findlay, her voice ringing loud and clear in her strongly accented English.

TWENTY-TWO

— · —

Dark, my life
And empty.
Bright the way
That leads to clearer skies.
It calls me.
Powerless, my will obeys.

VISIONS AND SAYINGS OF THE BLIND LADY SAGE

Our World, 2018
Near Inverness
The Grounds of a Stately Home

A curve of sun rose above the horizon, spearing fingers of light through the gaps between the thick trunks surrounding Findlay. Its newly risen glow illuminated the shadowed places of this dense woodland. The close growth slowed him down, the foliage of the non-existent path caught him with every step. He couldn't keep up with the trio who marched through as though they knew this part of the forest like the palms of their hands.

He strode along, puffing, eyes fixed on their backs. Something tugged at his jacket—a bramble, sticky with thorns, entangled the cloth, and the sharp prickles of blackberry caught his trouser legs. He dragged his legs forward, tugging the thorns with him. Nature's barbed hooks dug into his flesh, and his calves and thighs sparked with the fire of torn skin.

"Och! Damn it."

Rhiannon and her cousins—or whoever they were—were way ahead, through the wrought iron gate with the chain now dangling, broken by the young man with the bloody big sword. A mean bastard of a thing with a double-edged blade, similar to what he recalled of Rhiannon's boyfriend's weapon.

Findlay ripped his left leg free only to be stuck in the thorny thicket that wrapped spiked hands around his right foot.

He cursed.

The young people had lengthened their stride and were now in a smaller grassy clearing well past the wrought iron gate. They paused and glanced back at him, seeming to glow in the sunlight. Miss Ferguson's amber hair glimmered, and the morning sunshine traced her outline in gold. She looked like she shone from within. He sighed. She was an astonishing beauty.

Her lips curved in a delicate smile. She raised her hand in a brief wave, then, tugged on by the woman, followed the couple, their features also striking in the glow.

All three walked ahead toward...

Findlay squinted. Behind them, within a circular frame of silvery light, stood a clear picture of a different wood.

Findlay strained his vision past them to a sharp view of trees. Not this ancient forest, where thorns and thicket detained him, for the plants there were different. Not old and gnarled like those that grew here, but strappy. It was a smaller wood, the branches heavy with light green foliage. This copse had a natural beauty he'd never seen on this earth, despite growing up in Perthshire. The air burst through, pristine and shining with a different light, a brighter hue. Birdsong floated to him, their notes pure and tugging at his soul.

Innocence. Virtue. It was as though the view shouted these attributes at him.

What a place!

And then they were gone. The three young people and the beckoning view... disappeared.

Findlay slumped to the ground, numbness overcoming him, and the woody scent of nature filled his nostrils. The sun rose behind him, the angle of its rays growing wider, while the patch of grass where the young people had been remained bare.

He rubbed his brow above the bridge of his nose. He must've sat for a while because the shadows had shortened, so it would now be near midday.

No, they'd really gone.

He ran his hands through his hair and stood up, disentangling his trousers, jacket, and skin from the thorns. Their sting lingered.

"What *is* this place?"

He holstered his gun, then strode through the gate to the very spot where that *other* forest had been. He turned a full circle. The young people's boots had trodden the grass down flat. He retraced his steps, and at the gate to this section of the forest, he examined the chain.

Sliced through.

"Why was this part of the forest locked?"

He'd crossed the public walkways that were right of way paths through this property. A sign near the main gate of this estate advertised re-enactment days and such, so the laird mustn't be bothered about people crawling all over his land.

Findlay retraced his steps, got into his car, and drove to the main house of the estate, a good twenty minutes away. Travelling the long driveway, he changed his mind about calling it a *house*. The two-storeyed cut-sandstone double-tower gatehouse for a front entrance stood proudly at the top of the long gravel path. It was a newer build, maybe seventeenth century, with the crumbling remnants of the original stone wall of the main house—built God knows when—running along one side of it.

He got out of his car and trod along the gravel to the half-glassed front door and tapped on the pane. A man of late middle age, probably the laird, entered the atrium from the side, his kilt swinging as he strode along, shucking on his deep-green tweed jacket. Eyes wide with a querying expression, he opened the door.

"Good afternoon." His bushy eyebrows met in the middle with his frown, although it took little movement, such was the nature of their bush.

"Hello, I'm Detective Findlay from the Scotland Police and I've a couple of questions regarding your right of way paths." He held up his police ID.

The laird's brows dipped, then he gestured for him to enter.

"Och, we sorted all that oot a wee while ago." The pungent scent of stale urine wafted across to Findlay as he passed the laird.

Hmm. Tweed.

"Right of ways and such," the laird continued. "Damned annoying having strangers peering in your windows uninvited. Nae respecters of privacy. We have clearly marked the paths on which those nature enthusiasts may walk."

"Ah, it's just a quick question regarding the gate that locks off a certain section deeper into your lands, sir."

"Oh, aye?"

"The chain is broken, and you'll have to replace it, I imagine."

The laird stood straighter and rolled his shoulders, then slipped his hands into the pockets of his well-worn jacket.

"Broken, ye say? And the gate is open? You ken this how?"

"I was following a lead, nothing serious," Findlay added at the look on the laird's face, "and I noticed it broken. Thought I'd inform you."

"Aye, well thank you. I'll get my groundsman right on to it."

"May I enquire why you lock it, sir?" Findlay asked.

The laird ushered him toward the door. "We just don't want people in that older forest," the laird replied, barely lifting his head.

"Oh?" Findlay encouraged.

"Which station are ye from?" the laird asked.

"Perth, sir."

"Perthshire's police may not be familiar with the missing persons we've had up here in Inverness-shire. People seem to think our woods are the first place tae look. Silly old Highland fish-wifey tales o' people gone missing in the past." The laird paused and looked Findlay in the eye as though expecting a response.

Findlay remained silent.

"I had a superstitious ancestor who built that gate. Let's just say, it keeps the accusations away."

"Thank you, sir." Findlay nodded farewell then strode to his car, got in, and sat for some moments.

In his rear vision mirror, the laird stood at the front entrance, his bushy stare fixed on Findlay's car.

Findlay started the engine and drove to the nearest supermarket where he bought a light lunch. He returned to his vehicle in the carpark and ate the sandwiches and crisps, sipping at his coffee. He unwrapped the chocolate bar and opened his mouth to take his first bite but put it down. Aye, his clothes had got a bit snug lately.

Stress eating, his GP had called it.

Three teenagers in school uniform bounced past. They held polyfoam containers and shoved chips covered with gravy into their mouths in between laughter and foul language. One threw his fish supper into a rubbish bin. He missed, and the chips scattered around the base of the bin like thick-cut confetti. His companions' raucous laughter filled the carpark. They walked on leaving the mess behind.

Findlay gripped his steering wheel with one hand and his car door handle with the other, his muscles tight and tinnitus strumming in time with his pulse. He gritted his teeth. It was the usual sign that his blood pressure had increased. And that meant the medication, one of the milder antihypertensives—or so his GP said—had less and less effect on preventing his risk of stroke, heart attack, and so on...

He swore and eased back in his seat.

He was sick of this. Kids who didn't behave. And parents who didn't give a...

"I've had enough. This is a mug's game." His yell echoed back from his front windscreen.

Findlay turned the engine, drove out of the car park and past the high school kids now shoving one of their own to the ground. With the steering wheel digging into his palms, he drove till he found himself at the old back entrance to the property of the highland estate.

Miss Ferguson's car sat abandoned.

He left his car and walked along the pathway where trees skirted both sides. The wind blew, brushing his face with invisible fingertips, and the leaves above sang in its wake. A pheasant darted out of the bracken. He started, then laughed at himself. Birds flew from nearby trees, calling a warning at his presence. Brenda, his ex-wife, had loved all this nature stuff. She'd hill walk, and on weekends she'd climb Munros with friends while he worked. His marriage hadn't lasted long. He dragged a hand over his face.

"Bloody job." He kicked a stick lying across the path and hunched into his jacket.

Not even a son or daughter to show for our relationship.

His back teeth ground together. Years of working long hours bring people to justice—even *murderers.*

148

He huffed. Murder investigations—no respecters of people's personal lives. *And certainly not mine.*

He'd done it all not for any advancement in his career, although that'd come, but for the satisfaction of dealing with the wrong against a victim, and finding redress for their relatives.

Something put right.

And *right* mattered.

But then, the criminal returned to society all too soon. And often—though how he hated to say it—the corrections system hadn't achieved its goals. The person was released not reformed, only to re-offend. Yet another victim's hurt for him to put right.

It went on and on. And people were getting worse. He was sure of it. He pushed aside the dark cloud that threatened his thinking, his face growing tight.

He reached the gate, still shut with its chain lying on the ground, the laird's grounds-man not yet attending to the task.

He opened it and strode through to the place where the three had disappeared. Where Rhiannon's face and hair had glowed, and behind her was a perfect, pristine wood. A *different* forest.

Perhaps there was good in *that* place. There was barely little left in this one. He snorted at his cynical thoughts.

He took a breath, then blew out through his nose. Maybe being *good* wasn't worth it. No one else bothered. Or cared.

Findlay came to the exact spot where Rhiannon and her friends had vanished.

He stood still, checked his watch, and waited for *it* to open.

Twenty-Three

— · —

For to the king of noble heart,
Does the Fountain of all Goodness
Cover with his favour,
And surround with faithful warriors
As the dew saturates the grass of early morn.

POETRY OF A KING
ÀRD RÌGH RHONAN IUBHAR
(4030-4090 POST DRAGON WARS)

The World of Dál Cruinne
Post Dragon Wars Year 6083
Western Sovereignty of Dál Gaedhle
Craegrubha Broch, MacEnoicht Clan Lands
The Portal

Sunlight hit my skin.

It touched my face with weak morning warmth. Detective Findlay's expression was hard and his frown deep. He lifted his head, narrowing his eyes like he was trying to see past me. Then his eyes widened, and his mouth dropped open.

Morrigan strode by, clasped my hand, then tugged me... into nothingness.

My arms trembled and my whole body shuddered.

Light and sound assaulted me, my breath stilling in my lungs.

Morrigan, why didn't you warn me of the moments I'd travel through this white void?

I fell on all fours and dragged in crisp air, dewy with the sweet smell of early dawn—uncorrupted, like the very first morning.

A puff of wind floated past, laden with hints of honeysuckle and springtime. Of warm arms and comfort. Of a gentle woman's voice vibrating through her chest and caressing my infant ears, holding love and anguish.

I opened my eyes.

White trunks of birch saplings surrounded me, and my trembling hands spread on cool leaf litter. To my right on the horizon, a large sun shone with a silvery light, the colours of this world more intense from its reflective powers. The sky was the brilliant blue of Arlan's eyes.

Angus sheathed his sword, then helped me stand. "Come." He lifted his chin in the direction leading out of this small copse.

Sunlight was brighter here compared to Earth, and it silvered the edge of leaves wet with dawn's dew. Angus led me to a track beside a wide expanse of green patchworked with crops of yellow and cream. A mountain sat in the distance, but Angus and Morrigan turned me away from it and headed along to where the track widened to a road that could take two horses abreast.

"Yes, horses. No cars."

"Your pardon, my lady?" Angus' eyebrows rose.

A smile stretched my lips. "No cars here."

Morrigan chortled, and Angus speared her with a glare.

Ahead, a dark tubular building, the shape of a power station cooling tower, sat tall and imposing with a carpet of green grass leading to it.

"The same one as in my vision." The words left my mouth and floated on the wind that stirred my hair, the briny scent of the ocean hitting my face. Breakers crashed on a nearby shore.

"It is not far to Craegrubha Broch." Morrigan smiled at me. "The clan home of—"

"Lord Arlan Finnbar MacEnoicht," I finished for her.

I walked beside Morrigan for five minutes, the broch's situation becoming clearer the closer we came to it. It sat on an outcrop of rock almost in the sea with smaller stone buildings surrounding its base on the near side, where men and women attended their daily tasks. Dogs barked at our approach and horses nickered. Kilted, armed men milled around the entrance to the broch, and one spied us. He stood with his hands on his belt and shook his head.

"By the looks of Leigh, something has happened." Angus waved to the man at the door.

The man, Leigh, waved back, frowning.

Morrigan and Angus hurried their step. I had to walk double-time to keep up. Large dogs, like the breed of Scottish Deerhound, trotted around Leigh. The dogs barked again, then rushed for me.

"Heel!" Leigh shouted in a gruff voice and the dogs returned to him, sniffing the air at my approach. "We've had a wee bit of excitement," Leigh said. "Apart from your arrival, Lady Rhiannon." Leigh bowed his head. "Welcome to Craegrubha Broch and to Dál Gaedhle."

"Thank you, Lord Leigh," I said.

Angus laughed softly while Leigh's colour rose.

"Have I done something wrong?" I asked.

"Nae," Morrigan said. "It is only that Leigh is the youngest son of a lesser clan chief and is unaccustomed to being called by that title."

"Leigh will do fine, my Lady Rhiannon." Though Leigh's voice was gravelly, his smile was kind.

"Has Arlan won?" Morrigan asked. "He is àrd rìgh? Leigh, tell us this is so."

"Och, nae news o' that yet, aye," Leigh replied. "But the other master o' the broch"— he tilted his head in a way I'd seen many a Scotsman do— "has awoken, as I said he would, if ye all recall."

"Oh," Morrigan and Angus responded in unison, wearing matching frowns.

"The *other* master?" I asked.

"Lord Kyle," Leigh answered, then followed Angus and Morrigan inside.

I tagged behind them along a sloping stone staircase that led gently up between two drystone walls. At the curve in the inner stone wall, a man's shouts flew out of a doorway.

"Ah, Angus!" The man spoke with a husky voice, but it had volume. "Where is my brother and how did we get here to Craegrubha broch?" he asked in a bossy tone.

Morrigan and Angus marched straight into what looked like a private chamber. I hovered at the door, not sure if I should enter. A pale-looking young man, presumably the one who had just spoken, sat on the edge of the bed in a nightshirt that reached his mid-calf. Another man stood by the wall, deferring to Morrigan and Angus. The younger man had a bald patch with a round pink scar on the side of his head facing me, and dark ringed beneath his eyes. He was small and puny for the men of this world. Was this Kyle? He saw me standing back and leaned forward for a better view.

"Aisling?" He addressed me. "Is that you, Aisling? Are you here to make sure they have cared for me well? Come in, be not shy." He beckoned me in with a wave of his hand.

Morrigan turned and gave a slight shrug, opening her eyes wide for a second. So, I stepped closer.

"Lord Kyle," Morrigan said. "This is Lady Rhiannon, Lord Arlan's friend."

"Oh, don't be ridiculous." His tone held a reprimand. "It is Aisling, the lady sage. She has come to ensure you have all done right by me while I was sleeping. Have ye not, Aisling?"

"Lord Kyle, it is lovely to meet you," I said. "But I'm sorry, I'm not a sage."

Kyle blinked and sat mute for a moment while all stood in silence around him. Then he squinted.

"Why do you speak in such a way? Your accent... Where are you from and why do you pretend to be a sage?"

"I don't pretend, Lord Kyle. I'm Rhiannon. Not Aisling." I said, attempting to speak clearly in the Gaelic, holding my voice steady and trying to not let Kyle's tone intimidate me.

Kyle's shoulders rose in a deep inhalation, then his whole posture slumped. The dark rings under his eyes were more noticeable, and he pulled his feet up into his bed and lay down, his brow creasing.

"Lord Kyle." The man by the wall stepped forward. "Ye must rest. We are so pleased ye are with us again. And"—he looked at Morrigan— "there is much to tell ye of the happenings while ye slept."

"Aye." Morrigan turned to Angus. "Maybe I shall speak with Lord Kyle while you tend to Lady Rhiannon."

Angus nodded and directed me out. Behind us, Kyle mumbled, "Lady Rhiannon? Of which house is she?"

"We shall eat and prepare for our journey." Angus tugged me gently along. "For we should leave for The Keep this very day."

Leading me further up the sloping stairway, Angus entered a large, round hall with a fire raging in the middle. An older man in a kilt held a long fork with a piece of bread on its tines over the flames.

"Glen," Angus said to the man. "This is Lady Rhiannon, a guest of your clan chieftain."

Glen stood from the fire and nodded a bow, briefly casting his gaze at my clothing. "An honour to meet ye, Lady Rhiannon."

"Glen is a clansman warrior bonded to Lord Arlan," Angus explained.

"It's a pleasure to meet you, Glen," I said.

"Although at present, Glen is our *chef*," Angus added with a wink.

"*Chef?*" Glen squinted, then he shook his head in dismissal at Angus' comment. "Toast," he said, and placed the toasted bread on a plate then passed it to me. "Butter if ye wish, my lady. Freshly churned. Help yoursel' to the bacon and eggs on the platter there."

"Thank you." I went to the table Glen had pointed out and buttered the toast while the conversation continued behind me.

"I take it ye shall leave at once for The Keep," Glen said. "There is word *Tòireadh* goes well with many contesting and that Lord Arlan left just a touch shy of a fortnight ago. They know not where, for he departed under cover of night with his warriors and that once *murtair*."

"Aye, we shall leave soon. Nae, sooner," Angus answered. "How goes it for you, Glen, now ye are in charge of all the goings on in this broch and the clan lands?"

"It goes well, but certain issues have arisen." Glen cleared his throat. "I dinnae ken what to make of our new circumstance. Who is the chieftain now that yon lord has awoken?"

"Aye." Angus huffed. "Lord Arlan needs to inform us of his wishes."

"There are other wishes of which he needs to inform his clan." Glen stepped from the fire and walked to a bench by the wall. He shuffled through some loose papers and picked up a handful. "As I am appointed castellan of MacEnoicht clan lands, there's the matter of all the requests from clan chiefs for Lord Arlan to... ah"—he lowered his voice, so I strained my hearing to catch it. It was about Arlan, after all— "consider their noble daughters."

I stared down at my toast, the yellow blob of butter melting quickly to liquid—like my insides.

Arlan must *choose a clan chief's daughter.*

Shouting travelled down the passage and into the hall, then footsteps and anxious comments came closer. Kyle stumbled into the room with Morrigan and Leigh at his heels.

"You go to The Keep, Angus?" Kyle stood, one hand against the wide stone doorway. His shift was quite see-through, revealing skinny limbs. His legs shook as though he might fall over any second.

"My lord, ye are not strong enough for such a journey." His attendant rushed to his side.

"Even so," Kyle spat, "I shall go!" He stood straighter and glared at Angus, and then at me. "How dare they not wait for me! And they held the Quest without me?" He staggered. His attendant grabbed a nearby chair and placed it behind him just in time for him to collapse onto it. "And," he said through gritted teeth, "they let my younger brother contend in my place?"

"The Sàsaichean decided—" Angus began.

"Arlan is not the heir!" Kyle shouted.

I flinched at the vibration in the air from his voice. He looked so weak. How did he muster so much energy?

Glen stabbed another piece of bread with the long fork, and Angus examined his feet.

"Very well, Lord Kyle," Morrigan said. "You may accompany us, but only if your man attends and is responsible for you."

"Who are you to demand—?"

"I am Lady Morrigan of House Lùthas. I need not remind you that my clan is of equal standing with yours." Her voice rang out in the stone building, shutting Kyle's mouth. "Also, I am a sworn sword warrior of Lord Arlan MacEnoicht, and we have our lord's business to attend. You may accompany us to The Keep, but I beg you, hinder us not."

The fire crackled in the hearth and a dog whined by Leigh's side. Those present looked stunned. Had no one ever stood up to Kyle before?

For a moment it was like I'd returned to high school. The time I'd had enough of the taunts from Michelle Stone and the other popular girls. I'd turned away from them, stiffening against their derision. But my barrel of hurt had filled, and out of the overflow spout I'd spat back, informing them they could display their ignorance elsewhere. Kyle's face now held the same expression as Michelle Stone's: frozen for an instant, then slowly growing slack.

Go Morrigan!

"Very well," Kyle said, once he'd regained the use of his gaping mouth. "My man shall pack. We will be ready to leave within the hour."

Morrigan gave a slight nod, turned her back on Kyle, and accepted the piece of toast offered by Glen, her shoulders straight and cheeks dimpling.

TWENTY-FOUR

— • —

Stepping through, I leave all.
The past shuts behind me as a closing door,
Then is no more.
I face ahead, my brow set and determined.
I will claim it all:
Where my feet will tread, the air I will breathe, the time I will consume,
And the love I will receive.

CONTEMPLATIONS OF A TRAVELLER
GRAND MASTER LLEW
(POST DRAGON WARS 6000-CURRENT)

The World of Dál Cruinne
Post Dragon Wars Year 6083
Western Sovereignty of Dál Gaedhle
Craegrubha Broch to The Keep

Leather breeches and crop top sat smooth against my skin.

Standing in a small bedroom chamber of the broch, I threw my baby-rug over my shoulder and clasped it with the broach Leigh had handed to me, saying it was from Lord Arlan. A circle of silver in-laid with intricate knotwork and studded with rubies kept the swathe of material in place. Back on Earth—or the Other World as they call it here—this piece of jewellery would be priceless because of its beauty alone. It was just like that ancient Celtic broach found in Ireland—the Tara Broach now on display in their National Museum.

Exquisite.

A tingle ran right through me.

155

Morrigan stared at my plaid and skewed her mouth to the side. "Ye had better not wear the tartan of Gallawain."

"Arlan believes it's my clan. Probably," I added at the look on Morrigan's face.

"Ciarán is of Clan Gallawain," Morrigan said, then pursed her lips. "Or he was before the àrd rìgh stripped him of his chieftain title and sent him into exile. He causes the unrest disturbing our entire land."

A flash of cold passed over me. *I'm related to the bad guy?*

Morrigan left the small chamber and returned moments later.

"Here, ye should wear this." She held a plain maroon plaid-length of material out to me.

After swapping it with my Gallawain plaid and securing the Tara Broach-like clasp with trembling fingers, I tucked my jeans, jumper, and baby-rug away in my saddlebag, sheathed my sword in the baldric—like Angus had shown me—then set the belt over my shoulder. I followed Morrigan to the yard by the stables where Leigh tightened the girth strap on a white mare. Quietly, I approached the horse and stroked her long silky nose. She gave a soft nicker, her breath warming my hands at her grey muzzle.

"She's beautiful."

"Aye, and good natured." Leigh placed a sheepskin over the saddle. "And also yours, Lady Rhiannon."

"Oh, no. I couldn't possibly—"

"Lord Arlan told me she is for you." He cocked his head. "And I dare not argue with my lord. Her name is Bridie."

I tossed my saddlebags over Bridie's rump, fingers tingling, and my mouth stretched in a grin.

"Come." Angus flew onto his war horse. "It's a two-day journey to The Keep."

The ride was the longest I'd ever attempted. I'd only rode for half a day at the most with the riding school. My right thigh shook, and my seat... well, I was running out of ideas of how to describe that particular sensation when Leigh halted us at a small clearing a short way off the road and backed by maple trees.

I sat numbly on my saddle while Morrigan and Angus slid off their mounts. Kyle had slumped over his horse's neck and his man now fussed around him, asking Leigh for assistance to get Kyle down from his animal.

Morrigan approached me. "Ye are well, Rhiannon?"

"Nae, she loves her new mare so much she wishes to remain upon her." Angus winked at me.

"Let me help you down." Morrigan raised her hands to reach me in the saddle, giving Angus a sideways look. "Some of us have forgotten the hardship on a body during a first very long ride." There was a hint of reproach in her tone.

I grabbed the pommel and eased my right leg over Brodie's rump. My muscles were so tight, it seemed like I dragged my leg over in slow motion.

"Just ease yoursel' down, my lady." Leigh wandered past holding a rope. "Then bring your mare to the tether line."

With Morrigan's support, I landed. My ankles were so tight they cracked, and my legs were the proverbial jelly. I led Bridie to the line Leigh had strung between two trees. The other horses were already tied there. I removed my sheepskin, the saddle and bags, and the saddle blanket. There was a halter in one of the saddlebags, so I removed Bridie's bridle and slipped the halter over her head, tying it to the tether line. My mare bent her head to the grass and munched, swishing her tail behind her. I pulled some of the nearby deer grass, which was tough and dry, and made a wisp as I'd seen Arlan do, then brushed her down with the makeshift curry comb.

"Very good, my lady." Leigh was attending to his animal. "Ye ken how to care for your horse." He gave a nod of approval. "Aye, 'tis right braw."

Angus strode from the small cluster of trees with an armful of sticks and tinder.

"We have bread, cheese and cold meats from the broch, but warm tea would nae go astray, do you not think, Lady Rhiannon?" he asked.

My stomach growled in response. "Yes, a cuppa always goes down well."

"Then ye shall light the fire for us, if ye please." He grinned.

"Och, Angus, you know Lady Rhiannon may be unfamiliar with this skill," Morrigan chided. "Having different methods of heating water in the Other World." She turned to me. "Do you ken how to light a fire?" she whispered.

"Oh yes, of course. I had an open fire in my cottage. I used..." *Newspaper and fire starters.*

Morrigan's brow dipped, and I scrunched my lip to the side.

"Perhaps you'd better teach me how to light a fire the Dál Gaedhle way."

Morrigan nodded, screwing her mouth tight and suppressing a smile. She rummaged through the pile of twigs and tinder that Angus had dumped in the middle of our camp site and picked out the soft dry pieces of grass and lichen. Then she sorted the twigs into sizes, from smallest to largest, and arranged them in a stack on what was to be our fireplace.

"In the Other World," Angus said as he unwrapped the cold foods from the linen cloths and arranged them on a flat stone nearby, "I heard a lad boast of lighting his scouting campfire with only one match. We have flint, but one strike should suffice if Morrigan is good enough." He smiled a cheeky grin.

"You know very well that I am." Morrigan sounded affronted.

"So let your student try," Angus replied.

Morrigan sniffed, then turned to me. "Strike the flint with the iron stick, thus." She aimed it away from herself and sparks flew from the flint.

"Wow, boy scout style," I said. "I've only seen that in a movie."

"Now you do it but aim for the tinder," Morrigan said.

I struck the flint with the metal rod, aiming at the soft ball of dried grass, which Morrigan had placed in the centre of her square rack of wood. A spark flew from the flint, landing in the tinder. A thin stream of smoke lifted.

"Now blow," Morrigan said. "Pick up that ball and keep blowing upon it."

I lifted the ball of smouldering grass and blew. A flame shot up.

"Keep encouraging it while ye put it back next to the very smallest pieces of wood." Excitement laced Morrigan's voice.

I placed it in the nest of sticks and blew gently. The flames licked the twigs, and they took. My face warmed from their new fire, and I glowed within.

"I've never lit a fire that way before."

"Well done, my lady." Leigh had stopped tending to the horses and had been watching me. "We will make ye one of us soon enough."

I looked up from the fire. Angus placed a pan filled with water near it. The others had set out their bedding, with saddles for pillows, and arranged them around the fire. Kyle's man was laying him down on his blanket. Kyle flopped on his bed and was soon asleep. His man covered him with a tartan rug.

"The ride is too much for him," Morrigan looked over at the sleeping lord. "But he's always stubborn. More so now," she added in a much quieter voice.

Leigh had placed my fleece beside the other bedding, so I sat back on it, keeping an eye on the flames and feeding more sticks when required. Angus handed out portions of food, and Leigh joined us by the fire. Kyle's man took serves then sat by Kyle.

Angus sat beside Morrigan. "So, what do you think of Dál Gaedhle, Lady Rhiannon?" he asked. "Is she not the most beauteous of lands?"

"Yes. So fresh and clean, and almost like new." My answer was inadequate, but how could I describe... a near pristine world?

"Aye, 'tis cleaner than parts of the Other World, from what I have seen." Angus stared into the fire. "Ye will find our people welcoming." Angus gritted his teeth, and his mouth formed an awkward smile. "Ah, mostly."

"What do ye mean? Our warband will love Rhiannon," Morrigan said defensively.

"I'm not speaking of Lord Arlan's warriors. I mean, the sages. They always make my spine rattle." Angus gave a mock shiver. "Rhiannon is yet to meet the great Sage Eifion. And, aye, she will, for he is Arlan's wise counsel." He leaned toward me. "It's said the man is much older than he looks. And he looks old," he said with emphasis. "He knows things that many do not. A whole—what do ye name it—encyclopaedia is contained in his skull." Angus tapped his head with a finger. "He has advised great kings and mighty leaders."

"Arlan has spoken of him as though he's a good friend," I said.

"Oh, he is our lord's friend, and often in our company," Angus said, "but he is also Lord Arlan's wise sage."

A great leader needed a great adviser, and I would meet him, eventually. My stomach curled a little.

"I may have to get used to rubbing shoulders with important people."

Leigh looked across the fire at me. "Ye have left your world, my lady, and come to another, which from what my well-travelled friends here report, is vastly different."

I threw a thick stick on the now healthy fire and returned Leigh's gaze.

"I wanted to. My roots are here. I was adopted into the Other World." They all looked at me then. "Yes, through a portal. My adoptive parents died years ago but my real parents are here, somewhere. I'd like to find them. Know my origins. Whether they are clan nobles or a farming couple, they'll be my family. I... I need them."

"We saw ye had few acquaintances." There was sadness in Angus' tone. "Will ye miss anyone?"

"Yes, George," I said.

"The bespectacled man?" Angus asked.

"You saw him?"

"Nae, but Lord Arlan enquired of him."

"George was my closest friend. He... liked me very much—"

"He was in love with you?" Morrigan asked.

"Yes, and he never really got it that I... well, it wasn't like that for me."

The fire crackled and a soft breeze sent smoke into my eyes.

Leigh drew his knees up and rested his arms on them. "Ye leave all for this."

"Would ye go back, my lady?" Angus asked.

I shook my head. "No, I've left it all behind." *And here I am in my new life.* "I can have no regrets. There's no return for me. I'm here now, and I'll take the bad with the good and be part of making it better."

There, I'd said it. And saying the words out loud had made my arrival all the more real.

Morrigan leaned closer and rested her hand on my arm. "We will be your family now."

Her soft voice and the gentle grunts of agreement from the men travelled through the evening air and danced with the firelight flickering the trees.

And I knew I was home.

Twenty-Five

— • —

Be not foolish as to the thoughts of dumb animals.
Tho' they speak not your tongue,
They are wise.
And ye would be so to listen to their instincts.
For the heart of a man may be hid from your eyes
And yet exposed, as if naked and laid bare, to many a creature.

SAGE GLIOCAS
(2870-2962 POST DRAGON WARS)

The World of Dál Cruinne
Post Dragon Wars Year 6083
Western Sovereignty of Dál Gaedhle
The Keep

Please, may there be no other dragon eggs found.

Arlan rode toward The Keep after three days on the road, dust covering his plaid, his troop travel-dirty and tired, and his wee dragon needing food. It ate insects, but he'd kept small morsels of meat aside from his meals at the taverns of the inns that Bàn had insisted they rest in each night for the sake of his wounds. Arlan smiled at the clamp on his neck, a constant reminder of the tiny fellow hidden in his hair.

His calves were tender but didn't hurt as much as yesterday. And they did not sting as they had when Leyna washed them with her salted water.

He approached the meadow where Father's sentinel sat.

"Father, I trust I have won *Tòireadh*," he whispered. "And I hope I can live up to the part."

A crowd gathered at the edge of the road, looking up at him riding Mengus, many shading their eyes from the sun. They called out greetings, and he waved back.

160

"Lord Arlan, will we see more dragons?" a woman asked.

Arlan touched the wee one's tail, which curved neatly across his throat.

Vygeas trotted his stallion closer. "They fear the dragon, Lord Arlan."

"But it hides under my hair," he said out the side of his mouth.

"Nae, Lord Arlan, the one who killed your lord father and their beloved àrd rìgh," Vygeas whispered back.

Tight faces surrounded Arlan, with brows crinkled, and eyes fixed on him in hope.

"But they need not fear the beast responsible for the àrd rìgh's demise, Lord Arlan," Vygeas continued his whisper. "The mage who controlled the animal suffered badly from the experience and may not be in a hurry to repeat it."

Aye, and any self-respecting dragon would stay away from folk.

Arlan sat tall on Mengus and faced the crowd. "In truth, dear people, I believe we shall not see that beast again." Arlan spoke with authority. But should he mention the mage? Nae, they were scared enough. "The beast has done it's deed and now hunkers back in its lair, for they are solitary animals."

Faces eased, smiles emerged, and the villagers clapped while he passed.

"Welcome home, Lord Arlan," a man shouted, and the crowd joined in.

"Have ye found a dragon egg?" someone called from among the throng.

He couldn't answer. That decision belonged to the *Sàsaichean,* and he must waste no time in getting to the Great Hall of The Keep. Arlan led his troop across the bridge over the River Ruairidh and up the ramp to the caisteal, where the gates opened wide and the guards cheered him in.

He rode by the smithy's forge at the centre of the inner bailey, where a metal-crafter leaned over a mesh of tiny metal rings. He lifted his head from the forming maille garment and waved, then bent back to his task. The master sword-crafter strode from his forge toward him, the odour of charcoal smoke wafting from his leather apron.

"Ye are the first one home, Lord Arlan." He squinted an eye. "Och, the first one still breathin'."

"What do ye mean?"

The burly, sweaty man tilted his head toward a young sage standing by the rail for the horses.

"Lord Eifion says to come to the Great Hall at once, Lord Arlan, sir." The lad dipped his head in afterthought.

Arlan slid off Mengus, and his troop followed. He walked stiff-legged up the steps to the entrance of the caisteal. Here young warriors gathered, sombre faced. They lifted their heads at his approach and scowled. If looks were daggers, he would be stabbed a hundred times.

Eifion rushed toward him. "Lord Arlan, you have arrived at a sad moment." Eifion glanced aside to the warriors who continued their hate-filled stares now accompanied by growling murmurs. "Come with me. Come straight to the fore." He grasped Arlan's arm and glanced at his neck. "All is well, with...?"

"Aye," Arlan said. "Ye ken?"

Eifion nodded. He walked Arlan toward the platform of the àrd rìgh's throne where the sages of the Sàsaichean waited. Some sat at a bench table, others crowded in a group off to one side.

"And of Rhiannon?" Arlan spoke low for Eifion's ears only.

"Of that I am unaware," Eifion replied.

Arlan approached the *Sàsaichean,* and a gap opened in the cluster of sages crowding to the side. A shrouded body lay atop a wooden slab on the floor at their feet where the chief of Clan Callaghan stood red-eyed and stooped.

"Who's that?" Arlan asked.

"Seamus Callaghan has been lost to us through his efforts to win the Quest." Eifion bowed his head. "His followers report he was burned by a dragon in an ancient fortress near the Central Meadhan Mountains."

Arlan had continued to the group of sages seated at the bench, but now halted paces from them. He lifted his eyes to the ceiling and his shoulders sank. *Dragon's breath!* In his haste to leave, he'd left open the secret door to the dragon's lair, the key still on him. The pain of his own burns had overridden any thoughts to close what he had opened. Perhaps Seamus and his warriors were those Adele sensed tailing his troop as they first departed on the Quest. Hidden well, they must have followed his troop's tracks somehow and...

Poor Seamus.

How had the dragon fared? His own dragon stirred at his neck, tugging his hair, and becoming entangled, no doubt.

Arlan stepped aside to the group gathered around Seamus' body and bowed to his grieving father. "My condolences, Lord Callaghan, on the loss of your beloved son."

Lord Callaghan spoke his acknowledgement through a choke, his speech and movements slow, as though in a dream.

Arlan strode back to the bench where the sages sat, their talk ceasing at his approach.

"Lord sages of the Sàsaichean." Arlan's voice rang out beneath the high ceiling of the Great Hall, and all eyes rested on him. "I, Arlan Finnbar MacEnoicht, contender for Clan MacEnoicht in *Tòireadh,* wish to present to you the appointed prize required for success in the Quest."

Arlan pulled the empty dragon's egg wrapped in a cloth from his plaid, then handed it to the sage who sat in the middle of the table. The man received it and frowned, then unwrapped the cloth and laid the soft broken eggshell on the sage council's table.

"What is this?" The sage's eyebrows almost crossed as he inspected the object.

"A dragon's egg, my lord sage." Arlan spoke in a quiet tone, for a hush had descended on all those gathered.

"*Ahem.* May I see?" The sage sitting next to the one examining it, reached over and pinched it between her fingers. "The texts state that dragon's eggs are soft, unlike the hard shells of birds."

"It is a dragon's egg. I can assure you," Arlan said. "I have the burns to prove the mother dragon's displeasure at my theft." He bowed his head. "But I have fared better than my competitor."

"Please, pass it here." Sage Cénell's sharp tone boomed from the far end of the bench. He stood with mouth pinched and brow tight, holding out his hand for the head sage to pass the object in question along to him. "If it is an egg in the first place, a reptilian one *is* quite leathery to the touch."

"Lord Arlan states it is such—" the head sage began.

"Aye, I heard the man. But we must examine comprehensively, for though he is the son of the previous àrd rìgh, this does not make the acceptance by the Sàsaichean of his submission inevitable. Its veracity must be investigated thoroughly."

Cénell, joined by those seated next to him, scrutinised the eggshell. The sage sitting in front of Arlan surveyed him, his eyes resting on his throat.

"What is that which wraps your neck like a red torc?" he asked.

Arlan steeled himself. "It is the proof you seek that the object I have presented to you is indeed the shell of a dragon's egg." He put his hand up to his neck and clicked with his tongue. The hatchling stirred beneath his hair and crawled out onto his hand.

The sage leaped back from his seat, open-mouthed and eyes wide. Those near him, jostled by his movement, turned to Arlan. At their stirring, the tiny dragon curled its tail around Arlan's wrist and gripped tight to his fingers with its claws.

Gasps and exclamations ranging from surprise to delight to revulsion, dominoed along the table. Those behind Arlan strained forward for a better view. The dragon stared at them all, blinking. Warmth centred in Arlan, for an emotion he could only own as pride welled there.

"May we see?" asked the sage directly in front, now recovered.

Arlan's hand curled around his baby dragon and the hairs on the back of his neck stirred.

"Ye can see well enough what it is. It came from that egg, I promise you. Lord Bàn of Clan Lùthas will attest to it." Arlan glanced behind him where Bàn stood along with Vygeas and the rest of his warriors.

Bàn stepped forward. "I can vouch the egg was whole when Lord Arlan brought it from the cave and later it hatched, and this wee fellow came out."

"And a dragon's egg is required to win the Quest, aye?" Arlan's fingers still encircled his dragon like a protective cage.

"But we must see it." The sage held out his hand, wriggling his fingers.

"Aye, to verify, we must examine the whelp," Cénell demanded.

Arlan's shoulders tensed, and his dragon turned to him and blinked.

"I shall set him on the table."

Arlan put his hand out and lowered it to the table-top. The wee beast clung to him. With a finger, he nudged the tiny creature off his palm and onto the table for the sages to see. Cénell stood and slid along to be just behind the head sage, who peered closer at the dragon.

The dragon stood immobile, its wee red body lowered flush with the table-top, its tail still. Cénell reached over and grabbed it by the midriff and lifted. The animal let out a squeak, the dragon's cry tugging at Arlan's heart. It squirted a white substance from its back end, the thick paste-like stream streaking the arm of the sage standing nearest, who flinched. Arlan pressed his lips together.

Ma poor wee dragon has shat itself. It fears these sages so!

Cénell peered closer at the baby dragon, his grasp seeming to tighten.

Behind Arlan, Vygeas coughed.

Arlan made a fist and thumped hard on the table-top.

"No." His voice rang to the rafters, chasing the echoes of the crash his fist had made. Sages froze while Cénell's eyes rounded.

The officious sage dropped the creature onto the table and raised his arm to shield himself. Around Arlan, every sage and observer drew in a collective breath.

Arlan opened his hand on the table, palm upward.

"Drayce," he said. "Come."

The dragon scurried up his arm and into the safety of his hair then clamped on his neck, its whole body trembling.

"Lord Arlan," Cénell yelled. "You threaten me in the Great Hall!"

"Nae." Arlan strained to withhold a growl from his voice. "My apologies if I startled you, but ye would have harmed him."

Cénell lowered his arm. "But he is a dragon." His tone held venom.

"I doubt the fellow will last long." Eifion stepped beside Arlan. "Leave the poor creature be."

The lower lid of Cénell's left eye twitched. "Very well. But you must observe it closely, Sage Eifion." Cénell's expression relaxed somewhat. "I admit it would be interesting to hear of its progress and see how long it survives without a mother dragon."

The postures of all surrounding Arlan relaxed. He allowed his own shoulders to ease. Then the loud arguing speech of a man came from the back of the hall. He directed his challenging tone at the sages at the door, and many footfalls on the hard flooring accompanied his shouts.

The voice was very much like Kyle's.

Twenty-Six

— · —

A true brother's love is as steadfast as a loch.

Neither capricious, as love on a still summer day—a damselfly hovering over a pond who mates then darts away.

Nor as fleeting as a fickle friend who flees when the winds gather, and gales belie the canvas and snap tight the ropes.

SAGE GLIOCAS
(2870-2962 POST DRAGON WARS)

The World of Dál Cruinne
Post Dragon Wars Year 6083
Western Sovereignty of Dál Gaedhle
The Keep

I strode behind Morrigan as we approached The Keep's main building. The tall caisteal rose ahead of me, the stone at its entrance edged in Celtic-style knotwork. The intricate splendour shouted at me, and a sigh escaped my lips. I was in Celtic art heaven.

Kyle, with the help of his man, walked on shaky but determined legs up the steps to the doorway of the large hall, where many warriors milled about. I stayed behind Kyle and his man, Morrigan and Angus, and Leigh. We entered through the doors to a high-ceilinged space. Ahead sat a golden throne of... horses? I couldn't quite tell. In front of the throne and partly obscuring it, robed men and women sat at a long table. They'd be the sages Arlan had mentioned.

Shocked cries and loud talking carried down the hall to where I stood with Morrigan. I snuck a glimpse through the people milling about near the bench table. Morrigan edged forward, but I stayed back, keeping a pace behind. I would be intruding on an uneasy situation.

A thundering clap on a wooden table resounded through the hall, followed by a loud yell. My heart leaped at a man's shout of *No!* It seemed to vibrate the rafters.

It was Arlan.

He leaned into the table where one sage shielded himself with his arm.

"Drayce, come," Arlan said.

I almost stopped breathing.

There he was, the centre of attention. My pulse raced at the sound of his deep voice, and I forced my feet to keep me where I stood. Something tense was going on, and there was no way could I interrupt.

The sage who had raised his arm to shield himself, spoke. A nasty comment, by the tone, but I couldn't really make it out. Another sage, who stood next to Arlan, said something in a friendlier manner. Then the whole atmosphere in the hall changed and I exhaled, along with everyone else.

Kyle moved forward. "I wish to contest *Tòireadh*," he announced into the stillness of the now settled hall.

A sage stepped to Kyle, and he grabbed for her arm. He still wavered, like his man wasn't enough to help him stand, let alone walk, after our ride to The Keep.

The sage peered into his face, letting him hold on to her. "It is grand that ye have awakened, Lord Kyle. Do you wish to speak to the sage council?"

"No," Kyle shouted. "I *demand* to speak to the council."

The sage blinked and stiffened at Kyle yelling in her face, then she recovered and assisted Kyle's man to help him walk. Kyle, with the sage on one side and his man on the other, stumbled through the gap left by the parting crowd.

"I wish to declare the Quest null and void! Why did you not wait for me?" Kyle's surprisingly firm voice seemed to reach every corner of this grand hall.

At the end of the clearing crowd, Arlan turned to Kyle. For a flash, his face revealed a wrestling match of emotions, then his shoulders eased a little and his jaw hardened. He fixed his unblinking gaze on his brother.

My chest tightened. This looked difficult for Arlan. Man, Kyle was a pain! My conversation two years ago with Arlan about his brother came to mind. We'd sat on the bench in the park near my cottage and Arlan had revealed how Kyle had bullied him all his life and always seemed to make things tough for him.

Why stop now, hey Kyle?

If only I could've run up to Arlan and wrapped my arms around him and hugged away his hurts.

"This Quest is invalid." Kyle's voice rose. Everyone in the hall put their attention on his shaky steps as he continued his protests. "I am the representative for the Quest from Clan MacEnoicht. My brother's entry is fraudulent." Kyle's legs shook violently beneath his kilt.

"My Lord Kyle, ye are not well." The brow of the sage assisting Kyle scrunched above her nose. "Come, let us take you to your old rooms, where you can rest."

"What did *you* think you were doing?" Kyle ignored the sage at his side and yelled ahead of him toward those collected round the table.

"Hello, brother." The strain in Arlan's voice was palpable. But there was another element in his tone—a resignation. I'd never seen him like this.

No one in the hall moved and all whispered comments stilled. Kyle contesting the Quest would be a big deal. I glanced at Morrigan, whose nostrils flared. This wasn't just awkward, but dead serious.

My brow cooled.

Kyle stumbled and, with his shaky legs, collapsed to the floor, his two supporters' hands flailing in their efforts to hold him up. Arlan rushed forward and scooped his brother up in his arms, as though he were lighter than a child.

"I shall take him to his old rooms." Arlan strode to exit the hall. "Please, could a healer sage attend us?"

Arlan looked directly ahead, navigating his way through the crowd now pressing closer, not once glancing in my direction. I stretched out my hand to touch him while he passed with his face set hard and Kyle lying limply in his arms, but there were so many people milling around it was impossible to get near him.

Arlan's expression was one I remembered well. He was battling his feelings, trying to hold them in. Trying not to reveal a hurt, most likely, to these important-looking people in this grand hall. I couldn't speak. If only I could've reached him, but this wasn't the moment and definitely not the place.

A tall, blond man was at Arlan's heels. "Please remain here, friends." The man spoke to another in a grey cloak and a warrior, a woman, who stood next to some beefy-looking guys in leather pants and not much else.

Arlan had now barged through a group of warriors and long robed sages, who swished out of his way as he exited the hall.

The blond man stopped by Morrigan. "Och, ye are returned," he said to Morrigan.

His surprised comment drew my attention from Arlan's tense shoulders and his retreating back. The blond warrior's eyes turned to me, then widened. He looked so much like a male version of Morrigan.

"Ye must wait a wee bit till the *tadoo* is over," he said.

"Was he successful?" Morrigan grasped the man's arm. "Did he present the council with the egg of a dragon?"

"Aye, Arlan has given the sages the egg," he whispered. "But due to Lord Kyle's protest, it is yet to be decided if he has won the Quest." He ran after Arlan.

Morrigan faced me. "When this crowd clears, I will take you to Lord Arlan's rooms. He will return there after he has seen Lord Kyle in the care of the healer sages."

"Was that your brother?"

"Aye, that was Bàn," Morrigan answered.

"I see the family resemblance. Is everyone here movie-star gorgeous? Bàn would make any woman in my world melt at the knees."

Morrigan screwed up her face and laughed.

Warriors came to stand behind Morrigan. Arlan's warriors, I guessed. Some bore scars and one woman was massive, but they were all healthy-looking people. It must be living in this clean air with lots of exercise. And good genes. I peered around the hall. To the side, a group of men stood over a shrouded body, their heads bowed and resting their hands on the shaking shoulders of an older man who covered his face with his hands, sobs escaping from behind his fingers.

Injury and hurt and death belonged to this world, too.

Arlan had returned to prevent unnecessary pain and suffering. Had he won the place of àrd rìgh? Someone tapped me on the shoulder.

"Come with me, Lady Rhiannon," Morrigan spoke softly into my ear.

Morrigan led me up stone stairs with swirls and interlocking lines carved in every edging. Tapestries and weavings covered the stone walls. Up two flights, she led me along a landing where gaps in the stonework, windows of a sort but without glass, opened to a courtyard. On the opposite side, at ground level, stable hands tended to horses. One groomed my mare's pristine white coat and a horse whinnied loudly nearby. I leaned through a stone archway and chuckled. Mengus. I'd know that massive animal anywhere. Big and jet-black and muscular, but still a mean-looking war horse.

"Rhiannon, this way, please." Morrigan stood at a far door, and I strode along as she opened it.

"There's so much to take in." I walked through into a large room.

Morrigan remained by the door. "These are Lord Arlan's chambers. I will send a servant with food for you both. Lord Arlan has only just returned from the Quest, by all accounts, and he will require refreshment. There will be a room prepared for you, Rhiannon, but ye and Lord Arlan will need to talk. None will disturb you here."

The room had a fireplace on the outer wall and a double four-poster bed at the other. I sniffed the air and recollections of my trip to Ireland flooded back—peat burning in a grate brought George to mind. I'd never see him again. A soft sadness rose up and I gently pushed it away.

Sorry, George. I can have no regrets.

Chairs and a low table sat near the hearth and a rug covered most of the wooden floor. Tall windows with thick heavy curtains drawn and tied, looked out over a rushing river that ran beside this caisteal wall. Above it rose a moon, deep orange in colour verging on red and casting glitters where its light touched the moving water.

"Wow. You have a silver sun and a red moon?"

"Och, no. That is the beginnings of a blood moon predicted by our sages. The one afore which the competitors of the Quest had to complete their task. And Lord Arlan has. He was presenting the egg to the council as we arrived." Her voice dipped, filled with pride. "I will go now. I need to settle into my chamber and see how my fellow warriors fair. They will tell me the details of how Lord Arlan obtained the egg from its dragon mother." Morrigan's eyes softened with a smile. "Refreshments will come soon."

I placed my bag and sword by the wall then stepped to Morrigan and gave her a hug.

"Thank you," I whispered into her ear, then stepped back. "I'm nervous." My voice wavered. "I haven't seen him for two and a half years." I wrung my hands, my insides knotting. "What if I look older, what if—"

"Rhiannon, sister." Morrigan took my hands in hers. "Ye look wonderful and even if ye did not, it would matter naught to Lord Arlan." She gave my hands a squeeze and walked out.

No sooner had Morrigan left, than someone knocked at the door. I opened it to a woman dressed in a tartan skirt and plain cloth blouse laced at the front. She held a platter of fruit, cheese, and oat cakes in one hand and a jug in the other and strode right in and placed them on the table.

"Tha day tae ye, Lady Rhiannon." Puffing, she went straight to the cupboard at the side and got out horn cups and cloth napkins.

"Hello, and thank you," I replied. "Do you know when Lord Arlan will return?"

"Och, I dinnae ken much, only that he speaks with the sage council regarding his brother, Lord Kyle," the maid answered. "I ken with the way they sages blether I've nae idea when he'll get back tae his rooms, mi lady." She gave a short curtsy and left, closing the door behind her.

I rolled my eyes. If *blether* meant the same thing here that it did at home, Arlan would be ages. My vision landed on the wall opposite the windows. A fan of Lochaber axes alternating in a pattern with long spears adorned it, their blades shiny sharp silver edges against the grey body of the weapon. Below sat a chest, and by it rested daggers and swords of various sizes, and a battle axe. I picked it up, noting the similar ornamentation to all the handles—intricate swirls of knotwork.

My hands shook around the axe handle. These weapons were beautiful. And *everything* looked clearer, like I had new eyesight in this pristine, perfect, clean world of Dál Cruinne. A tremble arose within me. Soon Arlan would come to his room.

Any moment now.

I sought that place of calm and self-control. The place within, where I'd gone to think over what I would say to him.

And what I must insist upon.

TWENTY-SEVEN

— • —

Ye who hold me in your hands,
Strengthen mine to do my part.

POETRY OF THE WARRIOR
WARRIOR SAGE TAPHAÌDH
(4009-4059 POST DRAGON WARS)

The World of Dál Cruinne
Post Dragon Wars Year 6083
Western Sovereignty of Dál Gaedhle
Lord Arlan's Private Chambers, The Keep

I breathed in the peaty scented air of Arlan's chamber.

It mixed with those aromas that swirled around and gave off a hint of *him*. My hands ran over the smooth wooden axe handle. Squeezing my eyes tight, I pushed away any thought or emotion that would change what I'd determined to do.

The door creaked. I opened my eyes, and Arlan stepped into the room, his head bowed. He closed the door behind him and leaned against it, looking at the floor in front of him, like his mind was somewhere else. I stood still, holding my breath. Even my hands on the battle axe stilled. His shoulders weren't fixed in their usual broad military-look. He wore a kilt, his muscled torso bare, and cloths wrapped around each calf. A red necklace, maybe a torc or something to denote his clan chief status, sat around his neck.

Should I alert him to my presence? Surely someone would've told him I'd be here.

He sighed and looked up at the table set with food, then snapped to attention and swept the room, his vision landing on me.

"Hi." I leaned the axe against the wall, trembling to the centre of my being.

He strode toward me. It only took seconds for his arms to surround me, enfolding me in his body's musky perfume. Bands of warmth crossed my back, and his hot lips covered my mouth. They held longing and want and expectation and...

I forced my arms to obey me and put my palms on his chest, then I pushed gently. Our kiss broke apart.

"Arlan, we can't."

He jerked his head, eyes crinkling and his mouth still partly open. "Rhiannon..." His words trailed off, his eyes now widening but his brow slowly creasing. "But ye have waited for me..."

I released myself from his tight embrace, taking a step back, focusing on what I must say.

"And George... ye haven't seen him for six months." His voice was deep and masculine, just like I'd remembered. "Or so I'm told, and for this I am glad. I'm sorry my quest has prevented me from fulfilling my promise to return for you myself."

I pressed against the shaking in my centre. "Have you won the place of àrd rìgh?"

"Aye." His speech was hoarse. "Considering my brother's condition, they deemed his protests invalid." Arlan swallowed.

"So, you're their high king?"

He gave a silent nod.

"And as àrd rìgh, you must be with and... marry... a noblewoman." There was a quiver in my tone. "Which I'm not."

"Eifion searches for your roots. For your clan. For a missing girl babe of a noble house. Ye have brought your baby-rug?" His scarred eyebrow rose and so did the side of his mouth.

"Yes, I did, and I'll show it to whoever I need to but until it's proven that I belong to a clan of the standing worthy of an àrd rìgh"—I steeled myself and looked him in the eyes— "we can't be together."

"Rhiannon, I love you. I want you for my wife." He spoke tenderly. "Do ye want to wed me?"

"Yes." My answer came out tight. "But we cannot—"

"Forget tradition." He flung his hand out to the side and his mouth pinched. "If I'm àrd rìgh, I can do what I wish."

"Arlan, you're their high king. You can't disappoint your people. How will they feel if their king acts like he pleases? Will he be the same when push comes to shove? Save his own neck and not theirs?"

Arlan let out a sigh. The air passing through his lips broke the quiet of the room.

"I know you're not like that." I raised my eyebrows. "And you know I'm right." Arlan opened his mouth, but I placed a finger to his lips. I had more to say to this àrd rìgh. "We can only be together if Sage Eifion proves my parentage. So, until then, if there's ever a *then*, I want to be a Dál Gaedhle warrior. I've been training. I did as you asked. I've advanced in martial art classes. I can ride a horse and speak the Gaelic... in case you haven't noticed."

His mouth stretched into a grin, his eyes softening. "Aye, I had, Rhiannon." He spoke with pride in his voice.

"In a way, I'm here to discover who I am. Not only if I have noble Dál Gaedhle blood, but who I truly am. I know I was born to be more than mediocre. You made me believe that, Arlan. When I was me and naturally more than *just plain anybody* back in the mundane Other World, as you call Earth, people thought me weird. I'm now in the world you say I came from, and I feel that for certain. Here I'll find my purpose. Here I'll lend my strength to a cause. To Dál Gaedhle. To help keep it free from Ciarán Gallawain and his evil designs."

I ran over to my bag where I'd also rested my sword, my thighs shaking. Arlan let out a questioning grunt behind me. I turned. He'd followed and now we both stood in a clear space in his room. I unsheathed my blade, and he took a step back.

I knelt on one knee in front of him, and his eyes widened. I brought my sword to my lips, shut my eyes for a second, focusing. Then, holding my head up high, I kissed the flat side of the blade.

"I vow with all conviction that I will serve you, Lord Arlan Finnbar MacEnoicht, Chieftain of Clan MacEnoicht and now Àrd Rìgh of Dál Gaedhle, with all strength and will, in loyalty and truth, until my breath leaves me. And may the god of Dál Gaedhle bear witness to this pledge."

My insides stilled, and a peace settled within me while I never took my gaze from Arlan.

Moments passed. Arlan's shoulders rose and fell slowly, with his torso tightening in time with his breathing, and his navy-blue stare fixed on me.

"Rhiannon, I accept your vows." He swallowed, the soft gulp reaching my ears. "I am humbled that ye would pledge your life to serve me and Dál Gaedhle. It only proves ye are of the mettle of a Dál Gaedhle warrior and truly one birthed in this land." He fell to his knees, joining me on the floor. "We will prove who you are and then you will rule this land with me." His eyes searched mine. "Until that time, fight in my troop and be by my side, for you will never leave my heart."

Twenty-Eight

— · —

More is owed by those who reign.
To such who have gained honour and power
The more the right and duty to the risk.

WISDOM WRITINGS ON KINGSHIP
SAGE GLIOCAS
(2870-2962 POST DRAGON WARS)

The World of Dál Cruinne
Post Dragon Wars Year 6083
Western Sovereignty of Dál Gaedhle
Lord Arlan's Private Chambers, The Keep

Arlan poured ale, his grip tight on the cup, mirroring the clench of his gut and the swirl in his heart. He kept his back to Rhiannon, closing his eyes, seeking calm. Her body was so warm and yielding, yet she'd pushed him away.

Has she just rejected me and promised her life to me in one action?

He filled the other cup, willing the tremor of his hand to still.

Rhiannon was here. She would be by his side in his warband. He would discover her roots in Dál Cruinne.

All *would* be well!

He took a breath, held it and replaced the jug on the sideboard, then released it slowly through his lips. He raised his eyes to the crest of the àrd rìgh mounted on the wall above him. Surrounded by a circle of knotwork, the black horse standing rampant, reared over him. He picked up both drinks, turned, and walked to Rhiannon.

She sat by the fire, sheathing her sword with trembling hands. He placed the drink on the table. Avoiding his gaze, she thanked him, then selected a piece of cheese from the board, holding it but not taking the morsel to her mouth. A plain maroon plaid hung across her shoulder, and she wore the garb of a warrior. Her arm muscles had firmed,

173

and she glowed with health and was more alert to her surroundings. Aye, she had learned what it was to be a warrior, and she now had the demeanour of one. He suppressed anything else he would think of her, for yield to her wishes he must. He tightened his grip on his cup. To have her only as a warrior in his warband...

He bent his head back and sculled the drink, absorbing all she'd said and promised to him. The movement squeezed Drayce against his neck. His tiny dragon wriggled and scampered out from under his hair, along his arm and to his cup.

"What's that?" Rhiannon shuffled on her seat. "Is that a lizard? What's it doing in your hair?"

"This is Drayce, and he's a—"

"*Dragon!*" She stood, stepping closer. "No way!"

Drayce grabbed his cup with a claw and poked his head in to lap at the dregs.

"Och, nae ye don't. Ye shall have water." He went to the sideboard for the pitcher. "And there is nae meat on that platter." Arlan strode to the door where he ordered a servant to bring meat.

"Aye, Lord Arlan," the servant said, "The warrior lady, the one frae Dál Gallain, says she must tend yer wounds."

Arlan nodded, and the woman scurried off.

He turned back to the room. Drayce now sat in Arlan's palm, with his tail curled around his wrist.

"May I see him?" Rhiannon's eyes glittered, and the lambent light from the fire seemed to give her hair an inner glow.

He held Drayce out to her. The wee dragon peered directly at her, tilted his head, and blinked his double blink.

"Oh, he's gorgeous." Her hands came close to his dragon, and with one finger she stroked his head. He rose to her touch like a cat, increasing Rhiannon's fond exclamations. "He's even got tiny wings." Her hand froze, finger poised in her petting. "What are you going to do with him?"

Arlan lifted a shoulder. "Keep him for as long as he survives."

"What do you mean? You don't think he will?"

He pressed his lips together. "I've never had a dragon for a pet."

"Congratulations on winning the Quest and becoming àrd rìgh, by the way." She gave him a half grin.

He breathed a heavy sigh and slowly shook his head. "It's such a responsibility, Rhiannon."

She looked up at him, her head angled, and her warm eyes melted the lump that had formed in his throat.

"Now it's down to me," he continued. "All that is to come, and that which the sages will write in the history of Dál Gaedhle, and even of Dál Cruinne, henceforth will depend on every decision I make and every action—"

Somebody rapped on the door.

Arlan grunted. "Come."

The door opened and Bàn entered, followed by Eifion, Leyna and Vygeas.

"I hope we're not disturbing ye," Bàn said a wee bit hesitantly.

"I need to dress your wounds, Lord Arlan." Leyna bustled past Bàn, taking her bag from her shoulder.

"Wounds?" Rhiannon dropped her gaze to his bandaged calves.

"Aye, burned by that wee one's mother." Bàn pointed an accusing finger at the dragon clinging to Arlan's hand.

"Burned?"

"Rhiannon"—Arlan gestured to Eifion— "this is Sage Eifion."

Rhiannon bowed deeply. Standing in front of Eifion, she looked overwhelmed.

Hmm. Arlan was daily in Eifion's commanding presence. It was said, to meet the man in person for the first time could be an awe-inspiring occasion.

"I am Leyna." Leyna opened her bag. "I will take Lord Arlan to dress his wounds while you make acquaintance with his friends."

From her reassuring tones, Leyna had noted Rhiannon's discomfort too. Rhiannon's stiff posture seemed to lessen with Leyna's words. Arlan strode to the bed, Drayce's claws clamping on the back of his neck as the miniature dragon tucked himself into his hair once more.

"Thank you, Leyna." Arlan lay down on his front.

Rhiannon sat with Eifion and Bàn; their polite conversation hummed by the fire. Vygeas ambled over to him.

"I can hardly walk through the emotions in this room, Lord Arlan," Vygeas whispered by the bed. "Such conflict arises from ye both."

"Och, is nothing sacred around you, man?" Arlan hissed.

"I will tell ye this for naught: she loves you something fierce, my lord."

Leyna dampened her cloth and pressed cold onto the back of Arlan's calves. It stung like a deamhan's touch, and he drew in a breath. "Bàn. Whisky!" He pushed the words through his clamping jaw.

Bàn stood, interrupting Eifion and Rhiannon's low conversation.

"And you're his sword-brother," Rhiannon said to Bàn as he walked to the sideboard cupboard. "I've heard so much about you."

"Aye, that would be me." Bàn brought the bottle of whisky from the sideboard, then poured some into Arlan's cup. Bàn's dimples pitted.

Arlan squinted. Those dimples have melted women's hearts.

Just don't let Rhiannon see them.

"Morrigan informs me that Kyle called you Aisling?" Eifion said to Rhiannon, his brow creasing above his nose.

"Yes, he thought I was some sage."

Eifion's gaze turned inward, and his eyes moved as though reliving a scene from his past. Then his face paled.

"Eifion?" Arlan took the whisky from Bàn, drank, then held the cup out for more. "What ails you, sage? Ye look like ye have seen a ghost."

"I... I shall... let you young people be, Lord Arlan." Eifion stood. "I shall double my enquiries." He gave a curt nod, then turned to Rhiannon, giving her a thoughtful look. "Lady Rhiannon, goodnight."

The door had barely closed behind him when Vygeas strode to Rhiannon. "Lady Rhiannon." He gave a quick bow. "We have been acquainted for only a moment, but I sense you have disturbed our friend the sage in no uncertain way."

"What?" She turned her startled stare on Arlan. "What does he mean?"

Arlan stood from his bed and Leyna's ministrations. His legs, freed from their bandages, burned like the first fire had touched them. "Vygeas, explain yourself." He grimaced and walked over to be with Rhiannon.

"That old sage recognised her," Vygeas said.

"What!" Rhiannon stiffened. "I've never seen him before. And how could I have?"

"He knows you from somewhere, my lady. Or so it seems." Vygeas' tone was only slightly apologetic.

"Oh..." The word left Rhiannon's tongue with reluctance. "Maybe I *have* seen him." A small *v* formed between her eyebrows. "Possibly."

"When?" Arlan blinked.

"On the South Inch. In Perth. Where I work—worked. The same year I met you. That man was very professor-like, but the voice is unmistakable."

"Impossible."

"Is it?" She locked her gaze with his.

"Perhaps ye have a strong resemblance to a clan." Arlan grabbed at suggestions. His newest friends were unaware of portals. *How much to reveal?* "And now Eifion has seen you, he recognises family traits."

Arlan sighed. But the knowledge of portals and travels to Rhiannon's world would slip out soon enough.

"It has shocked him, whatever the case," Vygeas said.

"Perhaps he has..." She looked at Arlan, lowering her chin with one fine eyebrow cocked. He nodded for her to continue. "...already made that journey where he met me in the Other World." She blinked, her gaze on him intense.

"Blades and bloody double-sided battle axes!" Vygeas stepped closer to Rhiannon. "The *Other* World." Awe filled his voice.

Leyna's mouth dropped open. "The land of the Fae?"

"Nae, another world all together." Arlan spoke to Leyna, not removing his vision from Rhiannon. "I shall tell you all another time."

"Has Eifion told you about seeing me in the park?" Rhiannon asked Arlan, then glanced at Vygeas, who was studying her.

"Nae." Arlan shook his head. "Not a word."

"So, he hasn't been there yet?" Bàn asked.

Arlan rubbed the bristly whiskers beneath his chin. "He would've told me. I am certain of it. I'll go ask at once." He stepped to the door.

Bàn groaned behind him, Vygeas grunted, and Leyna called, "Come back here now, Lord Arlan, and let me finish!"

"Let it be for the present, my lord, for the sage still ponders it." Vygeas held his palm up. "Give the man time."

Arlan walked to the bed, dragging his feet, then lay down and allowed Leyna to bandage his legs.

"Vygeas, how do you know all this?" Rhiannon asked. "That he recognises me in some way?"

Leyna stilled her bandaging, and Vygeas' expression blanked.

Bàn coughed.

"She will take it far better than any you know, Vygeas." Arlan stood up, Leyna having finished her ministrations. "For, as ye have just discovered, she's from the Other World and therefore won't have the biases of ours."

"Hmm. It fully explains that which I see around her." Vygeas' fingers drummed his thigh.

"You see *what* around me?" Rhiannon's voice rose in pitch, and she drew her plaid tighter.

"It is well, Rhiannon." Arlan stepped over to her and sat, taking her hands in his. "There's magic in this world. I didn't tell you, for I was unaware of the strength of it. It seems to have emerged everywhere around me since my return."

"I thought there might be magic." She half smiled. "The portals were a dead giveaway."

"She is trustworthy," Arlan said to Vygeas, then to Rhiannon, "If Vygeas tells you, it's a secret to be kept. Will you?"

"Yes," she replied.

Vygeas' fingers danced on his thigh while he considered Rhiannon with an intense stare. Next to Arlan, Rhiannon squirmed a little.

"You can read people," she said. "Like a mentalist-illusionist?"

Vygeas twitched his head. "Aye, *read people*. That will suffice."

Heavy foot tread came along the corridor, followed by knuckles rapping loudly on the door. Bàn went and opened the door to a warrior standing outside.

"Lord Bàn, I am told Lady Leynarve of Monsae is here," the warrior said.

Bàn turned to Leyna, who was packing the dressings in her bag. She nodded back.

"Who enquires?" Bàn asked.

"A man, battle and travel worn, seeks entry to our gate, claiming he is a clansman faithful to the House of Monsae. He wishes to speak to his clan chieftainess."

"When I heard ye were alive, my Lady of Monsae, back frae the dead, or so they said, and in the company of lords of the west, I came with all haste." The clansman warrior, a battle-scarred veteran to rival Muir, knelt before Leyna.

Arlan moved closer to the Lady of Monsae. Shorter than Arlan himself and his people of Dál Gaedhle, this man had the same olive skin and tight, curly hair as Leyna. She'd been pleased to allow Arlan, Bàn, and Rhiannon to remain with her and Vygeas while she received the report from the man. He was dishevelled, dusty and reeking of horse sweat from a journey of many days from the clan lands of Monsae, on the coast of Dál Gallain's southwest.

"Please, drink before you relay your story, sir." Leyna offered him the pewter cup filled with the water she'd poured.

"Nae, my Lady Monsae, for I promised those I left behind I would faithfully report to ye. And that I will do afore I do aught else."

"Well, then." Leyna placed the cup on the table next to the kneeling warrior. "Please begin."

"There is nae other way to relay it but straight, so ye'll pardon my forthrightness, my lady."

Leyna nodded and Vygeas stepped to her side, his hand lightly brushing her lower back as though to reassure or comfort her. The man's gift gave him an uncanny knack of seeing a person's feelings before Arlan usually did. Arlan grunted to himself. He would watch and listen to the ex-assassin, for he gave off clues. A pre-knowing of sorts.

"After your parents were sae brutally assassinated..." The warrior placed a calloused, stiff hand to his forehead. "*Tobraichean na Beatha* bless their eternal rest."

Leyna stiffened and arched her back away from Vygeas' hand.

"Lord Ciarán came with a warband," the clansman continued. "The man himself, mind. This was five years ago, ken? When the man was nae the powerful lord he is tha noo'. Och, how he has forced the clan lairds under him..." The man shook his head. "Anyways, he sought to take Caisteal Monsae for his own, but we fought him off, my lady. Those of us faithful to your house and sorely grieving for the loss of our beloved clan chieftain and his family. Lord Ciarán retreated. Well and good, we thought, that's him given up. So, we left a steward to maintain the caisteal until it could be decided who tae be the next clan chief. An' then the clashes, and battles and general unrest started in Dál Gallain, and still goin'. Now Lord Ciarán again sets his sights on the Monsae lands, probably thinking, and not rightly I'll add, that—"

"An army sworn to the Laird of Caisteal Monsae accompanied the lands and titles he wished to win if he became the new laird by force." Vygeas finished the man's sentence.

"We are aware of the reason he tries again." Leyna glanced sideways at Vygeas. "He is aware of my survival, and I remind him of his past failure. Continue, if you please."

"Lord Ciarán sent his warriors again, not a fortnight past, taking us by surprise. We mustered in haste but were overcome." The man bowed his head, his cheeks bright red above his thick bushy beard, except where a fresh scar healed. "Caisteal Monsae has been taken."

Leyna's posture stiffened and she swayed a little. Vygeas supported her. This time, the lady didn't pull herself away from his touch.

"It's a strategic victory for Ciarán Gallawain, my Lady of Monsae," Arlan said. "The Monsae lands sitting along the border between Dál Gaedhle and Dál Gallain make it an ideal place to nudge his army past the long-neglected border forts and commence his taking of Dál Gaedhle lands."

Staring at her clansman warrior, Leyna paled and her hands trembled.

"Just after I met Lady Leynarve," Vygeas said, "our journey drew Lord Ciarán's attention to her, her lands and army, which he would seek to obtain through a forced marriage. He sent a mage after us, who failed in his task of killing me and seizing Leynarve." Leyna and Vygeas locked gazes for the briefest of moments. "In taking Caisteal Monsae, Lord Ciarán resorts to his usual hostile methods. And currently, the man controls most of the western section of Dál Gallain's coast."

"Aye." The Monsae clansman raised his head. "Except for the Isle of Eilean, with its harbour. It remains free of Lord Ciarán. He needs the assistance of those further east with ships and sea warriors if he wishes to take Dál Gaedhle with a sea force. He'll get nae joy frae the sea-rover-cum-conquering laird of the Citadel o' Cathair. Laird Lochlann detests the man—spits every time he is forced to say the name Ciarán Gallawain, or so rumour has it. Lord Ciarán's only course of action must be to battle on land."

"Then there is hope for Monsae," Vygeas said.

Out of the corner of Arlan's vision, Rhiannon stood transfixed by the whole scene. Dressed ready to fight, and eyes wide, her arms tensing at her sides. She itched to hold a blade; her posture told Arlan such. He warmed inside. Bàn, standing next to her, his loyalty never in doubt, would agree, along with his troop, with what he planned. He slid his gaze to Vygeas, and the man stared at him. The scarred side of Vygeas' mouth pulled into his version of a smile.

Och, I can keep nothing from him.

Arlan stepped to face Leyna, right beside the weary clansman, who now took the offered drink.

"Lady Leynarve of Monsae, in repayment for your services in my successful completion of the Quest, I give you my support to reclaim your clan lands, family caisteal, and title." Arlan gave a slight bow.

Leyna blinked, her expression changing in a flash from a frown of sorrow to one of consternation. "No, Lord Arlan, I do not presume—"

"Aye, I ken ye would nae. But I'm indebted to you. To you both. I wish to show my appreciation. But I wish to keep naught from you. Aiding you to win back your lands may ultimately assist in defeating Gallawain and halting his push west. I have the warriors." He glanced at Bàn.

"Aye, ye do," Bàn said.

"Leynarve." Vygeas' voice was soft, tender.

Leyna didn't look at Vygeas, her whole body tensing away from him.

"Thank you, Lord Arlan. It would mean everything for me to regain my lands and title. They have been lost to me for far too long. I was angry." From the corner of her eye, she flashed a hard look at Vygeas. "I left grieving and certain I would never return, but times change and so do people." She swallowed and glanced aside at Vygeas once more. "I accept, and I thank you. But you need not come, you will have much to attend now you are àrd rìgh."

"Och, Lady Leyna, I will go. I wish to see Ciarán's warriors and their tactics for myself. And as to being high king, this one will follow his father's example and lead from the front."

"I'll gather the warriors," Bàn said.

Beside him, Rhiannon looked from one to another, her feet as though on springs, bouncing.

"We will not require many," Vygeas said. "Maybe two warbands."

"Ye have a plan, Vygeas?" Arlan grimaced. "I beg you, not a siege. It is such an effort, and the resources within the caisteal walls usually destroyed, so the victor gains nothing but the expense of repair. Not to mention the shame in the loss of lives."

"I know the caisteal inside out." Vygeas cringed.

This once-*murtair*, so far, had flinched at naught. Leyna's narrowing gaze swung to him. Vygeas lowered his head, the dagger at his belt now absorbing his attention, his nostrils flaring.

"As do I." Leyna spoke in a firm tone. "There are entrances known only to the family and head servants. If they are still accessible, we can gain entry unnoticed and take them by surprise."

"Very well, we prepare." Arlan now stepped to where Bàn stood with Rhiannon. "We shall leave two days hence. I need to choose a second warband." He gripped Bàn's shoulder. "And you, my sword-brother, need to give Lady Rhiannon a crash course in fighting. On being a Dál Gaedhle warrior 101."

"One o' what?"

Twenty-Nine

— • —

This is the way of the blade.

WARRIOR SAGE TAPAÌDH
(4009-4059 POST DRAGON WARS)

The World of Dál Cruinne
Post Dragon Wars Year 6083
Western Sovereignty of Dál Gaedhle
The Practice Yard, The Keep

The morning sun sat low, just a scrap of its rim peeping over the outer bailey wall.

The Keep, still in partial shadow, bustled with activity. The clang of metal rang out in the bailey courtyard. At a blacksmith's forge, a man belted a long piece of steel with a mallet, his face glistening with sweat. Heat escaped the small building in the middle of the bailey yard, bathing me in warmth as I passed by.

I walked with Morrigan across to where the warriors practiced, clutching my sword close. My muscles were still tight and tense from sleep, and the skin on my bare arms now cool from the chill morning air. Deep within I shivered, the tremble shunting down every limb.

I had to psyche myself up. Be relaxed, but clear headed.

My mouth pulled in an irrepressible grin—I was about to start a quick course in sword fighting the Dál Gaedhle way.

I could hardly believe it.

A group of warriors examined weapons on one side of the sanded area, while others warmed up with wooden swords.

"Bàn has promised me he will be kind to you," Morrigan said.

"Why aren't you teaching me?"

"It is best if ye learn with an opponent the weight and size of a man. It will give ye more of an idea of a real fight." She put a hand on my arm. "Rhiannon, if ye come with us to retake the caisteal, it would be dangerous for you who have not seen combat. You have a belt in the martial arts, but my friend, that is not the same as... what would you call it? *Fighting on the street*." Morrigan's hand tightened around my bicep. "Och, ye are tense." She gave me a gentle shake of reassurance. "Ye'll be fine." Morrigan squeezed my arm again, then stepped toward warriors who I recognised from the Great Hall yesterday.

Arlan's warband.

Angus and Leigh were there, and a burly woman was pelting a sword onto the shield of a tall man with a crooked nose and a permanent cheeky grin.

"Adele"—Morrigan called to the man's opponent— "take pity on Douglas and come spar with me." She joined them, leaving me at the edge of the yard.

Soft sand covered the practice yard. Bàn waited in the middle with his arms crossed over a bare torso. He was only slightly shorter than Arlan, and just as muscled. I stood there until he nodded a welcome, giving me permission to enter.

"What have you there?" He pointed to my sword as I approached. "May I see?"

I handed him my broadsword. Arlan's comments of it having a pretty handle but being made for a man his size rang in my head. I huffed. There was sure to be a repeat of those words from Bàn.

Bàn unsheathed it, checked its balance, glanced at the handle and the blade, then stood back and swung it wide and fast on either side of himself. He moved it so quickly, it was just a blur.

"Hmm," he said.

"*Hmm?* Go on, say it's useless for me." I crossed my arms over my chest.

"Well, if ye are so attached to it—"

"I am." I puffed strands of loose hair away from my eyes—of course my frizz had come out of my hair tie already.

"Och, then it requires the master sword crafter to do nothing less than remake it but, despite the man being busy at present, I'm sure he will find time to attend to it."

"What does it *require*?" With that, I unsheathed my metaphorical sword, and pushed down the defensive grumbles.

My beautiful sword isn't good enough?

"For a start"—Bàn pointed at the tip— "the end is too heavy, and it wobbles. Most adversaries are moving targets already, without your sword tip wiggling and making it harder to aim." He squinted an eye at me.

I kept my face deadpan.

"The cross guard will have to be smoothed on the ends." He tapped the cross pieces above the handle that would stop an opponent's blade from slipping down the sword and cutting my hand.

"Why?"

"They're fancy, but the ends are sharp. Ye are sure to scrape your own forearm or even your thigh with them. Not advisable. Blood and wounds of yer own are distracting in a fight."

"Why would I do that? Scrape myself?"

Bàn stood back and gave a questioning sigh. "Have ye ever wielded this?"

"Yes. I tried to remember the sword exercises Arlan did and recreate them, but I haven't had lessons. I didn't want to mix up my fighting style. There are so many schools. I wasn't too sure if I should go with HEMA or even Kendo." I shrugged.

"Ken what?"

"Ah, no, um..." I wriggled my toes in my sturdy boots.

Bàn muttered something under his breath, but I didn't catch it. "And the pommel needs rounding. Ye will gouge an opponent but yer ain thigh, also. And hurt your hand if ye rest it—"

I flung my hands up. "So, I need a new sword!"

"Nae." Bàn sounded earnest. "It's a decent blade. Just a wee bit heavy for a woman and it requires sharpening."

"I spent hours honing that edge." I poked at the offending item.

Bàn ran his finger along one edge of my blade then held it up, uninjured. "The sword smith will sharpen it for you." Bàn's face hardened. "Ye must kill with this."

I gulped.

Bàn sheathed my sword, then walked to the side of the ring where a knave stood. He spoke to the boy, who then left with the sword. The clunk of wooden swords on shields drowned out what he'd said. Bàn strode back to me and smiled, his cheeks dimpling. A silvery scar tore through the one on the right.

"The master sword-crafter will turn your blade into a more suitable weapon for you, my Lady Rhiannon." He spoke my name softly, with affection even. Like he was hitting on me.

Really?

"Tell me what you know," he said, his tone now abrupt.

"Kicks, punches. Hand to hand. Disarming."

"Disarming...?"

"Guns and knives." *Oops.* I'd spoken before I'd thought.

"Guns?"

Ignoring his question, I continued, "I have only practised with my sword after Goog...You Tu... Ah, watching some fighters who know how to do it."

"And they never showed you? Nor gave you the personal instruction ye required?"

"Ah, well, no, 'cos they weren't actually... I wasn't there with them... at the time..." I cringed.

Bàn's blond eyebrows met in the middle and the corner of his mouth screwed to the side.

I grimaced inwardly. How much should this man know about the Other World?

Boy, I may have to censor everything I say to this guy.

183

"You'd better start teaching me how to do it, then," I said before he could ask any more questions.

He walked to the edge of the yard, where wooden swords leaned against a railing. He came back with two and handed me the lighter, shorter one.

"So, these warriors ye observed. They would give ye the theory. But I will tell ye one thing: all is forgotten in the midst of a fight. Fancy forms and routines dinnae happen. It's quick and it's sudden, and all over afore ye realise it. And"—he held up his index finger— "the hours ye have spent in the practice yard make your body do it without a thought. The moves, aye? But they're shorter, sharper, faster. Closer. It's strength, speed and a rapid response."

"Muscle memory."

He gave me a blank look.

I've done it again. "It's automatic."

His expression remained blank.

"Your body knows by instinct what to do."

He nodded, seemingly happy with that.

"So, attack me." He stood with his wooden blade lowered.

My heart thudded. I steadied myself and focused, then swung the wooden sword, hitting right then the left, again and again. I was clumsy, and he sidestepped many of my blows. Every time Bàn's sword connected with my swings, he blocked with no force behind it.

I am pathetic.

"Stop." He clanked his blade against my last swipe. "And stop thinking."

I stood back. Breathing, but not hard. *At least I'm fit.*

"Let me show ye how to swing this sword." He placed his blade on the ground, then stepped beside me, close. "Start with both hands on the handle, left nearest the cross guards. Raise the blade so the tip is up over your right shoulder, facing behind you. Like this." He raised my sword, so it pointed backwards over my shoulder. "Swing it forward, left arm in a straight line, and yer right hand moving the handle. Left hand stays in position while the blade comes forward." He held his hands over mine, directing the movement. "Then ye block your opponent's swing, or chop their shoulder... if ye are quick." He spoke close to my ear, his last comment lingering.

I blinked, then turned to face him. He stepped away, his throat pinking.

"Let's try that," he said.

I swung the sword a few times in the manner he'd shown me. "But I've learned this already."

"Aye then, so we'll spar."

Bàn stood opposite and raised his sword to his face. Then he roared and charged toward me, lifting his sword high and thrusting it down. I blocked automatically. The force of his strike jarred my shoulders, and my teeth clunked together. He came again. The power behind his blows was incredible. He pushed me back and down, grunting and yelling like an animal.

184

My heart pounded and my vision cleared. I met every blow with a block. Bàn paused a fraction, and I swung one back in return. He blocked and pushed my blade away. Within a second, his sword point was at my neck. I lifted my sword up to push his off. But couldn't move it. He pressed the tip onto my throat.

I pushed again, grunting with the effort.

"I'm dead, aren't I?"

"Aye." He lowered the sword.

I stood there, shoulders heaving, and heart fighting its way out of my chest. Tears pricked.

I'm a fool.

"I've less than two days to teach ye much, and my priority is to ensure ye do not die." His dimples showed again. "Ye have promise. And pluck, courage, and daring." He squeezed his mouth to the side. "Maybe, for the present, the daring needs to be tempered a wee bit with the will to survive."

He held up his sword. "Again!"

THIRTY

The hero's quest—a noble thought.
Wrought with battles, foes, and peril.
To gain the prize, to conquer all
And give the enemy terror.
But greater still and fiercer fought
With will, and heart, and mind
The quest for meaning, love, and joys,
That only the truest, noblest ploys
Of those who strive with courage bold,
Ensures the soul these treasures will hold.

POETRY OF THE WARRIOR
WARRIOR SAGE TAPAÌDH
(4009-4059 POST DRAGON WARS)

The World of Dál Cruinne
Post Dragon Wars Year 6083
Western Sovereignty of Dál Gaedhle
Lord Arlan's Private Chambers

The leatherworker spread the samples of leather armour over the furniture in Arlan's chambers. A yeasty animal odour hovered around the craftsman and his assistant. The toughened garment Arlan held rubbed hard between his fingers. Many pieces of leather overlapped each other to form a short tunic to sit just below the hips, and with a split section hanging low over the thighs. Leyna and Vygeas stood with him, while Leyna inspected the joins in another piece of armour.

"So, the layered leather makes for more protection?" Arlan asked.

"Slashes may be stayed," Vygeas said, "but a blade tip at the correct angle will pierce it. Even so, it is better than a bare torso, Lord Arlan, such as is the tradition of warriors here in the west."

"I have a metal worker constructing chain maille for me. Do you know of this garment?"

"Maille? Aye. Inberian warriors, the elite guard from a far kingdom in the east, wear it. I have only ever seen it on those warriors. It is an expensive item, taking a year of a crafter's life to make and, as such, is costly and highly valued. But it affords great protection and, in my opinion, is worth every expense."

Arlan gave a *hmm* of appreciation to Vygeas.

"Can ye have these leathers ready for my warriors by tomorrow?" Arlan asked the leather worker.

The craftsman gave a strained look. "I will try my best, my lord àrd rìgh."

The leather worker and his assistant gathered the garments, then hurried out, almost knocking over Eifion, who was entering the open door.

"Eifion, I am glad ye are here." Arlan pointed to the chair by the fire. "Please sit. We have much of which to speak."

"Lady Leynarve and I shall leave you." Vygeas took Leyna's hand, nodded to Eifion, then left.

Eifion sat, his face turned away from Arlan with his shoulders hunched, and he took in a faltering breath. Arlan sat in the seat opposite.

"What is it, Eifion?"

Eifion turned and faced him. "I suppose Vygeas told you I exuded some strong emotion last evening."

"Aye." Something about Rhiannon troubled Eifion. Arlan fought down the urge to force the information out of the man. He gripped the arms of his chair. He had a multitude of things to organise—*like a warband*—but whatever Eifion would tell him now, he would know. He wouldn't press the sage. He was too dear to him, and he would not risk upsetting him.

Eifion chewed his lips, as though he was chewing over a decision. "Do you remember much of your very young days? The people in your life when you were but a boy here in The Keep?"

"Such as?"

"Myself. And any other sages."

Arlan cast his thoughts back. "Aye, but mainly you, Eifion."

"Do you recall the sage, Aisling? The one for whom your brother mistook Rhiannon?" Arlan shook his head. "Sorry, nae. Why?"

Eifion returned his gaze to the smouldering peat fire.

"She was my first real love when I was young and freer and not so serious." He made a noise, a cross between a chuckle and a snort. "I did love her." Eifion turned to Arlan; his moistening eyes were full of memories. "I had to choose between her and my vocation"—he shrugged— "and you know my choice." Eifion lowered his gaze to the floor while the room filled with regrets. He rubbed his chin where grey stubble grew.

"I have a theory," Eifion finally said, his voice unusually quiet. "Mauve eyes are rare, but there is a clan that has a child born with such now and then. They are not a trait common to Clan Gallawain. The clan with mauve eyes is Cruithin, one of the oldest in the land."

"So, Rhiannon is not Gallawain? How then did she get my mother's clan tartan and crest? This makes no sense." Arlan slumped back into his seat. "I need to know her origins. I can forestall no longer answering the requests of chieftains to consider their daughters without them regarding my tardiness as an insult."

Arlan chewed the inside of his lip. Should he mention Rhiannon's thoughts on Eifion or no'? He leaned forward in his chair.

"But... Eifion. Ye have seen Rhiannon afore. In the Other World. For she relayed a meeting of a man whom she believes is you."

Eifion jolted. "Nae. I have *never* been to the Other World. Your lady is mistaken."

"Or... ye have not yet travelled."

"Aye, well, I would wish to learn much more before I myself use a portal." He chuckled. "But Rhiannon maintains I have gone through... So, in time, then, I do." Eifion returned his gaze to the fire, his eyes glistening in the light of its flames.

"Eifion, now you have identified this clan our task will be easier, aye?"

The sage stirred from his quiet thoughts. "I will investigate further. Firstly, I will visit the current Cruithin Clan chief in the north." Eifion's brow puckered. "But say naught to Rhiannon. Do not raise her hopes."

"I shall stay my speech, but in truth, I rest my hopes on this noble clan." He gave Eifion a direct stare. "For I love the woman."

Eifion sighed and his usual impressive posture slumped a little. "I will try my hardest. But understand full well, if she is not of this noble house, I can think of nowhere else to look. You must prepare yourself. For duty, Arlan, Àrd Rìgh of Dál Gaedhle, comes above all." Eifion rose heavily from his chair and left.

Arlan's gaze drifted to the fire, now a blur. His exhaled breath gusted into the flames and sent the peat ash swirling. Lifted by the heat of the embers, it rose to the chimney. His hopes of having Rhiannon for his love for a lifetime threatened to follow it and rise to be blown away by the wind.

The responsibility of leading people came with benefits... but oh so much more in personal sacrifice.

Father had shown him this was so.

He could not fail Eifion, nor all those who had put their trust in him to lead them to victory over Ciarán Gallawain and free Dál Gaedhle of his threat.

And, aye, how he wished for it so.

What must he lose now he'd won *Tòireadh* and gained the right to rule as àrd rìgh of the land? Perhaps he was selfish in wishing for his own happiness. Must duty to clan, chiefdom, and kingdom *always* come first?

Nae, to not have the freedom to give Rhiannon a place by his side—to be his wife—would break him. His breath stilled in his throat. *None should expect this of their leader!*

"I cannot lose heart... I will find a way. I shall not relinquish *this quest* until I succeed."

THIRTY-ONE

— • —

Fealty is a clan chief's right,
A lord and king's due honour.
But to have earned the love and loyalty of brave warriors and true,
Of such a one is rare.
Grasp him tight... and follow.

POETRY OF A KING
ÀRD RÌGH RHONAN IUBHAR
(4030-4090 POST DRAGON WARS)

The World of Dál Cruinne
Post Dragon Wars Year 6083
Western Sovereignty of Dál Gaedhle
The Practice Yard, The Keep

I gripped my remade sword. Jittering rose from my belly and bubbled into an uncontrollable squeal.

Awesome!

"The master sword-crafter has done a good job, my lady," Bàn said, grinning. "Hence his title."

I stood in the practice yard with Bàn a pace away. Around me, and covering every spare patch of sand, warriors honed their skills. Arlan stood in a corner of the yard with a very large, very grumpy, and very red-haired man, who Bàn identified as the war chief, Leuchars. He wore his upper torso and arms bare, like most of the Dál Gaedhle warriors. Many scars glistened silver along the exposed parts of his body, and he bore them like medals.

Drayce's head peeked out from Arlan's unbound hair; the dragon seemed to have grown overnight.

"Pay attention," Bàn commanded. "Wield your sword. Do some forms. Try it out. For ye must be proficient. By my blade, we leave tomorrow!" An uncertain edge snuck into his tone.

I cut through the air in wide, slow arcs, getting the feel of my improved weapon. It was lighter, and the wobble had gone. The sword tip went where I wanted it to go, nice and steady. And it moved so much quicker through the air. I trembled at the thought of the damage this blade could now do. Man, I had to be careful with it. Now I could actually hurt someone. Possibly, if I did it right.

Or, even hurt myself if I didn't.

"Watch your footwork," Bàn called. "Balls of your feet, lass! Now try closer swings. Ye don't always have that much room in a fight, and ye leave openings for your enemy."

I swung my blade through more forms.

"Dinnae swing too hard, aye?" Bàn advised. "The sword has its own momentum and ye'll over balance."

My arms were heavy. My shoulders killed me, and my thighs... I could feel muscles I would've thought had nothing to do with the movement of a blade. That meant ahead lay another disturbed night of waking due to a twinge in any position. My fingers were another matter. They curled numbly around the sword handle. I grunted, swapping hands, resting my sword in my left hand while I wriggled the fingers of my right. I had to regain *some* feeling.

Bàn stepped closer, rubbing his top lip with a hand that had the two outer fingers almost permanently curled.

"Remember ye have a pommel." He placed his hand over mine and lifted my sword handle, showing the now smoothed end. "Ye can break a face with it." His mouth curved in a sincere smile.

"You love this, don't you?" I couldn't keep the sarcasm from my voice.

His grin dropped. "I'm a trained warrior. I fight to keep Dál Gaedhle free." He moved his face close to mine, speaking low, his breath stirring my hair. "We're on the verge of war. I don't delight in killing, as ye imply. It is who I am. And what I must do. So, I do it with skill."

I gulped.

"The man ye love is the same, lass," he whispered.

"I know." I glared into his face. "And I'm not ignorant. I'm here to be part of this." I released him from my stare and looked around the practice yard. "I'll get there. I'll pick it up. It's not like I've never been in a fight. I know what it's like to have a knife at my throat."

Bàn stepped back from me, giving me a wary look.

Those who'd been practicing—I counted over sixty—ceased their activity and now stood near Arlan and Leuchars. Bàn walked toward them and gestured for me to come, too. Arlan's own special group of warriors were there: Adele and the man she'd fought with the other day, Douglas, along with Angus, Leigh and Morrigan. Plus, a scarred older man who had his hair in a bun and plaited his beard like a Viking. They stood close together, all wearing thick, padded cloth tunics and sleeveless leather jackets, tight and layered. Leigh was grimacing, tugging at the tunic sitting askew beneath his armour.

"The body armour of the south." Bàn followed my gaze. "Arlan wishes us to try it."

"Like Leyna and Vygeas wear?"

"Aye, that's where he got the idea."

"I don't think so," I replied. "We had armour like this centuries ago. Arlan saw our... histories," I added at Bàn's expression. I wouldn't explain documentaries. *That'd involve television.* I recalled my TV had once almost suffered death by broadsword. My mouth tugged at one side.

"What amuses you, my lady?"

"Oh, nothing," I whispered, straining away my grin.

Arlan stood on a wooden platform on the side of the practice yard where the warriors had gathered. He took Drayce from under his hair and placed him on a bench seat. The small dragon made a noise, like a mixture between a strangled squawk and a gecko's click, flapped its wings, and flew back to him. Arlan gave a surprised chuckle. Drayce crawled to Arlan's sword handle sitting above his shoulder and clung to it, curling its tail around Arlan's neck, and didn't budge. Awed comments and chortles came from those watching.

Bàn leaned close to me. "It's the first time it has flown."

The warriors stood on the sand in front of Arlan. His gaze flowed across the crowd, rested a fraction longer on me, then moved on. I pressed my lips tight, reminding myself I had determined I must be just another one of his warriors.

"Sword brothers and sisters." Arlan spoke and the murmurs among the group settled. "Tomorrow we leave to retake Caisteal Monsae for the Lady of Monsae. Some of you may ask why we help a clan of Dál Gallain. I will tell ye. Lady Leynarve of Monsae has pledged her warbands to ours in the fight against Ciarán Gallawain and what he seeks to take from us. For the man subdues the clan lands along the coast of Dál Gallain, conquering all on his way to our coast and border. Do not be deceived, this banished lord wishes all of Dál Cruinne to bow under his rule. And if ye wonder what life would be with him for your lord, ask any who daily flee from his mercenaries and warbands to enter the gates of The Keep, seeking refuge. We partake of this venture to support those in Dál Gallain who oppose the tyrant Gallawain and by this, protect our own border."

Murmurs of agreement travelled through the gathered warriors.

"We will not lay siege to this caisteal but use other means to gain it. We shall inform you of your part in due time. I ken not all of you have fought before. I mean a real fight, not just amongst yourselves." He grinned and laughter rippled through the group. "Or in the fighting pits."

Some warriors cheered.

Oh! They loved his comments. They nudged each other and nodded knowingly.

Bàn leaned closer again. "Arlan is famous for his wins in the backstreet fights," he whispered. "Nae more o' that now."

Goosebumps crept up my arms. The chuckles and murmurs of approval soon settled, then Arlan walked up and down the platform. His miniature dragon, sitting proud on his sword handle, didn't once flinch at the crowd and Arlan's loud speech.

"A warrior knows fear. A fool does not. Warriors are not fools. They are acquainted with fear, not allowing it to master them, for they wield it like a weapon and become *its* master. It will be like a friend that keeps you alive—if you ignore its cowardice and solely listen to its sense." Arlan's voice carried right to the back where I stood.

It was as though he spoke only to me, and the hairs on my arms slowly rose.

"This ally will advise you of the time to retreat, or to stay and hold your ground. But then this advisor changes. Your fear is now your new companion—bravery." He pointed at them. "Did you hear that? In its essence fear is *always* fear. It is what you do with it that makes you either a coward or the hero."

He stood tall and his gaze ran across his troops.

"Be brave. Fight well, and smart, my warriors, for we ultimately fight for Dál Gaedhle." Arlan raised his fist high. "For Dál Gaedhle!"

The warriors shouted back, "For Dál Gaedhle!" Then without a pause they cried, "For Arlan MacEnoicht and Dál Gaedhle! For Arlan MacEnoicht and Dál Gaedhle!"

"MacEnoicht! MacEnoicht! MacEnoicht!" rang around the practice yard and the loud shouts jolted my hearing. Those holding shields banged their swords against them, adding a clash to the rumbling thuds of feet stomping in time with their chant. Deep male voices reverberated through my body, and the surrounding emotion sent tremors into my middle.

Wow! They loved him. They'd follow him anywhere. I'd sensed something great about him, even while still in the Other World. Now it was real and pounding through me.

The shouting finally died down and most warriors dispersed. Only Arlan's own close troop remained. They frowned, tugging and adjusting leather body armour. Douglas let out a curse. Other warriors slapped Arlan on the back as he passed them. He nodded, acknowledging each one. One or two reached out to pat Drayce, but the dragon flapped his wings in alarm and scurried out of their way.

"How goes my newest warrior, Bàn?" Arlan spoke from a few paces away.

"Ye were right about her weapon, but the master sword-crafter has improved it."

"And the warrior?" Arlan asked, as he came to a halt in front of me.

I scuffed the sand with my boots, my guts churning. Now I would hear what Bàn really thought.

"She's raw. Don't put her in the vanguard," Bàn said.

I flicked my gaze up to land on Bàn.

"I'm honest, my lady. I wish ye to survive."

Arlan's warm hand rested on my shoulder. "Rhiannon, I want ye safe, but I want ye with me. There must be a balance. Och"—he moved his finger between himself and Bàn— "it has taken us from boyhood to learn to fight. Dinnae expect to be battle-hardened in but a moment."

I sheathed my blade.

So, I wasn't good enough to be with Arlan at the front? I repressed a huff. But I *felt* ready. The *readiest* I'd ever be for now. I'd do my best... fight with the skills I'd learned in martial art class if my sword skills failed me. I'd fight my hardest, cleverest. I glanced aside to Arlan.

To defend Dál Gaedhle was why I came here... *mainly.*

Arlan's mouth curled in an awkward smile. "Eifion wishes to speak with me in the side chamber. Will ye come with me, Rhiannon?"

I nodded. Of course, I'd go with him. I'd do anything to be near him. We walked through the bailey yard then into the Great Hall. Bàn strode behind us.

Arlan leaned close. "It's not imperative that ye attend this meeting. I only wish for you to ... be with me." He lifted a shoulder, his cheeks pinking.

Oh, he felt the same, but his blush could mean he's wondering if it's okay with me or not.

Brave warrior... nervous man when it came to a woman. *Cute.*

Doors opened off one side of the Great Hall and Arlan led me into a room where wooden bench seats sat informally around a glowing peat fire. Eifion and another sage sat on one, and Kyle and his man on another. Eifion stood and approached Arlan. Drayce squeaked and flapped his wings at Eifion, who stopped two paces away.

"That's his friendly noise," Arlan reassured him.

"Has it grown?" Eifion's tough hairy eyebrows drew together.

"Aye, it's the good food of The Keep. He fits under my hair nae longer."

"What will you do with him?" Eifion asked. "Will you take him to battle?"

"Ah, of that I'm uncertain, for he protests greatly if I place him only paces from me."

"He's imprinted on you," I said.

Arlan, Eifion and the other sage looked at me, all faces questioning.

"He thinks you're his mother," I explained to Arlan.

Bàn laughed and Eifion's brows dipped further.

"Like a bird, I think." *Don't they know about this?*

Eifion raised the now single line of hoary brow and opened his eyes wider. *Better put him out of his misery.*

"The first thing they see after they hatch, no matter what it is, they think it's their mum and follow it, or him, for life."

"For life?" Arlan clicked his tongue.

The dragon scurried away from his sword and crept along to his forearm. He rested there, looking around at them all, and double blinking at me.

"A dragon for life could be advantageous or a disaster." Eifion's commanding tones rumbled. "We must seek to protect him from the interference of a mage."

Arlan just stared at Eifion.

Eifion coughed. "One of bad intent," he added under his breath.

"Shall we attend to the issues?"

I turned at Kyle's clipped speech.

194

Drayce flapped his wings and Arlan stepped closer to his brother, wiping the superior expression off Kyle's face. Kyle's lids lowered a fraction. He briefly set his hooded stare on Arlan, then slid his gaze to Eifion, looking down his long nose at him.

"I saw Eifion have intimate relations with this woman." Kyle pointed his finger at me.

"Pardon?" I took a step back, a flash like an electric shock running across my now heating neck.

Eifion started. Arlan shoved Drayce to his left shoulder and grasped his sword handle.

"Speak brother, and clarify your statement," Arlan ground out.

"When he was younger." Kyle gave a slight nod in Eifion's direction. "I was but a child and knew not what took place." His smugness disappeared for a moment and a soft chuckle escaped his lips.

Kyle was odd. I'd read somewhere that sometimes after a head injury people lost, what was it—discernment? —and became impulsive, oblivious to the impact their comments and actions had on others.

"Kyle has something to say, no doubt," I said, then addressed him. "But I assure you, Lord Kyle, it was not I."

Eifion stood stiff, eyes riveted on Kyle.

"When I was a lad here at The Keep"—he pointed to Eifion— "you had secret trysts with Aisling, the lady sage. Then she left. And now she is back. She is the same sage, Lord Eifion. What do you wish to do with her?"

Eifion covered his face with his hand and bowed his head.

"Perhaps this is a conversation for more private circumstances," Arlan said.

"No, no, no, Aisling is aware." Kyle stared at me.

"I'm *not* Aisling." I had to stop myself from shouting.

"Aye, ye have violet eyes and long auburn hair." Kyle spoke with certainty. "You are she."

"Just think about it, Kyle. If I were her, how old would I be?"

Kyle's mouth opened and closed, his gaze searching the space just above my head.

"Can we attend to the matter of this meeting, Eifion?" Arlan's shoulders eased, and he lowered his hand from his sword. "Kyle has accomplished what he set out to do." Arlan's nostrils flared. "But why he wishes to upset people so, is beyond me."

I flicked my gaze between Arlan and Kyle, my insides twisting.

Boy, his brother is a problem!

Kyle seemed so intent on putting Arlan in his place. Maybe I shouldn't be so judgemental—he'd had a head injury, after all. I stood there scrunching my mouth, the heat in my face from his accusations to me—as Aisling—now dissipating. Kyle was far from the loving, protective big brother.

The expressions that'd tortured Arlan's face in the Great Hall now came back to me.

Ahh. Kyle's announcement that Arlan's participation in the Quest was null and void had sparked them. Arlan's painful look had only lasted a few seconds, but it now made *so* much sense.

Would Kyle care if he ruined Arlan's life? He was slandering those close and important to Arlan. Even if it was true about Eifion and this Aisling. Now that Arlan had won

195

the position of high king, had Kyle even thought twice about calling into question the integrity of the new àrd rìgh's advisory sage? I narrowed my eyes.

Doubt it.

Kyle's man placed his hand on Kyle's forearm, probably hoping to distract his master from his current line of thought. Kyle snatched his arm away.

"Nae, I am not finished. Arlan." He directed the full force of his now hoarse voice at Arlan. "I am clan chieftain, am I not?"

Arlan did not answer but bore his stare into Kyle.

"I am the eldest!" Kyle said. "I am head of the clan."

"The question of clan chief is exactly what I wish to discuss with you both." Eifion had removed his hands from his paled face.

Arlan's shoulders lowered a fraction.

"The sage council has discussed your situation," Eifion continued. "Lord Kyle will attend to the chiefly duties of Clan MacEnoicht, assisted by Glen, your castellan, plus an advisory sage, Sage Alder." Eifion gestured to the other sage present. "While you, Lord Arlan, are attending to the duties of the àrd rìgh."

Arlan stood the tiniest bit straighter, and the edges of his mouth relaxed. "This is excellent, Eifion," he said. "Kyle, would ye be content with that? Ye can be in charge of the lands and its produce. The administration of such." Arlan spoke with relief in his voice.

Kyle sat taller; his haughtiness accentuated by his still hooded eyes. "Aye, I would be." He glanced at Sage Alder, an approving expression emerging on his face.

Arlan untied the ornamented belt from around his waist and handed it to Kyle, who took it. Kyle allowed his man to assist him to stand, nodded to all then left.

"He's a handful after his head injury," I commented into the quiet circle.

Arlan sighed. "Kyle has always been difficult."

"Ye are generous to your brother," Eifion spoke to Arlan. "The sages who are expert in healing believe he will never be himself again," he said to me. "Thus, their negating any protests he has made regarding the Quest." His voice held strain and his face was now a healthier shade. "I leave tomorrow. I head north." Eifion turned away, his actions slow. So far, he'd moved spritely for a man his age.

Hmm. Kyle's accusations must've battered him. Was he ashamed of his relationship with Aisling, or had she really meant something to him?

"Will ye be anywhere near the Sage Hold of the Healers?" Arlan asked. "For I wish to give them a gift in return for the care both Kyle and I have received from their healer sages."

"I could head that way. It is close to the traditional clan lands belonging to those of whom I propose to enquire about"—he glanced at me— "that of which we spoke, Arlan."

"That is braw, Eifion. I shall get the gift organised to accompany you and your warrior guard."

"Ye may meet the Blind Lady Sage," Bàn said.

Eifion frowned. "Ye are fond of her, Bàn. What is her name?"

"Giorsal."

"That means *grey hair*. What is her real name?"

"They know her as such." Bàn lifted a shoulder and let it fall. "Ye will find her, and if she's well enough to take visitors, they might let ye see her."

"Giorsal told me not to harm this one." Arlan's dragon clambered over his sword handle again.

"Did she, now?" Eifion raised a brow.

"She named Arlan warrior king"—Bàn lifted his chin in Arlan's direction— "If ye recall."

"Well, maybe I shall endeavour to meet with her."

THIRTY-TWO

— • —

There is more to this world than that which is seen.
It sits behind the surface, lingering beyond the edges of sight.

BOOK OF LIGHT
MAGE TEXT. DATE OF SCRIBING UNKNOWN
BOOK LOST IN ANTIQUITY

The World of Dál Cruinne
Post Dragon Wars Year 6083
Eastern Clanlands of Dál Gallain
MacEnoicht Camp, Base of Caisteal Monsae

It'd taken a week to get here.

Saddle sore was not anywhere near the way to describe the ache in my seat and the stretch in my inner thighs—even with all the riding I'd done in the past two years. On dismounting at the end of the first day's ride, my right leg stuck on my white mare's rump as I drew it over. Arlan took the time to help me off, despite his need to attend discussions and plans.

I'd bedded down next to Arlan's warriors on my thin bed roll, the ground hard on my sore muscles and the cold seeping through. Leigh returned from one last check of the horses.

"Your mare has settled well for one not used to such a long trek. Nor being in a warband." He cocked his head. "I did nae ken ye were to warrior when I chose the mare for you. I beg your pardon for such, Lady Rhiannon."

"No, don't feel bad about it. She's such a gentle soul. I love her already." I gave a nervous chuckle. "I guess we both have to get used to being in a warband."

The breeze sighed in the treetops contrasting with the deep silence of the dark pool of sky above. It glistened with twinkling heavenly bodies. The stars and planets were the same awesome but tranquil beauty as in the Other World.

The hushed war council conversation drifted across from the fire. Arlan discussed with Vygeas, Leyna, and Leuchars the options for entering the Monsae castle undiscovered.

"It's imperative we stop Gallawain in his tracks," Arlan's deep voice rumbled over to me. "The boundary of your Monsae lands, Lady Leyna, being right where Dál Gallain meets Dál Gaedhle."

"Aye." Leyna's soft feminine tones now held a hard edge.

"If he retains the caisteal, it will nae take much for that bassa of a tyrant to barge through to our lands." Leuchars' gruffness sent a shiver through me.

I steadied my breathing. This was serious stuff. This war would be life and death. Not like in a dojo with blunt weapons and *tapping out* to show you submitted.

No one *submitted* here. You just died.

Cool night air brushed my arms and wood smoke wafted past my nostrils while the war council made strategies and escape plans. Leyna had sent word back to her faithful warrior clansmen informing them of their orders for their part of storming this caisteal. From the comments I'd managed to hear while Arlan and his team spoke around the campfire, good old Plan A and Plan B were even the *modus operandi* in Dál Cruinne. The cold settling on my bare skin met a spark within. I would be in an actual battle. And the *life and death* of it bellowed the spark to heated coals. I lay immobile, but my mind went through my fighting forms and reacted to every combat scenario I could think of.

The enemy would be brawny, tall, powerfully built men or women able to smash me to the ground with a swipe. I ran through everything I'd ever seen on YouTube, and all that Bàn had taught me about swordplay, as he called it. *Huh.* It was far from playing.

I didn't have the strength of most of the warrior women here, and honestly, I'd hate to fight even one of them. Especially Adele. But I could disarm someone. Kick and punch. If my sword skills weren't working, I'd resort to those I *was* proficient in.

I squeezed my eyes tight. Perhaps I'd surprise my opponent... no, my *enemy*... and gain the advantage that way.

Arlan had given me a dagger from the trunk in his room. I'd keep that tucked in my belt always. Tomorrow we'd reach Monsae, where I'd leave behind Rhiannon, the quiet librarian, and be reborn... a warrior.

Sweat collected and dribbled between my shoulder blades and down my back. The tunic and leather armour were stifling in the heat of another long day's ride. I squinted against the glare of the lowering sun. Arlan gave orders for silence. He and Leyna headed the combined warband through a forest, where we halted. Seagulls soared overhead, and once the horse tread hushed, the crashing of breakers came rhythmically through the trees.

Arlan and Leuchars dismounted, and the older man trod carefully to the second warband at the back of the queue of warriors two abreast to whisper last-minute orders. All slid off their horses, and I stood with Arlan's warriors.

"A small meal now," Arlan whispered. "Then we wait till night falls fully. Aiden will watch our horses and keep them ready. He's good at that, so I'm told."

"The entry is at the base of the hill, behind a copse," Leynarve continued in a hushed tone. "We go in there, with one or two to guard, for it is the best exit if we need to retreat. My warrior clansmen will enter by the eastward tunnel, which is also hidden and known to my war chief."

I searched the surrounds but found no evidence of a caisteal nearby. The tree foliage, thick with spring's life, chattered in the breeze that blew above our huddled group.

"Leuchars' warband will distract the attention of Ciarán's warriors," Arlan said, "keeping their archers occupied on the far side of the caisteal while we enter through the tunnel Lady Leynarve will find for us."

A young lad acting in the quarter master role, handed out cheese, dried meat, and bread from the stores on the pack horses and all ate in silence. Warriors tweaked leather armour, checked weapons, and allowed their eyes to adjust to the diminishing light. My armour was stiff and hard, like new shoes needing breaking in. It rubbed under my arms, even with the thick tunic close to my skin. That was the point of the hard leather that rubbed me, I guessed—for protection.

The sky dimmed of day and the lights of night appeared. High above me, sitting proud on the highest hill around, was a high square castle—Caisteal Monsae. Torches burning in sconces on the caisteal walls highlighted its rose sandstone, glowing it a dusky pink. A dark wall ran along the front of it a step lower. Not far below this, torches flickered at what would be the gatehouse. The fortress was still at least a half a mile away.

"We walk the rest." Arlan spoke quietly into my ear. "Night is our stealth. Our horses are too noisy for our intentions."

"Guerrilla tactics," I said.

"Aye?" He stood in shadow, holding my arm, his expression undecipherable, but his tone one of distracted concern.

Yep, he's got stacks on his mind. I mustn't side-track him. He shouldn't be worrying about me. He had a job to do.

Drayce squeaked and clambered down Arlan's arm, coming closer to me. I stopped my impulse to gasp in pleasure at this friendly action and stroked its cool, knobbly head instead. Vygeas came to Arlan's side, silent as a shadow in the deepening night and twice as dark.

"It is time, Lord Arlan." His words were quieter than a whisper.

"Come." Arlan tugged me to a walk and Drayce crawled back to his shoulder.

Arlan led his warriors, and I trekked a pace behind him along a clear path with no debris nor leaf litter to alert the enemy with snaps of broken twigs or slippery stumbles, and the trees above us provided extra cover. The other troop, holding shields and swords tight to dampen sound, moved away and to the opposite side of the fortress looming above. I sensed rather than heard their progress.

Next to a small wood, Leyna stopped at a grassy bank, the base of the caisteal's embankment, and we all halted behind her. At a tree surrounded by long overgrown grass, she rummaged through the undergrowth and then pulled. A wooden creak sounded like crashing thunder in the still night. I froze, my hearing stretching for any corresponding noise of recognition coming from the fortress above. None came.

In the dark, Vygeas shook his head and Arlan's shadowed form relaxed a fraction.

Vygeas was a weird man. He knew things but didn't want to share with me how he did. Didn't he trust me? Others spoke of his awesomeness as a fighter—although they never used that expression. Maybe I'd get to see him in action tonight.

Leyna entered the hidden doorway, and after a spark, torchlight glowed within revealing a tunnel carved through the base rock.

"Now we begin," Vygeas whispered, and he and Leyna stepped in.

Arlan turned to me, his dragon's head hovering close to my face.

"I wish you to stay here and mind Drayce," he whispered while his warriors filed past.

"You mean you don't want me in this at all?" My hackles rose a touch.

He gave a slight nod and moved closer. "I don't want you harmed. It's too soon for you."

I opened my mouth to protest, but my loud arguments against his decision would ring in the pre-attack hush. Besides, Bàn's opinion of my fighting skills now rang in my head.

"And I wish not my dragon to be sliced." Arlan ignored my intake of breath. "He sits close to my sword and... May I try something?" He unbuckled one side of his leather armour and then the top ties of the bulky tunic underneath, releasing a waft of his body's musky male aroma. "It works with the hounds, so it may do so for a dragon." He took a pace nearer. "I need to cover you with my scent."

Oh, Arlan was now so close, all thoughts of the imminent battle fled my mind. He wrapped his arms around me, chasing away the niggle in my gut that'd danced with the prickle on my skin. He brought me against his chest, now bared where he'd pulled his tunic partially aside. Arlan gently pressed my face and bare neck into him. His heart thundered beneath his ribs, his chest hairs crinkled against my ear, and his body heat warmed me.

This is so good.

"Are you doing this to get a hug?" My whisper faltered.

Drayce squeaked and small feet trod through my hair, his claws scratching my scalp as he clambered from Arlan to my shoulder. He was now the size of a large cat, and his weight rested heavily on me.

Arlan leaned back a bit. "There, it may work," he whispered, still holding me.

"Your speech was for me, wasn't it?" My shoulders drooped a little.

In the shadows, his head wiggled from side to side. "Och aye, it was. But some warriors I chose haven't seen battle. I have, and Leuchars, and Muir..."

"These warriors are fearless," I breathed out in a gush, still leaning close to him.

"Nae, dinnae believe that. It's when ye are fearful that ye must be brave." He glanced behind.

War cries carried from the other side of Caisteal Monsae. A Gallawain guard on the high turret of the main fortress yelled a warning, slashing cold down my spine.

"Vygeas has given the *all clear*." Bàn's loud whisper came from the entrance. "Those inside are unaware of our presence. Or so he says."

Arlan released me and tied up his tunic, leaving me with Drayce wobbling on my shoulder.

"No, Drayce." He put his palm up toward his dragon. "Stay."

He buckled his leather armour at the shoulder while I secured the buckles at his waist. I stepped back. Drayce squeaked in my ear and his claws gripped tighter, the clamp coming through my padded tunic at the shoulder.

"Stay here, Rhiannon. Guard this exit." He kept his hand up for Drayce to stay. "Keep out of the way. If anything goes awry, this is our way out. If we don't come out for you and... all is lost, take the horses and flee with Aiden."

"Flee?" My whisper was hoarse. "I'll stay and fight."

"Nae. Go." Arlan shook his head, now silhouetted against the light in the tunnel. "If I'm... overcome... save yourself."

Bàn stepped beside him. "We *must* go."

Arlan turned. My urge to follow him was as powerful as Drayce's, and I lifted my hand to the dragon to keep him on my shoulder, and myself in place.

"What if you don't return?" I was asking more than I was saying, and he would know it.

He faced me. "Go home." He spun into the tunnel and entered with Bàn on his heels. He meant back to the Other World.

Never.

They might take him hostage... demand a ransom. They did that here. His head held more value on his neck than on a spike.

And... "I couldn't be without him," I whispered into the night.

I'd ride to The Keep and get negotiations going. My brow cooled with sweat. I swallowed down bile and pushed those thoughts away, then turned my mind to fighting.

Drayce flapped his wings, and I held him down.

"Stay!" I deepened my voice as best I could. The dragon settled and squeaked and gecko-clicked mournfully then tucked his rough head into the side of my cheek. I leaned into the cool creature, sharing my warmth with him.

Then carefully drew my sword from its sheath... and waited.

THIRTY-THREE

— • —

When the pillars are struck, the world will crumble.
When good is good nae more, all will fall.

VISIONS AND SAYINGS OF THE BLIND LADY SAGE

The World of Dál Cruinne
Post Dragon Wars Year 6083
Eastern Clanlands of Dál Gallain
Caisteal Monsae

Findlay stood on the wall head at the top of the caisteal's battlement.

He leaned forward and rested his arms on the stone parapet, its cold seeping through the quilted sleeves of his padded gambeson.

Aye, Caisteal Monsae was quite the fortress, despite almost six years of abandonment.

He searched the night sky. An owl called in the forest beneath while the wind sighed through the pines. The stars were so clear and seemed to be so close he could touch them. For him, they'd only ever been bright and well defined like this on Earth that rare occasion he went camping in the Scottish Highlands years ago on a hill walking trip with Brenda.

For the first time since arriving at Lord Ciarán's door, the man had truly trusted him. Findlay shrugged. *Perhaps.* Ciarán had ordered him to stay by his side while they took the caisteal. A twinge of remorse raised its ugly head for those poor clansmen warriors who still regarded themselves part of Monsae! Lord Ciarán's mercenaries had finished off their fierce, faithful but futile attempts in no time, then sent the survivors cowering.

Lord Ciarán had returned to his tower, but not before appointing him official steward of this caisteal. Of course, Lord Ciarán had left a warrior to be war chief.

Findlay grunted. He wasn't much good at warrior-ing. He'd found he was okay on a horse, but when it came to a fight, he preferred a gun. That weapon of choice was out until Lord Ciarán could get his head around what he meant by gunpowder and how the lord could use it in the battles he'd planned. If Lord Ciarán allowed Findlay to return to Earth and retrieve some... but no. He didn't trust Findlay unsupervised through a portal. Their trip to the portal by the big river in the east, which opened up to the Zulu Wars, had proved that.

Bram the magician—*mage*—had discovered more portals. Lord Ciarán regarded these as opportunities, but would give no more away. There was a lot the man wouldn't reveal—yet. But he would bide his time and find out more about this MacEnoicht character, the son of an old adversary, who got up Lord Ciarán's nose so easily. And that assassin Lord Ciarán kept getting stuck on, who was helping this enemy with dragons. Also, something had happened when Bram had used a dragon to get rid of the high king in the west of this place. The dragon event had happened just prior to his arrival. But none spoke of it.

Well, not to him, anyway.

Findlay grunted. Anywhere you could find yourself, there was always politics.

He sighed. He still went in blind on many things, but so far, he'd stayed alive. And that was the name of *this* game. Information was power, though, and if he was going to continue to survive, he really needed to discover the whole story.

When he'd peered into this beautiful world behind Miss Rhiannon Ferguson on the verge of passing through the portal, he'd believed it would be paradise.

Wrong.

If he'd turned left instead of right once through that portal, he'd be in Dál Gaedhle, not Dál Gallain, and his life could've been a whole different story.

But he was here. In Lord Ciarán's service.

There was good and bad in this paradise, just like any world, he supposed. Lord Ciarán's methods weren't always the kindest though. Perhaps he wasn't any worse—or any better—than the scum Findlay used to put away.

This was a violent world. He'd seen that. Findlay snorted. Wasn't Earth a violent place? And the belief that good will always win just a fantasy? Because badness was the victor the majority of the time.

Sometimes it seemed like good would never win, and those who strived for it—like himself—were severely battered in the process.

So, what was the point of being on the side of good?

Findlay sighed heavily again, then returned his stare to the dark night sky.

Imperfect as this perfect world was, Lord Ciarán proceeded with his plans unrestrained by frustrating protocols and paperwork. An old but familiar buzz had stirred inside Findlay—a buzz he hadn't felt for a very long time. One he'd longed to feel again. So, he would grasp his circumstances by the throat, and make the most of them.

Roaring, like a war cry, rose from below the front bailey wall. The warrior beside him leaned over the battlement and swore.

"What is it?" he asked. "Are those clansmen back?"

"Aye. Fools." The warrior threw the gruff comment over his shoulder, then ran down the stairs to the main hall of the caisteal's keep. "Send the archers to the bailey wall!" he yelled down the stairway.

The warrior's warning shouts rang up the stairs behind him, along with the clatter of arms taken up and drawn. Findlay peered out into the night. Apart from the Highland battle cries that would chill a lesser man's soul, no other noises caught Findlay's ears. He'd been here before, and Lord Ciarán's warriors would deal with it.

He ran down the stairs. The ring of metal on metal ricocheted up the stairwell and out from the doors of the main hall below.

What? How had they got in so quickly? He scooted past a narrow window where the roaring from outside came through. More than one group?

No!

Disbelief echoed through his mind like the battle screams reverberating around him.

Findlay pressed his back to the wall, the cool from the stone kept pace with the ice dancing along each vertebrae. Warriors tore past him, joining their pals in the main hall. All he had was a dirk.

And knowledge.

Just as well castles had always fascinated him, with their secret passages and tunnels and escape routes. He'd found one here in Monsae quite by accident.

Another pair of warriors clattered past with arrows notched on bows, heading up to the battlement at the top of the tower.

"Get ye somewhere safe, Findlay," the older one cried, hurtling by.

Don't need to tell me twice.

Findlay darted down the stairs, pausing at the doorway to the main hall. Grunts and cries intermingling with the ring of sword on sword emanated from the opening. Prickling crawled across Findlay's scalp. He crept past the doorway, peeking into the hall.

Warriors, both men and women, strove against each other. Sweat ran down grim faces. A tall man with long, black hair and his back to Findlay, thrashed his sword at one of Lord Ciarán's men. The face of one of the enemies, a woman, was familiar. Findlay searched the others. Aye, there was one more he'd also seen previously.

Miss Ferguson's *cousins.*

The massive black-haired one turned in this mêlée, keeping his attention on his current foe with a broadsword. He now faced Findlay.

Miss Ferguson's boyfriend!

Oh! It all made sense now. Her reason for resisting a police watch on her house. This big guy turning up would surely have caused a stir.

One of the invading warriors, wearing dark grey, spun and slashed like the devil. Findlay's feet wouldn't move from the spot, nor could he take his eyes off this man who thrust and stabbed and hacked one opponent after the other, his blade a mere blur. His opposing swordsmen would barely move, and the man was there with a retort. His anticipation of his opponent's moves was faster than *lightning fast.*

A warrior belonging to Lord Ciarán, having just dispatched a Dál Gaedhle warrior, spun to be behind Miss Ferguson's boyfriend. In this close proximity, he lifted a dagger—a thin stiletto, like a misericord, but it would be no mercy killing. An assassination, going by his determined expression.

On the opposite side of the room, the grey-clad one had already set his scarred face toward the warrior with the dagger. His flying sword became a spear, stabbing the neck of Lord Ciarán's warrior. Blood gushed from beneath a face with eyes wide and mouth dropping open.

Findlay had seen enough. He willed his legs to move then ran down the steps and along to the kitchen with sweat dripping down his temples and a thankfulness in his heart.

He made a sharp left to bring him to the bread kitchen. Beside the oven, the entrance to what should be a clandestine tunnel, stood wide open and a breeze filled with fresh woodland scents blew across his face. On his previous encounter with the passageway, he'd walked to the end but had come to a wooden door. He'd shouldered it, but it hadn't budged. Then he'd searched for the door outside without success. It seemed someone else has succeeded here where he had failed.

Footsteps came behind him. He spun, pulling his dirk from his belt. One of Lord Ciarán's men grunted recognition. His lowered his blade.

"They must've come in this tunnel," Findlay said. "I've only a dirk. Come with me. There could be more of the enemy waiting to come in. At least if we go this way, we can cut any means of their escape."

Along the corridor beside the kitchens, boot tread thundered from the passage that contained the private apartments. Findlay peered round the corner. Dál Gaedhle warriors brandishing their weapons screamed toward where Findlay stood. Where had *they* come from?

Another secret passage?

The man beside him hesitated.

"Come." Findlay grasped the Gallawain warrior's arm. "We'll check the tunnel and block their escape, aye?"

Findlay grabbed a torch from the sconce and stepped into the narrow passage, the stairs inclining steeply. The draft blew his torch wildly and night calls echoed in from outside. A figure hovered in the darkness at the end of the tunnel.

He drew nearer, his torch lighting the exit where a warrior dressed in leather armour stood with some creature sitting on her shoulder. She peered in, attracted by the light, her expression hardening as he drew near. The woman yelled a command and moved off out of Findlay's line of sight.

He paused, pressing his back to the wall, allowing the warrior with him to go first. Gallawain's man strode past, weapon drawn, and a grim look on his face. Findlay followed and stayed at the tunnel's end, allowing the warriors to engage. He'd keep out of the way.

Damn. The thick bush just outside the secret entrance blocked his route past them.

The Dál Gaedhle warrior's sword flew, glinting in the light of Findlay's torch. The odd-looking creature that had been on her shoulder was now nowhere in sight. She matched the Dál Gallain swordsman's strikes blow for blow. Cold hit Findlay's stomach. *He'd* have to fight her off if she defeated Lord Ciarán's warrior.

The man held his ground, thudding down on the woman's sword. Their blades connected; sharp metallic ringing reverberated through the surrounding wood.

If Findlay stepped into this clash, he'd risk injury to himself. He wasn't proficient in sword fighting. Definitely not. He'd get in the way or get himself killed and be of no help to anyone.

And be dead.

The Gallawain warrior brought his blade down in a wide arc. His combatant caught his sword with her own, stepping in and keeping to the arc of the travelling sword, halting it very close to herself and the warrior. It was hard to tell, but she seemed to change her grasp on her sword, go for something at her belt. Then Ciarán's man screamed into the Dál Gaedhle warrior's face. Blood spouted from his thigh, pumping his life onto the ground.

The Dál Gaedhle warrior grunted and panted with her exertion. She pulled back a long dagger from under the apron section of her opponent's leather armour. The blade was black with blood.

Findlay gasped, gripping his weapon's handle tighter.

He'd be next. *And I only have a dirk!*

This woman was *glorious*, though. Her fighting was strong, clever. Gutsy. A heat rose within him, but he pushed it down. Not the time to be turned-on by a warrior chick!

"Sorry," she whispered, pushing the wounded man off balance.

Lord Ciarán's warrior staggered and fell.

She spun to face Findlay, the bloodied dagger and sword shaking in her hands, and her breath spurts of white mist in the cool night air. Her plaited hair glowed amber in the torchlight. Her wide-open eyes were violet.

And she'd spoken in English.

"Miss Ferguson?"

She held her sword and dagger in readiness, then lunged toward him.

"Stop!" he shouted in English.

Dropping the burning torch, he gripped his dirk with both hands, holding it up to block. Then he side stepped, only barely dodging her blow. He headed at a run toward the tree line. Her blade edge thumped on his leather armour at the back shoulder.

"Miss Rhiannon Ferguson, it's Sergeant Findlay. The detective. I'm your friend!" he screamed; his mouth thick around the English.

He swung away and turned. The light from the torch still burned at the exit behind her. She was a mere silhouette.

"Huh? What?" She'd now stopped, her panting voice also awkward around the English. "How?" she asked, her pitch now a notch higher.

"I followed you through the portal. Where've you been for the past two months?"

"Two months?" She shook her head. "I've been here about ten days."

"Really?" His pulse raced in his ears, throwing his comprehension slightly off.

"Yeah, the timelines are a bit screwed." She stood taller. "What are you doing with Ciarán's men? We'll rescue you." She nodded enthusiastically.

"Ah, no." He kept his hand round his dirk and took a pace to his right, where the torchlight now caught the smooth contours of her features.

"No?" She angled her head to the side, her eyes narrowing behind long-lashed lids.

Goodness me! She was still a beautiful woman... despite aligning herself with the pain in Lord Ciarán's rear.

"The man's brilliant—" he began.

"So I've heard"—her words crossed his— "but he's also evil."

He tweaked his head and lifted a shoulder. "That may be a matter of opinion. Why don't you come with *me*?"

Rhiannon gasped, and she adjusted the grip on her sword. "No, I can't. I'm with... the winning side."

"Och, maybe." He shrugged. "Lord Ciarán has some interesting things planned. He's got portals that go all over the place and all over time. I've seen them." *Well, one.* "You're on this MacEnoicht's team, aye?"

"Detective, don't be with Ciarán Gallawain. Arlan will beat him."

"First name basis, huh? You're in closer than I thought." The image of the black-haired warrior upstairs flashed through his mind. "Ah! Arlan MacEnoicht is your boyfriend, isn't he?"

Rhiannon's mouth shut tight, and her eyes hardened.

Footsteps echoed down the tunnel toward him.

"Time to part company. If you ever change your mind, I'll put in a good word," he said.

"Never." She grimaced, locking her stare on him.

He turned and ran.

A male voice spoke in a commanding tone from the tunnel, by Findlay didn't catch it.

"Aye," she answered the order.

The wind caught her grunt of frustration, then used it to chase him through the wood. A deep, clicking animal call came from a nearby tree.

Thirty-Four

*When the battle is lost
'Tis time to decide.
Flee with the wise
Or fall among the brave.*

*WARRIOR SAGE TAPAÌDH
(4009-4059 POST DRAGON WARS)*

**The World of Dál Cruinne
Post Dragon Wars Year 6083
Eastern Clanlands of Dál Gallain
Below Caisteal Monsae**

Findlay ran.

Screaming battle cries boomed from the windows and battlements. Dál Gaedhle warrior shouts echoed at Findlay's back while he tore through the wood behind the caisteal in the inky night.

Shudders sprinted to his core. He'd caught Rhiannon in the middle of battle-lust, and nearly worn it.

That was too close.

He brushed low-hanging branches away from his face and sped on into the dark forest, leaving the shouts and clamour of the stormed caisteal far behind. He slowed to a stop. His legs shook and calves burned. Breathing like a steam engine, he leaned on his thighs and let his pounding heart recover.

So, Arlan MacEnoicht was the boyfriend. *It all fell into place now.*

Something rustled in the trees nearby and a horse whinnied. Findlay straightened, his breathing almost back to normal. He still held his dirk, and he led with it as he approached the shadow of two men leading their mounts.

"Nae, Lord Kyle." The strained speech of a man deferring to another came across from the shadowed figures. "The caisteal is overcome. It is best we wait here until we know who the victor is," the man begged.

"I wish to be there," the other figure replied. "We will draw closer!" The timbre and quality of his voice, and his arrogant tone, were familiar.

Foot tread approached on Findlay's right, so he spun. The starlight glimmer of night revealed one of Lord Ciarán's men. With his sword at the ready, he strode past Findlay, not noticing him, and headed straight for the loud speech of the bossy-sounding man.

"Wait," Findlay called.

The warrior turned back. "Lord Findlay?"

"Aye. But who are they?" He pointed to the horsemen. "Stay your hand. We'll investigate."

"Who goes there?" By the softly nickering horses, the one with the haughty voice spoke in Findlay's direction.

Findlay walked with the warrior to the men by their mounts.

"More's the point, who are you?" Findlay directed the tip of his dirk at the men.

The one on the right, the servant-sounding one, reached for his sword and Lord Ciarán's warrior stepped closer, brandishing the point of his in the man's face and grabbing the lead reins from his grasp.

"How dare—?" the haughty one began, but it turned into a yelp as the warrior wrenched his mount's reins from his hand too.

"I'd prefer if you lived long enough to at least tell me your name, where you're from, and why you're here," Findlay said.

"I am Lord Kyle—"

"Hush, my lord," the man next to him hissed.

"Lord Kyle MacEnoicht?" the warrior asked.

"No, my lord is a Gallawain," his servant answered, speaking over the beginning of whatever his master was about to say.

"Ye shall wish to accompany us, then." The warrior kept his sword upraised.

Behind Findlay, cheers arose, the echoes spreading throughout the forest on the chilly night air. He exchanged glances with his warrior.

"Give us yer weapons and yer steeds," the warrior ordered. "We must make haste."

"Actually, mount behind us," Findlay said. "We need a ride out of here, but we'll bring these two with us."

He mounted, then his warrior pushed the haughty one into the saddle behind him. His companion took the manservant's mount and ordered him to sit behind. Ignoring the young lord's protests, Findlay kicked the horse to a canter out of the woods. The warrior followed with the lord's servant. The lord gripped feebly to Findlay's shoulder, and he had no sense of the need to remain quiet under the circumstances. Findlay elbowed him to silence.

"We'll return to Lord Ciarán's Tower the long way around," Findlay said.

They cleared the forest at a walk. The weak light from the distant caisteal lit them briefly, and the warrior stared past Findlay at the young lord mounted behind him.

"*Dragon's teeth*, but there is a strong family resemblance in the Gallawain clan, is there no', Lord Findlay?"

Findlay twisted in the saddle, then started. In the poor light, eyes that could be grey regarded him with a hooded expression Findlay had encountered every day since meeting Lord Ciarán. Fatigue lined his features, and the man was a weakling, but as best Findlay could tell, this one was driven by a determination from within that rang similar to another's. Findlay gripped the reins, turned, and dug his heels in the horse's flank.

Aye, Lord Ciarán would welcome meeting this one.

THIRTY-FIVE

— • —

Let the sword decide.
For it will have its say.

WARRIOR SAGE TAPAÌDH
(4009-4059 POST DRAGON WARS)

The World of Dál Cruinne
Post Dragon Wars Year 6083
Eastern Clanlands of Dál Gallain
Caisteal Monsae

Shouting settled and war cries ceased.

The ringing of steel on steel echoed no longer from the caisteal and my breathing, rhythmical and steady, filled my hearing.

Angus, whose presence as he ran down the tunnel had chased Findlay off, had ordered me to stay put until someone came for me. He'd nodded and grunted, impressed by the body lying on the ground just outside the tunnel. He'd returned inside, leaving me to guard alone.

Oh. He must've trusted me.

I turned away from the Dál Gallain warrior, splitting my attention between the tunnel exit and the surrounding forest edge. He'd groaned his last, moments before. The metallic scent of blood rose from him, and a rusty taste sat on my tongue. *Messy.* All this killing. His blood covered my trembling dagger hand and halfway up my forearm, and my tunic sleeve stuck to my skin where it'd soaked through.

Shouts came over the battlements. The clatter of horses' hooves headed in an easterly direction, and cheering echoed off the caisteal walls.

I stood tall, releasing my body from a fighting stance.

We had won? Already? That was too quick, surely.

Footfall marched along the tunnel and a light grew brighter.

"Rhiannon!" Morrigan exited the secret tunnel then glanced at the body beside me. "Och, I see ye have had your first kill. Arlan will be pleased." In the flickering torchlight, her grin-filled, blood-splattered face danced in ghoulish shadow. She took me by the wrist. "Come wipe the mess off your weapons. It spoils the inside of a sheath to put them away in such condition."

How can Morrigan be so calm and commanding?

"The caisteal is regained," Morrigan said. "It is true Monsae once more and Lord Arlan chases those who fled. Och, ye are shaking."

I wiped my sword and dagger in the long grass by the bank. They seemed clean enough in the poor torchlight, so I re-sheathed them, then ran my quivering hands and wrists along a patch of grass.

"The shaking takes some time to settle for women warriors, we have found. Men calm so much sooner." She shrugged. "I know not why. Come inside." Morrigan grasped my hand, and I followed. My insides shook with a persistent but gentle tremor and pounding rang in my temples. The tunnel filled my vision, looming long and narrow ahead of me.

The secret passage was steep, leading to steps, and then opened to a kitchen. Loud cries of jubilation, mingling with groans, echoed out of a large doorway further along. Adele stepped from it, dragging something behind her.

"We will place the slain in the bailey yard," she said to Morrigan and continued out the hall. The thing she was dragging was a lifeless body. "Help us clear the hall, you two."

My legs stopped mid-stride. Morrigan turned into the main hall, disappearing from my view. I tried to swallow, my mouth as dry as an empty swimming pool. I placed my hand on the closest wall, just to feel something real. The caisteal inner walls were a pink-tinged sandstone and gritty beneath my fingers. Quite attractive. It had markings, like the streaks in marble.

I drew closer—blood spatter.

I gulped, pushing a trickle of saliva down the dry swimming pool. Out of the corner of my eye, Morrigan came into view exiting the room and dragging another dead body. She dumped it outside the door and strode over to me.

"I can't... can't do this, Morrigan." I pressed my lips tight.

Morrigan's head tilted, and her expression softened. For a warrior who'd just killed and now disposed of bodies, she was the picture of compassion.

"I shall assign you another task. Lady Monsae has given Lord Arlan a private chamber in the passage yonder." She pointed to the first room in the hallway. The door was open, revealing a space empty of people. "His wounds will need tending. Get some water from—"

"Arlan's wounded?" My pulse spiked. "How bad?"

"Och, not very," Morrigan answered. "But his burns... Lady Leynarve is too pre-occupied to attend this night. Ye can do it, Rhiannon. Lord Arlan will need you."

So, according to Morrigan, Arlan was okay. I set my mind on what I'd need to tend his wounds... and off removing the dead from the hall.

213

I returned to the kitchen and found a bowl, and a small kettle of boiled water, and some salt. In a linen-press of sorts, I grabbed some clean cloths. On my way back to Arlan's room, I passed bloodied Monsae clansman warriors. Vygeas and Leynarve spoke quietly to them. I hurried into Arlan's room, closed the door, shutting out the gore and the stench of old sweaty fear and blood. I closed my eyes tight.

This was it. This was war.

And it wasn't even a large battle. I slumped against the door.

Get a grip, girl! You signed up for this.

I pulled in a breath and released it slowly, then opened my eyes. The chamber had a fireplace, a wide bed with fresh linen, a table and chair, but no rugs or tapestries. A wrought iron three-piece candelabra sat on the table and the only light in the room came from one lighted candle. It illuminated the room's contents in a soft glow. The dark wood furniture, the white sheets and the night poking through the window were like an old black and white movie, all adding to my surreal sense of things.

I lit the other candles and then took one to the fireplace, where kindling and wood were set ready. I knelt and tickled the soft stringy dried moss with the candle's flame, my hand steadier now. The kindling smouldered and caught the twigs and thicker pieces. I lifted my vision to the ceiling, which glowed with the new flames coming to life. My shadow jumped like a crazy animal.

"Oh!" I clamped my hand on my mouth. "Drayce!"

I ran to the window and flung open the panes. The forest sat to my right below the mound of the caisteal. He would still be in a tree if he'd obeyed when I'd commanded him to *stay*.

"Drayce!"

The murmurs of warriors and night calls of wildlife rose to me. But no dragon.

Arlan gave me one job: to watch Drayce. How could I have failed...?

I ran and opened the door, my hands fumbling with the latch. The torch in the sconce on the wall opposite shone into the room, and the shouted orders of warriors echoed along the passage with the clean-up still in progress.

I bit my lip. *Not going out there.* I shut the door.

The window remained open wide. I hurried to it, my heart thundering. What if I'd lost Drayce! Arlan would never forgive me.

"Drayce!"

The cool night answered in silence. Behind me, the clunking of furniture on wooden floors and the deep voices of the warriors travelled along the corridor.

I let myself drop to the floor and placed my head in my hands, tears dribbling their warmth into my palms.

Why be so upset about an animal? *People* died. People I'd spent the past few days getting to know. Arlan's warriors.

A man's life had ended tonight... at my own hands.

I'd stabbed him. A calculated, ruthless slice in the triangle of death to be sure he died.

Oh hell, this wasn't a martial art class. This wasn't even street fighting.

The shaking started again, along with so many feelings jumbling in my chest and gut.

I was empty, but at the same time I bubbled.

My shoulders heaved and my breath came in stutters while hot tears streaked my cheeks. The room was now a blurry glow. I'd managed to fight off the big guy. I sat a little straighter.

The wind blew in through the window, bringing with it the jingle of tack and male voices.

I forced control into my breathing, then stood and poked my head out the window, wiping away tears with the heel of my hand. Dál Gaedhle warriors returned and rode through the gateway, making their way to the bailey. An enormous black horse led them. Mengus. A man servant strode toward them and lifted his torch to give light for those who dismounted. Metal bits and buckles on bridles glinted in the torch's firelight. Arlan swung off Mengus, and Bàn dropped from his horse beside him.

My breath caught. With my own eyes I could see Arlan seemed okay. Unhurt.

He walked to the caisteal entrance beneath my window, with Bàn and the other warriors close behind, speaking amongst themselves. Arlan's rumbling tones lifted to me while the group strode out of my sight below and into the caisteal. A dark red shadow soared in silence toward them, then Arlan's voice echoed in surprise.

THIRTY-SIX

— ∘ —

The bold do win in enterprise and daring.
The chance they take, their endeavour to succeed.
The confident do fly upon their wings.
To soar, to glide, to ride the winds on high.
Though all intent is on the prize,
The nagging thought,
The silent doubt,
Does their discomfort ruffle.

VISIONS AND SAYINGS OF THE BLIND LADY SAGE

The World of Dál Cruinne
Post Dragon Wars Year 6083
Eastern Clanlands of Dál Gallain
Lord Ciarán's Tower

Fire crackled in the hearth, bathing Ciarán's back with warmth. The mage had passed a comment on the risks of frugality with charcoal and wood, and damp had now settled in a parchment smelling of mould. Decay. *Blast hell's ovens!* He would keep his library a warmer place or risk losing his collection, which had been a lifetime in the gathering.

A lone candle flickered on his desk, and he held the document on an angle so the fluttering glow passing across the text joined that of the fire's lambent illumination. With the lettering clearer now, he read more freely.

A faint clumping echoed up the stairs outside his partially open door. *By the antlers of Cernunnos!* He ground his teeth. He should have closed it fully. The clatter of his manservant's wooden shoes grew louder. Ciarán groaned.

216

It was always the way. No sooner did he immerse himself in the history this scroll relayed and either his man or Bram would come and pester him. The footsteps halted at his door, followed by a tentative tapping.

"What!"

"Mi lord," the gruff tones of his servant came through the crack, along with the glimmer of his lighted candle.

"Yes! Get on with it. What do you want?" With a gentle hand Ciarán placed the scroll onto the reading stand on his desk.

His man coughed and pushed the door further open, his bulbous nose twitching like a rabbit's. "Some news, Lord Ciarán. An item I'm sure ye would wish tae know."

Ciarán clenched his fist. "Well, do enter and enlighten me." He kept his tone a growl.

His man stepped in, then placed the candle stick on the edge of Ciarán's desk. Ciarán glowered at him, and the man snatched it back to his chest, then gave a short cough.

"'Tis about the new àrd rìgh of Dál Gaedhle—"

"They have finished their Quest already? From whence did you glean this information?"

"From the tavern, lord. Troubadours bring it. 'Tis all throughout the villages. All know. 'Twas only ten days ago, so 'tis said. 'Tis also said the man is perfect for the task."

"All know, but *we* only *now* discover it? It was for a dragon's egg, was it not..." Ciarán held his mouth open. Then shut it tight. "Damn him!" He fisted his desk with both hands. "I'll wager it was won with the information on my Ionan scroll. How I was relieved of the precious text is merely conjecture. That it coincides with the visit from that pitiful excuse for an assassin.... Vygeas must have sold it for gold." He stood. "I'll gut them."

"Who, mi lord?" His man swallowed, the gulp reaching Ciarán's ears.

He narrowed his glare. "The ones who stole it from under your nose, idiot! Who won? Tell me this, then remove yourself from my presence before I practice my knife skills on you."

"Arlan MacEnoicht, lord. The second son of—"

"I am aware of his station in life. Go!"

His man spun on his heel and left, stirring loose pieces of parchment that rested on the shelf by the door. Ciarán strode to the door and slammed it, catching a fluttering text before it fell to the floor, then held it in his stare.

The second son? Why did the eldest son not contend for the high kingship... Alana's boy... as is the custom? Was he injured still? Not recovered from the skirmish by that portal his own lordling warriors had bungled... and lost. Or had the lad succumbed to those injuries? He must discover *that* outcome.

He replaced the parchment on the shelves, then returned to his desk and lit another candle, the theme of the current scroll on his reading stand pulling at his thoughts.

On his stand, having been unrolled with care, lay a very old and very fragile parchment written on the occasion that an ancient sage had wished to record from the oral tradition the lore relating to high kings. It was interesting to him how cultures oft forgot the origins of traditions. Traditions which, in later years, became institution.

He held the newly lit candle above the text then read:

The man selected to lead the leaders of the families must be without fault. Chosen as chief among chiefs, he is to parade bare before those clans gathered on the moot hill. With a firebrand, the sage shall pass the flame over all his body, to reveal to the people the man's perfection for the task.

A string of expletives echoed in Ciarán's library.

"If I ever encounter that whelp who would be king of the west..."

Bram had described him as large and dark. Muscled and healthy, just like his sire, Donnach. Ciarán grunted. He would be the natural leader to whom all would flock, like the sheep they were. Ciarán stepped to the window and placed his hand on the cool windowpane. The night outside was dark; the courtyard lit by braziers glowed beneath a star-pocked sky.

"He would hate me for killing his sire." His voice bounced back from the glazing. "And be surely after my hide. My tower... and my promised kingdom." His fingers clawed at the window. "Perhaps Arlan MacEnoicht *is* capable of leading those who would thwart me. What then?" His nails scraping the glass sent a squeal through his library, squashing the thought plus the accompanying sinking of his bowels.

He straightened.

"*When* I encounter that whelp, it will not be death that I deliver, but humiliation. Let us see this *perfect* lad. And then make him live as an outcast. May he learn what it is to be the anathema which his father made *me*."

A tap came from the closed door.

"What? Did I not order you to go away?"

By Ceridwen's magic cauldron!

"Lord Ciarán?" Bram spoke through the door.

What could the mage possibly want at this late hour? He frowned. "Enter."

The door opened with a creak and the young man stepped into the room, his expression unreadable except for a tightness to his mouth and a glint in his eye from the fire. Or was it?

"Yes?" Ciarán halted his tapping foot.

"I have some news you will be pleased to hear."

"I have heard it, and I am not pleased."

"Pardon?"

"The new Àrd Rìgh of Dál Gaedhle."

"Ah, no lord, that is not my information."

Ciarán breathed a sigh. Minions! So frustrating at times.

"What report do you deliver to add to my manservant's news to disturb my peaceful evening?"

"I have found a portal not far from here, Lord Ciarán."

"Ah." He leaned forward into the mage's face until the lad flinched. "You have learned from your beating. I am pleased that you withhold not this discovery from me." He stood back. "Although on the previous occasion the words *not far from here* passed your lips, we ended up on the other side of the River Bàn-rìghinn."

"This one is to the north, perhaps a day's ride."

Was that a tremor in the young voice? "You are certain?"

"Yes, lord."

Ciarán's fingertips tingled.

"We must go without delay. Ready yourself to leave in the morn. I am sure we will manage minus the history lesson on the Other World from Findlay. I shan't wait for him to be fetched from Monsae. And tell young Galan I require his services once more. I am feeling magnanimous at present. I will give the lad another chance."

Thirty-Seven

—·—

Wipe clean the slate.
Words of condemnation wash away by grace.
Write anew the verse of love.

POETRY OF A KING
ÀRD RÌGH RHONAN IUBHAR
(4030-4090 POST DRAGON WARS)

The World of Dál Cruinne
Post Dragon Wars Year 6083
Eastern Clanlands of Dál Gallain
Caisteal Monsae

Vygeas stood in the main hall, the taste of ferrous touching his tongue.

Jubilance echoed from the walls though no one spoke. Necessity pushed aside dark feelings while warriors dragged the bodies of the slain to their place of burial.

Vygeas once more cursed the mage, Drostan, for giving him a gift without full explanation. But magic came with a price, they said.

Oh, for a way to turn it off when the feelings and intentions of others exhaust me so.
All I desire is clarity for my own!

He strode along the hall to the private quarters where the warned servants, who had fled earlier and now returned to their posts, assisted in the aftermath. They bowed and curtsied to Leynarve. Lime, the colour of admiration, glowed forth from each one as they gave her the respect the Lady of Monsae deserved. Relief filled the halls from local Monsae men and women and warriors alike—the dusky pink sandstone shone brighter.

Lord Arlan approached the door of the chamber at the head of the passage to the private quarters, while servants bustled past. MacEnoicht's warriors had fought well. The war chief, Leuchars, had earned every one of his scars in his past. That was a certainty. His skill had avoided no new scars this night. He was an asset to Arlan, and Vygeas would tell him so. Arlan could have none better for a war chief. As for the àrd rìgh himself, Arlan had fought bravely, his scent tinged with fear, but fighting on. Vygeas had glimpsed the vermillion of deep courage battling the dark throughout the àrd rìgh's aura.

Aye, Arlan had been in skirmishes, but the man had now tasted proper battle and the numb shock of those who sup of it for the first time hung around him.

Vygeas turned away. Leynarve stood at her chamber door, giving orders to her relieved and tired servants and warrior clansmen. Justification and a sense of rightness haloed a golden glow about her but streaked with an ache of crimson so deep it was almost black.

He had seen it before. He the cause, and he must address it.

"Leynarve." He touched her arm.

Shock accompanied the quick glare sent by the caisteal's housekeeper, then the woman covered her disapproval at his familiarity with their lady, curtsied and walked away.

Leynarve turned to him, her face haggard, her beauty tired and smudged with the lifeblood of another.

"Come to your chamber," he said. "All is in place. It is time to rest."

She nodded and turned into her room where a fire burned within a sizable hearth. A table laden with food and drink sat by the opposite wall and the four-poster bed, covered in drapery, was the grandest piece of furniture in the room. Light muslin curtains hung over a wide window that led to the balcony. Vygeas stood at the open doorway while Leynarve faced the fire and removed her sword belt then untied her leather armour, fresh with scratches and cuts.

"May I come in, Leynarve?"

She remained with her back to him, her head bowed, and gave a trembling nod. He removed his weapons and armour, then rested them by the wall.

"This is the Laird and Lady's room." Her voice was so soft that without his exceptional hearing, the words would be lost in the chamber. But she would have spoken them only for him.

Aye, it was the room—her parents' room.

His nose sensed the malodorous stench of old blood soaked into wood un-scrubbed. Thankfully, only a fume. Indistinguishable from the rest of the chamber's scents to another, but enough for him. Enough to plague him with guilt all over again.

An anger churning with hurt seeped from Leynarve's soul and wafted over.

Directed right at him.

She scratched at her curls, shaking out the plait that had held them restrained. Now they flew about her head, mingled with annoyance plus the pain that hovered, clothed in a grief so deep...

Her shoulders shook, and a wall of emotion, like a hand in his face, came from her. *Come no farther,* it said, without saying.

He smelled the salty tears. Heard the choked back sobs.

221

They would come, and he required not his heightened senses to know of them.

All throughout their preparation for the retaking of the caisteal, Leynarve had edged away from his touch. Had stifled her alarm at how well he knew her former home.

Of course he did. He pressed his lids together, tight against the fact. He had cased it, found numerous ways to enter unnoticed, and exit with much stealth after the deed.

The deed he'd performed the last time he'd walked these halls—the day he assassinated her parents.

He had confessed on the way to the Isle of Eilean, then begged Leynarve's forgiveness, and she had given it. The beginnings of the forgetting, she had said. He had trusted all he said and did from that point on had proved to her his changed life. And she the catalyst for it.

But here and now, he found himself in the very same room. The curtains of the wide double window ruffled gently in the breeze. He recalled his flight over the balcony that night.

The daughter had returned from the ball. The patter of her slippered feet upon the stairs. Her excited call to her parents, bubbling with the joy of all she would recount of her evening.

Then her scream. Her cry. Her sobs.

His eyes flew open. Those sounds had pierced his empty heart. Now the recollection stabbed his soul, which over the recent months had filled with love for *her*. The very same daughter.

"I cannot do this." Leynarve spun, deep brown eyes boring into his, their corners pinched with grief and hurt. Her lower lids pooled with tears—anger and hatred stifled in trembling clenched fists.

Anger at him. Hatred for the deed he had done.

He looked away, unable to face her. Leynarve's emotions were thrown like spears, despite her attempts to keep the lances in her grasp.

"This makes it all so fresh." Vygeas faced her. "We must rest in another room. Leave this shrine..."

Tears streaked through the grime and blood on Leynarve's cheeks—the remembrance of that night the watershed for her heaving shoulders and aching fountain now cascading down her face.

"Tell me again, for I so need to hear it once more. To aide my comprehension of the act." Her voice was barely a whisper. "Why did you do it?"

"Lord Ciarán deceived me. I accepted as truth his accusations of the Laird and Lady of Monsae's unjust conduct and cruelty toward their steading holders. I was young and naïve. And I was wrong. Believe me, if I could change the past, wipe this act from our mutual history, I would. Alas, my gift is not such a one."

Would this remembrance be the ruin of all he had wrought? His world stilled.

What if I lose her? Leynarve was now his whole world. His certainty in this uncertain life.

Please, no.

But if so, it was only what he truly deserved.

For the complete forgiveness he requested would come at great cost to Leynarve.

His hand drummed his thigh while the fire crackled, and the cheese on the platter warmed, sending its sharpness his way.

"You know I hate it." Her hands moved to her linen blouse, and she wiped her cheeks with the cloth. "That you are aware of what I feel."

"Nae, my love, for I am not only aware, but it pummels me as if ye yourself fisted me in the chest."

A log popped in the hearth while Leynarve's continually welling eyes never left his.

"I need you." Sobs choked her words. "Fool that I am, I need you to help me ease the very hurt you caused." Her voice was small. "You have become my strength."

Vygeas stepped to her, and she did not move away. His heart kicked, butting against the ache still flowing from her.

"Hold me together while I... clamber through this darkness once more." She sobbed, shaking with the weeping, then opened her arms.

He hurried the short steps to her embrace then wrapped his arms around her, her tears soaking his shirt, and her pain and confusion soaking into his soul where it matched his own.

He rested his cheek against her wild hair and kissed her head. She cried all the tears her eyes held, and only then, did he dare to speak.

"On the Isle of Eilean, you said you would work at the forgiving and forgetting." He blew out a slow sigh. "I understand now that it is like climbing a ladder. And you have taken one rung at a time. Here before us is yet another rung. I pray it is nearing the top."

The breeze susurrated through the delicate curtains and Leynarve nestled her head against his chest, saying naught.

He took a deep breath. "I am pleased you have your lands and title returned to you. I rejoice with you, Lady Leynarve of Monsae. It has not been easy to face again your home touched by tragedy"—he pressed down on his lips but had to continue— "with the man who wronged you so. Unintentionally, for I knew you not at the time. But I *am* no longer he..." His voice strangled, and he halted at the intensity of his own emotion. "Forgive me anew. Wipe my past from your mind. See only the man in front of you, who loves you, Leynarve."

"You are free." Her words muffled into his shirt.

Free of your grievance, or free to go?

"I will leave, then." Now the sole confusion he sensed was his own.

"No," she said, then stepped back, looking him in the eye. "If not you, then another assassin would have done Lord Ciarán's bidding and not spared me as you did. And I would never have known you on that road to Eilean." She reached her hands up to his face, small and warm, they rubbed through his scarred stubble. "And discovered that I love you."

THIRTY-EIGHT

— • —

Set the spark to the tinder,
Watch it catch aflame.
Once alight,
No water-filled loch, nor spring's fulsome rain,
Nor swelling mountain burn,
Can quench the blaze.
To try is to do so in vain.

POETRY OF SAGE GLIOCAS
(2870-2962 POST DRAGON WARS)

The World of Dál Cruinne
Post Dragon Wars Year 6083
Eastern Clanlands of Dál Gallain
Caisteal Monsae

A hand rapped hard on the door, then it opened.

"Ye would be the Lady Rhiannon, would ye now?" A servant woman entered and bobbed a short curtsey. "Here are some provisions and fresh water to wash... the stains of battle from ye." The woman's eyebrow lifted for a fraction of a second then she placed a trencher of bread and meat on the table. Another woman brought in a jug of beer and put it beside the trencher. She also carried a basin with a steaming pitcher and set it on the low cupboard by the side wall where cloths sat.

"Thank you." I squinted. "You are servants?" It was all so *civilised*.

"Aye, my lady." The woman curtsied again. "The servants were spared, and none molested."

"You are Ciarán Gallawain's servants?"

224

"Och no, my lady. We are faithful to House Monsae. I live in the village, and Lord Ciarán forced us to work here to tend to the needs of his steward, Lord Findlay."

"*Lord* Findlay?"

"Aye, but how grand it is to be serving the Lady of Monsae! What great rejoicing there is in the village on our wonderful news. How pleased we are that she sides with the Àrd Rìgh of Dál Gaedhle." She gave a sweet smile, then said, "The lad who minds yer horses with your bags o' claithes has arrived. I shall send your belongings up to ye soon." With another quick curtsey, she and the other maid left.

Fresh sweat mingled with that already dried while it ran down the centre of my back. The fire, now roaring, radiated its heat throughout the room. The hot water was so inviting. I undid the lacings of my leather armour and shrugged the garment off. It smelled of sweat and blood. I set it near the wall by the window and it stood up on its own. I took off my thick padded tunic, damp with perspiration, and wearing only my breeches and crop top, leaned over the bowl on the side table and poured in the hot water. A cloth sat beside it, and I drenched it in the water then washed my face and arms.

With the water now pink, my hands were clean. So, this was how Lady Macbeth felt. No, all the water in the world could not wash out the stench of bloodguilt. I let the thought of that Queen of Scots' madness flit around in my mind, but then I grabbed it and threw it away.

I can't be like that.

There'd be more ahead, and I'd have to cope with it if I would fight for Dál Gaedhle. "And I will."

I pushed against the sense of unreality. Like a Celtic re-enactment day that never ends. Where the battle was *real* and so was the mutilation and death.

The wind from the window blew cool on my back, and I washed as best I could. Chewing my bottom lip, I stared at the open window. I still had the problem of Drayce. I let my shoulders drop.

With a light tap on the door, a young servant woman came in with two saddlebags, mine and Arlan's, placed them on the floor and, without a word, stepped out, leaving the door ajar.

"Warriors guard the perimeter. They tend to the wounded." Arlan's deep, strong voice came through the gap while he held the door open. "The prisoners faithful to Monsae are released from the dungeon." He sighed; it ended in a groan. "They have put Leigh's body somewhere safe?"

Leigh's body? "Oh." My barely whispered word escaped into the room, but I couldn't take my eyes from Arlan standing in the partially open door.

"Aye, Arlan." Bàn's solemn voice came through the gap. "They will see to him."

"Rest, brother. The Lady of Monsae calls all to recover but stay alert, and she will address us in the morn." Arlan stepped in and closed the door behind him.

Arlan—my anchor of solid reality.

Drayce sat crowded on his shoulder.

"Oh, Arlan! I thought I'd lost him!" I took a pace forward, my hand on my chest, but stopped at his expression.

Blood smudged his face, and his eyes held a *look*. The same expression on soldiers in the TV news of battles in Afghanistan, and in the monochrome documentary film of the world wars—the look of a man who'd killed and seen death many times. His cheek bones stood out and his jaw muscles bunched, and his eyes were hard... no—stunned... but occupied, like behind them he weighed the cost of the battle. Balancing the victory with the loss.

Arlan would be feeling every injury and loss personally.

My breath caught, and I dared not speak. I couldn't express what he needed.

He took Drayce from his shoulder and placed him on the mat by the fire, grabbing some meat from the trencher as he did, then tossing it to his dragon. "Stay!"

Arlan's shoulders eased the longer he was in the room. He avoided my eyes, taking off his leather armour and bulky under tunic. In silence, he washed his hands and face in the pink-tinged water and pulled out the tie holding his hair at his back, the silky black cape falling across his bare shoulders.

I clasped my trembling hands, willing my feet to keep me where I stood. He drank from the jug of beer and released a breathy sigh.

He looked me in the eyes then, and every hard edge softened.

"Oh, Rhiannon." His voice came out gravelly, choked with emotion.

I ran to him and wrapped my arms around him, holding tight to his warmth and solidity. He was still alive and uninjured. His hands, rough on my bare skin, rested on the small of my back. Sweat's pungent odour clung to him, acrid and sharp. I buried my face in his chest. Blood's metal perfused his skin and mingled with leather's organic earthy scents.

And his heart beat beneath.

"Ye fought well, I'm told." His voice echoed through his chest. "Are you injured?"

"No." I lifted my head to face him and traced the navy ring that encircled his blue, navy-speckled irises.

Man, I needed him. But if I stayed here in his room, I'd break a promise to myself. Guilty. I'd be guilty of not holding true to my resolve.

But I don't care. I need him.

Arlan tilted his face closer and kissed me. Tentatively, with his mouth soft against mine. My lips melted onto his. His nose rubbed my cheek as he adjusted to make our kiss fit. He stayed there, mouth playing with mine, savouring.

I pulled him to me, holding tight. The length of his tall, hot body ran along the whole of mine. His arms drew me even closer as though to absorb me into him.

If only I could meld with him, share every thought of his. Every emotion, memory, idea. Every choice and regret—every part of Arlan I could know—and hold on to it forever.

Hold him forever.

I ran my fingers through his unbound hair and rested them on the nape of his neck. A shiver ran from his shoulders to his thighs and my answering shiver ran to my very

226

core. He moved his mouth from my lips and traced a path across my cheek to my throat, leaving my nerve endings firing. His hands glided down my back, shooting sparks that travelled much lower and deeper than his touch. His palms cupped my buttocks, lifting me. I hooked my legs around his waist, my arms smoothed over muscled shoulders, and my fingers ran further into his silky hair.

He moved his face from my neck and the tip of his nose traced a path to mine. He rested his forehead on my brow, his face so close I felt it only.

"I love you," he said in a deep, solid whisper that reverberated into my soul.

A soft, wordless sigh escaped my lips. Then he carried me to bed.

THIRTY-NINE

— • —

My home in this world; my haven in danger.
My body's warmth in the cold; my soul's security in threat.
My peace, my joy, my delight in the night.
My strength in this life and the place where I am me.
My other, my union, my wholeness—
You are she.

POETRY OF A KING
ÀRD RÌGH RHONAN IUBHAR
(4030-4090 POST DRAGON WARS)

The World of Dál Cruinne
Post Dragon Wars Year 6083
Eastern Clanlands of Dál Gallain
Caisteal Monsae

Dust motes danced in the beams of early morning sunlight streaming through the chamber window.

Arlan had tucked the crook of his elbow around Rhiannon, his hand resting on the curve of her warm waist. Her head lay on his shoulder. Fans of her hair crossed his chest, like fingers of burnt orange aflame with the light of dawn; threads of fine curled silk tickled his skin, stirring him to greater wakefulness.

They'd made love more than once. Rhiannon had given herself to him, as he had to her, without reservation, and completely.

They belonged to each other in body, mind, and soul.

Two now one flesh.

No going back. No more without her. None other than her.
Ever.

OF WARRIORS AND SAGES

The sense of her—and of himself, accompanied by an eruption of pleasure—had lingered from their lovemaking. Every touch of her soft skin, every sigh, her welcoming body, and her enjoyment of him—for aye, she'd delighted in their love... It had filled his body and crossed that space into his soul. He relished the waves of remembrance.

Rhiannon rolled away, her arm tracing a path of warmth as she turned onto her back, leaving in her wake a trail of gooseflesh across his abdomen. Argent light touched the curve of her breasts and the brush of her pubic hair, igniting his whole body with tingles.

One day he would cover Rhiannon in the plaid of his clan and pledge his life to hers in front of all.

Her chest rose and fell, her breasts moving with the evidence of her life. Hair covered her face while she slumbered...

And time. Stood. Still.

If but the battles were over, and *this* his life with her from henceforth. Waking to his love every morning and sharing their bodies' delights each night.

He sighed and dragged his eyes away, loathe to break his vision and thoughts from her. The battle for Monsae was but a start. More lay ahead. More chances for each time of love to be their last. He would never let her go. He would hold her with his devotion. Be the man, the husband, she deserved.

He turned again to gaze upon her. Leuchars had said a spouse and family were important to warriors—that which gave them the courage and the will to return home. And no point for some without them. He'd inwardly questioned his war chief. Surely the fight was enough? For the fight itself. For the land you love. For clan.

But what makes a clan family, and what makes the land live, but the man with his woman and their children to give it to?

A knowing came over him—he had found his *home* in Rhiannon. A truth from his first encounter with the young woman on the hill fighting her armed attacker, and unflinchingly facing a Dál Gaedhle warrior on his war horse.

He sunk deeper into the bed beside her, releasing a soft chuckle.

She stirred and woke. She traced his nude body from toes to face, where her gaze locked with his and her eyes rounded.

"Good morning." He kissed her warm lips that parted to receive his, and his desire roused. "How are you?" His voice came out husky deep.

She swallowed. "We can't do this." She shook her head.

He cupped her face in his hands and kissed her firmly. Her fingers caressed his chest, and she returned his kiss, mouth playing with his, then halted.

"We can't do this," she spoke into their kiss.

He pulled away until he could see her clearly, not just feel her gentle breath on his cheek.

"Ah, but we have *done this*."

She rolled out of the bed and searched for her clothes. He leaped out and stood behind her, wrapping his arms around her front, and pulling her back against him. Her warm flesh touched every sensitive part of his body now ready to love her again.

"I love you," he whispered into her ear.

"I love *you*, but this can't happen. Not until we are certain I am..." She spun in his embrace, her breasts tickling his skin, her expression set and determined, but pain sat behind her eyes. "I'll not be your mistress. I'll be your wife, or nothing." She pressed her hands to him and pushed herself away. "And if I can't be your wife, if I'm a *nothing*—of no clan nor noble house—it'll be more difficult each time we make love... harder to let you go." Emotion crowded her tight words.

His heart stopped beating for a moment, then ran as though in the midst of a fight.

"Rhiannon, heart of my own heart, you're of a noble clan. Eifion will verify it. Your eyes—"

"When? And where is he? What if I'm—"

"Don't say it," he said, voice hardening and fingers curling.

"So, you're angry at me? When I want to get this right? Look, yesterday was a high energy battle. Hormones were flying everywhere. They say it happens with soldiers and first responders. They're all fired up and then filled with relief that you're still alive. You just want to celebrate life and release some of those hormones and..." She let go a ragged sigh. "But I'll not dishonour you, the àrd rìgh. We'll do it right. We won't do this"—her hand flicked back and forth between him and her, and her breath drawing in faltered— "wonderful as it was, until we know... if we can marry."

"What are ye saying?" He sharpened his tone. How could he be with her and not be *with* her? Now they *knew* each other, not desiring her would be impossible. "We shall be fellow warriors and no more?" A rock had fallen into his guts.

Nae, it is my heart that has ceased its battle-dance in my ribs and lands with a thud in my belly.

She found her leather banding that covered a woman warrior's breasts and held it to herself while she searched for her breeches and tunic. She grabbed her saddlebags and hastily dressed, hair flying and tears streaming.

"I'll not have them thinking I'm your *piece on the side* from the Other World."

"Piece?" His brow tightened.

With her mouth a thin line, she flicked her fingers across her cheeks, ridding herself of tears. "I don't want your people thinking either of us is like *that*."

Arlan pushed back the ache, her words difficult to decipher. He let out a grunt.

"Or have you had other women, and everyone's okay with their àrd rìgh doing that? I thought in this world nobody cheated on their partners or used another person just for sex."

"Rhiannon!" His voice raised, and he was helpless to prevent the edge to it. "I'm disappointed you think I would do such things. It is nae that the opportunity has not arisen. I have refused many women."

Rhiannon started, her expression as though he'd slapped her. "Really? I can't believe you just said that!"

He took a step toward her, but she put her palm up to him. "No." She spoke low and firm, then she left the room, the door clunking shut behind her.

Arlan slumped onto the bed.

"What?" He forced the word out. The warmth that had sent him floating—now chased away.

What was that all about? If she would deny him... and herself of their love?

How could she feel what I have and now stop it? Their desire for each other bridled like a wayward beast!

He shook his head and his face ended up in his hands—his trembling hands moistening with sweat. What if mauve eyes were only a *freak of nature*—for that's what the Other World would name it—and she was not born of the Cruithin clan? Not of any clan, and the Gallawain tartan *baby-rug* given to her by her parents was just a mystery somehow. For it bore no connection.

"Eifion!" he shouted, then groaned.

Clicking came from outside the window, and a shadow in the sunlight on the wooden floor grew bigger. With a *thump*, Drayce landed on the sill, feathers sticking to his mouth.

Someone rapped on the door.

Arlan sighed. "Come in."

Bàn opened the door and stepped in. "Are ye well, Arlan?"

Arlan let the air blow slowly through his lips but gave no answer.

"Lady Rhiannon..." A *v* appeared above Bàn's nose.

"Aye?" His voice was hoarse, even to his own ears.

"She has just run to the stables—"

He shot off the bed. "She leaves?"

"I know not. I sent Morrigan after her." Bàn raised a hand to him.

Arlan stood still. The only sound in the room was his breathing and the murmured voices of people passing in the corridor.

"Ah," Bàn hesitated then asked, "what happened?"

He sat back on the bed, head resting in his hands. "I love an honourable woman."

"Ahh, if honour is her concern, all are aware of... you and Rhiannon... Well, we, your warriors, are pleased for your *happiness.*"

"I will not be happy if she is not noble, as ye have so rightly pointed out in the past. And she will not be with me if she is not. Och! *I* cannot be with her if she is not!" He lifted his head and ground the words out. "Cursed be duty. Cursed be any law, or mere tradition, that says I must marry into nobility."

"Arlan!" Bàn's voice echoed in the chamber. "Ye ken how it must be. And so does Rhiannon, for she is a sensible woman. That is why ye love her. So do we—your warriors. So do all, for we see ye love *her.*" He rubbed his upper lip. "Eifion?"

"Nae. So far, Eifion grasps at ideas. *Maybe this, maybe that.*" Arlan dropped his head into his hands again. "I'll die without her."

"Arlan, be ye not a player of drama! Ye'll marry another and do your duty."

"Nae, I will not! I will die a lonely old chieftain before I look at another woman, for there is none other like Rhiannon!"

Bàn remained silent for a span of heartbeats.

What? His friend and conscience would have spoken by now.

Arlan lifted his head. "So Morrigan is with Rhiannon?"

"My sister will attend to her." Bàn's answer collided with his question. "There's work to do, my lord àrd rìgh. Ye have warriors to bury"—Bàn's throat worked— "prisoners to question, thanks to give, and a celebration to prepare." His mouth screwed to the side. "But ye must first dress yourself, aye?"

FORTY

— ◦ —

Harsh decisions must a king make.
A life to keep... and one to take.
If ye do decree,
Your own arm it must be
That swings the blade.

WISDOM WRITINGS ON KINGSHIP
SAGE GLIOCAS
(2870-2962 POST DRAGON WARS)

The World of Dál Cruinne
Post Dragon Wars Year 6083
Eastern Clanlands of Dál Gallain
Caisteal Monsae

I hurried down the stairway.

My muscles were stiff from yesterday after fighting my hardest and I clutched my sword and dagger to my chest. Footsteps came rapidly behind me.

"Rhiannon." Morrigan tapped me on the shoulder. "Where are ye going?"

I shrugged. "The stables, to curry Bridie."

"Och, the stable hands have attended." Morrigan grasped my arm and turned me to face her. "Come with me. There is a cot for you in the quarters set aside for Arlan's warrior women."

I followed her back up the stairs and along the passage, glad to have her steer me away from Arlan right now. Arlan's door was closed and Bàn's voice rumbled behind it in reprimanding tones as we passed by. Morrigan turned into a chamber further along from the main bedrooms containing cots covered in sparse bedding. Adele was straightening the blankets on one.

Hmm. A real down-grade from Arlan's digs.

"Rhiannon will stay with us," Morrigan said to Adele, who looked around the cramped room with a scowl. "We will make space." Morrigan spoke in a firm tone.

My breathing hitched, Arlan's stricken expression still fresh in my mind. Adele glanced at me for a second and cringed, then strode out of the quarters. Warm tears flowed down my cheeks, and Morrigan pulled me into a hug.

"Rhiannon?" she whispered, "Lord Arlan was not rough with you? He did not force you—?"

"Hell, no!" My breathing hitched again. "It was very consensual. And absolutely wonderful." My shoulders shook with a stuttering breath. "It's just that we can't... until I know for sure we can..." I swiped tears away with my palm. "Morrigan, you more than anyone, would understand what I mean. With you and Angus? Nobility, and all that."

"Aye," Morrigan whispered, then released me from her embrace. Her lips pinched together, and her eyes misted. She cleared her throat. "I will get ye some water to wash. We have some time until the feast. Clean and sharpen your weapons, then rest. There are battles ahead and a warrior rests when she can, for when it is time to, you fight until ye drop or it is all over, and not before."

"What about the clean-up from the storming of this caisteal and the preparation for the feast?"

Morrigan cocked her head, frowning. "Och, the servants prepare." She left and soon returned with a jug of hot water and a basin.

I washed and dressed in fresh breeches and plaid, then picked up the used basin and walked out of the women's quarters. I passed Arlan's room, slowing at the open door. The chamber, still in disarray from our night together, sat empty. I squeezed my eyes tight for a second—*get a grip girl*—then increased my pace and headed to the kitchen, which was filled with cooks and scullery hands preparing food. I returned the basin and jug, then made a quick exit from the bustling servants.

I took the stairs and climbed right to the top of the caisteal. The aroma of roasting meats spiralled up the circular stairway with me. I stepped out onto the battlements to the wall head and leaned against the shoulder-high parapet. Until now, the roar of breakers crashing regularly to shore was the only indication of the ocean's presence. From here, facing the front of the building, spread a rocky shoreline and a narrow, sandy beach. Far in the distance, islands dotted the horizon with a grey-green ocean lying in between. Clouds filled a sunless sky, grey like the ocean that heaved and churned against the deep-brown rocks on the shore. Plumes of spray, like pure white geysers, rose up with every wave that crashed against the uneven shapes of the rock formations.

Birds scattered in the forest behind the caisteal, calling uneasily. I turned. A dark-red shape lifted from the trees. Wide, skin-tight wings flapped, and Drayce flew toward me. His wings were the span of a large eagle, and he headed straight for me. I braced myself for his landing. He soared to a halt on the parapet, and I jumped at the gust of wind accompanying his touchdown. He crawled along, then hopped onto my arm, his weight dragging me down.

"Wow, you're having a growth spurt!" A bloody scent of raw meat came from his open mouth. "Eww. What have you been eating?"

Drayce leaned in closer, tucking his cool head into the nape of my neck. I rested my chin on his knobbly head—it had grown scalier—and his cold tongue flicked against my skin. He made a soft clicking sound, almost like a cat's purr.

"I guess that means you're happy."

Loud male voices echoed from behind the caisteal, and I walked around to the section of the parapet that overlooked the bailey yard. Douglas and Muir held four Dál Gallain warriors, chained at the wrists and ankles, in a kneeling position. Blood patched the Dál Gallain warriors' tunics and breeches, purple bruises showed on their faces and bare arms, and they squinted at the daylight. Arlan and Bàn strode toward them, both armed. Arlan braced his shoulders and held his head stiffly. Bàn stayed close, speaking with him, their voices not rising to me.

Drayce pressed down on my arm as though to lift in flight.

"No! Stay, Drayce." I held him tight against me with my free arm. "Arlan won't want you down there. Those warriors have swords."

Drayce gave a guttural cry, then tightened his claws around my arm and settled his weight more fully.

Muir presented the man he restrained to Arlan. Arlan spoke to the prisoner, his voice an indistinct deep rumble. The Dál Gallain warrior set his face in blank determination. Muir made a comment and Arlan spoke again, his tone a question. The prisoner shook his head. Muir's expression was tight. Arlan spoke once more, and the man repeated his gesture.

Arlan nodded to Muir, who pushed the man forward with his boot in his back until the prisoner leaned forward with his neck extended. Arlan shook his head, drew his sword, lifted it high, then thrust it down onto the man's neck, cleaving the man's head from his shoulders. The prisoner's head fell to the ground and Arlan stepped away from the body. The corpse spurted blood rhythmically from the neck for a moment, then Muir dropped it.

I couldn't contain my gasp, startling Drayce, who squawked, and Bàn lifted his gaze to my position. I stood back, hand to my own neck, trying to settle my drumming heart.

Yuck. That was harsh. I guess dealing with the enemy was all part of Arlan being àrd rìgh. So, not all prisoners of war had rights here in Dál Cruinne? I swallowed down a sour taste. Yes, this world was severe in many aspects, and I'd probably discover more in the future.

Voices rose from below me once more, so I leaned against the parapet again.

Arlan stepped to the prisoners held by Douglas. Their faces turned to Arlan with trembling mouths, wide eyes, and chained hands clasped in front of them. Arlan spoke again and they nodded. Arlan stood back and Douglas dragged the men away.

So, there was mercy for those who would co-operate?

Arlan turned and walked toward the caisteal entrance, his face like flint. Drayce squawked and this time I let him go.

Warriors and servants in the garb of the caisteal, and some other folk who wore plain clothes—probably from the village below the caisteal—walked throughout the fortress, busily going about chores. The shrouded bodies of the fallen Dál Gaedhle warriors were on biers resting on carts in the bailey courtyard just below. Warriors patrolled the grounds and surrounding woods, and a group slung the bodies of the Dál Gallain dead into a mass grave by the wood without ceremony.

I shuddered and turned away. In the middle of a field about half a mile from the caisteal, sat a low round burial tor. Made of drystone, it had a turf roof in the same design as the grange I'd seen in Ireland. Men were opening it.

"We mourn, then we celebrate." Leyna's well-spoken voice came from behind me.

I jumped a bit, then faced her. She wore a dress with a snug bodice and a full skirt of a tightly woven woollen cloth, and she no longer had the appearance of a warrior but a true noblewoman.

"I haven't congratulated you on the regaining of your caisteal, Lady Leynarve." I gave a short bow.

"Thanks to your man. We would not have achieved this without the Àrd Rìgh of Dál Gaedhle and his warriors. Today we feast for luncheon, and most likely well into the night." Leyna smiled.

No. She glowed.

"You must be so happy to be home again," I said.

Leyna's smile broadened and cocked more to one side, giving her mouth a crooked look. "It is but a fraction of my happiness," she whispered conspiratorially. "I must beg your leave, for I have much to attend."

I bowed again, and she left the parapet. I gazed down at Muir who sat the head of the executed prisoner on the body, then dragged the corpse toward the wood. A shiver ran through me, sending me racing down the stairwell.

What would be the best way to approach what I haven't yet told Arlan?

I reached the door to the chamber where Arlan and I had slept. Now open, voices came from it, Arlan's one of them.

Good, Arlan won't be alone.

I knocked, keeping out of view of those inside.

"Come," Arlan said after finishing a comment.

I stepped into the room. Arlan stood from where he sat on the edge of the table set with a half-eaten breakfast. Leuchars and Bàn were the only ones in the room with him, and Drayce perched on the open windowsill, clicked at me. The servants hadn't yet attended the room and the bed lay dishevelled from our lovemaking. I swallowed.

"I need to report something to Lord Arlan." I kept my eyes on Leuchars, Bàn and the room in general and fought to keep my focus away from Arlan. Leuchars and Bàn started for the door. "Ah, you probably need to know this, too. It's about a Dál Gallain warrior."

They halted and stared at me. I felt Arlan looking at me, so I plucked up the courage and faced him.

"Lord Arlan, during the storming of the caisteal, while I was dealing with the Dál Gallain warrior, another escaped from the secret passage." I scrunched my toes in my boots and pushed away the pain.

Wow. So weird calling him Lord Arlan.

But it has to be like this...

"Many escaped, Lady Rhiannon." Arlan's tone was soft, forgiving. "It was your first battle and we left you to defend an exit on your own. Let it not disturb you."

"The thing is, Lord Arlan, I recognised the man."

All three warriors tensed.

"How?" Leuchars grunted beside me.

I stifled a flinch. "You know him too, Lord Arlan."

Arlan blinked and leaned forward.

"From... where I'm from," I said.

It was hard to decipher his expression. I couldn't decide whether I should mention I was from the Other World in front of the war chief.

Arlan frowned, his brows sharp. "George." Accusation laced his tone.

George in a battle? "No." A laugh burst from me at the notion, and I put a hand to my mouth for a second. "No. That policeman." *Oh hell, if Leuchars didn't know already, he will now.* "The one who came when my neighbour complained about your sword."

Arlan's eyes scanned the middle distance, and I could almost hear his thought processes.

"Detective Findlay followed us through," I said. "Morrigan, Angus and myself. But he ended up here a couple of months ago." I lifted a shoulder and let it fall. "Portals seem to have their own ideas about *when* to drop someone."

"And ye let him go?" Bàn folded his arms across his chest.

"I was occupied with killing another guy."

Boy! Women can multi-task, but I could only do so much!

"He recognised you?" Arlan's tone deepened and he stepped away from the table.

"Yes, I chased him. He headed for the woods. I cut his leather armour at the back"—I widened my stare at Bàn— "*as he fled*. But he knew me."

"You did well, Lady Rhiannon," Arlan said, and Leuchars grunted again.

"Thank you, but I'm not reporting it to receive praise. I need to tell you what he said."

"Aye?"

"Ciarán has portals that go all over the world. I think he meant the Other World, and all over time."

Leuchars narrowed his eyes at me.

My shoulders tensed. Did Leuchars think me disloyal? A spy?

Do they execute spies too?

"There was a lot going on. I—"

"It is well, Lady Rhiannon." Arlan spoke in firm and gentle tones. "It was your first fight. All can be confusion, even for one hardened by battle."

"What else was said?" Leuchars examined me through his hard expression.

I pushed against the shivers in my gut. *This guy's gotta be sure where my loyalties lie.*

"I told him he was on the wrong side and that Lord Arlan would win."

"Such a long conversation with one who fled." Bàn peered through his eyebrows.

"I'm reporting it, Lord Bàn, because the fleeing man hinted at Ciarán's aspirations." I faced Arlan again. "Lord Arlan, Ciarán may also know of gunpowder."

FORTY-ONE

— · —

Flare not to anger
When vision is short and wisdom is lacking.

SAGE GLIOCAS
(2870-2962 POST DRAGON WARS)

The World of Dál Cruinne
Post Dragon Wars Year 6083
Eastern Clanlands of Dál Gallain
Caisteal Monsae

Cool seeped into my back.

I leaned against a standing stone, one of many lining either side of the path to the burial tor where other mourners—nobles, warriors, villagers and servants—crowded around me. Arlan stood with Lady Leyna, Vygeas, Leuchars, and the Monsae war chief at the entrance to the tor, and Drayce perched on top of the stone nearest to him. Bàn, Adele, a couple of Leuchars' warriors and some local Monsae men, carried the biers holding Leigh, the Monsae warrior clansmen, and one of Leuchars' warriors to the torch-lit opening of the round stone tor. It was too far to take the Dál Gaedhle warriors home. Interring them in the caisteal's tor would be an honour.

Leigh's body was dressed in plaid and laid out on a bier, holding his sword between his hands resting on his chest. His complexion was grey and his features so still. In my head, his gravelly voice was giving me pointers on riding and his version of camp craft, just like he did on our journey to The Keep. His voice would never be heard again. My heart twinged and my eyes pricked with forming tears.

I lifted my gaze from Leigh's pale, lifeless form. Tears streaked Arlan's drawn face, and his eyes never left the procession while it passed him. We sang—well, they did. I didn't know the words, but the music was similar to some traditional Scottish folk ballads.

After saying prayers to the god of this world, those bearing the biers carried them into the burial chamber. Arlan entered after them and Drayce squawked. The dragon left his stone and landed at the opening, not following Arlan in, while flickering torchlit shadows danced at the entrance.

Some moments passed with shuffling and murmurs echoing out of the chamber, then Arlan emerged with the other leaders. Drayce flew to him, then Bàn handed Arlan a pewter flask. Arlan remained at the entrance of the burial chamber and looked out on the crowd. His dragon sitting on his shoulder surveyed all.

"To the slain." Arlan's voice rang clear and bounced off the standing stones lining the path. He poured the whole contents of the flask onto the stone wall of the tor. The full-bodied aroma of a strong whisky accompanied the splash and patter of the amber liquid hitting the rock. I breathed it in. It reminded me of the single malt scotch George had brought for Arlan's farewell back in the Other World. This one would have been worth a packet.

I followed the company into the caisteal, a heaviness sitting in my heart despite not knowing Leigh for long. Arlan's usually straight shoulders drooped and, even from behind, I could tell his hand movements were frequent eye-wiping. His dragon leaned into him as though comforting. Arlan peeled off with those at the front, then headed for his private chamber.

I walked along to the main hall, the dullness in my head sitting the same thick and heavy as the sensations in my chest.

Too much to feel all at once.

I held it like something solid in my centre—that determination to not want Arlan. To be content to just be near him. I couldn't—wouldn't—let my feelings cause my new resolve to falter. We couldn't make love again... no matter how much I needed him. I'd slipped, but now we—I—had to do it right. For his sake. For the honour of the position of àrd rìgh and the traditions of this world that I longed to call my own. And when I knew it actually *was* my own...

I shook my head. I'd have to wait till Eifion discovered the truth about me.

I walked with warriors from Dál Gaedhle and the Monsae Dál Gallain warriors and entered the hall.

Last night, in between making love, Arlan had spoken of my role in guarding the escape route with a gleam in his eye. His praise was enough. But how should I *be* around him now that we weren't going to be intimate? I'd been official with my report to him about Findlay, but at the memorial service, I'd ached to hug him in his obvious grief over Leigh's death. It was like he did take the losses personally.

I scanned the crowd, checking Arlan's position. Perhaps he'd emerged from his room. If so, I'd avoid him.

Monsae servants had scrubbed the Great Hall and arranged two long trestle tables on either side of it. A table sat at the top end on a plinth. Drayce now jostled at a window, emitting an anxious click, then rested on the sill behind the outer trestle table, then clicked in my direction.

Swords, daggers, money pouches, leather armour—some blood stained and torn—boots, saddles, and small items I couldn't name, sat on the bare floorboards in the middle of the hall. The odour of old leather, horse, and sweat rose from the pile.

"The horses are part of this too, but we do not bring them into the feasting hall." Stepping beside me, Adele grinned at her own joke. She seemed to have gotten over her problem with me cramming into the already cramped accommodation for the female warriors.

"So, this gets divided up?" I asked.

"Aye, partial payment for a warrior's service is the plunder of war, is it not?"

"Oh, yes, I guess it is."

"Ye have done well, Lady Rhiannon." Beside me, Douglas' eyes sparkled. The man's usual cheeky grin was kind of out of place following the sombre notes by the tor. "For your first battle. Impressive, I am told. I was busy myself killing Gallawain's warriors, so I could nae judge. But Angus spoke well of your kill. And ye ken bards will sing songs of the retaking of Monsae. They'll say our distant cousins are now new friends, all at the taking back of their home."

"Do ye compose for them, Douglas?" Adele asked.

"Aye." Douglas brightened at the idea. "And we sent the banished one back to his tower," Douglas sang in a simple tune.

"But Lord Ciarán wasn't even here," I said.

"Bards exaggerate. That's their job." Douglas winked at me.

I searched the empty upper table where Arlan would sit with those who led. He wasn't there yet, and once he did arrive, he'd better not invite me to sit with him. I'd say no.

Servants filled the tables with platters of roasted meats and vegetables, breads, and cheeses, and now bustled through the arriving throng with jugs of ale and wine. I caught Morrigan's eye and waved her to the table on the right of the room, near where Drayce perched, still clicking. Morrigan smiled at me, followed by Angus. They came to the table I'd pointed to and sat while I went to the window and stroked Drayce. His clicking was growing louder.

"He'll be here soon. Settle." I stroked his lizard-like scales and shushed him.

Arlan strode into the feast hall with Leyna, Vygeas, the Monsae war chief and Leuchars. They all sat at the head table. Drayce lifted and soared across the room, landing on Arlan's shoulder and wafting Arlan's hair in his face, sending those in his flight path ducking out of his way.

Sinking onto the bench seat, I blew out between my lips.

Leyna shone, looking totally the *lady* in her dress, and her hair an intricate coiffe of many braids. Her inner glow returned whenever she glanced at the scarred Vygeas, sitting beside her.

Other ladies wore full skirted dresses, some were made of tartan, all muted tones, others tweed.

"The heads of the important families in the village are attending," Morrigan said. "They are relieved Monsae has returned to her." She lifted her chin in Leyna's direction.

"And that their lady aligns herself with Lord Arlan. They know they will be well defended with the àrd rìgh of Dál Gaedhle on their side."

All the guests found their places and sat, then Leyna stood.

"Lord Arlan MacEnoicht, Àrd Rìgh of Dál Gaedhle, friends and warriors, people of Monsae, welcome. Dine and celebrate the successful reclaiming of Monsae and the ousting of those who belong to that tyrant, Ciarán Gallawain." She lifted her pewter chalice. "For Monsae! Eternal as the sea!"

I raised a pottery mug, which a servant hastily filled, and joined the toast, then sat down on the bench seat. It shuddered with another's weight, and I turned. Bàn smiled and took a drink from his mug. He smelled of lye soap and orange, for he, along with Arlan and the other warriors, had dressed for the funeral, with clean faces and fresh plaids and kilts.

"I have nae yet had the chance to say this, my Lady Rhiannon, so I will say it now. I commend you on your first kill, and how ye composed yourself during the retaking of Monsae." His dimples pitted.

"Thank you, Lord Bàn."

"And that ye did nae die."

Hmm. "I guess I have my teacher to thank for that." I raised my mug in salute.

Bàn inclined his head in reply, then leaned closer. "Ye are breaking my sword-brother's heart. I will forgive ye, though, for I understand the reason."

I stared into my mug, my neck warming. I should tell Bàn it was none of his business. But then... it was. Relationships were closer in this world. People were tied more strongly than anything I'd experienced. I swallowed down the ale.

Angus reached out to the nearest platter and ripped a leg off a roasted bird, put it to his mouth, tore chunks of meat, and chewed. Morrigan sliced a ham leg with her dagger and ate with daintier bites. On the other side of me, Bàn slipped his knife out of his boot.

"Shall I slice ye some mutton, my lady?"

"Yes, thank you."

So, he was being nice to me, even after the interrogation in Arlan's room?

"You know I'd never betray Arlan. I'd rather die."

"Aye." Bàn spoke like he'd never think otherwise.

"Then why were you so mean to me before?"

"Oh? About that Findlay cur?" A frown flicked across his brow. "Only being thorough, Lady Rhiannon. I ken not how it works in your world, but loyalty is highly valued here."

I opened my mouth to advise Bàn it was the same in *my world*, but at the head table, Leyna stood, sending the room into a hushed silence.

"I wish to toast, for in truth there is no way I could repay the man who came to our aid and fought by our side like a brother to regain what is ours." She raised her cup. "To Lord Arlan!"

All the guests rose, so I followed suit and shouted along with them, "To Lord Arlan!"

Arlan rose from the table, took Drayce from his shoulder, perched him on the back of his chair and ordered him to stay. He stepped around the plinth to stop in front of the pile of hoarded goods.

"Thank you, friends, warriors and people of Monsae, and especially our most gracious host, Lady Leynarve of Monsae."

Cheers rang around the hall, followed by a shuffle and scrapes on the wooden floor with all returning to their seats.

"It was my pleasure, even my duty," Arlan said, "to assist you in this task, for ye gave me aid when I was in need. I trust this is the beginning of a strong alliance between Dál Gaedhle and the House of Monsae of Dál Gallain. By our combined effort in restoring Monsae lands to you, my lady, we have secured this section of our joint border against our common enemy, Gallawain."

Cheers rose again along with the loud thunks of metal on wood while warriors banged knives and dagger handles on the wooden benches. Morrigan's cry hit my ears and Bàn thumped his dagger handle so hard on the bench, the vibration went right through me. Arlan waited, smiling, for the cheers to die down.

"I call Vygeas."

Vygeas rose and stood beside Arlan, his gaze on the floor, and he chewed the scar on the right of his lip. I leaned forward past Morrigan to see more clearly.

"Vygeas, for having my back in the thick of battle, ye may take first pick of the plunder. Forgive me for the paucity of it, for most belonged to Monsae, and we have returned it to the rightful owners. Please, take what ye wish."

"I thank you, Lord Arlan, but I need naught." Vygeas raised his face to Arlan. "To have served with you and Lady Leynarve of Monsae is all I need."

"So then, I cannot tempt you?"

Guests and warriors at the tables chuckled. Vygeas lifted a brief smile that twisted with the scarring at the right side of his mouth.

"Vygeas, of Clan Innësson, in gratitude for my life spared, I, Arlan MacEnoicht, Àrd Rìgh of Dál Gaedhle, bestow upon you the title of nobleman-warrior. We shall send to your father in the north of Dál Gaedhle this news that Innësson is now a noble house, with the right to obtain and own land."

A grin encompassed Vygeas' face. He turned to Leyna, who nodded a bow to him from where she sat. Some unspoken message passed between them.

"By this we will strengthen double the alliance between Dál Gaedhle and Dál Gallain through House Monsae," Arlan said.

The hall rang with cheers and clapping. Douglas wolf-whistled. Beside him sat Vygeas' knave, Aiden, whose eyes watered.

Bàn leaned into me. "Now they can wed," he said into my ear over the loud responses to this news.

My heartbeat went missing for a moment. *Huh? Now* nothing *makes sense!* My breathing tightened.

Vygeas bowed his head until the cheers died down, then looked at Arlan.

"It is with much regret that on first meeting ye, Lord Arlan, I did not do what I desire to do now." He unsheathed his sword, and on either side of me, warriors stilled. Bàn's forearm, resting on mine, tensed.

Vygeas dropped to one knee, placed his sword in front of himself, point buried in the rushes covering the floorboards, and grasped its handle. The muscles of Bàn's arm relaxed against mine.

"Arlan Finnbar MacEnoicht, Àrd Rìgh of Dál Gaedhle, I swear my sword to your cause and my life in faithful service to you."

Gasps of surprise tinged with approval rang around the hall. Arlan had not lifted his attention from Vygeas and now he nodded slowly.

"Vygeas of House Innësson," Arlan spoke with a husky voice, "I accept your allegiance, and thank ye for it. May I be worthy of all you have vowed."

Sighs and murmurs of support echoed through the hall and the guests' clapping grated on me, my forehead tight and my breath stuttering from Bàn's explanation.

"Lady Rhiannon," Arlan called.

My body stayed glued to the bench seat as Arlan's piercing blue gaze held me.

Bàn nudged my arm. "Ye must go to your lord àrd rìgh, Lady Rhiannon."

My legs obeyed me at last and I rose from the table with the stares of everyone present locked on me. I approached Arlan, my knees shaking. He smiled with his eyes and a corner of his mouth lifted.

"Be not shy, Lady Rhiannon." Arlan spoke loud enough for all to hear, but it seemed just for me. "We celebrate your first battle, and with a kill. Due to such, ye may choose what ye wish from the plunder."

I stopped a few paces from Arlan and turned to the pile of weapons and armour in front of him, my face heating in the deathly silent room. I scanned the pile and chose a dagger, the nearest one. Long and thin, its sharp edges shone silver. I could return Arlan's dagger to him if I had one of my own. I picked it up and Arlan grunted.

"I see ye chose the weapon that would have taken me if not for Lord Vygeas."

"What!" I leaned forward to throw it back onto the pile.

"Och, no. Keep it." He grasped my wrist with his warm, large hand, preventing me from returning it. "Ye deserve it. Besides, I am safe if this blade is in your hands." He picked something from the pile and handed it to me. It was the sheath that belonged to the extra-thin, long knife.

I stared at the dagger in my hand.

Someone tried to kill him with this! Why hadn't he mentioned that? Surely he would have told me of any close calls.

I mentally shook myself, bowed to Arlan, turned, and walked stiffly back to my seat. I hadn't yet reached my place next to Morrigan when Arlan called Muir to choose. With all eyes on someone else, I continued out of the hall and down the stairs. Sweat trickled between my breasts and my legs shook as I hurried the final steps to the cool air outside. I bent forward, hands resting on my thighs, still grasping the long, thin blade.

Heavy footsteps came behind me.

Oh, don't let it be Arlan. I can't face him now.

"Lady Rhiannon." It was Bàn. "Does something ail ye?"

I stood tall.

"Aye, something does *ail* me! I don't get it! How can he give Vygeas a noble title just like that"—I snapped my fingers under Bàn's nose— "but there's all this angst over me not being noble?"

Bàn opened his mouth.

"I know Arlan's not had his king making"—I threw my words at Bàn— "or whatever they do to make him official, but he can obviously dish out titles."

Why can't he just give me one and solve our problem?

Bàn never flinched but crossed his arms.

"Arlan was nearly stabbed to death? And I go and pick the very weapon that almost did it!" I shoved the thin dagger and its sheath at Bàn, handle first. "Here. You have it. I don't want it."

A torn dimple appeared on Bàn's scarred cheek.

"It's not funny." I clenched my jaw, my face blazing.

"My Lady Rhiannon." He unfolded his arms. "Lord Arlan, the Àrd Rìgh of Dál Gaedhle, can bestow the title of nobleman-warrior on Vygeas because he has links to the land and can name his clan."

My breath hitched, then I let my shoulders drop.

"And it was up to no one but Arlan himself," Bàn continued, "to inform ye of his narrow escape from death. And I believe he has nae because he wished to not upset you so."

"It didn't work." I spoke through gritted teeth.

The dimple in his cheek disappeared, and now his jaw muscles rippled.

"If ye did nae want tae be hurt, maybe ye should nae have jumped into his bed sae easily."

Heat boiled within me. *How dare he!* I took a deep breath, picking the choicest words I could think of in the Gaelic.

"Arlan rides tomorrow." Bàn interrupted my breath. "He wishes to gather support from those in north Dál Gallain who may waver in their allegiance to that cur, Gallawain. Well, that is what he announces to all. To me he says he'll wait nae longer for Eifion but will go and find the sage himself to hear his discoveries."

FORTY-TWO

— • —

Swords cross in a blade-edged kiss.
Yet their point can pierce a heart.

POETRY OF THE WARRIOR
WARRIOR SAGE TAPAÌDH
(4009-4059 POST DRAGON WARS)

The World of Dál Cruinne
Post Dragon Wars Year 6083
Eastern Clanlands of Dál Gallain
Caisteal Monsae

"Farewell, Vygeas. I would call ye friend." Arlan looked the ex-assassin in the eye.

The bustle in the bailey yard as warriors flung provision bags behind saddles, and Monsae servants shooed their children away from war horses' hooves, melted into the background. Arlan grasped Vygeas' outstretched hand in a wrist-on-wrist hold.

"I trust in time ye will call me sword-brother." Vygeas held his stare.

"Aye, ye are already." Arlan kept his grip tight, leaned in closer and lowered his voice. "Tell me. Why did ye do it?"

Vygeas quirked a scarred eyebrow.

"Determined yourself to be a warrior despite your station in life?"

Vygeas' hard lines melted for a fraction of a second, then his forehead returned to stretched leather. "Some men are born to fight, to know the joy of battle, to live in the moment and be alive at last... I am such a one. But I would not go to war equipped in the same manner as the other sons of steading holders, with pitchfork and scythe. I would go with a sword and fight with the blade." The corner of his mouth tweaked, and he drew Arlan yet closer. "Your woman," he whispered, "she longs for you. She stands aloof to protect herself. By Lugh Lámhfhada, I wish your sage all luck and trust Leynarve and I will hear news from you that gives us cause to celebrate."

Arlan swallowed. "I thank ye, Vygeas." He pulled away, but Vygeas clasped his wrist all the tighter.

"And"—Vygeas' torn eyebrow puckered— "I speak not only of your warrior's death, but you must not take the guilt of it all. Nor should you solely wear the blame. It walks around you like a shadow, though it need not." He stepped away, releasing his grip. "That is all I will say to you, Lord Arlan MacEnoicht, Àrd Rìgh of Dál Gaedhle."

Arlan left Vygeas' hazel stare. The man saw more than he could ever imagine. He nodded to himself in appreciation of the fact as he strode to Mengus.

He'd settled things with Leuchars in haste, ordering him to stay with his larger warband. Leuchars would reinforce the Monsae guard and encourage the regrouped Monsae warriors with some hard refresher training before returning to The Keep. Arlan's warband had prepared to leave, all wearing their leather armour, for encountering those faithful to Gallawain on their journey north was a high possibility. Rhiannon had packed her gear and now stood with her mare ready saddled.

So, she still regards herself as one of my own warriors.

He adjusted his new hardened leather gloves—found amongst the items plundered from the enemy—all the while a soft warmth glowed in his chest.

The guards at the caisteal's entrance tower spoke in questioning tones and their unsettled murmurs came into the bailey yard. Those about to mount stood still. A sage rode in, dusty and pale, his face creased to excess and sitting astride a horse with its head bowed low. It was Sage Alder.

Arlan strode toward the sage, who remained in the saddle. "Greetings, Sage Alder, but why are ye here and not at Craegrubha?"

"Oh, Lord Arlan, your older brother is indeed a determined man." The sage lowered himself from his horse and touched the ground with trembling feet. "Where is he? I will return him to the broch. He will take orders from you, for the young lord does not listen to me." Sage Alder drew himself up to his shaky full height. "And his manservant is weak and pliable. Why do you stare at me so?"

"Where is my brother?"

"Is he not here? He headed this way with all resolve and purpose. My strenuous efforts to stop him delayed him not. I come to beseech you to order him home."

"He's not here. And how have you lost him?"

Alder released a heavy sigh and glanced at his dusty boots. "I... We stayed at an inn a day's ride from here. I ate the fish. They dined on mutton. I emptied my stomach that night and my bowels for the next day. I recovered enough a day later to find he had left with his manservant for Caisteal Monsae. He wished to see the battle."

"Kyle. Is. Not. Here." Arlan ground out the words while within, burning and churning ground against each other. He would *not* delay his journey to find Eifion.

My brother, even in his diminished state, still seeks to obstruct me!

"Lord Leuchars." Arlan turned, and the war chief strode toward him. "I wish to be on my way. Naught must delay my mission to gather support from those in the north who waver in their allegiance to Ciarán Gallawain. I beg you, send a search for Lord Kyle and his man."

Leuchars answered with a wry smile. "My àrd rìgh, we've scoured the immediate vicinity whilst securing the caisteal and woods after the battle. If he were dead within bowshot of the caisteal, we would have encountered his body by now. Odds are, those who held Monsae have discovered him in their flight and taken Lord Kyle as hostage."

"Aye, Lord War Chief, for that is the way of war." Arlan swallowed. "Please send word when you have discovered where he is. It is sure to be Gallawain who holds him." Arlan turned and walked back to Mengus.

He wouldn't spend his life wearing the results of his brother's wilfulness and lack of discernment. He shook his head.

Aye, the issues with Kyle are as curly as a dragon's claw, and twice as sharp.

Arlan mounted his war horse, then he and his warriors rode, leaving Caisteal Monsae behind. Drayce flew for a while, soaring away to the forest skirting their path, then returning to land heavily on Arlan's forearm. The horses shied, and Mengus nickered a warning. With his free hand, Arlan scratched Mengus' forelock in a reassuring manner. His stallion twitched his ears.

"We cannot stay at inns on this journey, Arlan." Bàn rode beside him. "People will fear your dragon, and it would surprise me not if they sought to kill him."

Arlan's gut clenched. Drayce snuggled into his hair, tangling his knobbly head and neck in the strands. The dragon had grown, now almost the size of a hound, and much more difficult to conceal. Over the past few days, his hide had darkened to a deeper red.

"Aye, we'll camp. Well, I shall. The others can go into a nearby town."

"No, Lord Arlan." Angus rode with Adele behind Arlan. "We will stay with you and your beast. We fear him not, for Rhiannon tells us he is *cute*."

Arlan turned, Angus' face held a broad grin. Near the back of the line of warriors two abreast, Rhiannon rode beside Morrigan. She had spent most of her moments with Morrigan since... Well, she had a good friend and sword-sister in the noble warrior. It would do her no harm to bond with her further.

He faced ahead once more, pushing down an emptiness that competed in severity with that belonging to his thoughts of Father.

"Two day's ride north, ye say, Bàn?"

"We require a place to camp soon, Lord Arlan." Bàn's stallion plodded beside Mengus. "While the remaining light lingers for us."

"Aye," Arlan replied. "All must keep alert. We know not where those faithful to Ciarán Gallawain may hide."

"Gallawain's tower is that way, perhaps two long days' ride." Bàn pointed over his shoulder to his right. "We skirt the borders of Gallawain lands. Maybe none hereabouts will be predisposed, nor brave enough, to turn against him. For the lord has quite a reach."

"Aye, I plan to approach the caisteals even further north on our journey. Those nearer the border, and damaged in the skirmishes, may listen to me."

"Unless those lairds themselves were part of the raids."

"Aye," Arlan grunted.

He led his troop past yet another of the many steading farms and small hamlets that had lined their journey's path. He halted at a patch of green beside a forest of pine dotted with oak, a light breeze sweeping the tang of pine sap through the trees. He ordered camp set up. All supped on venison and rye bread supplied by the kitchens of Caisteal Monsae. With the meal clean-up attended to, Arlan assigned the first watch to Muir.

Sitting by the campfire, Arlan drained the last of his tea. Angus had set up a tether line at the forest's edge. Here, Rhiannon brushed down her mare's coat.

"Lady Rhiannon, would you please redress my wounds?" he called over to her.

In the night-shadowed darkness, Rhiannon's shoulders stiffened.

"I ken Lady Leyna has instructed you," he said at her hesitation.

She turned to face him. "Very well." Strain edged her voice. "But I don't have the supplies."

"I do"—he pointed to his kit— "and I'll be here by the fire when the others have settled."

Rhiannon finished grooming Bridie, then laid out her sleeping roll by a tree on the edge of the forest and near the tethered horses. The quiet bustle of Arlan's warriors settling down for the night surrounded him when she finally approached. He pointed to the saddlebag containing the dressings that Leyna had provided.

Rhiannon rummaged in the bag and brought out the small parcel of salt and a pan. She poured water into the pan from the pot, which had boiled over the fire and was set aside to cool, then threw a large pinch of salt into it. She wandered to Morrigan, the bag of bandages dangling from her hand, and whispered to her. Then both women returned to the fire.

Rhiannon, stony faced, set the bag on a patch of grass by the pot of salted water. Drayce trotted to her; his clumsy clamber led his face into hers.

"No, Drayce." She pointed to Arlan. "Go."

The dragon clicked mournfully and scampered over to him.

"You'll need to lie on your front, Lord Arlan." Rhiannon took a cloth from the bag.

Arlan spread his plaid on the ground, loosened his boots, and rolled his breeches up over his calves, then laid down on the woollen cloth. Rhiannon squatted beside him and gently removed the old bandages, then positioned herself so she could inspect his wounds by the light of the fire.

"How does it look, my lady?" He turned his head to face her.

The firelight caught the line of her features. Her glowing hair nestled above her creased brow and tight lips, but she said naught.

"Rhiannon?"

"Your burns have healed well, Lord Arlan," she said in official tones. "They look a healthy pink. No ooze or smell of infection and little rawness. You're a good healer. I won't need to do this again. When the bandages I apply tonight fall off, you can leave your legs bare. You must moisturise—put a salve on them." Her tone was clipped.

"You seem to you know of what you speak." An ache arose in his heart.

Where is the tenderness that once filled her voice?

"My mother burned her hand badly, and I had to take her to the clinic for her dressings. I watched the nurse and followed the progress of the healing burns. These might leave a thick silvery scar, like hers." She shrugged. "I've also got a St John's First Aid Certificate."

Rhiannon cleaned his calves with a deft hand. Her light touch sent shivers up to his buttocks and the cool liquid dampened the shivers. Her body's natural perfume, which always held a hint of floral, surrounded him. Her fingers were soft like silk where they touched his skin.

Rhiannon's silent distance pulled at his insides.

"There, done." She hastened away.

"Thank you, Lady Rhiannon," he said to her back as she walked off with Morrigan by her side.

For how much longer will it be like this? I can't get to the sage hold and Eifion fast enough!

He needed to breathe.

Drayce nudged Arlan, so he stood, leaving Rhiannon and his other warriors, and walked a short distance from the campsite. Drayce flew low beside him.

A bright moon shone, reflecting off the leaves of a nearby oak, and the damp spring air hung like a thin mist around him. He found a boulder by the tree just the right size for a seat and rested on it. Drayce glided to a branch and landed. Leaves shook, and the branch bowed with the dragon's weight, sending night birds scattering from the tree's shelter. An owl flew low past Arlan, a silent streak of movement.

Arlan reached over and picked a twig of oak, its developing acorns tiny, nut-like nobs between his fingertips. He should be on his way to The Keep and holding council with advisers. More warriors required training, for his warband must join with others. He must unite with clan chieftains, entreating them to add their warbands to become an army of a size to defend Dál Gaedhle. He would need to gather supplies, devise strategies and battle plans, and send scouts to monitor Ciarán Gallawain's activities. And he must also check on the sages' progress on producing gun powder. He huffed. Plus enlist the skills of one expert in smelting and moulding iron to help in the ways and means of making a cannon, like the sleek black beauties at Edinburgh Castle.

And there was also the question of maille, although it took an age to fashion into a useful garment. With a grunt he rapped his knuckles on his leather armour. He had grown accustomed to its earthy scent and the bulky tunic beneath. He nodded in acknowledgement of Vygeas' opinions on the garments.

Aye, it had forestalled injury in the battle for Monsae. To parts vital to life... *his* life. Though Leigh had not been able to stop the Gallawain warrior's blade from slashing his throat...

Arlan sighed, pushing away a heaviness in his chest, and forced his thoughts back to...

His diversion to this sage hold in the north would delay his planning, but he couldn't take another day not knowing of Rhiannon's heritage. He blew out between his lips. She *must* belong to a noble clan.

And if not?

A pressure built inside his heart as though it would tear. He was the àrd rìgh now. And his own desires must take second place. What a naïve fool to have thought, for even a moment, he could just wed Rhiannon without a care for her station in life nor the consequences of doing such. She had been more sensible, devoting herself to Dál Gaedhle's defence and not counting their relationship as a certainty just because she came to him through that portal.

No, his land and his people needed him. He'd promised Father he would serve until he slept at last with him. And he must keep that promise, no matter the cost.

He raised his eyes to the stars. He would do what he must. That was his destiny. The one he had *chosen*.

So be it.

He grunted, the tightness in his chest easing. He had more plans to consider.

Rhiannon's brief conversation with the policeman from the Other World had been fortuitous, indicating Ciarán had possibly discovered weapons from that world. He made a fist, stopping his thoughts travelling further on Rhiannon. The oak twig snapped in his gloved hand.

He must focus!

His warband had done well. He sat taller.

"Aye, I am proud of them," he said into the night.

How bravely they had battled. For most, their first proper battle. And his.

He'd only lost one of his own.

A weight, thick and dark like a moonless night, settled on him. He would visit Leigh's mother with a gift and an apology.

What would the hounds do now, for they would pine without Leigh?

He searched his recollections of the battle, seeking answers for any way to have prevented Leigh's loss. But each possible scenario could lead to death. No matter how he chose, it could always result in someone's death—one of his own who followed and trusted in him.

How did Father do it?

So much responsibility, and so much on him personally. And now on Arlan himself. He closed his eyes and let out a sigh that came from the depths of his being.

"I think I've never heard such a groan come from you," a voice came from the dimness of the night.

Arlan reached for his sword, grasping the sweat-moulded leather handle, then dropped his hand to his side.

"Och! Bàn!"

Bàn stepped beside him out of the misty moonlight. "Ye are taking the withholding of your woman's affections too hard."

"It's not only that... I lost Leigh." His throat threatened to close around his words. "My strategy was to surprise the enemy and lose none of my own."

"It was a battle." Bàn spoke in hushed tones, no doubt recalling Erin, a warrior he'd loved and lost in the skirmish beside a portal to the Other World. "Ye cannae save every one of your warriors in a battle, much less in a war."

"I could've prepared more thoroughly, trained my warriors harder. Made more efficient decisions... been a wiser battle chief... a cleverer àrd rìgh." He huffed, then shut his mouth tight, clamping down on the churning in his gut.

"Ye are not to blame for Leigh's death. Ye are not to blame for your woman withholding herself from ye. Arlan"—now a sharpness wove through Bàn's tone— "by my blade, you are not responsible for people's reactions." He seemed to collect his thoughts, as though they hung in the night air. "For their feelings in response to your orders. Nor the decisions they make to fulfil them. It goes how it goes, and àrd rìgh or no', ye cannot control everything." He flung his hands up. "Aye, and even how *they* feel about the *what* and the *why* of all our efforts against Ciarán Gallawain."

Bàn stood in front of him now.

"It's not just you as àrd rìgh. I ken ye take the responsibility seriously, and ye'll be a grand high king because ye do. But it isn't only *you*. We are all with ye. All of us behind and beside ye. Each with our own strengths and abilities. From your warriors to your sages to your servants and steading holders."

Bàn's hands rested at his belt, and he squared his shoulders. "Och, ye are being self-centred again. It's no' about you, nor the àrd rìgh. It's about the warbands of Dál Gaedhle against Ciarán Gallawain and all he intends to do—and all o' it is harm." His words hardened. "Ye must let us share the fault and the praise equally with yourself. For when the sages write the histories, they will say 'Arlan Finnbar MacEnoicht Àrd Rìgh of Dál Gaedhle led, *and with his warriors and advisors*, defeated Ciarán Gallawain... or were defeated by him'." His voice took an edge. "But he never did it *alone*." Bàn's breath blew into Arlan's face. "We are *all* part of what makes our story in *our* time. So, stop sulking!"

Bàn strode off without another word.

Arlan blinked and shut his mouth. Then he hung his head. Bàn was right. And Eifion had said it all along. *An àrd rìgh is not a one-person role.* He needed them all and couldn't do it without them.

All their destinies entwined with his. And his with theirs.

"But why does my task feel so...?" His deep rumble vibrated into the night.

His mind flew to a man content in his role. A humble farrier who did outstanding work on Mengus' enormous hooves. The man performed his tasks with joy. With pleasure, even.

If this is my life and my role in history, I must find the joy in it.

"Aye, if we must battle, I will receive great satisfaction in defeating Ciarán Gallawain."

On the branch above him, Drayce clicked, then lifted into the air.

Arlan's shoulders eased, like someone had removed a block of stone from him. He gazed into the night and let the tightness in his neck float away.

"Drayce has been gone too long." Arlan had ordered an early start to the day's journey, well before the sun had curved above the horizon. Now, with the silver orb's travels across the sky almost done, Arlan searched the late afternoon sky. "I worry he's injured himself."

"Or met another dragon and flown away with his love." Beside him on his war horse, Bàn's face lifted.

"Nae, there are no other dragons roaming free."

"Are you sure?"

Screeching and gusting air drew closer, then Drayce glided past Bàn, a hand span from his head. Bàn ducked and cursed, his war horse curvetting.

"He heard you," Arlan chuckled.

Mengus whinnied. Arlan tightened the reins and stroked his neck. "*Mo dheagh charaid*," he crooned. *My dear friend.*

Drayce glided from the other side and landed on Arlan's shoulder, where he jostled, blowing Arlan's hair across his face.

"Och, ye are well too large for my shoulder now. *Phew*. What have ye eaten?" Tufts of wool hung from the dragon's pointy teeth, and the stink of raw meat and lanolin wafted from his mouth. "I must devise a way of keeping Drayce from depriving another steading holder of his livelihood."

The dragon perched in front of Arlan on the saddle, tail draped down one side of Mengus. The stallion nickered, flicking his ears back.

"Stay, Drayce," Arlan commanded, holding the dragon in place with one hand until he settled, and rubbing his war horse's neck with the other.

Mengus turned his head to peer behind at the dragon's tail, giving the disdainful look and grunt he usually reserved for the hounds.

Douglas trotted his horse near. It tossed its head and snorted at the dragon. "Shall we camp by this burn, lord? We've spied hare. Muir and I will hunt."

"Very well, but please count Drayce as a mouth to feed."

They halted near the burn. Douglas took his bow and arrow, and Muir his spear, *Sleaghach*, and headed to the nearby field the group had just passed. Arlan assisted the others to make camp, and when dusk fell, the two hunters returned. They held two brace of hare, enough for a decent meal, and a couple of scraggy young ones for Drayce. Both warriors wore furrowed brows, and Douglas sent sidelong glances to Muir.

"What is amiss?" Arlan directed his question to Douglas.

Douglas spat. "There may be folk around... and... Deamhan's balls! I'll let the old man tell ye, lord. For it makes nae sense to me."

Arlan bore his stare into Muir, who handed the hare to Douglas and cleared his throat.

"I thought I saw something, Lord Arlan. Nae, someone." Muir looked to the ground and shuffled his shoulders.

"This is not like you, Muir. Tell me, what disturbs you so?"

"Lord, perhaps the descending sun, removing her light from our day and casting shadows, tricked me into thinking I glimpsed Lord Ciarán walk the field where we hunted."

Ciarán Gallawain *here*?

"You doubt it?" Arlan asked Muir. "Why?"

Muir rested *Sleaghach*'s shaft end to the ground and leaned on the haft. "I saw him, then I did nae."

"The man disappeared?" The hairs on the back of Arlan's neck rose.

"Aye. 'Tis strange to begin with. Why would the man be here, far from his tower when he has others to do whatever he bids?"

Rhiannon had drawn close to the conversation. Adele stood by her, tightening her baldric straps, preparing for her turn at the watch.

"What made you think it was him?" Rhiannon asked.

"Aye," Douglas grunted. "For all I spied were hare aplenty."

"Ye began your warrior service in my father's own troop." Arlan spoke above Douglas' protests. "You would have seen my cousin, would ye not, Muir?"

"Aye, lord. I ken the man." Muir stood tall. "And I saw him just now. But then not." He shrugged.

"We had better investigate," Adele said. "I'll go, lord. 'Tis my watch."

"Not only you, Adele. Douglas, Muir, Angus. Scout and return with surer information." He lifted his chin in command and the warriors spread out from the campfire to inspect the four quadrants of their immediate surrounds. The cooling evening air tickled a mist from the nearby burn. It rose and surrounded their small camp, swirling throughout the fields beside them.

Rhiannon assisted Morrigan to skewer the hare on fresh green sticks and cook them over the fire. The aroma of roasted meat with a charcoal tinge filled the air by the time the scouts returned. Muir approached Arlan, his brow scrunched.

"My lord, forgive an old man's imaginings." He shook his head. "There is naught to be found out there the noo."

"Och, no. I trust you, my most experienced warrior." Arlan kept his tone gentle. "If ye saw him, he was there, but has retreated from our view. We must still be vigilant. Bàn, Douglas, you are on watch with Adele."

His warriors went to their task, melting into the gathering mist.

Arlan stood by the campfire opposite the others, his sword remained strapped to his back, within hand's reach. Arlan finished his serve of spit-roast hare, and Drayce, sitting beside him, had eaten two raw. He patted his dragon's cool, scaly hide.

Angus looked up from where he sat on the other side of the firepit, licking the last of the meat juices from his fingers. "If Ciarán Gallawain is nearby, does he follow us?"

"Nae, the man has spies." Morrigan dismissed Angus's question with a wave of her hand. "If it is him, he is up to no good so close to the northern edge of our border, aye?"

"Why does he wish to crush you, lord?" Angus interrupted. "Does he truly desire Dál Gaedhle for his own?"

Arlan rested his hands on his belt and his gaze drifted to the crackling coals in their firepit. Perhaps Gallawain wished to burn this land and every trace of its àrd rìgh. Just as he had burned Father from it, using a dragon's breath. Until he engaged with Ciarán, he could only gauge the rebel lord's desires by his current actions. Subjugating many eastern lairds and their clans and creating enough disturbance to send a continual stream of refugees over the border, only spoke of a conqueror bent on taking all he could spy.

"Outright war is such a waste." Morrigan broke the thoughtful silence. "Of warriors and equally those who fight not. For the disorder and the starvation it brings destroys lives as much."

"Lord?"

Arlan looked up from the fire. Opposite him, Angus' intense expression demanded a response.

"I have never met Ciarán Gallawain. Nor did I know of his existence until the àrd rìgh's council meeting that sent us on our reconnaissance mission to the border. I put nothing past the man. Although he is my mother's cousin and of her clan, I see none of her in his actions. Nor any family traits."

"What would ye do if ye met him?" Angus asked.

"I know not how I would feel if I met the man. But I'd endeavour to speak some sense into him. We need not a war. Morrigan is correct. It is such a waste. Negotiation must be the better way."

"But ye are a fighter, lord." Angus' brow beetled. "Our warrior king."

"Aye, I wish to fight with my words and save us all from needless battles. But if the man reasons not..."

In the camp hearth, coals seethed heat into Arlan's face and released wisps of smoke while his thoughts swirled. Rhiannon sat opposite, gazing into the dying embers, her face aglow in the lambent light. He tore his gaze away from her and out into the low hanging fog. Those on watch had reported naught.

Nothing to find, then? Muir imagining things?

Hmph.

"I shall go see what the others are up to." He strode away from the camp through a small copse, the night mist speckling his cheeks with cool.

Close and to his left, the tall, shadowed figure of Douglas waved, then strode in another direction, his foot tread diminishing as he increased the distance between them.

Many paces away from the camp, a distant glow caught Arlan's eye. The fog thinned around an illuminated henge of upright stones, a cromlech. The tall stones, ancient and worn, in the light-scattering mist looked like the teeth of a giant, its jawbone left in the ground to rot. In the still night air, a familiar sound arced across from it. A strange noise to his world, and one he'd not come across since leaving the Other World.

The grunt of an engine.

FORTY-THREE

— • —

Darkness or light, tangible or elusive, of matter or of spirit—
Or both.
We all choose the god for whom we serve.

SECRET SACRED WRITINGS OF THE SAGES

The World of Dál Cruinne
Post Dragon Wars Year 6083
Eastern Clanlands of Dál Gallain
North

Arlan ran toward the light and sound.

The henge of upright stones stood an arrow shot away, shimmering amber in the light of a flickering torch.

Och, no. He skidded to a halt, slipping on the dewy grass.

"I need my warriors." He spun from the direction of the large sandstone monoliths and sprinted, reaching the campsite in no time.

Adele kept watch not far from the fire pit, surveying the mist-shrouded night. Angus and Morrigan had their heads bent together in quiet conversation.

"Bàn!"

Arlan's youngest warriors by the fire rose at his shout.

Muir darted from the tree line on the far side of their camp, his creased brow a runnel of shadows in the glow from the pit. "What is it, lord? Have ye seen him?"

Rhiannon was rummaging in her saddlebags with her back to Arlan and turned at Muir's question.

Bàn and Douglas emerged from the misty night, Douglas coming at a run toward him.

Drayce flew to Arlan, who ducked, and the dragon screeched, landing beside him on the ground.

"Your wee dragon is wee nae longer, lord." Douglas panted.

"Aye, Douglas, and ye shall mind him for me." Arlan patted Drayce's head in passing.

"Ah... Does Rhiannon no' hold the wee beastie?" Douglas' frown glowed in the firelight as he followed Arlan's progress.

"Nae, not tonight, for I need Rhiannon." He strode to her, his voice thudding with each step.

Rhiannon's eyes widened as he neared.

"What's wrong, Lord Arlan?" Angus gripped his sword handle over his shoulder.

So did Morrigan, and Rhiannon grabbed her own sword.

"Ye must come. There's a portal nearby, and I hear an engine," Arlan said, looking only at Rhiannon.

"A what?" Muir asked.

"A portal?" Rhiannon's eyes grew even wider. "Is it Ciarán Gallawain?"

"Then ye will need us." Douglas spoke over Rhiannon.

"I need stealth and those who know portals, and the tongue of the Other World may be required," he replied to Douglas. "You and Adele stay watch. Break camp and be ready if we retreat. Mind my dragon, for he will try to fly to me. I wish no harm to come to him, and if Ciarán Gallawain is near and sees Drayce, he will desire him."

Arlan turned and ran. The others were close behind. Grunts and curses and a dragon's squawk echoed from the campsite, but Drayce didn't follow.

Not long after leaving the campfire's light, through the sketchy silhouette of a clump of gorse, the glowing view of the henge ahead grew clearer. Arlan ran to the rush of a burn and followed it. The babbling water, covered in a drift of fog, led toward the revving engine and the ring of standing stones, which was roughly the diameter of his broch's round hall. Shouts travelled across to him through the night air. An older man's voice yelled orders and the engine roar ceased.

Thirty paces from the glow, Arlan could make out the scene. Illumination, from what could only be a wide-open portal, emanated in the centre of the ring of stones. Through the portal, the golden sunlight of the Other World shone, touching with a yellow light the vehicle parked between two of the standing stones. A young man sat in the driver's seat. The conical beams of the headlights of this vehicle caught the moist air and lit a middle-aged man's outline while he stood in front of the vehicle, shouting. Tall with long greying hair, he dressed in leather armour with a sword strapped to his back.

Arlan directed his warriors to hunker down behind a clump of gorse beside the burn. He turned to Rhiannon, who'd crept closer and peered at the scene.

"That's an armoured jeep with a machine gun!" she whispered. "Who's driving it?"

A long tube, like a small cannon, fixed to the back of the vehicle, had a belt of spiked metal draped from it and curled in the tray at its base. Metal plated most of this car and the wheels were chunky.

The engine's roar had stopped, and the burn's babble rose above the quiet. The older man gave orders in the tongue of Dál Cruinne and the young man answered, but the words weren't clear.

"They're from this world," Arlan whispered over his shoulder. "The one who drives has—"

"Been shopping in the Other World, but I doubt he paid for it," Rhiannon finished.

A gasp came from the burn beside them. A dark figure dressed in a black hooded robe stood in water up to their waist in the swift flowing current. The person turned, revealing a young man's face stretched in discomfort under the hood.

"Lord Ciarán!" The man's deep voice rang over the rush of the burn. "We are discovered." The light glowing from the portal went out while it slowly closed.

"What are you doing?" the grey-haired man roared across the way to the man in the water. "Keep it open, fool!"

Dragon's breath! The one in the burn was a mage!

"That's why I saw, but did nae see, Lord Ciarán," Muir rasped. "His mage must have covered him."

Metal hissed as swords flew from sheathes.

Arlan sprang forward, running hard toward the standing stones, trusting his warriors to follow. Grunts came from behind him, and he glanced over his shoulder. Bàn stood with sword raised as though pressed against a clear wall. Beside him, Rhiannon was poised mid-stride, her face contorted and lips moving rapidly, but no sound reached him. Morrigan pointed her weapon at the mage in the burn, who now held his arms out in their direction.

"Drive, you fool! Get it out of here," the older man ordered—was it *really* Ciarán Gallawain? "I won't waste the bullets on them."

Arlan continued ahead, his neck cool with sweat, while the standing stone circle sitting in a swirling mist loomed closer.

The jeep engine's roar rang through the night, then it drove away off to the east. The thud of booted footsteps came toward Arlan, along with the hiss of a sword drawn swiftly from its sheath. Both belonged to the figure of the middle-aged man who had stood by the jeep. He now advanced with speed, backlit by a burning torch that sat at the place where a portal had stood open. Light shone in Arlan's eyes, and he squinted to gain a better view of the swordsman marching toward him.

"Ha! I cannot believe my luck!" The older man spoke in superior tones. "I have never met you, cousin, but you are the spitting image of Donnach." He spat the name as though it tainted his mouth, and he could not rid himself of its taste soon enough.

Damainte!

Arlan pressed his lips tight against the ream of expletives that sought to escape them. This warrior could *only* be Ciarán Gallawain. He was certain of it now.

Arlan raised his weapon, adjusting his grip, readying to fight, but said nothing. His breath came steady, and his pulse thundered in his temples. He ground his teeth against the vitriol rising in his mouth.

This one killed Father.

"What? No greeting? Very well, let us begin." Ciarán stepped forward, his broadsword's blows flying fast.

Arlan blocked each one with Camhanaich.

Ciarán stepped back. Arlan circled his sword on either side of his body in protective arcs, watching.

Ciarán's blade spun and flew around him, flashing in the torchlight, his contact with Arlan's blade was fast. Arlan returned each stroke. He stepped, parried, and thrust. The metallic ring of each sword clash filled his ears. Ciarán swiped and hacked, holding the broadsword with one hand as though it were a mere short sword. Arlan blocked and jabbed, thrust and swung, swiped and ducked.

Ciarán flowed back, his steps graceful, and now with both hands, held his blade high above his head, intimidating but leaving himself wide open. Arlan side stepped. It was a trap into which he would not go. Ciarán would slice down without hesitation.

"Ah, Donnach taught you well. Or was it Leuchars? How is the red-headed beast?"

Arlan focused on Ciarán's eyes, waiting for the tell-tale flicker of eye movement that would give away a hint of Ciarán's next move. He held his peripheral vision ready to catch any twitching muscle.

"Yes, I know them all." Ciarán's teeth gleamed white in the lantern's glow. "And I knew your mother *very* well. There is none of her in you. You are MacEnoicht through and through." He stepped forward, blade flying, spinning.

Arlan fanned his sword in defence, covering every opening, returning with counter thrusts and blows. He swallowed.

The man was good. *More than good.*

He gulped air, sweat dripping down his brow while the stabs and slashes continued. Ciarán skipped back and Arlan pressed forward, focusing on any gap or opportunity. The man's circles were tight and fast, and his balance perfect. Ciarán stopped, poised on the balls of his feet.

Able to hold them in no longer, Arlan's hoarse words burst out. "Why did you kill my father?"

"Oh, it was not *I* who killed your father." Ciarán's sword did not waver, and his mouth drew into a leer. "Did you not hear? 'Twas a dragon."

Heat coursed through Arlan's body, driving him forward, his sword locking with Ciarán's, who pushed against it. The force Ciarán exerted seemed out of proportion to the man's build and apparent strength. Then Ciarán eased his resistance, leaving Arlan's momentum to force him unexpectedly closer. Ciarán sliced down across Arlan's left arm, tearing through his padded tunic, the razor-edged blade cutting deep, then stepped back. Retreating a step, Arlan's footing skidded on loose stones among the dew-wet grass.

This master swordsman is better than I.

Kyle must be right—I will never be good enough.

Arlan regained his footing, then pushed forward, turning his blade's arc tight and left, chopping down, forcing Ciarán through a gap between the standing stones. Their blades connected along their lengths. Ciarán angled his blade and slid it down Arlan's sword edge, pushing Arlan's blade away and skipping the tip of his own along the neckline of Arlan's armour, then landing at his throat. Ciarán's sword point pressed in, sharp and cold.

Arlan flinched back. Ciarán pushed harder, going with the flow of Arlan's momentum. He forced Arlan backward, tipping his point of balance. Unsteady now, Arlan held his upper torso at an awkward angle to avoid a slice to the neck. Arlan skidded for some paces, the grass slick beneath his boots. His footing gone, he fell with Ciarán's blade at his throat all the way to the ground.

Barely managing to keep his sword in his grasp, he skittered backward on all fours. Ciarán followed his slithering retreat with a twisted smile on his lips. Hard rock thudded against Arlan's back, clunking his head, knocking his teeth together. Ciarán halted his advance and hovered over him, keeping his body well out of reach of Arlan's blade.

Arlan grabbed Ciarán's sword with his gloved left hand, his upper arm burning with the previous cut, but his sight crystal clear. Blood's metal hung in the air. The side of Ciarán's face shone in the torchlight. Stone-grey eyes looked down at him along Kyle's aquiline nose. Arlan gasped and blinked back the wave of hurt that surged from childhood memories. He gritted his teeth. He would *not* be distracted by the uncanny similarity between the two men.

Arlan sought a way to move from the blade. With his back against a hard sarsen, no manoeuvres came without the real risk of his throat cut. He must break his immobility.

"What do you want, Ciarán?"

"What do *I* want?" Ciarán's tone held the same power as Kyle's voice.

A sense of worthlessness rose from deep within Arlan's soul, its ascent nudged by the pain of Kyle's bullying now ghosted in the actions of Ciarán.

"The answer to your question consumes too much time." Ciarán glared at Arlan down his sword's shaft.

Arlan's past surfaced, threatening to blind him to the present. He forced against it.

I must come out of this, and not only for myself.

"What do you want of *me*?" Arlan spoke with force.

The point of Ciarán's icy blade remained pressed, sharp, and piercing the skin at his throat, pinning him in place.

"I desire nothing of you. *You* are a piece on a playing board." Ciarán sneered. "The tail end of a cloud passing. A mist burned off by the sun." Scorn tainted his voice. "After my great battle, no one will remember the son of Donnach MacEnoicht. Just as *his* memory is but a passing shadow."

Arlan panted against the blade's edge. If only he could breathe in deep and gain some clarity.

"Ye want fame? Your name recorded for time immemorial?"

"You mean a monument to my memory?" Ciarán snorted a derisive laugh. "No. That is a standing stone. A menhir, which in millennia from now is an oddity in a field. A farmer will plough around it, ignorant of the words its runes speak. The crop will grow, and the stalks cover the name and accolades."

Arlan's forehead tightened, chilling with the sweat he dripped.

"For what, then, do you seek? What is the reason for the striving? Why will you inflict destruction, devastation and *death* on our world?"

"To beat it," Ciarán snarled.

Arlan breathed out his incomprehension.

"To beat Death, the King of the World. None can deny his tax. None can disobey his command. No one is free from his mortgage. The insignificant and the esteemed finish the race in the same position—residing in the grave as neighbours. None return from it." The blade pressed harder and Ciarán bore his stare further into Arlan. "No, young MacEnoicht, High King of Dál Gaedhle, I seek to cheat it."

"By slaughter and conquest!" Arlan's stomach churned, and his head grew light. Still grasping Ciarán's blade, he pushed against it with his gloved hand. The cool metal edge wouldn't budge, stinging his throat. A trickle of warmth came from where its point pressed in.

"We all serve someone. None is masterless." Ciarán stood taller now. "My lord and I have an agreement."

A screeching rent the air, echoing through the night, and gaining in volume. Ciarán looked up, the point of his blade at Arlan's throat not lessening its force. A shrieking animal cry and flapping of wings in the night sky drew nearer.

"What? A... dragon?" Awe filled Ciarán's exclamation. He flashed a look at Arlan. "On with the game, young king. But here's a little something to mar that beauty so like Donnach's." Ciarán wrenched his sword from Arlan's grasp and the sharp point at his throat disappeared. The cool edge of the blade sliced his left cheek, leaving a sting.

"Come, Bram!" Ciarán's deep, arrogant voice slipped away in the night, far to Arlan's right.

Arlan's mouth dried. He gulped air and shaking overtook him.

"Arlan!" Rhiannon's and Bàn's strangled voices choroused.

Arlan turned to the burn.

Empty.

Released from their magic restraints, his warriors ran to him.

Drayce landed by him and spread his wings like a shield, screeching and roaring like a *deamhan* beast.

FORTY-FOUR

— • —

For behind this world's physical realm there sits another where two principalities reside in opposition. The climax of our world's history will be the conclusion of their conflict.

SECRET SACRED WRITINGS OF THE SAGES

The World of Dál Cruinne
Post Dragon Wars Year 6083
Eastern Clanlands of Dál Gallain
By a Portal in the North

"Arlan!"

My scream vibrated back to me from the clear shield blocking me—us—from Arlan. I pounded against the *nothing* that stung my hand with pure energy. It seemed to go on forever on either side of us. No way around it.

I shrieked his name again. He fell to the ground with Ciarán's pointed blade at his throat.

Everything inside me melted.

This was the end.

Arlan's done for.

The older man had spun like a top, his sword invisible in the whirl of his fighting.

"No!" Bile scorched my mouth. My ribs were tight from screaming—burning.

I bashed the pommel of my sword against the unyielding shield of power that prevented me, Bàn, Muir, Angus, and Morrigan from stepping any closer.

Drayce tore from the sky. Behind this magical shield I couldn't hear a thing, but with his mouth opening and closing, I guessed he was screeching. Ciarán swivelled his gaze up to the sky and his mouth dropped open, as though he'd lost interest in Arlan for a moment. His expression, shaded by the half-light, was of amazement. His attention

262

returned to his sword pointing at Arlan's throat. He pulled it back and flicked it up past Arlan's face. Drayce flapped closer. The dragon's bared teeth were like spikes aimed at the older man. Ciarán turned and ran, almost twisting in two to keep his eye on Drayce while he did. Drayce landed by Arlan and spread his wings.

The wall evaporated, filling my hearing with Drayce's shrieks directed at the retreating lord and his mage.

I reached Arlan before Bàn, my pulse thudding in my temples and visions of Arlan forced to the ground at the point of a sword doing slow-motion replays in my mind. Arlan sat up, still leaning on one of the standing stones, grasping his left upper arm while blood spilled between his gloved fingers. A metallic scent hit my nose.

"Grab that lantern over there," I yelled.

Angus ran to the lantern sitting where the portal had remained open well past sunset. He grabbed it and sprinted back to us. The approaching glow lit a cut in Arlan's cheek weeping blood with pink flesh visible beneath the sliced skin, plus a small cut at the base of his throat.

I dropped my sword.

"Loosen your fingers from your arm. I need to see if it's a bleeding artery." I manoeuvred the lantern for the best light, ignoring my shaking limbs.

Arlan lifted his hand from his wound. His blood soaked the torn edges of his tunic sleeve, obscuring my view. I unsheathed my dagger and cut away the damaged sleeve. No spurting, only ooze came from the wide injury to Arlan's now exposed arm. But constantly.

"Okay, so it a vein, not an artery. It'll need to be sutured soon, though. Within six hours. Your wounds need dressing, and your arm requires a firm bandage." I turned to Bàn. Deep creases etched his face. "Help me get him to our camp. I have Leyna's dressings there."

"I am fine." Arlan shuffled to stand, only managing a half crouch. "I can walk!"

Bàn grabbed Arlan's uninjured arm and helped him stand upright, then we both walked beside him. Muir and Morrigan joined us and we made our way back to camp.

"He and his mage are nowhere in sight," Muir said, his sword in one hand and spear in the other.

"No trace of them." Morrigan strode ahead, turning to the way we had come and walking backwards, scanning the stone henge behind us. Her sword remained drawn.

Arlan didn't speak, only his raspy breath filled the night air. He gripped his injured arm tightly to his chest and blood dripped from his cheek. We were all speechless around him, his warriors' concern palpable in their silence. Drayce flew close, circling above Arlan's head.

Adele saw us first. "What is amiss?"

"Put more wood on the fire," Bàn ordered. "Lady Rhiannon needs light by which to tend to Lord Arlan's wounds."

Douglas jumped into action and threw small logs on the diminished campfire while Arlan sat near it. I ran to the saddlebags and dug into Arlan's, fumbling for clean bandages. I gripped them tight, closing my eyes.

Get a handle on it, girl!

I dashed back to Arlan by the fire. Blood covered his arm, his gloved fingers sticky with it. He looked pasty. From the blood loss of his injuries?

Or, maybe, from meeting Ciarán Gallawain face to face.

I ignored the trembling threatening to consume me and pressed on. "Remove your hand." My command came out sharper than I'd intended.

He's bleeding. He'll get an infection. They don't have trauma hospitals here. Or antibiotics!

Stop it! Get on with this now. Cover his wound.

I swallowed past a desert for a mouth and willed my shaking hands to obey. I had to think.

A neat slice from the sharp blade separated the skin of his blue tattoo-covered arm. The gash ran across his outer upper arm and cut through part of the bicep muscle. It continued to ooze. I took a breath.

"Okay. Whisky." I turned to Bàn. "You always have some. I need to clean this before I cover it with a firm bandage." I spoke to his back.

Bàn had already run to his saddlebags. "Prepare the horses," he ordered Angus and Morrigan. "The sage hold is half a night's ride. We leave as soon as Lady Rhiannon has bandaged our lord."

Morrigan scurried to the horses, but Angus just stood there. He looked from Arlan's arm to Bàn, then back again. "What if the sages cut it—"

"Hush!" Striding by, Bàn glared at Angus.

Angus spun on his heel and ran to Morrigan.

What? I shook my head briefly. I didn't have time to wonder what they meant. I grasped Arlan's bearded chin and turned his cheek to the light.

"It's not deep but will also need suturing." I stared intently at Arlan. "Do you do that here?"

"They're skilled at the sage hold." Bàn had returned with whisky. "They can sew it, if that's what ye mean."

I grunted in reply and took the flask of whisky from him, then focused on Arlan's arm.

"This may sting, but I don't want you getting an infection." Straight away I poured the whisky over open wound in Arlan's arm.

"Ahhh!" Arlan bit down on his lip and rocked back and forth for a minute. Drayce flapped wildly at Arlan's gasp.

"Somebody get Drayce, please," I asked.

Douglas reached for the dragon, who dodged and flapped, avoiding his grasp.

"Don't hurt him," Arlan said, then bit down on his lip again. "Wait until he settles near me, then hold him."

Drayce lifted and flew, circled the group, then, on seeing we weren't reaching for him, glided and landed next to Arlan. Douglas grabbed the dragon and spoke to him in soothing tones like he would to a startled horse.

I wiped the blood and alcohol off Arlan's arm, cleaning it with what I had, then wadded a clean piece of linen and got a bandage ready.

"Bàn, put your hand on either side of this cut and press the edges together."

Bàn placed his hands on Arlan's freshly wiped skin, avoiding the trickles of blood that'd started already, and pushed the edges of the wound closer to each other.

"Keep your hands away from the exposed muscle," I told Bàn, then covered the gaping wound with the wad of clean linen.

I wound the linen bandages firmly, around and around Arlan's arm, leaving a section of bandage at the end, which I ripped down the middle longways and tied to secure it. I slid my belt from my waist and made a sling.

"You need to keep your arm immobile. Any movement will tear your wound wider. And if you're riding..."

"Aye, he is." Muir led Mengus, who he'd saddled ready.

"I'm going to wash your face with alcohol," I said to Arlan.

He gave me a guarded look. "I thank ye for more forewarning this time."

I tilted his head back and trickled the whisky over his cheek. The fluid ran down his beard, neck, and armour. He groaned but didn't move. I placed a wad of folded linen over his cheek and bandaged it in place around his head and chin.

"Your throat's... cut. Though not so bad as the other cuts. J-j-just skin." I stuttered through my adrenalin surge, then wadded another piece of linen and held it in place with a thin bandage around his neck. "Now your left hand. You grabbed his sword, yeah?"

"Aye, but—"

I pulled the thick leather glove off his hand. It was more like a gauntlet.

"—my new glove protected my fingers," Arlan finished.

I inspected the slices along two fingers. "They're only shallow, but I'll bandage them too."

I ripped a bandage in half lengthwise and bound each wounded digit separately. He'd need to hold the reins. I giggled, the shaking from my centre now flowing out with my jittery laugh.

Ah, adrenaline.

"What's sae funny?" Arlan's words were tight, his jaw less mobile now bandaged.

"Sorry. You look like the walking wounded."

"He *is* the walking wounded." Bàn spoke into my ear. "By my blade! While we all remain whole." He gave an exasperated grunt.

"Why *does* only our lord bear wounds?" Adele tore her glare through the gathered group.

Arlan stood. "Ciarán's mage held them back," he said, his voice grave. "I must enquire of Eifion why the man stood waist deep in a rushing burn."

"Let me help ye mount, lord." Muir held out his hand.

"Why did he not finish ye, Arlan?" Bàn asked, and the horse saddling, camp packing, and torch making halted.

I searched Arlan's face while all looked to him. He straightened up and reached for Mengus, his Adam's apple bobbing.

"Why? Aye, a good question, for the man could have. It seems he has plans, and me remaining alive—for now—would be part of them." Arlan dropped his gaze to the ground. His bandage didn't hide the ache in his eyes, like he'd lost something essential.

Oh, Arlan thinks he'll fail. He doubts we can win.

"Arlan." I gentled my voice, raging against the whirlpool rising from my gut. "We'll beat him. Your army against his."

Grunts of agreement surrounded me. Arlan tilted his head to the left, his usual action when thinking.

"Not only is he a far superior swordsman than I, but he's also a tactician. The man wants his day of glory. I am... *we* are... only a means to Ciarán Gallawain's finale, and merely actors on his stage. He wishes for our spectacular end on a Mòr Cath Làraich of his determining." He sighed heavily.

My face grew tight while I madly pieced together the Gaelic words for their meaning.

"In the Other World"—Arlan faced me— "ye would name it Armageddon."

FORTY-FIVE

— • —

The man selected to lead the leaders of the families must be without fault. Chosen as chief among chiefs, he is to parade bare before those clans gathered on the moot hill. With a firebrand, the sage shall pass the flame over all his body, to reveal to the people the man's perfection for the task.

FROM THE ANCIENT HISTORIES OF DÁL CRUINNE

The World of Dál Cruinne
Post Dragon Wars Year 6083
Western Sovereignty of Dál Gaedhle
Sage Hold of the Healers

I held Drayce tight in front of me on the saddle.

He'd squawked and clicked his distress for most of the journey and I often had to stop him from leaping onto Arlan while I rode beside Mengus. We crossed the border during the long night and now the edges of the horizon tinged with light. We reached rows of grapevines and Angus sped ahead, leaving a trail of dust in his wake.

The vineyards went on and on until finally an ambling group of wooden structures surrounded by a high slatted fence came into view, and Bàn slowed the group to a fast trot.

Green-robed sages stood in front of the main building, and I pulled Bridie up sharp with the others. Angus ran from the cluster of sages, then he, with Bàn and Muir, helped Arlan down from Mengus. Arlan moved awkwardly with one arm bandaged, and lines etched his brow. The sages directed them to some smaller buildings off to the side. Drayce squawked an agonising noise.

"Here, you take him." I gave him to Douglas, who grabbed the flapping dragon and clucked softly to him.

I raced to the group of robed men and women hovering in the doorway of the room where they'd taken Arlan. Eifion stood there, about to enter. The crowd had parted and stood back with respectful expressions on their faces.

"Sage Eifion"—I grasped his arm— "please let me come in with you."

He nodded sharply, taking me by the hand and leading me into the room. The door shut behind us. The room looked like the sage's equivalent of a *medical clinic*, with a treatment table and another with leather satchels arranged on it. A peat fire burned in a small hearth in the corner where a sage stirred a steaming pot while another ground something with a mortar and pestle.

Bàn and Muir sat Arlan on the waist-height table, hovering anxiously with Angus by their side. A dozen frowning sages looked on while a tall man with thick, greying hair peered at Arlan's arm while another unwrapped my makeshift bandages.

The main sage examined Arlan's arm and tutted. "Is it ready?" he asked the sage by the fire.

The woman poured a hot liquid into a mug and brought it to Arlan.

"This is for the pain, Lord Arlan. We prepare for what we must do." The grey-haired sage spoke gruffly, obviously the one in charge of the proceedings.

With his uninjured arm, Arlan raised the mug and drank, his face pinching at the taste. A sage placed a pillow at the head of the table and encouraged Arlan to lie down. Before he lowered himself, Arlan called to Bàn, who bent over him, then whispered into Bàn's ear. Bàn frowned and helped Arlan to lie down on the wooden table, then stepped away, leaving Arlan with Muir and Angus, and headed toward me and Eifion in the crowd.

"Now, the young lord's men," the sage in-charge said, looking at Angus and Muir, "we will need you to hold him down."

"Sage Phelan, what do you plan?" Eifion moved away from the gathered observers, still holding my hand, and approached the table where Arlan lay, bringing me with him.

Arlan's lids slowly closed, his eyes glazed over.

Must be some *strong herb.*

"We will take it as briskly as possible." Sage Phelan spoke with authority.

"You will remove it?" Eifion's tone barely held on to politeness.

"Aye. Otherwise, 'twill fester and poison him."

"Ye may not have heard. This young lord has won Tòireadh. He will not be àrd rìgh if—"

"You're not cutting it off!" The room silenced at my announcement.

Bàn turned and edged me to a corner, dragging my hand from Eifion's. Sages unrolled leather satchels and laid out instruments that could've come from a butcher's shop. Bàn moved to stand where he blocked my view.

"Bàn, you can't let them." I widened my stare at him.

"If it saves his life?" Beads of sweat shone on Ban's forehead.

"But all they need to do is be clean."

"They'll do the best they can—"

I pushed past him and headed for Sage Phelan. "You can't amputate. You can save his arm."

Arlan's eyes shut, and his chest rose and fell slowly.

"Sew it up, please. I cleaned the cut well with alcohol immediately after Lord Ciarán sliced him."

The sages surrounding me let out a collective gasp. Hopefully it was at hearing that bastard's name and not at my first aid.

"You can do the same to all your instruments. And rinse your hands in strong alcohol beforehand, too."

Sages shook their heads quietly, and Sage Phelan peered at me beneath a heavily hirsute eyebrow.

Eifion stepped to my side. "Ye are sure of this course of action ye propose?" he whispered.

I nodded.

He leaned closer. "Very sure?"

I widened my eyes and nodded again.

"The Lady Rhiannon is right to suggest this," Eifion said, his voice holding a deep resonance and his tone one of authority.

Thank heavens he pulled rank now.

"I beseech you all, please try." He let his plea fall directly onto Sage Phelan.

Phelan's eyebrows met. One or two of the other sages held dubious expressions.

"We would have this man be our high king," Eifion continued in *that* tone. "Please do all you can to sew his arm."

"The bones are still okay." I added, "He just needs muscle sewn—"

"Festering may still—" Sage Phelan began.

"Not if you sew with clean needles and thread. And wrap it in clean bandages like I've explained. And cutting it off gives you the same risks of infection, anyway. Plus, the blood loss..."

Sage Phelan's glare halted my sentence. "Ye would advise me?" Sage Phelan's words were brisk.

I bowed my head. "No, lord sage. I just ask you to reconsider."

After a moment, Sage Phelan gave a reluctant nod.

I strode to the table and explained how to soak the instruments they would use in strong alcohol, and to use clean linen to wrap his arm. The sages who were women nodded at my instructions, like clean bandaging was common sense to them. They had fresh bandages on hand in a cloth-lined basket. Sages whispered orders amongst themselves and two quickly returned with stone jugs of whisky.

"An exceptionally strong distilling, young lady." Sage Phelan observed. "I trust this will be sufficient."

I stepped back. They'd caught on to what I'd meant, and they were more open to my suggestions than I'd expected. I'd leave the suturing to them.

Definitely not in my skill set.

Sage Phelan and two other sages held their hands over a bowl while a woman sage poured the whisky. Even from where I stood, the pinching scent of a strong scotch flew up my nostrils. Arlan moaned once or twice. A sage directed Angus to hold him down by his uninjured arm, and Muir to hold him by the shoulders. They began to wash and suture his wound, and Arlan's groans continued.

Bàn stood against the wall beside me, and now leaned so his arm rested on mine.

"Ye ken, he cannae be àrd rìgh if maimed. Our leader is to be unblemished. The wee cut to his face will nae count. But Arlan must be fit to lead a warband. Wield a sword or spear. Carry a shield. Tasks he cannae do without the use of both arms." Bàn gentled his voice, and he held a confidential tone. "Ye may have saved him to serve us yet."

My breathing stilled. The leaders in this world must be a fully capable warriors? *He can't be àrd rìgh if they regard him* incomplete?

I should let them take his arm. *Then he'd be* mine. If only I'd just shut my mouth.

I bowed my head and screwed my eyes tight, my shoulders cringing and my face burning at my thoughts. Dál Gaedhle needed him, and my wants must come second.

Or maybe, not even at all.

The soft whisper of a breeze blew through the open window and filled the chamber with a sweet floral perfume. The air tickled Arlan's bare arm with its warmth. He opened his eyes to a blurry room. Bandaging covered his injured arm and held it firmly in place against his trunk.

He strained for recollections.

A *stramash* had occurred. He searched his foggy memory.

Eifion was there... arguing with the sages.

His voice had joined with Rhiannon's, their tones... pleading.

Arlan blinked his vision clear, then wiggled his lips, flinching at the tight soreness of his cheek. Vague images of sages hovering over his face returned to him, commenting on fine muscles and expressions affected if not repaired adequately. Then murmuring about tendon damage to his arm and the depth of the cut, and the risks they took by not...

Not doing what?

He grunted. The sewing had hurt more than the blade slice.

Sunlight, angling as it did at late afternoon, beamed in through the window. His vision of the room faded out, replaced with the long angular face of Ciarán Gallawain. The sweet birdsong floating through the window took on the man's philosophical tones. He would consider him a monster if he wasn't so eloquent, so skilled with the sword, and so much cleverer and more intelligent than himself. His cousin was everything he was not...

Arlan blinked the blurry window back into view and breathed away the tightness in his chest.

How to beat him? For beat Ciarán Gallawain, he must.

He threw his head back on the pillow, neck muscles burning.

But I am not on my own.

Aye, it was so during that one on one. But he would lead his army against this tyrant. An army of skilled, faithful clan chiefs and warriors who all, like he, loved Dál Gaedhle more than their lives.

And with their lives would keep it from the deamhan's greedy grasp.

All of us together.

"Oh, Bàn, sword-brother and wise friend. Ye are right," his gravelly voice whispered to the balmy breeze flowing through the window.

Footsteps and voices travelled past the opening, Bàn's among them. Someone rapped lightly on the door.

"Come." The words came out throaty.

Bàn opened the door and stepped in, his face lined, but frown relaxing.

"How are ye, Arlan?" He pulled the chair from the nearby table and sat down.

Arlan shrugged. Pain shot up his arm and he groaned, tight muscles screaming at him.

"Take your time, Arlan. They worked on ye from morn till after midday and—"

"How long have I been here?" He moved to sit, but with his left arm strapped to his side, and burning muscles shooting pain down his arm and back, he succeeded in only a small shift.

"It's the third day since we rode here. They kept giving ye some herb-drink to help ye sleep. Ye needed it," Bàn added.

"Where's Rhiannon?"

"She's helping with the harvest." Bàn looked down at his hands and picked at his palms. "I've never heard a cry of pain and anguish such as that which came from her lips when she thought that Gallawain cur would slay you."

"She was not the only one with that opinion." Arlan ignored his throbbing muscles and slipped his legs over the side of the cot. "Drayce?"

"After they brought you here, he stayed at your door all day with Rhiannon. Did ye no' hear his whining both nights? Not even Rhiannon could console him."

"Where is he now?"

"In the orchard with Rhiannon, she drew him away with morsels of food. The sages are fascinated by him."

"Och, I'm sure they are." Arlan eased his feet onto the floor.

"Where are ye going?"

"I need tae move, Bàn." Arlan ground his teeth.

Footsteps pattered to his door, and a hand knocked with purpose. Bàn rose and went to the door just as it opened and Eifion stepped in.

"Ye are awake." Eifion strode across the floor and patted Arlan's uninjured shoulder.

"When did you arrive, lord sage?" Arlan asked. "I dreamed ye were here."

Bàn gestured to the chair, then Eifion sat.

"I arrived not long before you all. And what a *tadoo* that was." Eifion leaned back in the chair and pursed his lips. "Ciarán injured you but left you alive."

"The man hates me. It exuded from him with every movement. And, he said he had a master." Arlan leaned forward. "Do ye ken who that might be?"

271

Eifion sat immobile, his eyes widening, then a slow lowering of his shoulders and thinning lips chased away that expression. "It is said that after his banishment, he made a pact with an evil force." His lips now danced in his face. "It must be so, then. Arlan, son of my heart, ye will need sage counsel. And"—he glanced beside himself to Bàn, as though deciding on his next statement— "protection of other sorts."

"Och, do I not know it? I heard the man was brilliant, but he bested me in sword combat. In strategy. In tactics. I am insufficient for the task." Defeat wove through his words, and he shuddered against it.

Bàn uncrossed his arms and lowered them, and looking Arlan in the eye, hardened his stare.

"But," Arlan continued, "I have my warriors and your wise guidance. And... we will discuss your other gifts, my lord sage. We will do this together, using all our resources, for we *must* defeat him. I will unite the clan warbands under the banner of the Àrd Rìgh. Some name me Warrior King, so I shall use it."

Bàn's shoulders broadened, and his mouth lifted in a smile.

Eifion nodded in his sage-like way. "Ye have the Lady Rhiannon to thank that ye still have an arm."

"What?"

"I supported her pleas for the healers to not remove it."

Cold flashed through Arlan, his bandaged limb growing heavy.

Oh, aye. Here he was, thankful it was not his sword arm when all along Ciarán had calculated for the maiming to cost him the high kingship.

"Ciarán Gallawain would have the winner of the Quest shamed. Especially with you being the son of the man he has hated most in life." Eifion's eyes hardened. "Unable to assume your place as the High King of Dál Gaedhle, you would be less of a threat to him on the battlefield."

"If I had lost my arm as he wished, I would also be a useless warrior on the field."

"And leave you with little purpose. Not able, nor permitted, to assume the role you have won, nor use to the full skills you have spent your lifetime in training." Eifion slipped his arms up his sleeves.

"But we've thwarted him." Victory resounded in Bàn's voice. "Ye have nae lost your arm. But ye mustn't fester."

Eifion gave Arlan a knowing look, pulled one hand from a sleeve and pointed his finger at his bandaged arm. "Aye, I ... work on this."

"He does nae want ye to warrior, but he doesn't wish ye dead?" Bàn's brow beetled "But you will still lead the army against Gallawain," he grunted in affirmation.

"The man is smart," Eifion said. "Wicked, but strategic and ever the opportunist, and therefore, there must be a particular reason he wishes you alive."

"Ciarán spoke of what he named *his great battle.* I will be there. And he knows nothing would keep me away from it. Not now. Naught will prevent me from crushing that cur, injured shield arm or no."

"What does the bassa plan?" Bàn asked.

"Aye," Eifion said. "For he does have a plan. The man always did."

"We will remain wary. I will send scouts to spy on Gallawain's activity. We need warning of his future moves." Arlan blinked to clear the confusing thoughts Ciarán's wounding him had brought. "Eifion"—Arlan reached out and placed his hand on his sage's— "my heart aches to know what you have discovered of my Rhiannon's clan?"

The sage smiled. "I have discovered Clan Cruithin sent Aisling here after she became depressed in mood. This sage hold is renowned for their care of those unwell in spirit as well as in body. Now I am here, I will enquire further of Aisling. For her clan chief and cousin know not what became of her these past thirty or so years."

"How does Aisling relate to Rhiannon, apart from the similar eye colouring?"

"That is what I shall discover here." Eifion rose and Bàn opened the door for him. "I go to speak to Sage Byard now." He turned to Arlan. "You both have been here before. Do you recall a lady sage with violet eyes?"

A memory of opaque, white irises flecked with mauve flashed through Arlan's mind. "Giorsal," Arlan said.

Bàn spun to him with recognition in his eyes.

"The Blind Lady Sage?" Eifion asked.

"Aye." Arlan and Bàn spoke together.

FORTY-SIX

—•—

Scattered throughout the worlds
Are doorways to each other.
Sentient and yielding
Bent to the will of those who seek access.

SECRET SACRED WRITINGS OF THE SAGES
LOCKED SCROLL 34 BROCH OF THE ANCIENTS

The World of Dál Cruinne
Post Dragon Wars Year 6083
Eastern Clanlands of Dál Gallain
Lord Ciarán's Tower

Ciarán dug his heels into his stallion's flanks.

His pulse raced in time with his horse's galloping hooves. The wind streamed his hair behind, whipped his face and cleared his mind. He grinned into the breeze. Ciarán savoured the lingering pleasure of forcing young MacEnoicht to the ground. A hard ride through the night had done naught to lessen it.

The MacEnoicht lad was his sire all over. So easy to hate him.

A gifted swordsman.

But... perhaps the one who takes in stature after the father, would be like the mother in nature. Arlan had fought with determination.

Yes... Alana could put up a fight...

He had forced Donnach's son back against a standing stone. *Ha!* He would cower through the rest of his life with the maiming Ciarán had wrought.

Arlan would lose his place as high king. Another would lead Dál Gaedhle's defence. Ciarán's grin tightened. He had weakened the warrior. He would cringe on the battle-field, and that would only occur if the warrior sages permitted him to fight at all.

Ciarán snorted a laugh. A one-armed warrior—most ineffectual.

He nudged his stallion on. Sweat foamed at his horse's bit and stained his black neck with patches of white. Now Ciarán's laugh contained joy, for taking the kingdom due him would be a simple task. He would give them no chance to Quest again and find another high king to lead them against him in battle. He, Ciarán Gallawain, would be king of *all* the land. No Quest for him.

The dragon egg the lad had found to win *Tòireadh* for the high kingship... was now a dragon.

The small, dark creature had guarded MacEnoicht like a savage hound. Ciarán had kept his vision on the wee beast while making his retreat. The mage saw it too. Ciarán would have insisted Bram seek to enter and control, but the beast was yet too small, and it took years of growth to be of any useable size. This one was fierce, though. Perhaps...

Surely no one from Dál Gaedhle, especially the son of Donnach, would employ a mage to direct the dragon's protection?

Ciarán caught up to the moving cart, but his steed baulked at the roaring coming from the front section of this beige, grey, and pale-green splodge-covered metal cart. Galan had done well deciphering the means of its momentum and drove it efficiently. Bram had gifted the lad with speaking the foreign and difficult tongues of the Other World, and Galan's natural abilities in sneaking and stealing had come to the fore in the acquiring of this moving structure he called an *armoured jeep*. Galan maintained that when used, the chain of spiked metal attached to this miniature *cannon*, as Findlay would name it, would slay warriors in but moments.

Hmm. A successful night on many counts. A new portal, the closest to his tower, opened to a world at war. A desert war, Galan had said, where sand covered the land as at a beach and little grew there. Bram had proven his value by perfecting the ability to hold a portal open longer than the brief moments of dawn or dusk.

His tower lay ahead, every window glowing with light from within. He tugged the reins, slowing his horse to a canter, and let Galan speed the jeep to the flagstone courtyard. A figure ran from the entrance to the tower, illuminated by the jeep's light.

Findlay!

Ciarán pulled his stallion up.

"Lord Ciarán." Findlay glanced aside at the jeep while Ciarán dismounted. "You've found a jeep from the Gulf War, by the looks of it. I'm sure you will be very happy with that."

"What are you doing here?" Ciarán snapped. "How fares Caisteal Monsae?"

Findlay pressed his lips together and bowed his head for a fraction. The light spilling from the tower entrance caught his strained expression.

"Retaken, Lord Ciarán."

"How?" He narrowed his eyes, heat flaring within.

This fool had best explain how he lost such a strategic resource or—

"No, I wish to meet him!" A voice with an authoritative air echoed from the circular stairs and out to the courtyard. "You, his man, shall introduce me, for the other one—Findlay—has made himself scarce." The tone held pique, and footsteps descended.

"Who comes down the stairs, Findlay?" Ciarán stifled the heat within from his loss. Now Findlay owed him an explanation for strangers in *his* tower.

Findlay snapped his head up, his shoulders no longer held taut. "Your cousin, I believe. Kyle MacEnoicht. Although he first introduced himself as a Gallawain."

The chatter continued while this cousin finished his descent and exited the tower, followed by a servant and Ciarán's own man.

"Oh, there you are." The young man strode toward him, the light from the tower stairwell capturing the strong lines of Gallawain in his features.

He had the complexion of Alana, with the kink of Ciarán's own hair in the short waves that covered this young one's head, apart from a bald, scarred patch on one side. Ciarán's breath caught. Here was a living truth that he and Alana had had something. Something more than mere cousins shared.

The man held himself like any young lord would, reminding Ciarán they had raised him as a prince and son of the Àrd Rìgh of Dál Gaedhle. Kyle stepped into the lights of the car, apparently oblivious to the oddity parked on the flagstones. He held his head high and locked gazes with Ciarán, then ran his vision over Ciarán, appraising him from head to toe and back again. His step faltered, and he came to an abrupt halt with his mouth slightly agape.

"Lord Ciarán?" He gave a slight bow. "I am Lord Kyle, Lady Alana's firstborn and that makes us cousins." While he spoke, his brow pinched, and his head trembled. "And I can't but help noticing how closely we resemble one another."

Ciarán put forth his hand in greeting and Kyle grasped it with a weak, thin grip, but the man held his stare.

"Welcome, Lord Kyle," he said, "but I must correct you. For we are not cousins. Our relation is closer than such and, indeed, is the closest blood tie one man can have with another."

"No!" Kyle's breathless word held nothing but awe.

FORTY-SEVEN

How I waited for this day.
I saw you in my dreams
But ye were far away.
And now, as visions stream,
Ye are here, and I trust ye will be with me to stay.

VISIONS AND SAYINGS OF THE BLIND LADY SAGE

The World of Dál Cruinne
Post Dragon Wars Year 6083
Western Sovereignty of Dál Gaedhle
Sage Hold of the Healers

"Giorsal has been quite disturbed these past three days." The sage, who had granted Arlan, Bàn and Eifion permission to visit the Blind Lady Sage, led them down a passageway lined with doors, padlocks on each.

Arlan exchanged strained glances with Bàn.

"She may not be co-operative." The sage gave a tight smile. "But at your insistence, Lord Sage Eifion, I shall comply." She unlocked the door and opened it.

Arlan entered the room after Eifion with Bàn close behind him. Light spilled in through a glazing pane from the courtyard onto which this small room faced.

Giorsal had been pacing, but now stood still. The tall woman's loose russet hair mingled with grey, fell in waves over her shoulders and down her slender back. She faced them, and her hand wringing ceased. White eyes flecked with purple bore into Eifion.

She walked toward him and placed her hands on his face, tracing the contours of his features, just as she had to Arlan on their first meeting. Eifion gasped at her touch.

She sniffed him and continued softly touching his face with her fingertips. Eifion stood still, his posture stiff but yielding to her examination.

"Eifion," she whispered, and then embraced him.

Eifion's arms wrapped around her, his shoulders shaking with a sob.

The carer sage blinked, and her cheeks reddened.

"I think we should give Eifion and Aisling some time by themselves." Arlan lifted his chin, indicating the doorway, and the sage and Bàn followed him to stand outside the open door.

"How do you know her real name?" the sage asked.

"Just a guess," Arlan replied. "How did she come to be here?"

"After childbirth she became low in mood." She shrugged. "Some women suffer such, but circumstances forced Aisling to give up her babe..."

I placed the basket by the apple tree. Strawberry's sweet but sharp tang filled my mouth from the fruit I'd savoured. The dust and fine particles from the straw surrounding each berry plant, in the rows and rows of strawberry plants, floated through the air and tickled my nose. The sun warmed my head and shoulders. I sighed. It all was so normal and safe here in this sage hold.

Arlan would heal well and be able to use his arm, the healer sages had said. Sage Phelan had even thanked me for my insistence and stated in the future they'd *deliberate* on their options in similar circumstances.

They weren't too sure about his face and how the scarring would affect his features. *Whatever the case, he will always be handsome.*

No one could be idle with plenty of chores to do at the sage hold. I'd needed activity to take my mind off Arlan. I could do nothing other than let him heal. And mind Drayce. The dragon sat huddled on a branch, fretting for Arlan. I planned to see if the sages would allow him into Arlan's room today.

"Oh, look at that full basket of strawberries! For a warrior, you make a good market gardener, Rhiannon." Sage Isla had taken me under her wing after she'd found me at a loose end waiting for Arlan to be well again.

She walked toward me. "Come, rest and eat," she said, then sat under the nearest tree.

The outdoor life had taken its toll on Sage Isla's middle-aged skin, now tanned and wrinkled, with sunspots dotting her face and covering the backs of her hands. She offered me a small bread roll filled with cheese, inviting me to sit beside her.

"Something weighs heavily upon you, Rhiannon." Isla leaned against the tree trunk, with her head angled toward me. "We give counsel here. Talking over your problems often helps." Her voice held warm notes of friendship. I'd heard them more than once since arriving at this place, and her interactions with others in the sage hold had shown me her wisdom when it came to people.

I bit into the roll. Isla waited, holding her gaze on me. She seemed to be someone I could speak to. Someone who'd listen.

But where do I start and how much do I tell?

I swallowed my mouthful. "I... need... to know who my parents are. That will solve a whole lot of issues. You see, I was adopted, but my birth parents are from here."

"You know not your clan?"

I shook my head.

"It is most definitely Cruithin," Isla said, "for no other clan has purple eye colouring. So ye can start there."

"Eifion is investigating, but he hasn't told me anything yet."

Isla's eyes widened, and she sat forward from the tree and faced me square on. "Ah, so that is why Eifion Iubhar, the sage counsellor to the àrd rìgh these past thirty years, is here visiting us now."

"Yes," I said, only now hearing Eifion's clan name for the first time. "Eifion is looking for an Aisling."

"*An* Aisling?" Isla peered at me, then blinked a few times, scrunching her bottom lip with her teeth.

"Yes. Lord Kyle mistook me for her the first time he saw me." I let a nervous laugh escape.

This sage must know something, and with her lip-chewing, it was as though she struggled with whether or not to say it.

"Have you heard of the Blind Lady Sage who lives here?" Isla asked.

Wow. Talk about a change of subject.

"Bàn speaks of her, and he believes what she says." *Like how Arlan will be known as the warrior king.* "Isla, if you're aware of something that could reveal my roots, please tell me."

"I will break a confidence," she swallowed. "But you must know who you are. For you can be none other. You look like Aisling when she arrived here." Isla knelt closer and grasped my hand. "Aisling suffered a deep depression as some women do after childbirth," Isla whispered. "In fear of her father's reaction, Aisling hid her pregnancy once she showed and until the babe was barely a month old. Of her own volition, having no man to support her, she gave her babe away. On her arrival here," Isla looked upwards, as though recalling the time, "about thirty years ago, she relayed her situation to the sages who cared for her but never told us, nor anyone, who fathered the child. We protected her, for there was a risk her pregnancy might somehow be discovered." Isla's gaze rivetted on me. "It is almost impossible to keep such a secret. Our fears were grounded, for soon after she came here, members of her clan had discovered she had been pregnant. Some servant, wishing to keep in her lord father's graces, I expect. The servant accused Aisling of harming the babe, suggesting she had murdered the infant, for Aisling would not name those who had received the babe into their care. Thus, her accuser named the adoption a fabrication. It was only the àrd rìgh's wife, the Lady Alana, speaking up for her, that spared Aisling from any harm. And her father banished her, in a sense, by ordering her to stay away, so she remained here. Neither Lady Alana nor

Lady Aisling would tell of the babe's whereabouts, only that she was now in the care of a childless couple."

Oh, that so fitted in. But...? My mind grasped at thoughts leading in many directions.

Drayce drummed some clicks and flew from the tree across from me, leaving the branches rocking in his wake. Shouting came from the end of the line of fruit trees.

Arlan turned down the avenue between the trees, yelling my name. Drayce flew to him squawking and adding to the clamour. A bandage held his left arm tight, and a dressing flapped on his cheek. His unbound hair, like a jet-black cape, lifted around his shoulders in the breeze. His face looked a little haggard, but my mouth stretched into a smile.

I couldn't take my eyes off him. My shoulders eased. I hadn't realised how tight they were until now.

Those working in the orchard, or seated eating, all stopped what they were doing and stared at the flying dragon and the yelling warrior. I rose and stepped amongst the orchard workers. He scanned those standing along the row of apple trees, then spotted me.

"Rhiannon!" He loped awkwardly toward me. His hope-filled smile changed to a pained frown, then back again.

"Arlan, are you well enough?" I asked, but his yelling drowned me out.

He shouted my name again. Everyone looked from him to me, to the flapping, squawking dragon flying in circles above him, now shattering the orchard's peace.

But why now? Isla was divulging information that resonated with me. It could be all about me, my mother, my origins. Crucial stuff to know.

I gripped hard on the bread roll in my hand.

He reached me and stretched his hand out to grasp mine, but I pulled away.

"Come with me." It was an order, by the sound of it.

"No, I'm speaking with the Sage Isla," I answered. "You're interrupting something important. Can you wait a wee bit?"

"*This* is important. You must come with me." The orchard rang with his deep voice. *Now,* his eyes begged me.

Drayce flew above his head, emitting softer squeals.

I didn't move, and Isla sat back by the tree, her posture stiffening. He was making her uncomfortable. I bit down on a retort. This lady sage may have revealed more of this confidence she breached, but not now this big, loud man had interrupted.

"I've something to share with you that is vital for our happiness." Arlan took my hand in his.

I faced Isla. The sage smiled, and an understanding expression filled her face. "Go," she said.

FORTY-EIGHT

— • —

Come away with me, my love
To a forest glade.
Lay beside me on a bed of moss.
Let our love transport us to worlds beyond.

POETRY OF A KING
ÀRD RÌGH RHONAN IUBHAR
(4030-4090 POST DRAGON WARS)

The World of Dál Cruinne
Post Dragon Wars Year 6083
Western Sovereignty of Dál Gaedhle
Sage Hold of the Healers

Arlan held my hand tight, his warmth surrounding my fingers.

His whole body vibrated, but he didn't speak while he led me at a pace to the main buildings of the sage hold. We reached the hall then veered off to the left. Arlan guided me along the path lined with lavender and orange nasturtiums, and a clematis in purple flower trailed up the wall near the door of a smaller wooden building, fat bumble bees dancing in between the large blooms. Buzzing filled my ears.

"Where are we?"

"Eifion is here." He continued to stride forward at a pace. I'd double stepped to keep up with him all the way from the orchard.

I planted my feet, and he skidded to a halt.

"Tell me where you're taking me." I lifted my chin. He spun to face me, so I continued, "I'm not moving another pace until you do."

The air whistled out of Arlan's nose and bruising showed at the edges of the flimsy bandage on his cheek, now half off with the black stitches poking out beneath.

281

"We are going to the place where the sages care for those who are not happy in their minds." He spoke slowly, looking directly at me, like he gauged my reaction. He still held my hand.

"Why?"

"It's safe. They have minders." He inclined his head in an encouraging gesture.

"Why?" I repeated.

He hesitated for a moment. "Ye will want to meet the woman here. Eifion is with her. And Bàn," he finally said.

"Is it Aisling? She's still here?"

"Aye," he said softly, "but her mind is..." He shrugged then turned.

I went along with him, and a sage let us into a closed section of the hold.

"Giorsal is still with Sage Eifion." The sage took us to where Bàn stood by an open door. I trod on the rushes covering the floor, the scent of lavender wafting up to my nose. Bàn smiled a greeting, then lifted his chin, pointing into the small chamber.

"She is calm—" The sage interrupted herself and, looking at me, widened her eyes. "By all that is good..."

"Hush," Arlan ordered. "Allow the lady to meet her."

Arlan stepped in ahead of me. Dampness from his hand covered my fingers, and he let go once I'd entered the room. Eifion sat on a bench seat with a woman beside him. They held hands and Eifion's eyes were moist. The woman's eyes were white.

"The Blind Lady Sage," I murmured.

She stood tall. Glorious waves rippled through her long hair, and deep red peppered the grey. She trod across the floor, intent on me. Her eyes had a faint hint of purple where her irises should be, and she was kind of looking at me.

"My baby girl," she whispered.

She closed the space between us and wrapped her arms about me. The woman's warmth surrounded me, her thin arms held me tight and her whole body trembled.

I couldn't move. Could barely breathe.

Eifion sat on the bench, smiling. I'd never seen him smile. This one held happiness and relief. He blinked back tears and his mouth stretched further.

"So, are you saying"—I spoke over the woman's shoulder— "this is Aisling? And she's my mother?"

Eifion nodded.

Things I'd wondered my whole life now spun in my head as a lightness filled me. It all came out in a single question. One that required an answer.

"But how did I get to the Other World?"

With a jolt, Aisling let go of me and paced around the room, babbling to herself. Her minder sage frowned, watching her closely.

"What did I do?" I asked.

"It is well," the sage said. "She has but rare moments of clarity these days."

Eifion stepped across the room and reached for my hands. I let him take them, his bony fingers wrapping around mine.

"Rhiannon, it is almost certain that Aisling is your mother," he said.

My stomach flipped. "Then I'm from Clan Cruithin?"

"There is more." Eifion's gaze pierced me. "I am your father."

"What? Wow." I staggered.

Arlan supported me with his right hand under my elbow.

"I am from a noble house also," Eifion said. "I declare you mine and give you all the rights belonging to a daughter of Clan Iubhar."

My world seemed to still. This wise old man was my father? The visionary woman, my mother?

Awesome.

And, they were *my* people. My family. My belonging. I'd found the ones I needed.

A soft trembling rose up from my belly, and a peace came with it. Then the meaning of Eifion's clan name came to me.

"*Yew*, as in the tree," I whispered. "Thank you." I took my hands from Eifion's and covered my mouth, my vision blurring with welling tears.

"Aye." Eifion patted my back.

A brawny arm came around my waist. Arlan pulled me close to him, nudged my hands from my mouth and kissed me deeply. Tears mingled on our lips but Arlan continued his kiss undeterred.

He finally released me and rested his forehead on mine. "Will ye marry me now?"

Aisling's babbling grew louder, shouting unintelligible words. She turned to us, wringing her hands and pacing. Arlan held me closer and Eifion stepped beside us. Aisling's minder sage moved toward her.

"No!" Aisling put up her hand to her. "I would have them know. He needs to know. She needs to know... Alana's son needs to know."

Aisling stepped a pace nearer, spreading her arms, inviting an embrace. She moved to us, including all three of us in her arms.

Then my mind went to another place. To another time.

I trudge along behind Alana, as I have for the whole day. The ride was long.

How does Alana have the energy to get straight back on her horse after riding this far north?

Alana said she had a plan. She had hastily wrapped my baby girl in her clan's maroon tartan plaid that she wore over her shoulders, then scooting me out of my place of hiding, ordered me onto my horse. That was at midday.

The sunlight angles through the trees while we tie our mounts at the forest's edge, and we follow a narrow path for a time.

"Are ye sure this is the way?"

"Have I ever let you down?" Alana's green eyes hold mine.

"Nae."

"Come on, Aisling. It is not far. The woman at the house of worship at Dun Drochaid assured me this couple will take her." Alana turns and strides straight ahead.

I shake. It comes from my inner being. I look down at the wee head covered in russet fluff and an ache stirs in the centre of my chest, and right where my heart should be, a hole appears.

Now my heart is wrapped in a Gallawain plaid.

My friend—my best friend in the world—is correct. Alana is always right. I could never be strong like her. But then, Alana had had a man to wed, and the means to cover her illegitimate pregnancy. I push down a grumble. A clan chief. The makings of an àrd righ, they'd said.

And they were right.

I had never told my man of his wee, beautiful daughter. I shake my head. He chose the life of an advisory sage. An important role, where study and meetings and advancement took much time and energy. Especially if the sage wished to be the adviser of kings.

No room for a wife. Let alone a child.

Eifion will never know, and I will never see him again.

The hole in my chest grows larger.

Now the wife of the àrd righ leads me to the place where she will resolve my shame and inconvenience, and the lives of a childless couple will be made happy.

"Hasten, Aisling! Night draws near." Frustration flies out with Alana's words. "We will walk back to the horses in darkness!"

My baby cries. My cherished one. I shush and rock her while I walk. The midwife who delivered me of my precious babe in secret spoke of bairns feeling the emotions of those around them. Drawing off their mother's feelings. Surely, my wee girl knows we will soon part.

The forest thickens, and it is more difficult to see the track. Low branches of beech swipe my face and tangle in my hair. The wind stirs through the leaves that now whisper among themselves, and the sun lowers, withdrawing her light from the forest.

"We must find our way through this, Aisling." Alana turns slowly on her heel, searching for the path.

"Ye have lost our way." A chill creeps through me.

We will be in a wood at night, two lone women and a suckling babe—with night predators, forest stalkers, and wandering sidhe.

A beam of light opens up before us and pours in the last rays of day. A man and woman, much older than myself, peer at us through the glow. Their mouths break into smiles. It is the couple for the bairn and, though they dress oddly, they are both homey.

I push the pain aside and follow Alana. I lift my babe for them to see and the woman's smile broadens.

"Oh, may I hold her?" the woman asks. She speaks with an accented tongue.

"Aye," Alana answers for me, and takes my babe from my arms, ripping away my heart.

The wind blows through the treetops, roaring like an ocean, and the circle of light goes out, leaving a bare space in the wood, my arms empty, and the people gone.

The wind swirls around us, picking up leaves from the forest floor, and lifts my hair across my face. In the sudden darkness, a storm of grief at necessity's harshness blows through my whole being.

FORTY-NINE

— • —

My soul to join with yours.
My strength in your weakness,
Provision in your need,
And company while we walk this world.
My mind to ponder the ways of you,
Mine heart to enjoy the delights of you,
And my body to love and protect you.
My love to warm, comfort and uphold you.
My will to love despite imperfection.
And my life to live with yours until 'tis done.

TRADITIONAL MARRIAGE VOWS OF DÁL GAEDHLE

The World of Dál Cruinne
Post Dragon Wars Year 6083
Western Sovereignty of Dál Gaedhle
Sage Hold of the Healers

Eifion's soul floated within him.

This sage hold contains a paradise.

Trees and plant life dominated its grounds and a forest lived on the hill to its rear. Eifion strolled through the tall beech trees with their grey trunks mottled in white, leaves chattering their song in the breeze, and their clear, crisp scent filling him with living energy.

A fortnight had passed with Arlan healing well. With Rhiannon, Eifion had experienced precious moments of Aisling's clarity for a reunion, of sorts. He had signed and sealed the formal documents declaring Rhiannon his, assigning her place in his clan. His mouth tugged tight in a smile.

That had brought joy to all their hearts.

Eifion stopped by a tree in the centre of the forest, its branches sprouting high above his head and the trunk, its north facing side half covered in moss, a sufficient size for his needs. He placed his hands on it, spreading fingers wide, its bark rough and white beneath his fingertips.

He stood closer, leaning in, drawing the energy that warmed his soul and washed away the ache of his joints. He embraced the tree, his body against its trunk ensuring complete contact—then he let his spirit go.

The tree's spring sap rose in the excitement of life and the energy of growth flowed through the channels within the trunk. He rode the sap to the top and soared through the leaf canopy, enveloped by its soft tang, stroking the small, gentle foliage with his spirit's fingers, and lingered at the treetops.

Away to the east stood the stone henge of which Arlan spoke. Eifion went there and hovered.

Aye, there was a hum. A thrilling thrum, slumbering until awakened by the sun's emergence or departure from day. Then 'twould be a roar.

He moved on and to the south of Dál Gallain where a short journey would bring a rider to a tower.

So close, yet his soul halted. Unseen, a border stood. Entry forbidden. A magic surrounded this tall tower and its associated buildings. A pungent odour assaulted him, like that emitted from a tar pit.

A mage at work.

Ciarán's mage, for it could be the fortress of none other.

Eifion peered to the fullest extent of his inner sight. Servants at the tower went about their tasks. A strange cart sat on a flagstone courtyard, clad in sheeted metal, with spring's sun reflected from patches of clear glazing. Perhaps the armoured jeep of which Rhiannon spoke. Workers laboured in the surrounding fields, planting and harvesting side by side. Activity in a nearby smithy's had the heavy hint of arms forged.

Eifion scanned the country further, reluctant to send his soul past this point. It may not be safe. Grey mists of conflict rose from north and south, but far, far east, beyond the saw-toothed mountains that cut Dál Gallain from the rest of the land mass, not so.

Ciarán's reach incomplete, then?

Eifion withdrew and returned to his conduit. The yielding tree was generous in its flow of *source* while he hovered over the forest. He then searched through the sage hold and rested his intention on the small reptile.

Drayce flew above Arlan and circled its master who strolled with Rhiannon. Arlan stopped and sat on a bench seat surrounded by spring blooms, and Rhiannon joined him. Eifion followed the dragon, who landed at their feet and inclined a scaly head to them. Drayce's focus, desire, and attention was on the one sensed as *self.*

Arlan.

Drayce saw no distinction, no separateness from him.

Eifion drew nearer. The dragon tensed and turned. Eifion sent forth comfort, and Drayce received the same.

Eifion examined the creature's being.

Drayce was a female!

As such, her defending instincts were great and directed solely at Arlan.

Eifion concentrated, drew from the tree on which his body leaned, and surrounded the wee beast in a *protection*.

She shuffled her wings, clicked a soft sound, then settled.

I sat beside Arlan, leaning close, on a bench seat in a cottage garden section of the sage hold. Most plants grew for eating or healing, but some pockets of the gardens grew flowers for their beauty alone. This being one of them. A tiny hover fly darted from blossom to bloom, like a miniature dark helicopter. It stopped right over a rose, eyeing up the aphids on the narrow stems. I drew in the perfumes of roses and fuchsias: they filled me with a lightness.

Life couldn't be more perfect. Could it?

The sages had removed the stitches on Arlan's face, leaving red dots of healing flesh spaced evenly along each side of the neat cut made by a sharp blade. The wound would leave a scar. And the band of Endless Knot on his bicep wasn't so endless anymore. Arlan healed well and was recovering from his ordeal with Ciarán.

And boy, am I glad I'm not related to him!

"So, what is it with Eifion and trees?"

Arlan put his arm around my shoulder, and I snuggled closer.

"He's a mage."

"A mage? Mages here are like magicians, yeah? And I don't mean a prestidigitator."

Arlan blinked. "Aye, I think, for I know not the term ye use. He uses an energy from..." He waved his hand around. "I am uncertain, but he declares it's good. I believe him. And he's your father, so you should too."

"I don't have a problem with that. You're going to need a mage. That guy in the burn, freezing his... off, is a mage. But a bad one, isn't he?"

"Aye." Arlan's mouth skewed to the side. "Eifion protected me when I went to your—the Other World—though I knew it not at the time."

I rested my head on Arlan's shoulder. Drayce sat at his feet, gazing up at him with adoring eyes then did the cute double blink thing.

"What will you do about Kyle?" I asked.

"Keep the warriors I sent to search for him at their task until he's found. If Ciarán took him hostage, we'll receive a demand for ransom soon enough."

I played my lip between my teeth... but I had to ask. "How do you feel about the fact that he's not your full brother?"

Arlan scowled, and the birdsong from the nearby trees was deafening.

He lifted his head and gazed at the sky. "He's still my brother." A soft gulp came from Arlan. "But my mother..."

"Was unfaithful to your father," I said it for him. He expelled a loud breath, his brow furrowing as he lowered his face to mine, but I continued. "But what if... it wasn't... consensual?" Arlan's chest stilled beneath my hand. "You know Ciarán's not nice. What if..." I shrugged. "That'd be a deep shame, and maybe your mother couldn't admit to it. She was going to marry an àrd rìgh. It would've caused a stir, and if she really loved your dad—"

"She would have told him." He sat straighter, his movement dislodging my hand. "Ciarán's betrayal of my father was her chance. But she didn't take it."

"I'm not familiar with this world enough yet, but it would've been really hard for her to live with it anyway, and especially difficult if the truth came out."

Arlan's face went hard as stone.

"Just saying... don't condemn her when you don't know what actually happened."

Arlan's expression softened a touch and at his feet Drayce made that clicking noise and shuffled his wings, stretching like a bird. The breeze blew a strand of hair across my face and Arlan opened his mouth like he was about to speak, his head tilting to the left.

"What?" I asked.

"We need to return to The Keep. My king making awaits. And a wedding."

I placed my hand back on him, and played with the plaid draped across his chest. "I've been thinking about that."

"Aye. For this I am glad."

"Does the wedding have to be a big deal?" I cringed.

"Nae," he said gently.

"Really? Good. Because I... well... my family's here. I'd like to be married with both my mother and father present. I know that means all the clan chiefs and nobles won't—"

"That matters not. My parents are gone and, well, we know not where Kyle is." He tucked a lock of hair behind my ear. It sprung back, *unkempt* being its default setting, and the breeze blew it back into my face. "My warriors are my family," he continued, "and those close to me are all here."

"It's decided then. Yes?"

"Aye."

Sage Bayrd officiated over the unpretentious wedding ceremony. Arlan draped a MacEnoicht tartan plaid over my shoulders and we promised our lives to each other till the end of time.

Simple.

We left the feast early, leaving our friends and family to celebrate without us, and we feasted in other ways.

Birds chirped in the trees settling for the night outside the window of the room supplied for Arlan and myself, now the bridal suite. I lay nude, full length along Arlan's warm bare skin.

"I love you." My voice echoed softly into his ribcage where his heart still pounded from our love making.

"And I you, my wife."

"I'm a woman of Dál Cruinne from Clan Iubhar."

"Aye, an ancient and once royal clan."

"Really?"

"Aye." He pressed his lips together and the rise of his ribcage slowed, his breathing halting for a moment, then he spoke. "Until Eifion discovered your roots, I feared I may have had to give you up. That becoming àrd rìgh would mean a sacrifice more than I could bear. I found I had to be willing to lose you to have you."

I slid my arms around him, surrounded by his scent, the aroma of heaven—my heaven.

Some of Dál Cruinne's ways were still a bit strange to me. I gave a small shrug, nudging his arms while he hugged me. But other aspects rang *oh-so-true*. I'd found my place here. And found *me*.

"I love a man who is a king," I whispered softly. "A warrior king, according to my mother."

"Aye, and ye are my warrior queen." His arms tightened across my back, moulding my body into his where his hollows and lines fit neatly with my curves.

"I *am* a Dál Gaedhle warrior." I lifted my head. "Aren't I?" My mouth stretched in a grin.

"Aye, and a brave one." He kissed me, letting it linger.

"I will be the mother of your child." My heart thudded against his chest. With his face so near, those deep blue irises speckled with navy filled my vision.

"Aye, we will have many. Be not anxious for that."

"I'm not anxious, but I'm late."

"Late?" His brow scrunched.

I nodded. "*Late.*"

— • —

Epilogue

The World of Dál Cruinne
Post Dragon Wars Year 6083
Eastern Clanlands of Dál Gallain
Lord Ciarán's Tower

A servant had lit the fire in the Great Hall. Striding towards the fire's heat, Ciarán loosened the ties of his leather armour. The young one, Kyle, and his man sat in the large chairs placed beside it while Findlay stood back, close to the hearth. Lambent light etched Kyle's face, drawing memories of Alana's features to mind. This one was his. He would take measures to learn more of Kyle and encourage him to divulge useful facts about Dál Gaedhle. Kyle's comments became clearer as Ciarán approached.

"...is not so large nor ornamented as The Keep, but much more civilised in its apartments than Craegrubha Broch." Kyle raised his goblet to Ciarán. "My congratulations on such a fine tower, my lord host."

Ciarán nodded his appreciation, then a figure in a dark robe caught his attention. It was the mage making a fast retreat from the hall.

"You will excuse me," he said to Kyle. "I have a small matter to attend."

Ciarán left the men by the fire and exited through the same side door the mage had used. The hallway sat empty. He strode to the stairwell, the flutter of a dark robe ascending the curved steps catching his vision.

The mage had eluded him, behaving as he did when guilty.

But of what?

Ciarán strode up the stone stairs two at a time and arrived at the door to the mage's workshop as it closed. He pounded on the wood, then stopped himself.

"'Tis my tower," he growled grasping the handle, then thrust the door open and burst in.

291

The mage spun from his work bench, a scowl filling his young face. A grunt came from beside the window, where the mage's new young assistant stood, mouth agape, a sheaf of weeds in his hands.

"Yes, I invade your workshop," Ciarán yelled at Bram.

It took only two strides to reach the mage, grab his robe collar and shake.

"Leave us," Ciaran spat at Bram's assistant. "Bram and I have business."

The lad dropped the weeds on the bench then ran out, slamming the door behind him.

"Why did you retreat so hastily from the hall? What do you hide from me, mage?"

"Nothing, lord." The lines on the mage's face set hard.

"I know you. Tell all."

Bram stared at the floor, his hands by his sides grasping his robe. A fine sheen of sweat glistened on his brow.

Heat ran through Ciarán's veins, and he placed his mouth close to Bram's ear.

"Do not lie. I am aware your herbs and potions"—he gestured with his free hand to the dried vegetable matter that adorned the racks hanging from the workshop's ceiling—"are but a smoke screen for the methods you use to achieve your purposes. The genuine magic occurs in your stone bowl there." He flung his hand toward the offensive object sitting in pride of place in the chamber. "Have you seen a thing that will disturb me, and you wish not to reveal it?"

Bram stood mute; the neck of his robe so tight in Ciarán's grip it would surely choke him.

Ciarán shook Bram. "Well?"

The lad barely whimpered. "What do you want, lord?" His deep voice held clear.

Is that insolence in his tone?

Ciarán let go and the mage dropped to the floor.

"Why the reluctance? You know I have a contract with your master. You will tell me—"

"Arlan MacEnoicht lives." Bram stood.

"Of course this is so. That was my plan. I restrained myself on meeting the spawn of MacEnoicht. I have left him with an injury to think upon. He would have led an army against me. I have ensured he will lead nothing, and mayhap never be a warrior again, with luck."

"But..." Bram bit his lip.

"What?" Ciarán yelled into Bram's face.

Bram flinched but regained himself in an instant. "Healer sages repaired his arm. They sewed it. He is whole."

The heat in Ciarán's veins became fire. He clenched his fists and forced them to remain by his side. "Then I shall send an assassin to kill him," he said through gritted teeth. "The progeny of Donnach will not become my nemesis. He will die and be done with!"

"No, my lord, you cannot." Bram's shoulders hunched in a cringe, as though awaiting the beating he should receive.

"Why not?" Ciarán spat. "I have failed in my attempt to humiliate the son of Donnach." Ciarán spun from Bram, not awaiting an answer. He roamed the room, dodging dried plants and clay pots. "Thwarted in my attempt to repay the father, through the son, for all he stole from me," he said to himself.

"They name him Warrior King." Bram's words were but a whisper.

Ciarán spun. "He *will* lead them?" He scattered his gaze around the room, looking at nothing. "I despise him but must admit he takes so after Donnach. Arlan will be a leader all will follow. He is by far a greater threat than the other benighted candidates. I must make haste to rid the land of him."

"Ye must not." Command came through in the mage's tone.

"Tell me. What does your master say, for you have surely had some direction from your conversations in your wee stone bowl. Inform me of the reason why I must endure MacEnoicht's continued success."

"My master says Lord Arlan must be present at the last battle." The mage stood straighter.

"Why does our master insist? MacEnoicht is still their warrior king, is he not? I have failed in that regard." *And oh, how that smarts.* "What is so special about the lad?"

"It is in relation to the eternal reward promised to you." Bram looked him in the eye.

Ciarán stood back, blinking at the piercing nature of the mage's stare.

There it was again, though. The mention of the eternal reward. It was immortality of which this master spoke, he was sure of it. *Certain of it.*

Life forever. No more the prospect of death.

"What has this young warrior king to do with my reward?"

Bram's cheek muscles rippled.

Why reticence once more? "Must I beat the information out of you, mage?"

Bram swallowed, his soft gulp reached Ciarán's hearing.

"He is to be sacrificed." The mage clamped tight his mouth.

A human sacrifice as payment for life forever?

"Ah, yes, I have read this in an ancient scroll... Well, a translation of such. A wonder from another land in Dál Cruinne. Far from here some believe in this. Or they once did." His voice took on a philosophical note. "It is far back in that land's history. But here in Dál Gallain?"

So that is how I will gain life immortal. Beat death with death.

"Now I must face the upstart once more." He set his hands on his belt and tapped his foot. "But it will be in the theatre of war?"

"Ye are to make it so."

Ciarán's brow tightened in a frown. "Why Donnach's son?"

"He is perfect."

"But I have maimed him. He will scar." Ciarán's yell shook the rods hanging from the ceiling, sending the dried herbs quivering. "He is no longer perfect, even by the ancient standards of Dál Gaedhle. Besides, he is only a man. Who can claim perfection in *any* aspect of character? Morals? Behaviour? Thought?"

"Even so," Bram spoke with gravity, "he is perfect for our master's purposes."

THE CLANS of the SOVEREIGNTY of DÀL GAEDHLE

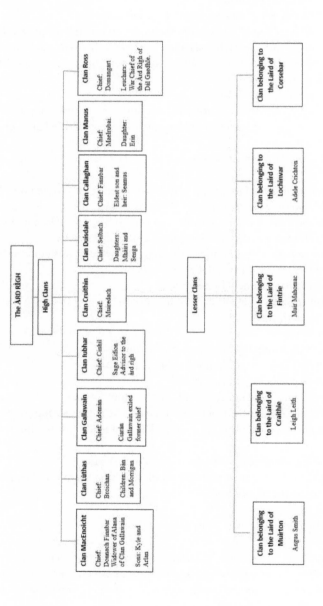

The ÀRD RÌGH

High Clans

Clan MacEnoicht

Chief:
Donnach Finnbar
Widower of Alana
of Clan Gallawain

Sons: Kyle and
Arlan

Clan Lùthas

Chief:
Brochan

Children: Ban
and Morrigan

Clan Gallawain

Chief: Adomán

Ciarán
Gallawain exiled
former chief

Clan Iubhar

Chief: Cathil

Sage Eifion
Advisor to the
àrd rìgh

Clan Cruithin

Chief:
Muiredach

Clan Duisdale

Chief: Sethach

Daughters:
Mhàiri and
Senga

Clan Callaghan

Chief: Finnbar

Eldest son and
heir: Seamus

Clan Manus

Chief:
Maelrubai

Daughter:
Erin

Clan Ross

Chief:
Domangart

Leuchars:
War Chief of
the Àrd Rìgh of
Dàl Gaedhle.

Lesser Clans

**Clan belonging
to the Laird of
Muirton**

Angus Smith

**Clan belonging
to the Laird of
Craithie**

Leigh Leith

**Clan belonging
to the Laird of
Fintrie**

Muir Mahomac

**Clan belonging
to the Laird of
Lochinvar**

Adele Crichton

**Clan belonging to
the Laird of
Corsebar**

GLOSSARY of GAELIC and SCOTS WORDS

A gràidh chridhe	love of my heart
Am fuath	the fae
Àrd Ghliocas	high wisdom
Àrd Righ	high king
Bayrd	sings
Beul an latha	the dawn of the day
Beul na h-oidhche	the dusk of evening
Boireannaich	woman
Braw	Scots for good/great
Broch	round tower of iron age construction
Burn	a small watercourse, creek, brook
Cernunnos	Celtic god of beasts and wild places
Creagrubha	rocky outcropping
Cruinne	the globe/world
Cumhachd Adhar	power of the air/bad spirit
Dál	denotes belonging or ownership
Damainte	damned
Deamhan	demon/evil spirit
Dearg	to redden/draw blood
Dreich	Scots for dreary/ bleak

Droch dhuine	bad man/reprobate
Eilean	island
Fàistinnaech	wizard/prophet/diviner
Fannlag	weakling
Giorsal	grey hair
Gliocas	wisdom, prudence
Heid	Scots for head
Murtair	assassin
Muir	sea
Oidhche mhath	goodnight
Phelan	wolf-like
Ruairidh	red king
Sàsaichean	council
Sleaghach	spear
Stramash	Scots for disturbance, uproar
Tapaidh	clever smart brave heroic
Tobraichean na beatha	the fountain/source/issue of life
Tòireadh	a quest, diligent search
Trobhad	come here!
Uisge beatha	malt whisky
Weesht	Scots for *shush*

AUTHOR'S NOTE

A VISIT TO TAPPOCH BROCH, TORWOOD, SCOTLAND

It was the last day of November. The midday autumnal sun, sitting low in the sky, sent long shadows across our path. Our son, another forest lover, and myself climbed to the pine plantation that carpeted the hill on which Tappoch Broch has sat since long before the Roman Empire ever knew there was a Britain to conquer. The path would have been slushy but a cold snap from an impatient winter had frozen the mud. The ground crunched beneath our walking boots with every step.

We reached the shade of the forest where pine needles now carpeted our tread, adding to the silence, for no birds called in between the trunks on this shaded hillside. Sun beams illuminated the trees at the edge of the wood, lighting my peripheral vision with a golden hue, but my attention was to the front of me where lay the ruins of an ancient building, Tappoch Broch.

Halfway up the slope a sign indicated we were in the right place and heading in the correct direction. Ahead there seemed to be a mound, but the closer we came the more we saw stone interlocking stone, like a drystone wall made of giant blocks. I spied no entrance, so I climbed the mounded soil at the side then walked along the top of a dirt covered wall. It was circular, and looking into the pit below me, I saw grass, wild heather, toppled large cut-stones and a young fir tree. Then I noticed the narrow lintels, one of which I walked across, and doorways. I scampered down the mound of round wall, which was about ten feet high, and found a lead-in tunnel to one entrance, a stairway covered in weeds. The walls are reportedly twenty feet thick and certainly seemed so.

I ducked and went in, careful of my footing for what was once the ground floor of the broch was now rubble overgrown by wild years. I pivoted on my heel and took in the walls surrounding me, imagining the floors above, the hearth stone and fire, and perhaps the people who lived here. I found that somewhat difficult as we only have history books and archaeology finds, and their interpretations, to guide us as to what the peoples of the past were like.

Although these structures are estimated to have been built between 400 BC and 200 AD, many ruins still stand dotted across the Scottish mainland and the Isles. They would

297

have been impressive, making a statement regarding the wealth and importance of the families who had built and lived in them. From the size of the lintel over the doors of Tappoch, and the faint dents showing where a large bar could be placed across the main entrance of this one, they were also quite defensible. Tappoch Broch sits right at the top of this high hill, where its inhabitants would have had a clear view of all who approached, friend or foe, for miles in every direction. Now, a plantation occludes the view.

In my mind, I drew the walls high, lit a fire in the hearth and saw Arlan warming his hands over the glowing peat, his warband drinking mead and ribbing Angus over his performance in a recent hunt. I had used a structure based on Iron Age dwellings similar to this one to provide a home for Arlan's father, the chief of Clan MacEnoicht. It fit the world I had imagined, and I hope I have represented this impressive building adequately, and described it enough for the reader to have a true sense of these intriguing structures.

I also elaborated a bit to make a three-broch structure connected by covered walk-ways, which would be the extensive library of the Broch of the Ancients. Through my research on these buildings, I discovered most of them have voids in the dry-stone walls, especially the double walled ones further north. These voids allowed for air to breeze through, dragging heat from the animals that were stalled in the lower floor, plus the heat from the hearth fire, through the stone walls, staying off the cold and damp. I imagined, and hopefully correctly, that structures such as these would be ideal for preserving artefacts and parchments.

If you are a lover of the past as I am, I can thoroughly recommend a walk to these brochs in Scotland, some of them surprisingly not too far off a main road.

Suggested reading:

Towers in the North. The Brochs of Scotland.
Ian Armit. The History Press 2011.
Scotland's Hidden History.
Ian Armit. The History Press 2009
Celtic Scotland
Ian Armit. Birlinn Limited 2016
The King in the North. The Pictish realms of Fortriu and Ce.
Gordon Noble and Nicholas Evans. Birlinn Limited 2020

ACKNOWLEDGEMENTS

A novel isn't written overnight, and this one has seemed like an age in its development.

I date the commencement of all my manuscripts, and I started this section of Arlan's and Rhiannon's story on the second of May 2020.

Yes, *that* horrible year. I still had to work, being a health care worker, thankfully not on the front line. I give my thanks to all my colleagues who were, and acknowledge the price paid.

Social gatherings were out during that year (and more), and this provided plenty of time at home to write. It still took a while to complete, as did *Of Myths and Portals*, due to back logs in all the process of getting a novel to publishing stage. I also wrote the first draft of *Of High Kings and Mages* in that year.

Added to this, my husband and I decided (after COVID) to move back to the UK and resettle closer to family, an endeavour which took over eighteen months in the process, causing another delay in *Of Warriors and Sages* completion to publication stage.

But here it is.

Firstly, thank you to Candida Bradford of *A Place of Intent*, my editor who gets my stuff and stretches me and my stories. So glad we met.

Thank you to my cover designer, Fiona Jayde Media, for great covers for this series and flexibility with the title changes.

I'd like to thank the beta readers of four years ago:

Jill Williams, Sue Jacka and Ileana Noble.

And a recent one. A fellow writer: Joanne Smith.

My Word Menders critique partners: authors SL Dooley, M D Boncher, Karen Sweet and Philip Wilder who worked through the manuscript with me for over a year.

Also, the support, mentoring and advice I receive from Realm Makers, their Realm Sphere (of which Word Menders is part) and annual conferences.

My brother in-law, Gary. Thank you for the finer points of police officer rank designations and mug shot usage.

Thanks to author Eliza Hampstead for the hints on the techniques in the HEMA fight scenes.

I acknowledge the authors of the history of Scotland books I've read. These books have helped me in my settings(See Author's Note). Also, *Am Faclair Beag* the on-line Scottish Gaelic dictionary.

Thank you to my husband Frank, who understands why I have to write, to create stories to express what's going on in my head as I interpret the people and the world around me.

And always, thank you God, the Creator, who puts that creative spark in us all, for giving me the joy of storytelling.

If you enjoy my novels please leave a review.
Reviews help independently published authors by getting the word out about their novels.
Thank you.

ABOUT THE AUTHOR

Jenn Lees writes fantasy.

The Crossing: Arlan's Pledge Book 1, (Re-released as *Of Myths and Portals*) achieved the finals in the OZMA Book Awards for Fantasy Fiction CIBA 2021 (manuscript). *Restoring Time* (Book 4 of the *Community Chronicles Series*) reached the finals in the CYGNUS Awards for Science Fiction CIBA 2021.

The Quest manuscript (now published as *Of Warriors and Sages: Arlan's Pledge Book Two)* achieved semi-finalist in the OZMA Fantasy Book Award 2023 (Chanticleer International Book Awards)

An Ink & Insights Competition judge says of her writing:

'Beautifully crafted, full of rich setting descriptions, tension that caught my attention and kept it, and characters that leapt off the page. This author is a skilled storyteller.' (Melody Quinn).

Retired nurse, Jenn has travelled extensively and lived on three continents.
Scotland remains her source of inspiration. Jenn loves walking through a forest and climbing a mountain to experience the view.

Her only disappointment in life is that time travel is not possible... apparently.

Find out more about Jenn Lees and her novels.

Sign up for the newsletter and receive *Running with the Stags*, a free novella in the *Arlan's Pledge Series.*

www.jennleeswriter.com

Discover Vygeas' and Leyna's story in *Murtairean: An Assassin's Tale* , another novel by Jenn Lees set in the world of Dál Cruinne.   RECOMMENDED READING PRIOR TO *OF WARRIORS AND SAGES*

Also by JENN LEES

OF MYTHS AND PORTALS
ARLAN'S PLEDGE BOOK ONE
DESTINY MUST CLAIM THEM

AND COMING SOON

OF HIGH KINGS AND MAGES
ARLAN'S PLEDGE BOOK THREE

A KING MUST DIE

NOVELS IN THE WORLD OF DÁL CRUINNE

MURTAIREAN: AN ASSASSIN'S TALE
RECOMMENDED READING PRIOR TO OF WARRORS AND SAGES
AN ASSASSIN'S TWO HITS: ONE FROM THE PAST TO HAUNT HIM. ONE TO FREE HIM

A MAGE WHO PURSUES ... AND A WARRIOR WOMAN WHO LINKS IT ALL

THE COMMUNITY CHRONICLES SERIES

THE CRASH
STOLEN TIME
SAVING TIME
RESTORING TIME

COMMUNITY CHRONICLES NOVELS ARE
ALSO AVAILABLE IN AUDIO
APPLE BOOKS (AI NARRATED)

Milton Keynes UK
Ingram Content Group UK Ltd.
UKHW030351240824
447344UK00005BA/564

9 780987 644879